Analyzing Digital Fiction

Written for and read on a computer screen, digital fiction pursues its verbal, discursive and conceptual complexity through the digital medium. It is fiction whose structure, form, and meaning are dictated by the digital context in which it is produced and requires analytical approaches that are sensitive to its status as a digital artifact. *Analyzing Digital Fiction* offers a collection of pioneering analyses based on replicable methodological frameworks. Chapters include analyses of hypertext fiction, Flash fiction, Twitterfiction, and video games with approaches taken from narratology, stylistics, semiotics, and ludology. Essays propose ways in which digital environments can expand, challenge, and test the limits of literary theories that have, until recently, predominantly been based on models and analyses of print texts.

Alice Bell is Senior Lecturer in English Language and Literature at Sheffield Hallam University, UK.

Astrid Ensslin is a Professor of Digital Culture and Communication at Bangor University, UK.

Hans Kristian Rustad is Associate Professor in Scandinavian Literature at Hedmark University College, Norway.

Routledge Studies in Rhetoric and Stylistics

Edited by Michael Burke

Analyzing Digital Fiction

Edited by Alice Bell, Astrid Ensslin,
and Hans Kristian Rustad

Routledge
Taylor & Francis Group

NEW YORK AND LONDON

First published 2014
by Routledge
711 Third Avenue, New York, NY 10017

and by Routledge
2 Park Square, Milton Park, Abingdon, Oxon OX14 4RN

*Routledge is an imprint of the Taylor & Francis Group,
an informa business*

© 2014 Taylor & Francis

Library of Congress Cataloging-in-Publication Data

Analyzing digital fiction / Edited by Alice Bell, Astrid Ensslin and Hans
    Kristian Rustad.
        pages cm. — (Routledge studies in rhetoric and stylistics ; 5)
    Includes bibliographical references and index.
    1. Hypertext fiction—History and criticism.   2. Experimental fiction—
History and criticism.   I. Bell, Alice, 1979– editor of compilation.
    PN3448.H96A43   2013
    809.3'911—dc23
    2013010784

ISBN: 978-0-415-65615-3 (hbk)
ISBN: 978-0-203-07811-2 (ebk)

Typeset in Sabon
by Apex CoVantage, LLC

Printed and bound in the United States of America by Publishers Graphics,
LLC on sustainably sourced paper.

Contents

SECTION III
Semiotic-Rhetorical Approaches

Afterword

List of Figures with Figure Captions, Cases, or Illustrations

Acknowledgments

The editors wish to thank The Leverhulme Trust for funding the Digital Fiction International Network (DFIN) (Ref: F/00 455/E) from January to December 2009 and from which this project originated. The DFIN project brought together scholars from the UK (Alice Bell and Astrid Ensslin), Norway (Hans Kristian Rustad), the United States (Jessica Pressman), Canada (Jess Laccetti), and New Zealand (Dave Ciccoricco). The grant funded two research visits by the Investigators to Otago, New Zealand (Alice Bell) and to Yale (Astrid Ensslin), and a workshop also attended by the President of the Electronic Literature Organization, Joseph Tabbi, that initiated a number of sole- and joint-authored publications including this volume.

The authors and editors would like to thank the following for allowing reproduction of their copyright work: screenshot of *10:01* by Lance Olsen and Tim Guthrie reprinted by permission of Lance Olsen; screenshot of *Radio Silence* by Stuart Moulthrop reprinted by permission of Stuart Moulthrop; screenshot of *afternoon, a story* by Michael Joyce reprinted by permission of Eastgate Systems, Inc. http://www.eastgate.com/; screenshots of *The Path* reprinted by permission of Tale of Tales; screenshot of *Flight Paths* reprinted by permission of Chris Joseph (original image by Paul Hart, http://www.flickr.com/people/atomicjeep/); screenshot of *Don't touch me* reprinted by permission of LAL Annie Abrahams; screenshot of *Anonymes v.1* reprinted by permission of anonymes.com; screenshots of *Loss of Grasp* reprinted by permission of Serge Bouchardon; screenshots of *Zeit für die Bombe* reprinted by permission of Susanne Berkenheger. Every effort has been made to contact copyright holders. If any there are any errors or omissions, we will be pleased to make a correction at the earliest opportunity.

Finally the editors would also like to thank Michael Burke (Series Editor), Felisa Salvago-Keyes (Editor at Routledge), and all at Routledge for their assistance in the preparation and production of this book.

Introduction

1 From Theorizing to Analyzing Digital Fiction

Alice Bell, Astrid Ensslin,
and Hans Kristian Rustad

Why write a book on analyzing digital fiction? Twenty-five years after the publication of the first hypertext fictions, we might assume that a substantial body of in-depth analyses of digital fiction exists. In our many discussions as members of the Digital Fiction International Network[1], however, we established that it does not. Indeed, we were struck by how few systematic analyses of digital fiction are to be found. We realized that while authors have been experimenting with different modes and media, creating different structures and forms, and writing in different genres and styles, the scholarship surrounding digital fiction hasn't yet caught up. We concluded that the field needs more analyses of digital fiction and more replicable approaches through which they can be methodically analyzed.

We were also surprised to see how few of the existing approaches to digital fiction put their trust in the literary work itself, and to acknowledge that these works and their authors say something important about literature as an art form, about the media ecology of our time, and about our society and cultural practices. Too often, we felt, arguments about the importance of digital fiction are found, not within the text, but outside the fictional work. The mainstream media heralds a digital age in which we read literature differently (i.e. on screen), in which digital technologies will make readers fit for the twenty-first century (i.e. on trend), and in which literature needs to be where the readers are (i.e. online). We believe that these arguments are important and that digital fiction should and must have a place in our increasingly digital lives. However, claims about the timeliness or cultural relevance of digital fiction are not alone sufficient for justifying the value of and the position of digital fiction in our education system, in scholarship, or in society generally. Digital literature is a form of *literature*, and digital fiction is a form of *fiction*. Research in digital fiction thus needs to return to, to hold onto, and to expand the core practice of literary studies, and that, to our minds, is the methodical *analysis* of texts.

To that end, this volume provides a collection of systematic, comprehensive, and explicit applications of different methodological approaches to digital fiction. It offers analyses of digital works that have so far received little or no analytical attention and, in the spirit of the Routledge Studies in

Stylistics and Rhetoric series, profiles replicable methodologies that can be used in the analyses of other digital fictions.

SCOPE

Digital fiction, as defined by the Digital Fiction International Network, is "fiction [that is] written for and read on a computer screen [and] that pursues its verbal, discursive and/or conceptual complexity through the digital medium, and would lose something of its aesthetic and semiotic function if it were removed from that medium" (Bell et al. 2010). It is fiction whose structure, form, and meaning are dictated by, and in dialogue with, the digital context in which it is produced and received.

The roots of digital fiction can be seen in the Interactive Fictions (IFs) of the 1980s. IFs such as Infocom's (1980) *Zork* and Adam Cadre's (1999) *Varicella* require the reader to type text commands in order to navigate the fiction, with the storyworld changing in response to their input. Later digital fictions, which were produced pre-Web, in software such as HyperCard and Storyspace and then in Web technologies such as HTML and Flash, take a range of forms but, like IFs, require that the reader engages with the digital technology either corporeally and cybernetically through mouse clicks or cognitively by making decisions about her or his journey through the text.

Aarseth (1997) defines digital fictions as "ergodic literature". In such texts, he argues, "nontrivial effort is required to allow the reader to traverse the text" (1). While Aarseth's definition does not explicitly exclude print texts, his concept of nonergodic literature shows why a linear and bound print text does not satisfy the criteria associated with ergodic literature. In nonergodic literature, he states, "no extranoematic responsibilities [are] placed on the reader except (for example) eye movement and the periodic or arbitrary turning of pages" (1–2). The nontrivial effort that Aarseth identifies in ergodic literature generally is characterized in digital fiction by the role that readers have to play in its navigation so that their reading experience is much more active or "nontrivial" than that associated with their print counterparts. Some demand that the reader follows hyperlinks in order to navigate the text. In Michael Joyce's (1987) Storyspace fiction, *afternoon, a story*, the choices that are granted to the reader result in different and sometimes contradictory narrative outcomes. In Lance Olsen and Tim Guthrie's (2005) Web-based fiction *10:01*, the reader can navigate the text using either a chronological timeline along the bottom of the screen or by clicking on an image of a particular character. Readers can also choose internal and/or external links as their curiosity dictates. *10:01* does not contain the narrative contradictions of *afternoon*, but the navigational choices mean that it is different each time it is read either by the same or a different reader. Kate Pullinger and Chris Joseph's (2007) *Inanimate Alice* does not permit the same level of choice as *afternoon* or *10:01* insofar as the reader is only offered one pathway through the text. However, readers are required to interact with the narrative by clicking on moving images, completing puzzles or selecting icons. Other digital fictions, such as geniwate and Deena Larsen's (2003) flash fiction *The Princess Murderer*, require that readers choose their own path through the text but also verge on literary games as they reflect subtextually on stereotypical ludic semantics, such as misogynist teleology (Ensslin and Bell 2012). Indeed, creative new media are increasingly blurring conventional generic boundaries, thus becoming hybrid forms of experimental literary and media art. Kate Pullinger and Chris Joseph's (2010) *Flight Paths* is a prime example of digital fiction in participatory Web culture, as it integrates readers' story versions in its collaborative paratextual website. Each reading of a digital fiction is different, either because the reader takes a different pathway through the text or because the text offers a different version of itself.

LOGISTICAL DIFFICULTIES

That multilinear digital fiction is different each time it is read means that determining a "reading" of these texts is inherently problematic. Higgason (2003a) defines hypertext fiction in particular as a "scholar's nightmare" because of the logistical problems associated with its analysis, but the same could apply to a range of digital fictions because of the role that the reader plays in their construction. Higgason warns that "many of the old concepts of what it means to do criticism will be challenged by and changed to address new types of texts, and the standards by which we judge academic rigor will need to change in the process". It was perhaps the novelty of the digital fiction reading experience that led the first wave of digital fiction scholars to look toward poststructuralist textual models in order to understand the new forms of literature that were emerging, particularly hypertext fiction. Because the reader has a role in constructing the narrative, hypertext has been described as an example of Barthes's (1990 [1974]) "writerly" text; Deleuze and Guattari's (1988) concept of the "rhizome" text has been applied to the branching structure of hypertext; Derrida's (1979, 1981) theory of "deconstruction" has been used to conceptualize the multilinearity that hypertext permits (see Bolter 2001; Burnett 1993; Delany and Landow 1991; Landow 1994, 1997, 2006 for full accounts). Perhaps most famously, hypertext has been described as "an almost embarrassingly literal reification or actualization" (Delany and Landow 1991: 10) of contemporary literary theory. While poststructuralist models can be used to conceptualize the hypertext structure, the association of hypertextuality and these particular theoretical models has not necessarily led to literary-critical readings of individual digital fictions. Rather, the metaphoric mapping of theory and textuality has remained mostly at an abstract level—a blueprint from which few, if any, analyses have since materialized.

In what has proved to be a more influential approach, first-wave theorists situate hypertext fiction readers in a binary relationship with their print counterparts (e.g. Coover 1992; Douglas 1992; Liestol 1994; Simanowski 2002) and, as noted above, the role of the reader represents an important and distinguishing facet of digital fiction and its reception. In Douglas's (1992) article, "What Hypertexts Can Do That Print Narratives Cannot", the hypertext reader is compared to the print reader in terms of the choices that each medium allows. Whereas, "in print narratives", Douglas argues, "our reading experience begins with the first words of the narrative and is completed by the last words on the last page" (2), in hypertext fiction, "readers are unable to begin reading without . . . making decisions about the text—where their interests lie and which pathways through the text seem most likely to satisfy them" (2–3). Douglas's observations about the choice granted to the reader are based on examples from Storyspace hypertext fiction but could also apply to a range of other digital fiction including Web-based hypertext fiction, Flash fiction (fiction produced in Flash software), and videogames. For example, the Web-based hypertext fiction *Inanimate Alice* has a linear structure so that the reader is not granted any choice in terms of her reading path. However, she has to click links and play mini-games to move between different episodes so that nontrivial effort is still required to read the text. The reader of Jason Nelson's (2003) *Dreamaphage* must navigate a collection of floating texts within a 3D environment, using the cursor as a kind of steering wheel and deciding which of the documents he or she would like to explore first. From a methodological perspective, however, irrespective of the text type, Douglas's observations—though accurate—do not yield either a critical analysis or a means of conducting such an analysis for any type of digital text. This is somewhat ironic, as it is precisely because the reader has such an interactive role in digital fiction that transparent and replicable approaches are so necessary for the critical field that surrounds it. If a particular approach to a particular digital fiction is to be useful to a range of readers who all experience a different version of the narrative, then the method of analysis needs to be visibly and overtly articulated.

A MULTIFOCAL PERSPECTIVE

As Douglas notes above, digital fiction is different from print fiction because of the affordances that digital media permits, and, consequently, analyses of digital fiction must be sensitive to those differences. Primarily, reader-players of interactive narratives have to learn and "submit" (cf. Walker 2000: 48) to the mechanics of the text to read or play successfully. What is more important to a *literary* analyst, however, is the relationship between a digital text and the reader, and the way the text causes a certain (subversive as well as immersive) response. According to Hayles (2007), deep attention allows subjects to focus on an artifact like a print novel for an extended period of time without, however, losing a sense of the actual world surrounding them. Hyper attention, on the other hand, is based on natural or artificial primary needs (such as food, drink, and sleep in actual life and the "artificial" basic need to finish a video game level or quest before being able to focus on any other activity) and occurs frequently with young people immersed in game worlds. It frequently results in the prioritization of virtual world over actual world needs or concerns and "is characterized by switching focus rapidly between different tasks, preferring multiple information streams, seeking a high level of stimulation, and having a low tolerance for boredom" (Hayles 2007: 187). As Rettberg (2009) observes, "[N]o literary medium [is] more suited to straddling the divide between hyper attention and deep attention than electronic literature", and writers of digital fiction have experimented with this divide in uniquely creative ways. To comprehend and critically reflect on the aesthetic interplay between hyper and deep attention, we need methods that can capture the way the text invites those kinds of attention. We need to look at the text, but we will also need to consider media-specific attributes such as interface design, software versus hardware mechanics, links, images, sound, and so on. Moreover, digital fiction becomes textualized (and/or tactile and audiovisual) for the reader in a way that print literature does not and cannot.

NARRATOLOGIES

The media specificity of digital fiction causes blind spots in some narratological frameworks because they are to a great extent developed based on readings of print literature. So, for example, while narratological models can be used to analyze the narrative structure of a hypertext fiction, categories as simple as "story" and "plot" are immediately problematized by hypertext fiction's multilinearity; they sometimes have multiple plots, multiple stories, multiple beginnings, and multiple endings (cf. Laccetti 2008). Ryan (2004) argues that "the question of how the intrinsic properties of the medium shape the form of narrative and affect narrative experience can no longer be ignored" (1). Given the diversity of narrative forms that we experience daily, ranging from exclusively oral to exclusively textual, Ryan's statement could (or perhaps should) be considered a truism. Yet while analysts are becoming increasingly more aware of media-specificity, few replicable approaches exist that can be used to analyze digital fiction as a form of *digital* narrative as opposed to a form of digital *narrative*. We caution the unmediated application of print-based frameworks. Instead, this volume offers a number of approaches that seek to outline and promote methodologies for the media-specific study of digital fiction. These methods may well prove to be useful for the analysis of other types of text and thus contribute to the development of a transmedial approach to narrative (cf. Ryan 2004), but their primary purpose here is to address the idiosyncrasies brought with digital media in particular.

MULTIMODALITIES

Over the last fifteen years, new forms of digital fiction have emerged, seeking to explore, transcend, and deconstruct the default functions and uses of new digital technologies. As a result of the continuous development of digital fiction software has quickly followed. While early versions of Storyspace, for example, were limited in terms of its color and sound capabilities, the Web and its ensuing technological developments offer authors a wider variety of modes of representation. The development of multimedia and hypermedia software such as Flash, Dreamweaver, and Quicktime (as well as standalone applications such as recent versions of Storyspace) has led to a wave of digital fiction that combines verbal text with graphics, pictures, animations, and music in increasingly dexterous ways. Hayles (2002, 2008) defines this in terms of a shift between a first and second generation of digital fiction (cf. Ciccoricco 2007). While the first generation can be identified largely in terms of the link-lexia structure (cf. Landow 2006) as epitomized by early Storyspace fiction, the second generation of digital fiction has evolved with technology to contain more sophisticated and semiotically varied navigational interfaces.

Art and literature have always explored and transcended media borders, and the development of all forms of digital fiction can also be seen as both aesthetically and technologically motivated. For example, hypertext existed both as a phenomenon and as a concept long before the computer became a literary medium or commercialized, and a number of print works, retrospectively collected under the term "proto-hypertext," are often seen as the print precursors of hypertext fiction (e.g. Bolter 2001). B.S. Johnson's (1999 [1969]) *The Unfortunates* comprises a box containing twenty-seven pamphlets—each acting as an individual chapter. The reader must begin with the prescribed first and last pamphlet, but she or he can then choose to read the other chapters in any order. Also packaged in a box, Marc Saporta's (2011 [1963]) fragmented novel *Composition No. 1* is comprised of unbound pages that the reader can read in any order she or he chooses. In both cases, different reading orders deliver or imply different narrative outcomes so that the reader is assigned some responsibility, as in a hypertext, for selecting which path to follow. In this sense we might say that these early print literary hypertexts—or proto-hypertexts—demonstrated the need for a medium that was suitable for and adaptable to multilinear and multimodal storytelling. Likewise, the new generation of multimedia digital fiction has reacted to and developed alongside technological advancements. However, they can also be seen to remediate (cf. Bolter and Grusin 2000) the multimodal aesthetic strategies found in well-established modern (and pre-modern) art and literature. Thus while comparisons can be made between nondigital forms of art and literature and digital fiction, in realizing new aesthetic strategies, multimedia digital fiction does offer something new and different from earlier forms. Thus while we advocate, in accordance with Ensslin (2007) and Ciccoricco (2007), that works of digital fiction should be seen as part of a continuum rather than as belonging to discrete and potentially conflicting categories, we, like Hayles (2002), also acknowledge that a second generation of digital fiction, or what Hayles later has also "postmodern" or "contemporary" electronic literature (2008: 7), has emerged, which contains more visual and auditory attributes.

From an analytical point of view, while early digital fiction can be said to challenge established concepts such as authors, readers, and literature, more recent digital fiction also investigates the borders between different modalities and art forms, such as the borders between literature, music, graphics, and photography. In works such as *Flight Paths* (Pullinger et al. 2010), *Nightingale's Playground* (Campbell and Alston 2010), and *Loss of Grasp* (Bouchardon and Volckaert 2012), for example, these different modes are combined to create a multimodal reading experience in which different modes work with and against each other. Accordingly, scholars of digital fiction must also be sensitive to the multimodal dimension of the works. Thus not only must each mode be taken into account independently, but the relationship between different modes and art forms is also important for the work's meaning potential.

More specifically, multimodal literature tests the interpretative traditions and methods of close reading that have been inherited from print literature so that, as Hayles (2008) advocates, "the multimodality of digital art works challenges . . . critics to bring together diverse expertise and interpretive traditions so that the aesthetic strategies and possibilities of electronic literature may be fully understood" (22). Close reading of the multimodal dimension of digital fiction involves perspectives less familiar in literary theory but highly acknowledged in visual theory and discourse analysis. Such an approach involves the reading of the interplay between semiotic resources, a relation that might be characterized as symbiotic, parasitic, antagonistic, or subversive, and that can be described more systematically through semiotic concepts such as "anchoraged" and "relay" (Barthes 1977: 39–41), as "congruency" and "deviation" (Schwarcz 1982: 14–19), or as "elaboration" and "extension" (van Leeuwen 2005: 230). At the same time the interface and/or the spatial composition on the screen call for the analysts' attention and competence. Hayles (2008: 7) points out that an understanding of digital fiction involves a focus on a work's interface metaphors, while the social semiotic theory of multimodality (e.g. van Leeuwen 2005; Machin 2007; Martinec and van Leeuwen 2009) provides us with some analytical tools for approaching multimodal compositions, such as salience (tone, color, foregrounding, etc.), compositional principle (left-right, top-bottom, center-margin, etc.), positioning of the reader-viewer, modality, transitivity, and framing (that is, the sense of connection-disconnection through the use of frame lines, empty spaces, etc.). The second generation of digital fiction analysts can use multifocal approaches to digital fiction by combining perspectives from different fields and diverse tradition, but the field must also acknowledge that print-based methods are not necessarily to be neglected.

NEW GENERATIONS

In addition to Hayles's second generation, Ensslin (2007, 2010a) suggests that a third generation of digital fiction exists, which she defines as "cybertext". Based on Aarseth's (1997) original use of the term, which denotes "ergodic" textual artifacts (digital and in print) that require, for their perusal, nontrivial, playful, and exploratory reader activity, Ensslin narrows the meaning of "cybertext" to a specific type of digital literature. Cybertexts, according to Ensslin, are designed so as to diminish readerly agency to such an extent that the underlying machine code seems to be either fully or partially in control, while, at the same time, deluding readers into expecting high levels of agency. Simultaneously, Aarseth's and Ensslin's notions of cybertext allow an inclusion of ludic features in the analysis of the ever-growing body of digital fiction, as well as the inclusion of poetic and literary-narrative elements in the analysis of the ever-growing body of indie and art games (cf. Ensslin 2012a). In *Digital Litteratur* (2012), Rustad further suggests that a fourth generation of digital fiction has emerged, which he defines as "social media literature". This is literature that is created and read in social media environment, such as Facebook poetry and Twitterfiction (see Thomas's and Klaiber's articles in this volume), where the platform is a significant part of the aesthetic expression and the meaning potential (also see Bogost 2007: 14).

ADDRESSING THE PARADIGM SHIFT

Some attempts have been made to produce media-specific methods of analysis for digital fiction as well as generate a body of criticism that will be useful to other readers. In a special edition of the *Journal of Digital Information* dedicated to hypertext fiction and criticism, the editors assert that the journal should "contribute to this area by publishing criticism of specific works and discussions about the state of hypertext criticism" (Tosca and Walker 2003). Somewhat disappointingly, however, the articles largely comprise the latter. Higgason (2003b) calls for "a body of criticism [which] can provide various readings of the texts"; Miles (2003) concedes that the field is "hobbled by the lack of examples of such simple things as what an individual hypertext might mean"; and Larsen (2003) notes that "to understand nuances in Dante's language, culture and story, we have a myriad of commentaries, translations and keys. Where are these supporting works for hypertext?"

In projects that seek to address these media specific concerns, scholars have begun to offer a range of tools. Ensslin (2007) draws up a dynamic canon of digital literature, including fiction, offering close readings with a view to demonstrating the much-debated critical and analytical "value" of literature born digital. She has also applied multimodal and cybersomatic approaches to Kate Pullinger et al.'s *The Breathing Wall* (Ensslin 2010b, 2011) and analyzed digital fictions from two generations with respect to unreliable narration (Ensslin 2012b). Ciccoricco (2007) applies narrative theory to a range of digital fiction and has also shown how cognitive theories can be used in the analysis of video games (Ciccoricco 2008); Pressman (2008) reads works of digital literature in relation to literary modernism, taking in particular a new critical approach to a variety of digital fiction including Flash fiction and Storyspace hypertext; Bell (2007, 2010, 2011) has provided a methodological approach for the analysis of Storyspace hypertext fiction, which is based on possible worlds theory and has used post-classical narrative theory to analyze second-person narration in a range of digital fiction (Ensslin and Bell 2012, Bell and Ensslin 2011); Rustad (2008, 2009) argues for the need to close read digital fiction before jumping to any consistent conclusion about the readers' reception of the works. He is approaching multimodal hypertext fiction using concepts from text-play theory. Thus while it remains a slow process, the scholarship surrounding digital fiction continues to undergo a significant paradigm shift. Research has moved away from a "first wave" of pure theoretical debate to a "second wave" of scholars interested in critical analysis. Significantly, as the second wave of scholarship bourgeons, collections that offer replicable methods of analysis are slowly emerging either in the form of field-specific journals, such as *dichtung-digital* and the *Electronic Book Review*, or as edited volumes (e.g. Van Looy and Baetens 2003; Simanowski et al. 2010; Page and Thomas 2011). However, such projects are still relatively few in number.

As a means of further addressing the field's analytical and methodological deficiencies, some scholars have been exploring new avenues of defining and implementing approaches to analyzing digital fiction. In particular, the DFIN's commitment to analytical transparency has been articulated in their "[S]creed for Digital Fiction" (Bell et al. 2010). In this document, the authors argue for a "bottom-up approach" to digital fiction analysis in which conclusions are based on examples, and critical assertions are substantiated with evidence. Taking this logistical premise as a starting point, the DFIN promises to produce a body of exemplary analyses of digital fiction substantiated by robust theoretical and terminological conclusions.

In the spirit of the DFIN's agenda, this volume offers a range of analytical tools and associated terminology for digital fiction analysis and, in so doing, provides a body of analyses based on systematic methodological approaches. Rather than imposing a single methodology, this volume exploits the latest research by the current generation of scholars and comprises a diverse selection of essays in which an analysis of digital fiction is conducted transparently whether that that be narratological, new critical, stylistic, or semiotic.

STRUCTURE AND CONTENT OF THE VOLUME

The volume comprises three strands: Narratological Approaches; Social Media and Ludological Approaches; and Semiotic-Rhetorical Approaches, and it closes with an Afterword. In Narratological Approaches, theorists use tools from narrative theory to analyze digital fiction and debate the extent to which tools that have traditionally been developed using examples from print must be adapted when used in a digital context. In "Media-Specific Metalepsis in *10:01*" Alice Bell analyzes Lance Olsen and Tim Guthrie's *10:01* to show that digital fiction facilitates new types of metalepses. More specifically, she shows that both ascending and descending metalepses occur via sound effects, external links, and, visually, via the cursor that the reader uses to select links. She shows that possible worlds theory provides a better approach to metalepsis than the Genettean model, particularly in a digital context, because it allows us to analyze the reader's role in the metaleptic jump more accurately. Adding a hermeneutic dimension, the chapter concludes that the metaleptic ontological breaches are related to the text's thematic concern with commerce and consumerism in contemporary Western society. In "Digital Fiction and Worlds of Perspective" David Ciccoricco also interrogates narrative theory's ability to analyze nonprint fiction. Beginning with an overview of classical theoretical models of focalization, he presents an analysis of Judd Morrissey's (2000) *The Jew's Daughter* and Stuart Moulthrop's (2007) *Radio Salience* to show how and why narrative theory must be revisited if it is to be applied to narration in digital texts. Completing this section, Daniel Punday shows that the user interface (UI) is a key element of digital fiction that has received little attention and draws on possible worlds theory as a means of analyzing it. Using examples from interactive fiction and literary hypertext, he shows that the UI is a key component of our understanding of the fictional world.

The contributors to the second part of the volume, Social Media and Ludological Approaches, examine collaborative fictions and narrative computer games from the perspectives of social and interactive media, as well as game studies. In "Playing with Rather than by the Rules", Astrid Ensslin offers a reading of Tale of Tales's (2009) quasi-fictional art game *The Path*—a remediation of Perrault's folk narrative "Little Red Riding Hood"—from a functional ludo-narrativist perspective. Her analysis is informed theoretically by the Situationist concept of *détournement* and looks in particular at elements of metaludicity, allusive fallacy, and illusory agency. In "140 Characters in Search of a Story", Bronwen Thomas asks whether Twitterfiction offers a new kind of storytelling experience. Contrasting two distinctive varieties of the form, her analysis focuses on the narrative strategies employed and the usage made of the affordances of the medium, while also discussing the stories' reception and patterns of following. Susana Tosca follows with a study on *Amnesia: The Dark Descent* (2010), an atmospheric horror game that encourages immersion. In her chapter *"Amnesia, the Dark Descent*: The Player's Very Own Purgatory", she analyzes the game by applying her methodology of pragmatics of links (Tosca 2000) to the video game medium so as to explore the viability of hybrid digital narratives. The second section of the volume concludes with Isabell Klaiber's chapter, "Wreading Together", which provides an in-depth analysis of two collaboratively written stories from *1000000monkeys.com* and *protagonize.com*. Her study demonstrates how in multilinear collaborative online writing projects, narrative (in)coherence on the textual level is subject to the dynamics of collaborative interaction, and that narrative coherence in online collaborations thus proves to be unstable, progressional, reversible, and collective.

The main scope for the third section, Semiotic-Rhetorical Approaches, is to show the value of approaching digital fiction using semiotic theory. The section deals with the play of signs in digital fiction, as they appear in combination with other signs and sign systems and/or as they appear as a consequence of the readers' performative action. In "(In-)Between Word, Image, and Sound" Hans Kristian Rustad offers a reading of Kate Pullinger's (2010) *Flight Paths* and argues for how and why the work can be read as a cultural encounter. By approaching the work from aesthetic theory and semiotic theory, the chapter considers how cultural differences and Homi Bhabha's concept of the "third place" emerges in the play between verbal language, music, graphics, animations, and movies. The chapter also offers a discussion of the importance of paying attention to the multimodal aesthetic of digital fiction and suggests a theoretical framework for how to approach this multimodal dimension. Serge Bouchardon in "Figures of Gestural Manipulation in Digital Fictions" makes the claim that readers' gestural manipulation in digital fiction is in itself a sign, a part of the process of meaning making in the work. He points out that we lack the tools for analyzing the role of the gestural manipulation and suggests a model based on semiotic and semiotic-rhetorical theory. Through the reading of two digital works, *Anonymes v2* (2000) and *Loss of Grasp* (2010), Bouchardon argues for the use of a five-level analysis model to better understand what he calls figures of manipulation in digital fiction. In the third article in this section, Alexandra Saemmer also pays attention to the significance of the readers' gestural manipulation in digital fiction and offers a close reading of Bergenheger's (1997) *Zeit für die Bombe*, based on semiotic and semiotic-rhetorical theory. In particular, she shows how figures of manipulation, animations, and the characteristics of the reading device contribute to the immersive potential of the work, as they concurrently disturb and confirm the readers' expectations.

In the Afterword, Roberto Simanowski assesses the state of digital fiction scholarship and suggests future areas of research for the field. He shows how and why more work is needed if we are to comprehensively analyze digital fiction.

NOTE

1. The Digital Fiction International Network (DFIN) was funded by The Leverhulme Trust from January to December 2009 (Ref: F/00 455/E) and brought together scholars from the U.K. (Alice Bell and Astrid Ensslin), Norway (Hans Rustad), the U.S. (Jessica Pressman), Canada (Jess Laccetti), and New Zealand (Dave Ciccoricco). The grant funded several international exchanges and a DFIN workshop, held in August 2009, which was also attended by the President of the Electronic Literature Organization, Joseph Tabbi.

WORKS CITED

Aarseth, E. (1997) *Cybertext: Perspectives on Ergodic Literature*. Baltimore, MD: Johns Hopkins University Press.

Anonymes (2000) *Anonymes*. Last accessed 8 February 2013 at: http://www.anonymes.net/index.php

Barthes, R. (1977) *Image, Music, Text*. London: Fontana Press.

Barthes, R. (1990 [1974]) *S/Z*. Richard Miller (trans). Oxford: Blackwell.

Bell, A. (2007) " 'Do You Want to Hear About it?' Exploring Possible Worlds in Michael Joyce's Hyperfiction, *afternoon, a story*". In: M. Lambrou and P. Stockwell (eds). *Contemporary Stylistics*. London: Continuum.

Bell, A. (2010) *The Possible Worlds of Hypertext Fiction*. Basingstoke: Palgrave-Macmillan.

Bell, A. (2011) "Ontological Boundaries and Conceptual Leaps: The Significance of Possible Worlds for Hypertext Fiction (and Beyond)". In *New Narratives: Stories and Storytelling in the Digital Age*. R. Page and B. Thomas (eds). Lincoln, NE: University of Nebraska Press, pp. 63–82.

Bell, A. and Ensslin, A. (2011) " 'I know what it was. You know what it was': Second Person Narration in Hypertext Fiction". *Narrative* 19. 3: 311–329.

Bell, A., Ensslin, A., Ciccoricco, D., Rustad, H., Laccetti, J., and Pressman, P. (2010) "A [S]creed for Digital Fiction". *electronic book review*. Last accessed 13 February 2013 at URL: http://www.electronicbookreview.com/thread/electropoetics/DFINative

Bergenheger, S. (1997) *Zeit für die Bombe*. Last accessed 8 February 2013 at URL: http://www.wargla.de/index1.htm

Bogost, I. (2007) *Persuasive Games: The Expressive Power of Videogames*. Cambridge: MIT Press.

Bolter, J. D. (2001) *Writing Space: Computers, Writing and the Remediation of Print* (2nd edition). Mahwah: NJ: Lawrence Erlbaum Associates Publishers.

Bolter, J. D and Grusin, R. (2000) *Remediation: Understanding New Media*. Cambridge: MIT Press.

Bouchardon, S. and Volckaert, V. (2010) *Loss of Grasp*. Last accessed 8 February 2013 at URL: http://www.lossofgrasp.com

Burnett, K. (1993) "Toward a Theory of Hypertextual Design". *Postmodern Culture* 3. 2. Last accessed 3 February 2013 at URL: http://www3.iath.virginia.edu/pmc/text-only/issue.193/burnett.193

Cadre, A. (1999) *Varicella*. Last accessed 13 July 2012 at URL: http://adamcadre.ac/if.html

Campbell, A. and Alston, J. (2012) *Nightingale's Playground*. Last accessed 13 February 2013 at URL: http://www.nightingalesplayground.com/

Ciccoricco, D. (2007) *Reading Network Fiction*. Tuscaloosa, AL: University of Alabama Press.

Ciccoricco, D. (2008) "*Play, Memory*: Shadow of the Colossus and Cognitive Workouts". A. Ensslin and A. Bell (eds), *dichtung-digital* [online] Special Edition: "New Perspectives on Digital Literature". Last accessed 21 May 2013 at URL: http://www.dichtung-digital.org/2007/Ciccoricco/ciccoricco.htm /

Coover, R. (1992) "The End of Books". *New York Times Book Review* (June 21) 1: 23–24.

Deleuze, G. and Guattari, F. (1988) *A Thousand Plateaus: Capitalism and Schizophrenia*. Brian Massumi (trans). London: Athlone Press.

Derrida J. (1979) "Living on". In *Deconstruction and Criticism: A Continuum Book*. J. Hulbart (ed). New York: Seabury Press, pp. 75–176.

Derrida J. (1981) *Dissemination*. Barbara Johnson (trans). Chicago: University of Chicago Press.

Douglas, J.Y. (1992) "What Hypertexts Can Do That Print Narratives Cannot". *Reader: Essays in Reader-Oriented Theory, Criticism, and Pedagogy* 28: 1–22.

Delany, P. and Landow, G.P. (1991) *Hypermedia and Literary Studies*. Cambridge: MIT Press.

Electronic Book Review. Last accessed 13 February 2013 at URL: www.electronic-bookreview.com/

Ensslin, A. (2007) *Canonizing Hypertext: Explorations and Constructions*. London: Continuum.

Ensslin, A. (2010a) "From Revisi(tati)on to Retro-intentionalisation: Hermeneutics, Multimodality and Corporeality in Hypertext, Hypermedia and Cybertext". In *Reading Moving Letters: Digital Literature in Research and Teaching*. R. Simanowski, P. Gendolla, and J. Schaefer (eds). Bielefeld: Transcript, pp. 145–162.

Ensslin, A. (2010b) "Respiratory Narrative: Multimodality and Cybernetic Corporeality in 'Physio-Cybertext'". In *New Perspectives on Narrative and Multimodality*. R. Page (ed). London: Routledge, pp. 155–165.

Ensslin, A. (2011) "From (W)reader to Breather: Cybertextual De-Intentionalisation in Kate Pullinger et al.'s *Breathing Wall*". In *New Narratives: Stories and Storytelling in the Digital Age*. R. Page and B. Thomas (eds). Lincoln, NE: University of Nebraska Press, pp. 138–152.

Ensslin, A. (2012a) "Computer Gaming". In *The Routledge Handbook of Experimental Literature*. J. Bray, A. Gibbons, and B. McHale (eds). London: Routledge, pp. 497–511.

Ensslin, A. (2012b) "'I Want to Say I May Have Seen My Son Die This Morning': Unintentional Unreliable Narration in Digital Fiction". *Language and Literature* 21. 2: 136–149.

Ensslin, A. and Bell, A. (2012) "'Click = Kill': Textual *You* in Ludic Digital Fiction". *Storyworlds* 4: 49–73.

Frictional Games. (2010) *Amnesia: The Dark Descent*. Helsingborg, Sweden: Frictional Games.

geniwate and Larsen, D. (2003) *The Princess Murderer*. Last accessed 21 May 2013 at URL: http://www.deenalarsen.net/princess/

Hayles, N.K. (2002) *Writing Machines*. Cambridge: MIT Press.

Hayles, N.K. (2007) "Hyper and Deep Attention: The Generational Divide in Cognitive Modes". *Profession* 2007: 187–199.

Hayles, N.K. (2008) *Electronic Literature: New Horizons for the Literary*. Notre Dame, IN: University of Notre Dame Press.

Higgason, R.E. (2003a) "A Scholar's Nightmare". S. Tosca and J. Walker (eds). *Journal of Digital Information* [online] 3. 3. Last accessed 16 July 2010 at URL: http://journals.tdl.org/jodi/article/view/117/116

Higgason, R. E. (2003b) "A Body of Criticism". S. Tosca and J. Walker (eds). *Journal of Digital Information* [online] 3. 3. Last accessed 16 July 2010 at URL: http://journals.tdl.org/jodi/article/view/117/116

Infocom. (1980) *Zork*. Last accessed 13 February 2013 at URL: http://www.infocom-if.org/downloads/downloads.html

Johnson, B. S. (1999 [1969]) *The Unfortunates*. Basingstoke: Picador.

Joyce, M. (1987) *afternoon, a story* [CD-ROM]. Watertown, MA: Eastgate Systems.

Laccetti, J. (2008) "Where to Begin? Multiple Narrative Paths in Web Fiction". In *Narrative Beginnings Theories and Practices*. B. Richardson (ed). Lincoln, NE: University of Nebraska Press, pp. 179–190.

Landow, G. P. (1994) "What's a Critic To Do? Critical Theory in the Age of Hypertext". In *Hyper/Text/Theory*. G. P. Landow (ed). Baltimore, MD: John Hopkins University Press, pp. 1–48.

Landow, G. P. (1997) *Hypertext 2.0: The Convergence of Contemporary Critical Theory and Technology* (revised edition). Baltimore, MD: John Hopkins University Press.

Landow, G. P. (2006) *Hypertext 3.0: Critical Theory and New Media in an Era of Globalization*. Baltimore, MD: John Hopkins University Press.

Larsen, D. (2003) "You Can Get There From Here". S. Tosca and J. Walker (eds). *Journal of Digital Information* [online] 3. 3. Last accessed 18 July 2010 URL: http://journals.tdl.org/jodi/article/view/117/116

Liestol, G. (1994) "Wittgenstein, Genette, and the Reader's Narrative". In *Hyper/Text/Theory*. G. P. Landow (ed). Baltimore, MD: John Hopkins University Press, pp. 87–120.

Machin, D. (2007) *Introduction to Multimodal Analysis*. London: Bloomsbury.

Martinec, R. and van Leeuwen, T. (2009) *The Language of New Media Design*. London: Routledge.

Miles, A. (2003) "Reviewing versus Criticism". S. Tosca and J. Walker (eds). *Journal of Digital Information* [online] 3. 3. Last accessed 18 July 2010 URL: http://journals.tdl.org/jodi/article/view/117/116

Morrissey, J. (2000) *The Jew's Daughter* [online]. Last accessed 20 August 2011 at URL: http://www.thejewsdaughter.com

Moulthrop, S. (2007) *Radio Salience* [online]. Last accessed 20 August 2011 at URL: http://iat.ubalt.edu/moulthrop/hypertexts/rs/

Nelson, J. (2003) *Dreamaphage* (version 1). Last accessed 14 February 2013 at URL: http://collection.eliterature.org/1/works/nelson__dreamaphage/v1/opening.html

Olsen, L. and Guthrie, T. (2005) *10:01*. Last accessed 13 February 2013 at URL: http://www.lanceolsen.com/1001.html

Page, R. and Thomas, B. (eds). (2011) *New Narratives: Stories and Storytelling in the Digital Age*. Lincoln, NE: University of Nebraska Press.

Pressman, J. (2008) "The Strategy of Digital Modernism: Young-Hae Chang Heavy Industries' Dakota". *Modern Fiction Studies* 54. 2: 302–326.

Pullinger, K. and Joseph, C. (2007) *Inanimate Alice*. Last accessed 13 February 2013 at URL: http://www.inanimatealice.com/

Pullinger, K., Joseph, C., and participants. (2010) *Flight Paths: A Networked Novel*. Last accessed 13 February 2013 at URL: www.flightpaths.net

Rettberg, S. (2009) "Communitizing Electronic Literature". *Digital Humanities Quarterly* [online] 3. 2. Last accessed 13 February 2013 at URL: http://digitalhumanities.org/dhq/vol/3/2/000046/000046.html

Rustad, H. K. (2008) *Tekstspill i hypertekst*. Kristiandsand: Agder University.

Rustad, H. K. (2009) "A Four-Sided Model for Reading Hypertext Fiction". *Hyperrhis* 06. Last accessed 13 February 2013 at URL: http://www.hyperrhiz.net/hyperrhiz06/19-essays/80-a-four-sided-model

Rustad, H.K. (2012) *Digital Litteratur: En Innføring*. Oslo: Cappelen Damm Akademisk.

Ryan, M.-L. (2004) "Introduction". In *Narrative Across Media: The Languages of Storytelling*. M.-L. Ryan (ed). Lincoln, NE: University of Nebraska Press, pp. 1–40.

Saporta, M. (2011 [1963]) *Composition No. 1*. Richard Howard (trans). London: Visual Editions.

Schwarcz, J.H. (1982) *Words and Pictures: On the Literal and the Symbolic in the Illustration of a Text*. Chicago: American Library Association.

Simanowski, R. (2002) *Interfictions*: Vom Schreiben im Netz. Frankfurt a. M.: Suhrkamp.

Simanowski, R., Gendolla, P., and Schaefer, J. (eds). (2010) *Reading Moving Letters: Digital Literature in Research and Teaching*. Bielefeld: Transcript.

Tale of Tales. (2009) *The Path*. Last accessed 13 February 2013 at URL: http://tale-of-tales.com/ThePath/downloads.html

Tosca, S.P. (2000) "A Pragmatics of Links". *Journal of Digital Information* 1. 6. Last accessed 13 February 2013 at URL: http://journals.tdl.org/jodi/article/viewArticle/23/24

Tosca, S. and Walker, J. (2003) "Hypertext Criticism: Writing about Hypertext". S. Tosca and J. Walker (eds). *Journal of Digital Information* [online] 3. 3. Last accessed 13 February 2013 at URL: http://journals.tdl.org/jodi/index.php/jodi/article/view/116/115

Van Leeuwen, T. (2005) *Introducing Social Semiotics*. London: Routledge.

Van Looy, J. and Baetens, J. (eds). (2003) *Close Reading New Media: Analyzing Electronic Literature*. Leuven: Leuven University Press.

Walker, J. (2000) "Do You Think You're Part of This? Digital Texts and the Second Person Address". In *Cybertext Yearbook 2000*. M. Eskelinen and R. Koskimaa (eds). Jyväskylä, Finland: Research Centre for Contemporary Culture, pp. 34–51. Last accessed 13 February 2013 at URL: http://cybertext.hum.jyu.fi/articles/122.pdf

Section I
Narratological Approaches

2 Media-Specific Metalepsis in *10:01*

Alice Bell,
Sheffield Hallam University, UK

INTRODUCTION

As the relatively small but diverse sample of texts analyzed in this volume shows, digital technologies offer writers and programmers a whole array of tools with which they can build narratives, many of which are unavailable to authors who write in print. Hypertext provides a linking structure within which lexias can be connected in both linear and multilinear configurations; the Web, as an ever expanding hypertext system, allows digital texts to be linked to other digital texts; software allows sound, image, film, animation, and code to be incorporated into digital fiction works. Whether in terms of structure and navigation or in terms of modes and media therefore, digital technologies add something to narrative and, as analysts are keen to show, they challenge, or at least problematize, the theories of narrative that have until recently been predominantly developed in relation to print.

Yet while we must be mindful of "media-specificity" (Hayles 2002), narrative theory can provide tools that we can use in our analysis of digital fiction, and if we are to develop a truly digital toolkit, then we need to evaluate the effectiveness of print-based methods for our field (and where these tools fail, suggest modifications, amendments or alternatives). This chapter contributes to that process by using narrative theory to analyze what I will show are media-specific metalepses in digital fiction. It begins with an overview of the theory of metalepsis before showing how metalepsis can manifest in digital fiction. The chapter will provide a method for analyzing metalepsis based on possible worlds theory (c.f. Bell and Alber 2012) before applying it to *10:01*, a hypermedia fiction by Lance Olsen and Tim Guthrie (2005), in more detail. The application of the theory to *10:01*, a digital fiction that relies thematically on metalepsis, will show why and how it needs to be modified if it is to be used as a comprehensive approach to metalepsis in digital fiction more generally. In line with the aims of this volume, the method profiled in this essay is replicable so that while I will show how possible worlds theory can be used to analyze metalepsis in *10:01*, the overt application of the theory will also reveal how the method works in general. Thus readers of this study should be able to abstract the method used in this analysis and apply it to other texts.

WHAT IS METALEPSIS?

A metalepsis, as initially defined by Genette (1980) in his seminal work *Narrative Discourse*, is "any intrusion by the extradiegetic narrator or narratee into the diegetic universe (or by the diegetic characters into a metadiegetic universe, etc.), or the inverse" (234–235). Metalepsis is thus a term that describes the movement of fictional entities between diegetic levels, either from the narrating space into the narrated space or from the narrated space to the narrating space. Providing a useful means of conceptualizing the two types of metalepsis that Genette identifies, Pier (2005), following Nelles (1997), has divided the term into two types: "descending" and "ascending", respectively (also see Bell and Alber 2012). In a descending metalepsis, a fictional entity moves from a diegetic level to a hierarchically lower one as in, for example, Woody Allen's short story "The Kugelmass Episode" (1980), in which university professor Kugelmass hires a magician to help him enter the storyworld of *Madame Bovary*. In an ascending metalepsis, a fictional entity moves from a diegetic level to a hierarchically higher one as is the case, for example, in Flann O'Brien's (1939) *At Swim-Two-Birds*, when the characters that are invented by the fictional author, Dermot Trellis, check themselves into his hotel to torture him. The preceding examples show how metalepses take place across borders *within* a fictional world, but as Herman (1997) notes, metalepses can also "dissolve the border not just between diegetic levels, but also between the actual and the non-actual—or rather between two different systems of actuality" (134). Thus "metalepsis" is also used to describe instances in which authors are represented in their own works (e.g. Ryan 2006: 208; Chen 2008; Feyersinger 2010; Kukkonen 2011: 2) when, for example, Martin Amis appears at the end of his novel *Money* (1984) to play chess with the protagonist John Self, and also in instances of second-person address (e.g. McHale 1987: 223–235, 1997: 89–95; Fludernik 2003: 389, Wolf 2005: 94), such as the narrator's invocation of "you" in the opening line of Italo Calvino's (1979) *If on a Winter's Night a Traveler* or the protagonist's address to the reader at the beginning of Michael Joyce's (1987) *afternoon*: "do you want to hear about it?" (see Bell 2007).

METALEPSIS IN NARRATIVE THEORY

Some narrative theorists have devised typologies that can be used to distinguish between different types of metalepsis (e.g. Nelles 1997; Herman 1997; Malina 2002; Fludernik 2003; Pier 2005, 2011; Ryan 2006; Kukkonen and Klimek 2011; Bell and Alber 2012). Fludernik (2003), for example, argues that metalepsis manifests in four different ways. In "authorial metalepsis" the author-narrator addresses the audience in order to foreground the inventedness of the story and in "rhetorical metalepsis" the author-narrator pauses the action to speak about his characters. Correlating with Pier's categories of descending and ascending metelapses, Fludernik then suggests:

ontological metalepsis (type 1), in which the narrator (or a character) jumps to a lower diegetic level, and ontological metalepsis (type 2), in which a fictional character jumps to a higher narrative level. Ryan's (2006) categories are more limited than Fludernik's, but she too discriminates between "rhetorical metalepsis", in which the author "may speak *about* her characters, presenting them as creations of her imagination" (207), and "ontological metalepsis", which "opens a passage between levels that result in their interpenetration, or mutual contamination" (207). According to both Fludernik and Ryan, then, in cases of ontological metalepsis, entities transgress ontological boundaries, while in rhetorical and also authorial metalepses, fictional entities remain in their original positions with the narrator drawing attention to his role in the fiction making process while not moving across any ontological boundaries. This essay is concerned with ontological metalepses, in which world boundaries are transgressed rather than with rhetorical and/or authorial metalepsis, in which communication between narrator and reader takes place but during which no actual boundary crossing occurs.

Fludernik and Ryan, following Genette, refer to diegetic levels in their typologies, but in ontological metalepses the entities' maneuvers suggest that *world* boundaries are breached. In the real world authors, readers, narrators, and characters cannot really move between ontological domains; this would involve, for example, authors physically entering their own texts, characters speaking to readers, or heterodiegetic narrators interacting with the characters to which they have no ontological association. When ontological metalepses occur, however, we are asked to imagine that these interactions or movements do take place. Thus terminology that describes the domains of existence as "worlds" rather than the more abstract concept of diegetic "levels" more accurately describes what we are asked to imagine happens during the cause of ontological metalepses. Consequently, there has been a general tendency in the scholarship surrounding metalepsis to use "worlds" as opposed to Genettean "levels" to describe what happens during a metaleptic jump (e.g. McHale 1987; Wolf 2005; Kukkonen 2011; Bell and Alber 2012).

The use of "worlds" as opposed to "levels" might appear to be a terminological issue only, but it also has ramifications for the method of analysis. Adopting the term "world" as opposed to "level" allows analysts to utilize tools that are specifically designed to analyze the relationship between worlds in fiction (cf. Herman 1997; Wolf 2005; Kukkonen 2011; Pier 2011; Limoges 2011; Bell and Alber 2012). In particular, we can utilize established concepts and terminology from possible worlds theory, a systematic and comprehensive framework that is designed specifically to analyze worlds and the interactions between them.

METALEPSIS AND POSSIBLE WORLDS THEORY

As a theory that is founded on propositional modal logic, possible worlds theory is fundamentally concerned with the relationship between the "actual world"—that is, the world we belong to—and "possible worlds"—that is, worlds that are constructed through imagination, hypothetical situations, dreams, wishes, etc. While possible worlds theory originates in philosophical logic, it can also be used in a narratological context because the worlds described by fictional texts represent a particular type of possible world. In narrative theory (e.g. Doležel 1998; Pavel 1986; Ronen 1994; Ryan 1991; Bell 2007, 2010, 2011) concepts of ontology, reference, and modality have been appropriated from possible worlds logic (e.g. Kripke 1972; Hintikka 1967; Lewis 1973; Plantinga 1974) and applied to the worlds built by fictional texts. As a methodological approach it is extremely proficient at elucidating very complex ontological configurations, and it provides appropriate terminology for labeling different ontological domains. It is therefore especially effective for analyzing fictions that play with ontological structures in both print (e.g. Ryan 1992; Ashline 1995; Punday 1997) and digital texts (e.g. Koskimaa 2000; Ryan 2001, 2006; Bell 2011), but it has also been used to investigate the truth value of fictional narratives (e.g. Pavel 1986; Doležel 1980; Ryan 1991); evaluate the ontological status of fictional worlds and their inhabitants (Pavel 1979; Margolin, 1996, 1990); and construct taxonomies of fictional possibility relative to genre (e.g. Traill 1991; Ryan 1991). More relevant to this study, possible worlds theory can also be used to explain how fictional entities move from one domain to another (e.g. Ryan 1991; Bell 2010) and thus can be used to explain what happens to entities during the course of different types of metalepsis (see Bell and Alber 2012).

In possible worlds theory, an individual is said to possess "transworld identity" when she moves from one ontological domain to another (e.g. Rescher 1975; Kripke 1972; Hintikka 1967; Plantinga 1979; Pavel 1979). Using this concept in a fictional context can explain some examples of ontological metalepsis. For instance, in the ascending metalepsis in *At Swim-Two-Birds* described above, when the characters torture Dermot Trellis, they move from the world *in which* they were created to the world *from which* they were created. We are asked to imagine therefore that fictional entities have made a permanent transition from one ontological domain to another; in possible worlds terminology, the characters are therefore said to possess transworld identity. In other examples of ontological metalepsis, the concept of "counterparthood" is required. For example, when Martin Amis plays chess with John Self in *Money*, readers are asked to believe that, ontologically, Martin Amis has moved from the actual world to the fictional world of *Money*. However, in order for readers to recognize the figure that John Self plays chess with as Martin Amis, they must also know that Martin Amis exists as the author of that text in the actual world. Martin Amis's descending metaleptic jump in *Money* is therefore not an example of transworld identity because he has not made a permanent transition from actual to fictional. Instead it is an example of what is known in possible worlds theory as "counterparthood" (e.g. Lewis 1973; Margolin 1990). Martin Amis exists in the actual world as the author of *Money*, and Martin Amis also exists in the fictional world as John Self's opponent. The two Martin Amis figures are thus counterparts of one another.

METALEPSIS ACROSS MEDIA

Most theories of metalepsis, including the possible worlds approach as outlined above, have been developed predominantly in relation to printed prose narratives and thus focus on verbal manifestations of the device. Yet as Kukkonen (2011) notes, "[M]etalepsis . . . occurs in a variety of multimodal media" (18), and different media "allow for different ways of depicting the fictional and the real world, of drawing and identifying the boundary between them and of realizing different types, effects and functions of the transgression of these boundaries" (18–19). In the context of hypertext fiction, for example, in Stuart Moulthrop's (1991) *Victory Garden,* a lexia entitled ". . . and . . ." describes the demise of a character named Emily as she slips into unconsciousness during a missile attack. The succeeding lexia, also entitled ". . . and . . .", contains the same text as appears in the preceding ". . . and . . ." lexia, but with cracks and fissures as though the screen has been smashed. Visually, therefore, the hypertext suggests that the blast in the fictional world has physically influenced the typographical materiality of the text on the computer screen in the actual world. Corroborating Kukkonen's assertions above, in this case of ascending metalepsis, the fictional world appears to invade the actual world by taking advantage of the visual affordances that the hypertext medium brings to fiction (c.f. Bell and Alber 2012).

The preceding example is taken from Storyspace hypertext fiction, but research is emerging that seeks to understand metalepsis across a range of other media including graphic novels, painting, comics, film, television, role-playing games, videogames, and code poetry (e.g. Wolf 2005; Ryan 2006; Klimek 2009; Feyersinger 2010; Kukkonen and Klimek 2011; Thoss 2011). Within this work, theorists are increasingly concerned with showing the extent to which the affordances of different media affect the nature of metalepsis and also how print-based tools can be used to analyze them. Of course, metalepsis can, as in print fiction, also be enacted verbally in nonprint contexts. In Richard Holeton's (2001) hypertext *Figurski at Findhorn on Acid*, for example, emails are exchanged between several of the characters and a writer called "Richard Holeton". Thus in an example of descending metalepsis comparable with the example from the print fiction *Money* above, a counterpart of the author is verbally depicted in the fictional world of *Figurski*. While metalepsis can be represented verbally, nonprint media also provide a context for media-specific metalepsis. The citations above show that transmedial studies do exist, but, as Pier (2011) suggests, there are "only occasional forays into the visual media or into works employing multiple media" (269), and much work remains to be done to understand how metalepsis operates in different types of text.

With the issues discussed above in mind, this essay has two aims. First it will show how the means of navigation and representation in one particular Web-based hypertext fiction—Lance Olsen and Tim Guthrie's *10:01*—allow metalepses to manifest via a range of nonverbal modes. More specifically, using possible worlds theory, I will show that sound effects, external links, and the cursor that the reader uses to select links are all metaleptic because they suggest that entities from the fictional world can intrude into the actual world or vice-versa. Moreover, I will argue that metaleptic jumps are hermeneutically significant in *10:01* because they make explicit the thematic relationship between the fictional world described in text and the world to which the reader belongs (cf. Bell 2013). In a second step, this essay will examine the extent to which current narrative theory, and the possible worlds approach in particular, which has been primarily developed in relation to print fiction, can be used to analyze metalepsis in a digital fiction context and suggest ways in which the model needs to be modified or expanded to accommodate the affordances that Web technologies bring to fiction.

10:01

Originally published by the *Iowa Review Web* in 2005, *10:01* is a Web-based version of Olsen's print novel *10:01*, which was published in the same year. Both narratives are set in a movie theater in the Mall of America in Bloomington, Minnesota, and both document the ten minutes running up to the beginning of the main feature. In both versions, *10:01* is narrated by an omniscient third-person narrator who, somewhat uncannily, has access to the thoughts and feelings of the characters, and both narratives are primarily concerned with the internal musings, memories, and speculations of the movie theater audience members. In each text, during the ten-minute buildup to the feature, the characters muse over their personal circumstances and/or watch and speculate about the other moviegoers as they take their seats. Toward the chronological end of the narrative in both versions, an explosion occurs. It is not clear, however, as to whether the blast happens within the movie theater, on the movie trailer, or in the mind of one of the characters.

While the two versions of *10:01* share many narrative elements, there are certainly some ontological, representational, and navigational differences between them. As a codex, the print version exists as a series of bound printed leaves, and as a hypertext the digital version exists as a collection of lexias that are connected by links. As is typical of novels, the pages in the print version are fixed, and the reader navigates the text from front to back. Chapter titles also trace the narrative chronologically in terms of hours, minutes, seconds, and milliseconds with the first entitled "00:00:00:00" and the last "00:09:54:27". By contrast, as shown in Figure 2.1, the digital version of *10:01* houses two different navigational tools, which result in

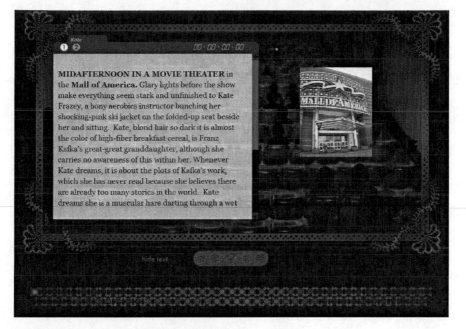

Figure 2.1   Screenshot of lexia 00:00:00:00 in *10:01*

two different navigational structures: a timeline at the bottom of the screen and a visual representation of the moviegoers in the theater. To date, no analyses of the digital *10:01* exist, but in his review of its print predecessor, Martin (2006) writes that the narrative "revolves around the ongoing tension between the cinematic time of frames moving in a linear, mechanistic sequence and the human time of subjective experience moving freely, in many different improvised patterns". In the digital version of the text this tension is encapsulated via the two different means of navigation. Using the timeline, the reader can, as in the print version, read the narrative chronologically but by clicking on the different points on the timeline rather than by turning pages. In addition, the reader of the digital version can also select from any point on the timeline and can thus read the narrative in any temporal order that she chooses. Alternatively, the reader can click on the silhouettes in the visual representation of the movie theater and focus on the characters' thoughts, feelings, and actions as opposed to their place in the overall chronological sequence. The lexia titles also reflect the dual navigational structure by containing both the temporal point in the narrative—in Figure 2.1 this is "00:00:00:00"—and also the character's name—in Figure 2.1 this is "Kate". Thus while the reader of the print version experiences an exclusively linear structure, the reader of the digital version can navigate the text temporally by using the timeline to select a chronological point in the narrative or spatially by selecting a particular character about whom they want to read. Although unlikely, the reader of the print version could of course flick between chapters at her leisure and thus navigate the narrative in a nonchronological order. However, the navigational features afforded by Web technology explicitly encourage navigational exploration in a way that the codex does not.

In addition to the different navigational structures, the two versions of *10:01* also utilize distinct modes of representation. The print version is comprised of text only, but the digital version also contains a number of nonverbal modes. The lexia shown in Figure 2.1, for example, contains a photographic image. That image does not appear alongside the corresponding text in the print version. In fact, the print version contains no images at all. In addition, while not possible in codex form, the digital version of *10:01* is intermittently accompanied by music and/or sound effects. It also contains numerous external links, which, if followed by the reader, take her away from the *10:01* website to external Web domains. Thus while the print version is exclusively text based, the digital version utilizes a range of different visual, aural, and hypertextual modes and media.

The preceding overview has shown how the digital and print versions of *10:01* are very different both from a navigational and representational point of view. Yet while these differences certainly result in different versions of the same narrative and will inevitably result in a different type of experience for the reader, from a narratological perspective the two texts are almost identical. Consequently, in both the print and digital *10:01*, the same heterodiegetic narrator narrates, the same characters appear, and despite a few omissions the same events occur. Thus, while the nonverbal elements in the digital *10:01* certainly play an important role in producing a multisensory experience for the reader, they actually add very little to the narrative structure of the text. Significantly, however, the thematic message of *10:01* is profoundly affected by the digital context in which it is presented. Of the print version, Martin (2006) writes that "the process of over-consumption in the mall is depicted . . . through an aesthetic strategy that emphasizes the people in the theater and not the manipulative power of the mall or the movie". Conversely, in the following analysis I will show that media-specific metalepses accentuate "the manipulative power of the mall or the movie" *as well as* the "people in the theater" and, perhaps more significantly, I will show that we as readers might be as susceptible to, and as responsible for, "the process of over-consumption" as the characters in the movie theater.

THE METALEPTIC CURSOR

Whether the reader of the digital *10:01* (henceforth *10:01*) explores the text via the links on the timeline or the silhouettes in the movie theater, the reader and her choices are symbolized onscreen by the cursor, which she uses to hover above and/or select links. The cursor is a commonplace navigational tool that is deployed in most, if not all, computer systems. In fact, Bizzocchi and Woodbury (2003) suggest that "we are so accustomed to this correlation [between hand movements and associated cursor movements] that it is perfectly transparent—we don't think about it, we don't question it, we don't even notice it" (558). Yet while the cursor may have become a normalized form of navigation in computers generally, the relationship between the reader and the cursor in *10:01* is ontologically significant because *10:01* is a *fictional* digital text. When reading any type of fictional text, the reader is situated in the actual world, and the characters are situated in the fictional world, but when reading a digital fiction, the reader is also represented onscreen by a cursor. In *10:01* an additional dimension is added because if the reader of *10:01* selects links by clicking on the characters' silhouettes in the movie theater, as opposed to selecting points on the timeline, she appears to be able to reach from the actual world in which she is situated to the fictional world in which she is represented.

The ontologically intrusive nature of the cursor in *10:01* can be understood by theorizing the relationship between cursor and reader in digital fiction more generally. Ryan, for example, suggests that the cursor is either "an extension of the proprioceptive boundaries" (1999: 20) or "the representation of their [the reader's] virtual body in the virtual world" (2006: 122, cf. Ryan 2001: 54). She thus suggests that the cursor is either an extension or a copy of the reader. In possible worlds terms, the former correlates with the reader possessing transworld identity because it suggests that she can literally reach into the fictional world, and the latter correlates with counterparthood because it suggests that the cursor represents a copy or version of the reader in the fictional world. Clearly transworld identity is not an appropriate way of conceptualizing the reader's presence because it is ontologically impossible for the reader to reach into the computer screen. Instead, we regard the cursor as a counterpart of the reader. Ensslin's (2009) concept of "double-situatedness" confirms the applicability of the counterpart approach to the reader-as-cursor relation in digital fiction. "On the one hand" she argues, "user-readers are 'embodied' as direct receivers, whose bodies interact with the hardware and software of a computer. On the other, user-readers are considered to be 'reembodied' through feedback which they experience in represented form, e.g. through visible or invisible avatars (third person or first person graphic or typographic representations on screen)" (158) (cf. Ensslin 2012). Readers are thus double-situated in both the actual and the fictional world.

Yet while the reader of *10:01* is certainly represented visually onscreen and thus doubly situated, the reader-as-cursor does not have the same ontological status as the characters in the fictional world. Instead we might think of the cursor as intruding into a world that exists between the actual world and the fictional world of the characters. We might call this part of the fictional world the "mediating space" because it is equivalent to the space from which the omniscient heterodiegetic narrator observes the characters and events (cf. Bell 2010: 31–38). The reader of *10:01* is thus doubly situated in the actual world and mediating space: when she selects links she is projected into the mediating space visually, via the cursor, but as reader of the fiction she also exists, corporeally, in the actual world. She thus exists in two different ontological domains at the same time, or, in possible worlds theory terms, the cursor and the reader are counterparts of one another.

While terminology from possible worlds theory can be used to explain the reader's dual ontology in *10:01*, the framework requires some alteration if it is to be applied to this example because, while the cursor does represent the reader visually, it is not a counterpart of the reader in the original possible worlds conception of the term. In *10:01*, as in any other hypertext, the reader is represented onscreen by a digital icon, which is thus a representation of the reader rather than an exact copy or counterpart. As Margolin (1990) notes in his exposition of counterpart theory, "[Q]uestions immediately arise about whether there is a minimum degree of similarity required for counterparthood and what it may be" (866). It is therefore important that the lines of cross-identification are established if possible worlds theory is to be applied in this case.

In possible worlds theory, some theorists argue that proper names should be used as a means of cross-identification (e.g. Pavel 1979; Ryan 1991) because they can act as "rigid designators attached to individuated objects, independent of the objects' properties" (Pavel 1979: 185). In this approach counterpart relations are established on the basis of proper names, irrespective of the characteristics that the two individuals possess. In *10:01* a proper name is not available as a means of cross-identification because the reader is represented visually. As a method that is based on verbal representations of counterparts, therefore, it is not appropriate in this case. Other possible worlds theorists (e.g. Kripke 1972; Doležel 1998) suggest that individuals can be considered counterparts of one another if they share what are known as "essential properties". In this case, sufficient evidence can be gathered on which to base an association as opposed to using linguistic signifiers. In the context of *10:01*, uniting the reader and cursor on the basis of essential properties is a more appropriate method because it does not rely on verbal clues. Instead, the reader and cursor can be cross-identified via their shared spatiotemporal positions and functions: when the reader moves the mouse, the cursor moves, and when the reader clicks the mouse in an appropriate space, the cursor selects a link.

As the analysis has shown, it is possible to utilize concepts and terminology from possible worlds theory to describe the relationship between the reader and the cursor in terms of ontological parallelism. Crucially, however, since the reader appears in the mediating space of the fictional world—albeit in virtual form—she enacts a form of descending metalepsis. Since all digital fictions utilize some form of onscreen navigational aid, the cursor-as-reader counterpart relation and associated metalepsis is not necessarily exclusive to Olsen and Guthrie's text. However, the analysis does show how the reader of the digital version of *10:01* can intrude into the fictional world in a way that is certainly not possible in the print version and thus reveals how the cursor represents an exclusively digital metaleptic jump. Moreover, the metaleptic cursor in *10:01*, while primarily based on an ontological intrusion into the fictional world, also emphasizes the reader's epistemological perspective in relation to that fictional world. When the reader selects a character as a link, the omniscient narrator divulges what is often quite intimate information about that individual's life. For example, we learn that Trudi Chan has gone to see the film as a break from her work. The omniscient narrator also tells us, however, that Trudi's husband has recently left her and that "suspended in unsuspecting Trudi Chan's uterus floats a two-month old fetus" (00:06:07:18). More disturbingly, we learn that Max Watt has committed a series of violent and probably sexual crimes against women. He intends, the omniscient narrator informs us, to kidnap one of the women in the cinema in order to do the same again. In each case, we spend only a short time with each character so that our relationship with them is shown as very transient. At the same time, however, we learn a lot about these individuals' social backgrounds, their current thoughts and emotions, and aspects of their personal histories.

While privy to this often distressing if not disturbing information, the reader is unable to influence the characters' circumstances because they belong to a different ontological domain than the reader. As link chooser, the reader is granted some degree of agency and is also given access to the characters' thoughts, fears, and wishes. Ultimately, however, because the reader in the actual world and characters in the fictional world are ontologically incongruent, the reader has no mandate to intervene; she remains a voyeur. The tension between epistemological access to intimate thoughts and the simulated ontological access and actual ontological exclusion from the world in which they have most impact is striking. As link chooser, she exposes private information—some of which is unknown to the characters—but as an ontological foreigner, she is powerless to help.

AUDIBLE METALEPSIS

By reaching into parts of the fictional world, via a metaleptic cursor, the reader unearths details about particular parts of the fictional world and its inhabitants. The following example of metalepsis shows how sound effects in *10:01* produce metaleptic effects that intensify the reader's omniscience but that work in the opposite (ascending) direction. Rather than the reader reaching into the fictional world, therefore, the fictional world appears to intrude into the reader's space.

Ranging from the buzzing of fireflies to the bodily functions of characters to the sound of a spinning movie reel, the sound effects in *10:01* offer audible representations of the fictional world that complement the descriptions given by the narrator. For example, as Miguel Gonzalez and Angelica Encinas "feel each other up" (00:00:03:13) while Miguel "closes his eyes to savor the moment" (00:03:27:29), sounds of heavy breathing can be heard. Miguel's breathing also quickens as his and Angelica's sexual encounter becomes more intimate (00:07:27:22). Similarly as the narrator describes the aftermath of the explosion in the movie hall, the sound of a thumping heartbeat can be heard (e.g. 00:09:31:24 and 00:09:36:18). The different sound effects in *10:01* constitute a form of ascending metalepsis because in each case a noise that originates in the fictional world crosses the ontological boundary to reach the reader in the actual world (cf. Limoges 2011; Keazor 2011: 109–110).

It is important to note that these examples of what we might call "audible metalepses" are distinct from cases of "rhetorical metalepses" (Fludernik 2003; Ryan 2006) in which the author-narrator pauses the action to speak to the reader about his characters. In a "rhetorical metalepsis" the narrator speaks to the reader *about* the characters, but in the case of the sound effects in *10:01*, audible components from characters in the fictional world exceed the ontological threshold to reach the reader in the actual world directly. It is as though part of the fictional world leaks into the actual world crossing what McHale (1987) has termed a "semipermeable membrane" (34) through which both worlds seem to be uncannily accessible to one other. While readers inevitably have access to the fictional world, the sound effects in *10:01* imply that the characters' physiological noises can be heard in, and therefore can access, the actual world. More specifically, because a constituent of a character—a perceptible sound in particular—moves from the domain *in* which it was created to the domain *from* which it was created, the noises possess transworld identity.

Yet while possible worlds theory can explain the transition, it is important to note that its use in this case also necessities a modification of the method because rather than the whole character moving from one domain to another, the sound effects in *10:01* represent only one part of the character. As a means of categorizing this example in which part of the character, representing the whole, crosses the ontological divide between one world and another, I suggest the term "synechdochical metalepsis". This means of conceptualizing the transition acknowledges that a metalepsis takes place but that it is only partial. That is, it is a component of the character—the character's breath or heartbeat in this case—rather than the whole character that breaches the ontological threshold and possesses transworld identity.

The ascending audible metalepses in *10:01* imply that the fictional world can intrude into the reader's physical-sensory space. However, that the reader can hear the characters' heartbeat or breath also means that she is intruding on the characters' private and personal (corporeal) space. The audible metalepses, like the metaleptic cursor, thus accentuate the reader's voyeuristic position in relation to the fictional world. It also reminds her that she exists, not in isolation, but as witness to a society to which she would have some responsibility and connection if she were ontologically congruent with them. The heavy breathing that she witnesses, for example, might be an expression of desire, but it might also be a response to danger. That she sits in a separate ontological domain to the action in *10:01* paralyzes her from taking action, but as the proceeding analysis will show, it does not mean that she can divorce herself from its significance.

METALEPTIC LINKS

As shown in Figure 2.1, *10:01* begins, chronologically at least, with the following description of the fictional world: "Midafternoon in a movie theater in the Mall of America. Glary lights before the show make everything seem stark and unfinished to Kate Frazey, a bony aerobics instructor" (00:00:00:00). In *10:01*, the "Mall of America" text is formatted as an external link, and if followed, it takes the reader to the Mall of America website. "Welcome to the Mall of America" the greeting reads, and a series of images depict the latest fashion trends and shops from where they can be purchased. From the Mall of America homepage, internal links provide access to individual stores' websites as well as information about opening times, events that are scheduled to take place, a map of the mall, and a list of guest services. Other external links in *10:01* lead to websites including multiple stores and cafes that are housed in the Mall of America; tourist information sites; a religious website to which users can submit questions; a website into which readers can enter information in order to calculate their projected date and time of death.

Clearly, the external links do not appear in the print version of *10:01* because they are an exclusively Web-based phenomenon. They do, however, add extra detail to the narrative because, if followed by the reader, they are used primarily as sources of contextual information. For example, the Mall of America website provides information about the location of the movie theater as well as implicit and explicit cues about its target market and the associated demographic of its visitors. In the print version, readers do not have direct access to this source, but in the digital version the extra Web-based information can be used by the reader as she builds up her knowledge and understanding of the fictional world. Thus while in the print version, the reader's knowledge of the fictional world is provided only by the words on the page, in the digital narrative readers can leave the *10:01* website and, potentially at least, explore an entire chain of extra-textual sources of information.

Like the sound effects, the external links in *10:01* have a primarily epistemological function. However, the external links are also ontologically significant because when the reader follows a link, she is taken from the fictional world to a source of information that originates in the actual world. Since this information, which exists in websites external to *10:01*, is meant to be used in the reader's understanding of the fictional world, she is asked to imagine that the characters in *10:01* also belong to the same ontological domain as she does. It is as though the fictional world reaches out into the actual world to cannibalize information before retreating back to its onto-logical origin. More specifically, from a possible worlds perspective, when the reader clicks on a link that describes a location in the fictional world, she is led to information about a location in the actual world. The external links thus suggest that the characters in *10:01* possess a form of transworld iden-tity. While not exclusive to *10:01*, this kind of metaleptic jump is peculiar to Web-based hypertext fiction because it requires links for it to be enacted. The external links in *10:01* thus represent another media-specific form of ontological intrusion that can only occur in digital form.

Of course the characters in *10:01* do not really belong to the same do-main as the reader, and the fictional world of *10:01* does not really have access to the actual world. Yet it is precisely because the external links sug-gest that they do that this form of ascending metalepsis is so unsettling. As the reader learns from the omniscient narrator as she selects links via the metaleptic cursor, many of the characters in *10:01* are extremely unhappy either because they are in dysfunctional relationships, because they work in unsatisfying jobs, or because they feel generally misunderstood or under-valued by the world in which they live. The world to which the characters belong is, as Martin (2006) observes, "dismal". Martin continues, "[M]any of Olsen's characters are controlled by outside influences that assault, in-habit or consume them" so that "their freedom to dream, to construct their own temporal realities, is restricted and shaped in ways they are powerless to resist and often not even aware of". That the characters' unhappiness is caused by their surroundings is pertinent because the metaleptic links suggest that their world is an extension of our own. Like the sound effects, the external links suggest that the fictional world and actual world are not so separate after all. In fact, the way in which the two worlds slide into one another asks the reader to question whether they are so separate after all. More specifically, *10:01* asks the reader to consider the extent to which her life resembles the character's existence and whether she, like them, is ad-versely influenced by the twenty-first century capitalist milieu in which the links and destination websites suggest they both live.

CONCLUSION

In her overview of metalepsis in popular culture, Kukkonen (2011) hypoth-esizes that "narrative research into hypertext forms . . . will certainly reveal a wealth of what I would call 'interactional metalepsis'" (18) and, while Kukkonen does not define this term, the metalepses that have been analyzed in the digital version of *10:01* might constitute at least some examples. In particular, the analysis of three different kinds of media-specific metalepsis has shown that the affordances of Web technology can produce varying types of ontological violation. Sound effects act as ascending metalepses that suggest that elements from the fictional world are able to cross into the actual world. While audible metalepsis could be found in other types of text that incorporate sound, the analysis of the cursor and external links has shown that *10:01* also contains metalepses that are exclusively digital. The cursor acts as a descending metalepsis in which a counterpart of the reader can be traced in the fictional world, and external links act as a form of ascending metalepsis in which the characters from the fictional world possess a form of transworld identity. Interestingly all of the metalepses within *10:01* take places across the fictional-to-actual boundary. That is, there are no instances in *10:01* in which any fictional entities move to other ontological domains within the fictional world. This is perhaps connected to the fact that the reader must interact with the text throughout her reading experience, and thus a relationship already exists between actual and fictional domains. Yet the discrepancy between epistemological access and ontological disparity that the metalepses represent is striking because it highlights the ontologically ambiguous position that the reader occupies in relation to the text. Like readers of all fiction, she has access to information about the fictional world and its inhabitants. That this world seems to melt into hers at times brings them uncannily close.

The analysis has also shown how possible worlds theory can be used in the analysis of metalepsis. In particular, the concepts of transworld identity, in which an entity moves from one world to another, and counterparthood, in which an entity exists in two different worlds at the same time, can be applied to both ascending and descending metalepses. During the course of the analysis it has been shown that possible worlds theory requires some modification if it is to be used in the analysis of Web-based fiction and thus become a transmedial approach. The analysis of the metaleptic cursor advocates that the conditions on which counterparthood is established may need to be relaxed if it is to be applied in all cases; the analysis of sound effects suggests that the scope of transworld identity requires modification if it is to accommodate the movement of particular components of an individual across worlds; the analysis of external links shows that transworld identity can be a temporary process in which entities oscillate between one world and another.

Metalepsis can be found across media including print and digital fiction, film, television, theater, videogames, and comics, and as this article has shown, metaleptic jumps can manifest in various different modes. Not only does the study of metalepsis refine our understanding of this narratological device in particular, but it also contributes more generally to the study of "unnatural narratives" that present "physically impossible scenarios and events" (Alber 2009: 80; cf. Bell and Alber 2012; Alber et al 2010; Nielsen 2004; Richardson 2002). Unnatural narratives, like digital fictions, challenge and problematize theories of narrative because they contain phenomena that challenge the real-world parameters on which these theories rest. This essay has shown how possible worlds theory offers a systematic means of analyzing examples of "unnatural" metalepses in one digital text, but more research is required if it is to provide a truly comprehensive means of analyzing metalepses across media.

WORKS CITED

Alber, J. (2009) "Impossible Storyworlds and What to Do with Them". *Storyworlds* 1. 1: 79–96.
Alber, J., Iversen, S., Nielsen, H. S, and Richardson, B. (2010) "Unnatural Narratology, Unnatural Narratives: Beyond Mimetic Models". *Narrative* 18. 2: 113–136.
Allen, W. (1980) "The Kugelmass Episode". *Side Effects*. New York: Random House, pp. 41–55.
Amis, M. (2005) *Money* [1984]. London: Vintage.
Ashline, W. L. (1995) "The Problem of Impossible Fictions". *Style* 29. 2: 215–234.
Bell, A. (2007) "'Do You Want to Hear About It?' Exploring Possible Worlds in Michael Joyce's Hyperfiction, *afternoon, a story*". In *Contemporary Stylistics*. M. Lambrou and P. Stockwell (eds). London: Continuum, pp. 43–55.
Bell. A. (2010) *The Possible Worlds of Hypertext Fiction*. Basingstoke: Palgrave-Macmillan.
Bell, A. (2011) "Ontological Boundaries and Methodological Leaps: The Significance of Possible Worlds Theory for Hypertext Fiction (and Beyond)". In *New Narratives: Stories and Storytelling in the Digital Age*. R. Page and B. Thomas (eds). Lincoln, NE: University of Nebraska Press, pp. 63–82.
Bell, A. (2013 forthcoming) "Schema Theory, Links and Hypertext Fiction". *Style* 47 (3).
Bell, A. and Alber, J. (2012) "Ontological Metalepsis and Unnatural Narratology". *Journal of Narrative Theory* 42. 2: 166–192.
Bizzocchi, J. and Woodbury, R. F. (2003) "A Case Study in the Design of Interactive Narrative: The Subversion of the Interface". *Simulation Gaming* 34: 550–568.
Calvino, I. (2007) *If on a Winter's Night a Traveller* [1979]. Random House: London.
Chen, F. F. (2008) "From Hypotyposis to Metalepsis: Narrative Devices in Contemporary Fantastic Fiction". *Forum for Modern Language Studies* 44. 4: 394–411.
Doležel, L. (1998) *Heterocosmica: Fiction and Possible Worlds*. Baltimore, ML: The Johns Hopkins University Press.
Ensslin, A. (2009) "Respiratory Narrative: Multimodality and Cybernetic Corporeality in 'Physio-cybertext'". In *New Perspectives on Narrative and Multimodality*. R. Page (ed). London: Routledge, pp. 155–165.
Ensslin, A. (2012) "From (W)reader to Breather: Cybertextual De-Intentionalisation in Kate Pullinger et al.'s *Breathing Wall*". In *New Narratives: Stories and Storytelling in the Digital Age*. R. Page and B. Thomas (eds). Lincoln, NE: University of Nebraska Press, pp. 138–152.
Feyersinger, E. (2010) "Diegetic Short Circuits: Metalepsis in Animation". *Animation* 5. 3: 279–294.
Fludernik, M. (2003) "Scene Shift, Metalepis and the Metaleptic Mode". *Style* 37. 4: 382–400.
Genette, G. (1980) *Narrative Discourse: An Essay in Method*. Jane E. Lewin (trans). Ithaca, NY: Cornell University Press.

Hayles, K. (2002). *Writing Machines*. Cambridge, MA: MIT Press.

Herman, D. (1997) "Towards a Formal Description of Narrative Metalepsis". *Journal of Literary Semantics* 26. 2: 132–152.

Hintikka, J. (1967) "Individuals, Possible Worlds, and Epistemic Logic". *Nous* 1: 33–62.

Holeton, R. (2001) *Figurski at Findhorn on Acid* [CD-ROM]. Watertown, MA: Eastgate Systems.

Joyce, M. (1987) *afternoon, a story* [CD-ROM]. Watertown, MA: Eastgate Systems.

Keazor, H. (2011) " 'I had the Strangest Week Ever!' Metalepsis in Music Videos". In *Metalepsis in Popular Culture*. K. Kukkonen and S. Klimek (eds). Berlin, Germany: Walter de Gruyter, pp. 104–26.

Klimek, S. (2009) "Metalepsis and Its (Anti-)Illusionist Effects in the Arts, Media and Role-Playing Games". In *Metareference across Media: Theory and Case Studies*. W. Wolf, K. Bantleon, and J. Thoss (eds). New York, NY: Rodopi. 169–190.

Koskimaa, R. (2000) *Digital Literature: From Text to Hypertext and Beyond*. Unpublished Ph.D. Thesis, University of Jyväskylä, Finland. Last accessed 13 February 2013 at URL: http://www.cc.jyu.fi/~koskimaa/thesis/coverp.htm

Kripke, S. (1972) *Naming and Necessity*. Oxford: Blackwell.

Kukkonen, K. (2011) "Metalepsis in Popular Culture: An Introduction". In *Metalepsis in Popular Culture*. K. Kukkonen and S. Klimek (eds). Berlin, Germany: Walter de Gruyter, pp. 1–21.

Kukkonen, K. and S. Klimek (eds). (2011) *Metalepsis in Popular Culture*. Berlin, Germany: Walter de Gruyter.

Lewis, D. (1973) *Counterfactuals*. Oxford: Blackwell.

Limonges, J.-M. (2011) "Metalepsis in Animation Film". In *Metalepsis in Popular Culture*. K. Kukkonen and S. Klimek (eds). Berlin, Germany: Walter de Gruyter, pp. 196–212.

Malina, D. (2002) *Breaking the Frame: Metalepsis and the Construction of the Subject*. Columbus: Ohio State University Press.

Margolin, U. (1990) "Individuals in Narrative Worlds: An Ontological Perspective". *Poetics Today: Narratology Revisited II* 11. 4: 843–871.

Margolin, U. (1996) "Characters and Their Versions". In *Fiction Updated: Theories of Fictionality, Narratology and Poetics*. C. Mihailescu and W. Hamarneh (eds). Toronto, ON: University of Toronto Press, pp. 113–132.

Martin, S. P. (2006) "Already Too Many Stories in the World". *electronic book review*. Last accessed 13 February 2013 at URL: http://www.electronicbookreview.com/thread/endconstruction/cinematic

McHale, B. (1987) *Postmodernist Fiction*. London/New York: Routledge.

McHale, B. (1997) *Constructing Postmodernism*. London/New York: Routledge.

Moulthrop, S. (1991) *Victory Garden* [CD-ROM]. Watertown, MA: Eastgate Systems.

Nelles, W. (1997) *Frameworks: Narrative Levels and Embedded Narrative*. New York: Peter Lang.

Nielsen, H.S. (2004) "The Impersonal Voice in First-Person Narrative Fiction". *Narrative* 12. 2: 133–150.

O'Brien, F. (1967) *At Swim-Two-Birds* [1939]. London: Penguin Books.

Olsen, L. (2005) *10:01*. Portland, OR: Chiasmus Press.

Olsen, L. and Guthrie, T. (2005) *10:01*. Last accessed 28 February 2013 at URL: http://www.lanceolsen.com/1001.html

Pavel, T. G. (1979) "Fiction and the Casual Theory of Names". *Poetics* 8: 179–191.

Pavel, T. G. (1986) *Fictional Worlds*. London: Harvard University Press.

Pier, J. (2005) "Metalepsis". In *The Routledge Encyclopedia of Narrative Theory*. D. Herman, M. Jahn, and M.-L. Ryan (eds.). London: Routledge, pp. 303–304.

Pier, J. (2011) "Afterword". In *Metalepsis in Popular Culture*. K. Kukkonen and S. Klimek (eds). Berlin, Germany: Walter de Gruyter, pp. 268–276.

Plantinga, A. (1974) *The Nature of Necessity*. Oxford: Clarendon Press.

Plantinga, A. (1979) "Transworld Identity or Worldbound Individuals". *The Possible and the Actual: Readings in the Metaphysics of Modality*. M. J. Loux (ed). Ithaca, NY: Cornell University Press, pp. 146–165.

Punday, D. (1997) "Meaning in Postmodern Worlds: The Case of *The French Lieutenant's Woman*". *Semiotica* 115. 3/4: 313–343.

Rescher, N. (1975) *A Theory of Possibility*. Pittsburgh, PA: Pittsburgh University Press.

Richardson, B. (2002) "Beyond Story and Discourse: Narrative Time in Postmodern and Nonmimetic Fiction". *Narrative Dynamics: Essays on Time, Plot, Closure, and Frames*. B. Richardson (ed). Columbus, OH: Ohio State University Press, pp. 47–63.

Ronen, R. (1994) *Possible Worlds in Literary Theory*. Cambridge: Cambridge University Press.

Ryan, M. L. (1991) *Possible Worlds, Artificial Intelligence and Narrative Theory*. Bloomington, IN: Indiana University Press.

Ryan, M. L. (1992) "Possible Worlds in Recent Literary Theory". *Style* 26. 4: 528–553.

Ryan, M. L. (1999) "Introduction". In *Cyberspace Textuality: Computer Technology and Literary Theory*. M. L. Ryan (ed.). Bloomington, IN: Indiana University Press, pp. 1–30.

Ryan, M. L. (2001) *Narrative as Virtual Reality: Immersion and Interactivity in Literature and Electronic Media*. Baltimore, ML: John Hopkins University Press.

Ryan, M. L. (2006) *Avatars of Story*. Minneapolis, MN: University of Minnesota Press.

Thoss, J. (2011) "Unnatural Narrative and Metalepsis: Grant Morrison's Animal Man". In *Unnatural Narratives, Unnatural Narratology*. J. Alber and R. Heinze (eds). Berlin, Germany: de Gruyter, pp. 189–209.

Traill, N. H. (1991) "Fictional Worlds of the Fantastic". *Style* 25. 2: 196–210.

Wolf, W. (2005) "Metalepsis as a Transgeneric and Transmedial Phenomenon: A Case Study of the Possibilities of 'Exporting' Narratological Concepts". In: *Narratology Beyond Literary Criticism: Mediality, Disciplinarity*. J. C. Meister (ed.). Berlin, Germany: De Gruyter, pp. 83–107.

3 Digital Fiction and Worlds of Perspective

David Ciccoricco,
University of Otago, New Zealand

Our unflinching fascination with newness, with what Michael Joyce (2000) has called the allure of "nextness" characteristic of today's upgrade culture, threatens to reduce any act of literary innovation to *mere* experimentalism.[1] Digital fiction is not only vulnerable to the same threat, but is, ironically, also susceptible to becoming culturally passé or technically obsolete before it can coalesce into recognizable forms or genres. But once we look beyond "nextness", so to speak, it becomes clear that there is much to be gained from analyzing digital fiction. Most immediately, perhaps, are insights revealed through distinctly digital aesthetics. Newness often goes hand in hand with reflexivity, as novelty—either uncomfortably and self-consciously, or deliberately and audaciously—draws attention to itself. In this sense it still holds that any narrative written *in* digital environments is also always in some way a narrative *about* digital environments. Analyses of digital fictions, then, promise to yield a significant commentary and critique on the present cultural and media-historical moment. Outside of aesthetics, pedagogical justifications arise: Rettberg (2009), for one, argues that digital fiction marks a potential convergence of the "configurative desires and cognitive behaviors of Generation M" on the one hand, and the "contemplative and interpretive demands" of literary reading practices on the other. Referring to Hayles's (2007) distinction between "hyper" and "deep" attention, which contrasts the growing exposure to and desire for dynamic participatory media with the sustained, concentrated attention associated with more traditional media such as novels in print, Rettberg writes, "I can think of no literary medium more suited to straddling the divide between hyper attention and deep attention than electronic literature" (16).[2]

But there is also much to be gained from what digital fiction can tell us about narrative and literary theory, which is to say, meta-critically, about our models for and conceptions of narrative and literary texts. Many recent examples of digital-literary scholarship seek to offer "new perspectives on digital literature",[3] and the current collection states its commitment to a "multifocal" approach to analyzing digital fiction. But if we seize on the narrower notions of *perspective* and *focus*, it is true that digital fiction, via its dynamic graphical interfaces and topological structures, provides new perspectives on narrative itself and the acts of narrative communication staged in and through storyworlds. The present chapter thus considers aspects of perspective taking or "focalization" rooted in classical narrative theory that can be revisited in light of digital fiction, and illustrates how these aspects inform the process of interpretation. Specifically, I will consider hypertextual links as taking on a perspectival function in or beyond the narrative discourse in Judd Morrissey's *The Jew's Daughter* (2000), and a ludic and layered focalization that arises through the remediated frame imposed by a meta-discursive, cybertextual agent cycling through radio stations in Stuart Moulthrop's *Radio Salience* (2007). I will further argue that perspective in digital fiction is inevitably informed by the movements of the interface, or what is best described as a process of "cybernetic narration".

DEFAMILIARIZING CRITICAL VIEWS

Perspective has long been a preoccupation of literary theory given that it guides the reader's understanding of the ethical relations that inhere in storyworlds and our identification with or alienation from certain characters or narrators. Attention to perspective and points of view in contemporary literary theory is commonly traced back to Henry James's (1881) metaphor of a "house of fiction", which accommodated innumerable views through a million windows out on to the "human scene" of the storyworld.[4] Over half a century later, Frank's (1945) "Spatial Form in Modern Literature" marks the beginning of a more concentrated emphasis on the sort of perspectives readers can glean from a text's formal structure. His essay describes works of modernist literature that convey a distinct spatiality comprised of "reflexive relations" among "units of meaning" (231). For Frank, these units of meaning depend on spatial patterns that emerge from views of narrative characters, scenes, and actions. Of course, when the narrative moves from the page to the screen, we can no longer take the material supports of textual structure for granted, and we must find meaning amid the spatial patterns that emerge from a networked database.

Major innovations in literary theories of perspective coincide broadly with the rise of a formal critical discipline of narrative theory in the 1970s, which aimed to study story grammar much in the same way linguists study grammar at the level of sentences. For Genette (1980), perspective is a function of "mood", one of the categories (along with "tense" and "voice") by which he analyzed narrative. His foundational distinction that the agent who tells the narrative is not necessarily the same one who perceives it led to his model of "focalization", which has contributed substantially to the discourse on perspective and point of view. Focalization is generally understood as the process of filtering narrative information, with varying degrees of subjectivity, via any number of vantage points of characters and narrators. In terms of narration, Genette refers to those narrators who are also characters at the level of the story action as "homodiegetic" and those who are not present in the story as "heterodiegetic". In terms of focalization, Genette proposes the triad of zero, internal, and external focalization. Zero focalization is closely tied to omniscience in that it refers to a narrator who knows (and can see) more than any of the characters; internal focalization restricts the vantage point to a particular character (or characters) and is thus the most subjective mode; and external focalization denotes an objective view whereby the narrator does not have access to characters' thoughts and can only report their actions.

Historically, there has been confusion with regard to framing focalization in terms of either a restriction of vision or knowledge. Bal (1997) has critiqued Genette's model on the grounds that both zero and internal focalization, in terms of filtering vision as opposed to knowledge or perceptions, refer to focalizing subjects, whereas external focalization—like the external reportage in behaviorist narrative—refers to objects focalized. Furthermore, given her stance that focalization is an inevitable rather than an optional element of narrative (1997: 142), Bal argues that zero focalization is not a logical possibility. Her model deletes Genette's zero focalization and maintains a distinction between internal, or character-bound focalizers, and external narrator focalizers, keeping the latter term but redefining it. Bal's pairing of internal and external is commonly adopted in typological analyses, likely for its intuitive division along intra- and extra-diegetic lines, and is adopted herein. Franz Stanzel's (1984) articulation of "narrative situations" has also greatly influenced contemporary approaches to perspective in narrative texts. Stanzel's narrative situations include "first person," "authorial," and "figural." His first-person narrative situation aligns with Genette's notion of homodiegetic narration and popular conceptions of this "voice" position in literary texts. Both "authorial" and "figural" texts align with heterodiegetic narration, but Stanzel's "figural" texts dovetail with focalization theory in that they are identified by their use of story-internal focalizers or, in his terms, "reflectors."

New or newly foregrounded aspects of perspective taking arise in contemporary literary criticism with the proliferation of texts rich in visual media. The relationship between narrative text and image—whether in the form of illustrations, navigational cues, or paratextual maps—has long been an important aspect of narrative analysis (see Ryan 2003; Drucker 2008). But it has received heightened attention in the wake of cultural studies and visual culture scholarship across media and even more acutely given the extent to which today's cultural production is made for screens (Bolter and Grusin 1999; Hocks and Kendrick 2003; Mitchell 1986, 2008). Aspects of textual perspective involving the manipulation of narrative discourse, formal structure, and visual design are all integral to analyzing digital fiction. But beyond these aspects, digital fiction further prompts a revisitation of print-based models of perspective and focalization given the need to attend to the phenomenological process of reader intervention in visual, aural, and kinetic interfaces.

Some extant readings of digital fictions have treated image and sound as semiotic channels that serve to intensify the focalization dictated by the text. For instance, in Page's (2008) discussion of Kate Pullinger and Chris Joseph's Web-based coming-of-age novel *Inanimate Alice* (2005), she describes how the "visual and aural stimuli that mimic Alice's focalization leads to a multi-semiotic experience beyond that found in offline print literature"; she adds, "[T]he use of sound and image to *amplify* verbal focalization draws attention to the complexity of the reader's corporeal and psychological interplay with the text" (my emphasis). From this observation alone it is not clear how the multimodal elements highlight the participatory ("corporeal") nature of the text, at least in a way that transcends what is accomplished through the interplay of the semiotic channels found in cinema. After all, there is a host of filmic devices that endow characters and narrators—or a qualified sense thereof—with perspectival powers and limitations (see Chatman 1990: 154–160 for examples). Soundtracks can accomplish much by way of reflecting a character's emotions, not to mention the familiar external camera-eye focalizations analogous to behaviorist narrative description in print, and visual focalizations of a character's mental state in cinema might resort to stylized or surreal renderings and meta-diegetic inserts. Where digital fiction transcends or at least troubles these conventions is in its language-driven quality and, more specifically, the fact that the text driving the narrative can orchestrate focalizations through language *and* this text itself is open to animation that can transmit additional semiotic signals. If the text includes image and/or sound, these elements can certainly orchestrate focalizations in an expressly filmic manner—be they corresponding, contradicting, or much less direct and determinate in relation to the textual channel. But given the presence—and, indeed, primacy—of the textual channel, the effect is invariably more layered and complex.

Even in some of the earliest segments of *Inanimate Alice*, we find instances of this complexity. The visual material does not signal a simple intensification of what Alice sees or imagines; rather, there are variable focalizations in some scenes that move above or away from Alice, and there are multiple possible interpretations of the perspective suggested by the visual material in others. For example, in the opening sequence Alice, an eight year-old girl living with her parents in Northern China, explains that her father, who works in the oil industry, has not returned from a working expedition for over two days. The screen is at this stage split horizontally. The textual narrative, in units of one or two sentences, appears at the top: "He goes by himself, in his jeep, while mum and I stay at base camp." In the bottom half, a triad of animations is displayed depicting a jeep driving across a barren terrain while frenzied instrumental music instills a sense of urgency. Several factors make it highly unlikely that we are seeing what an eight-year-old girl is seeing in the mode of an internal focalizer: Alice has just told of her father's absence; she has mentioned that she stays at home when he goes to work anyway; and the view of the jeep is "traveling" at the same speed as the jeep, suggesting a nonhuman "camera-eye" vantage point. In fact, after navigating a few passages forward, the camera angle changes to a subjective though still mobile camera angle, with only the gravel road in view, as if to approximate the sightline of its driver. These images might be understood to portray what Alice *envisions* as she narrates, and the soft focus and slightly pixelated renderings of the jeep would support this reading. Even so, if it makes sense to read these images as her imaginings, then the next segment, which includes a detailed architectural diagram of her base camp's floor plan, is not likely to be something she can readily summon with her own cognitive armature, nor would it appear to be something meant to reflect her conscious meditations.

In any case, in digital fiction an analysis of any graphical element in isolation is often insufficient for even a "local" understanding of the narrative—which is to say, of any one of its parts (unlike comics, where an individual panel, framing a discrete image-text relation, can in turn frame a coherent focalization) (see Herman 2009). It is thus necessary to undertake a reading of the interface that not only integrates semiotic elements but also accounts for their dynamic, performative nature. In a text such as *Inanimate Alice*, that might include the fact that the words displayed in the opening sequence pulse and fade in and out to the sound of muffled static, as if suffering from interrupted reception—an effect that might evoke both the stifled transmission of her father's work radio and, reflexively, her own attempt as an eight-year-old to "transmit" her story (we are told she communicates with the world through a portable electronic "Player"). Or such a reading might include the fact that the visual images of the jeep depict it driving at changing angles, which may suggest either a movement toward Alice and back home, or—for some more ominous reason—further away from it.

UNDERLINING A VIEW OF LINKS: *THE JEW'S DAUGHTER*

Early hypertext theory sufficiently established the potential of links beyond that of a glorified navigational device. The rhetorical effects of linking strategies on the process of composition and reception were considered in contributions such as Parker's "A Poetics of the Link" (2001) and Rettberg's "The Pleasure (and Pain) of Link Poetics" (2002). These digital-literary critics—many of whom, as was commonly the case, were also digital artists—demonstrated that the link could stage (often ironic) juxtapositions and enjambments that could inform the mood, tone, and themes of the narrative. Clearly the link brings with it, in the words of Harpold (2003), an "excess of narrative possibilities." A consideration of links more specifically as a perspectival tool, however, remains to be fully explored.

Links already perform a somewhat unusual role in Judd Morrissey's *The Jew's Daughter*. The design of the interface consists of a single screen of black text on a white background in which everything from the conventional font to the text breaking in the upper right- and lower left-hand corners suggests the appearance of a printed page. These "pages" are also numbered, a quality that is unusual in itself for digital fictions typically comprised of networked nodes. The one obvious difference is a single word (or part thereof) or a phrase that is highlighted in blue, which looks much like a hyperlink but behaves much differently. Rather than clicking on the blue-colored text—an act naturalized in the domain of digital textuality—it responds to the reader's "rollover" with the mouse pointer/cursor by calling up new textual material that is integrated, almost imperceptibly, into the existing page. Thus, in the same gesture, Morrissey's text adopts conventions of the printed page and subverts expectations of Web-based hyperlinks.

The Jew's Daughter, moreover, is already a veritable play of perspectives. The story opens and closes with a first-person narration by an unnamed male student and writer who has recently returned to his troubled apartment in Chicago from a trip overseas. The source of the trouble is both an uncertain and insecure relationship with his partner, Eva, and the fact that she has been staying in the apartment during his absence without the permission of his landlord, an Italian countess named Josephine, and her hired hand, John Austin, whose violent and obsessive temperament makes every knock at their door a fearsome experience. What we know of the story often comes from the direct thoughts and observations of the student narrator as he walks the city streets as well as his recounting of conversations he has with various members of the city's homeless population. But given the shifting nature of the text and the volatility of the discourse itself, the narration can at times belong to more than one character or no one character at all, and a definitive analysis of the narrative situation is ultimately elusive.

There are shifts in focalization in turn, some of which occur from sentence to sentence. In one passage (reproduced here in numbered sequence), the student narrator appears to filter not only the point of view but also the speech of a bartender named Annie who is nervous about a belligerent patron:

1) And he says to me, he says Annie, give me one on the house.
2) My throat's dry like sandpaper.
3) Can you believe it?
4) I told him all I gots just gonna make you thirstier.
5) I can't help your thirst, I says.
6) She pushed her dumb blue gaze first at the man in the brown fedora and then at me, seeking out our approval. (134)

In the first five sentences, we have Annie focalizing the narrative but recounting what we presume is more or less what the bar patron has said at an earlier time, with sentence three momentarily returning to a present tense direct address to what is, at this stage, an indeterminate addressee. But in the sixth sentence, we realize that the student narrator, presumably sitting at the bar, has been filtering what Annie has been saying (in her own dialect) *about* what the bar patron has been saying.

Other shifts in focalization result from the dynamic transitions between "pages". Hayles (2008: 76–77) identifies a significant pronominal shift in the movement from the first page to the second. In the opening passage, the student anchors the narration: "I rarely slept and repeatedly during the night, when the moon was in my window, I had a vision of dirt and rocks being poured over my chest by the silver spade of a shovel" (Morrissey 2000: 1). But after the new text is introduced on page two, we see the final part of the passage has changed to: "She had a vision of dirt and rocks being poured over my chest by the silver spade of a shovel" (2). Likening the effect to shifts in focalization that occur in Shelley Jackson's *Patchwork Girl*, Hayles notes how they set up a tension between the male and female characters that is continually deferred throughout the narrative. In Morrissey's text, the "vision" can suggest opposing interpretations: either his fear that she may want him dead or her fear that he may die. But perhaps the most dramatic comment on this perspectival play comes in the form of the dream the student has in which he is looking over the shoulder of his lover, who is standing "on the top of an enormous tree" (239). He finds his vision morphs into her own: "And then I could see through your eyes and it was I who was standing, my feet perched where the tree tapered to a point, maintaining balance against a violent wind" (239). In fact, if the student is indeed seeing through her eyes in these dreams, then it is possible that, contrary to Hayles's reading of the opening sequence in which the focalizer appears to change from him to her, he actually retains the role of both speaker and seer at this moment.

A more detailed reading of the links, however, yields an even more comprehensive interpretation of perspective. For example, in the passage where the student describes his dream, the highlighted link on this page is located on the word "eyes," but only on its final three letters, spelling "yes." Even though the toolkit of traditional narrative theory does not account for shifts in focalization that are introduced in such a (visual and hypertextual) manner, it is possible to read this link as part of the story's play of perspective. At this late stage in the narrative, which is effectively linear in its page progression despite its vertiginous shifts, we know that the student is conflicted about his lover, and specifically the possible infidelity that might have occurred in his absence. The intertextual parallels between *The Jew's Daughter*, Joyce's *Ulysses*, and, by extension, Homer's *Odyssey* are relevant here (the student, much like Joyce's protagonist, is a self-described "Irish-Jew", and the text takes its name from the anti-Semitic ballad that Stephen Dedalus sings in Leopold Bloom's presence during the Ithaca episode of the novel).[5] After all, we know that Odysseus returns home to Ithaca, Leopold Bloom returns home to 7 Eccles Street, Dublin, and the protagonist of *The Jew's Daughter* returns home to his troubled apartment in Chicago. But whereas Odysseus returns to a wife who has been faithful, and Bloom to a wife who certainly has not, the student is left tortured with uncertainty. At one point he even refers to "the crimes you've committed" that "swell up and then the missing swells up, and one outdoes the other"—a phrase followed by the (recurrent) fragment: "Precious time away" (239). A reading of the link pushes us further toward an incriminating scenario. In seeing through her eyes in his dream state, and thus appropriating her—albeit fantastically—as a focalizer, he is also in a sense seeing that her eyes say "yes" in a manner highly reminiscent of Molly Bloom. In other words, the presence of the link suggests that the student is not simply seeing what she sees but also what she thinks and desires. Furthermore, we can recall that the link on the very first page is located at the word "criminal", and is there used as an adjective in its initial context to refer, vaguely, to the student's negligence and potential failure "to come through" (1). But if she has, in his eyes, committed crimes (239), then she might also be the nominal "criminal" referred to obliquely—perhaps unconsciously—here as well. That she adopts the vision of his burial in the movement of the next transition supports the notion that her subjectivity, if not her presence, is being announced.

The presence of another character is "announced" in similar fashion earlier on. The linked text on page 230 is the single letter "j" in the word "joined." Linguistically, the act of severing the word "joined" feeds into a network of allusions to decapitation that forms a prominent theme in the narrative, likely stemming from the suicide decapitation of a woman on a railway line that Eva had witnessed during a trip to Indonesia. The image recurs in varied forms throughout the narrative and continues to haunt both the student as well as Eva. In fact, in the several scenes that lead up to the link at "joined", the student has been wandering the city with a bag under his arm containing notes for the book he is working on, which he refers to as a "decapitated head" (223–230). He is eventually intercepted at his front gate by a homeless man who asks to be invited in for a drink. The man introduces himself to the student as "J" (234), endowing the earlier link on "j" the effect of foreshadowing—though exactly who, if anyone, sees or senses his imminent arrival remains unclear.[6]

During the same exchange, the student is fixating on the homeless man's head—a fixation reinforced by the presence of the link at the word "head" in the student's description of "his head tilted, his eyebrows tight, and his dark eyes looking at me as though they were sincerely curious, even bewildered" (234). That the head of the homeless man preoccupies the student here, as do other heads elsewhere throughout the narrative, speaks to the same decapitation trauma, and establishes a clear diegetic significance to the link present. That is, the links become meaningful in terms of who sees what *in* the storyworld, rather than being mere navigational devices. Moreover, they are not easily explained as transgressive, metaleptic effects occurring at a separate (higher) level of narrative communication (cf. Bell's chapter in this volume). But like the curious source of the link at "j", the notion of *attributing* the link in relation to the diegesis remains problematic. It could be either a) an authorial perspective making use of the link to provide a further commentary on the student's state of mind, or b) a sort of layered focalization whereby the student's thoughts are represented on top of his own representation of his thoughts, visually, via the presence of the link. If, in another possible reading, the student narrator is not only telling this story but also writing it, then he could quite literally be *writing* these links as well. The interpretation is complicated not only by the fact that the rhetorical register that mediates the links changes throughout, but also the fact that all of the references to his own writing process—his "notebooks" (223) and "pages" (23)—are confined to the print medium. Of course it could be none of the above.

Thus, if we accept the diegetic significance of these links, we inevitably raise another question: how do we account for the placement of these links in this vein? In most cases our answer would depend on where we locate a narratorial and authorial consciousness. In cases of heterodiegetic narration, it would be entirely reasonable to assume that links serve to emphasize the vantage point of the narrator, whether that vantage point refers to physical or ideological orientation of vision. But the ontological status of these interpolations is more problematic for a character-bound focalizer who does not have an awareness of, let alone access to, the narrative's discourse. At the very least the presence of these links complicates an understanding of a single perspectival filter *at any given moment*. There are clear precedents for such synchronous multiple filtering in extant narrative theory, from the notion of "collective focalization" commonly employing the first-person plural "we" (see Banfield 1982: 96; Stanzel 1984: 170–172)[7] to what Jahn (1999) has more recently described as "ambient focalization", in which more than one agent can serve as a spatio-temporal anchor for a given scene at any one time. But the presence of links in digital fiction that are at once elements of the text's structure, design, and diegesis present an indelibly different case.

Nonetheless, it is logical to attribute the placement of the suggestive links in the text to the same agent responsible for selecting which textual material will be added and subtracted in each transition.[8] In order to account for this agent, we do not need to resort to a mystical notion of a ghost in the machine or an equally problematic notion of an implied author (or, for that matter, implied programmer).[9] Just as Chatman refers to a "cinematic narrator", which is the "composite of a large and complex variety of communicating devices" (134) that ultimately organizes the varied semiotic channels of cinema into an act of narration, we can refer to this agent as a "cybernetic narrator" that fulfills an analogous role in fictive narratives that unfold in programmable and networked media.[10] Or, in deference to those who reject the idea of a composite narrator *per se* (see Bordwell 1985: 61–62)—we can at least refer to the process of "cybernetic narration". The notion of cybernetic narration is not put forth to challenge or counter claims for the empowerment of the reader so often celebrated in digital environments or in any way a disavowal of the "nontrivial" work they undertake in directing the semiotic sequence of digital fictions (Aarseth 1997: 1). Rather, it provides an economical way in which to *attribute* the operational output of digital fiction, one that coherently integrates the thematic and programmatic design in equal measure. The same notion can account for the additional recursive exchange between reader and computer in digital fiction, which is to say the algorithmically orchestrated loops comprised of human input and computer output. Cybernetic narration, of course, can conceal just as much as it reveals. In *The Jew's Daughter*, much in the same way that the "fog-breath of the carriage horse on Michigan Avenue would rise impenetrably" to obscure the student's view of the city (9), our own view of the narrative discourse is perpetually obscured by the ever-shifting interface.

PLAYING FOR PERSPECTIVE: *RADIO SALIENCE*

The force of cybernetic narration is even more pronounced in Stuart Moulthrop's *Radio Salience* (2007), which is motivated by different demands on reader participation and engages with a play of perspective in a more direct sense. Graphically, the text presents four vertical panes with images that fade in and out. Audibly, the text presents fragments of radio channel content from snippets of music to news radio, talk radio, and even court or evangelical radio, in at least a half dozen languages. The segments are interrupted by blasts of static, reflecting the experience of a listener cycling through stations. As Moulthrop's "Rules" for the text indicate, "[w]hen two or more of the four panes belong to a single set, click the mouse. You'll see the full image, accompanied by a gloss or reading" (2007). This "reading" consists of a column of text generated dynamically in tandem with a robotic-sounding voice-over (rendered by various text-to-speech applications), which gradually occupies the middle two panes of the screen. Verbal material is thus introduced only in response to user action. But if human intervention affects the textual output in *Radio Salience*, human error can also suspend it; as the "Rules" make clear, "if you click while none of the four images match, play is over," and we hear one of many "game over" messages before being shunted back to the start page.

If we insist on the text's status as a language-driven work, we must confront the paradox that of all the semiotic channels, the textual one is still the most difficult to access, and when we do locate it we are at the mercy of its transience. The text involves "forced participation" (Walker 2000) or what Bell and Ensslin (2011), in order to emphasize coproduction over coercion, have more recently described in the context of "actualized input/output". Indeed, we can listen to and watch the text unproblematically; but if we want to read it, we have no other choice but to play it.

By invoking the lyrical significance of radio waves for poetic imagination, Moulthrop's text taps into a literary tradition that would include Ezra

Pound's radio opera experiments of the early 1930s and, several decades later, Jack Spicer's poetics of radio transmission and, more specifically, his notion of the poet as a receptive host for expressive language rather than a creative agent (Schoenbeck 2010). As Moulthrop's introduction to the text states, the project "takes as its muse the breathless voice of the airwaves, or radio" (2007). At the same time, by reframing that tradition in the media environment of digitally networked computers, the idea of a "breathless voice" takes on added meaning. Here, the computer-generated voice-over, given that it is potentially synthesized artificially by a machine rather than a product of a prerecorded human voice, represents the ultimate disembodied speaker.

That speaker, furthermore, changes from one scene to the next, not only in terms of place and time in a fictional field (as there is no "storyworld" per se) but also in terms of jumping narrative levels, at times occupying a position at the level of the diegesis and at others external to it. Thus, if the ludic demands of the interface challenge our ability to view the text in the most immediate sense, then the discourse poses similar challenges to an understanding of the points of view that are portrayed. Narrativity—the degree to which, in Ryan's (2005: 347) articulation, the text can "inspire a narrative response"—remains extremely low, and readers are never able to establish a clear sense of subject in the form of a narrator or character. In fact, unlike the webs of interrelationships constructed by some earlier digital fictions, including Moulthrop's own *Victory Garden*, characters mentioned in any one of the given textual segments of *Radio Salience* do not resurface in any of the others.

The focalization is also variable, as a sample of opening lines from textual segments suggests:

1) We managed a few words with Ozzy and Harriette Marcuse, known to circus fans everywhere as the Flying Cutlery.
2) The logic of this picture is the Discourse of the Divided Subject, as-/-if-/-within the Virtual Body.
3) Hello world. The birth of novelty in the eruption of what was and will again forever be, as if this return to the self is once more refabricated in its image, so what else is new?[11]

The first example is internally focalized, and presents a homodiegetic speaker who recounts an interview he or she conducted with circus performers, and goes on later in the passage to quote them directly; in the second, a heterodiegetic speaker can be said to assume an externally focalized position, but the speaker refers not necessarily to a storyworld but rather directly to the image displayed; and the third involves what might be construed as a direct address to a notably wide audience or at least an indeterminate one, but it is most likely the effect of an (internally focalized) interior monologue.

But unlike the obfuscations of Morrissey's shifting interface, the images that accompany these texts can elucidate a reading of the text. They can in turn convey more information about the vantage points represented—if not as a coherent narrative, then at least as a network of thematic connections reminiscent of Joseph Frank's "reflexive relations". At times, the text functions more or less as a "gloss or reading" (Moulthrop 2007) of the image displayed, thus constraining our own gloss or reading. In the second example above, the use of the demonstrative pronoun in "this picture" sets up an immediate connection between text and image, which is a computer graphic–generated depiction of two naked ladies asleep in a bed. A reference to the "artist's perhaps idiopathic aversion to technique", moreover, establishes the speaker's treatment of the image *as* an image, which is to say as a creative artifact. The opaque theorizing on the "Discourse of the Divided Subject" is ultimately undermined at the textual segment's conclusion by a comparatively unequivocal observation: "To the merely observant, of course, this will look like a couple naked ladies in bed".

Other segments involve a mutually informing relationship between image and text.[12] For example, in one segment the text begins with a question about the content of dreams and then continues with what resembles a description of the content of a dream itself (see Figure 3.1). The accompanying image shows a man with his eyes closed, conceivably dreaming and quite possibly the dreamer in question. The grammatical coherence of the passage

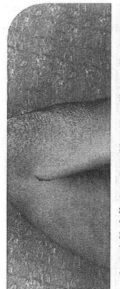

Since when were we responsible for the content of our dreams? On the last day of December they showed up in little boxes, encased in too much bubble-wrap. Unpacking them took days. So much bubble-wrap. Each tiny cell a stolen breath. Break one open, and the world changes ever so much: a release of content for which I am not responsible. By the middle of March, the system had begun to make sense even to the most innocent. We could follow the interplay of all its gears and levers, appreciate the heft of its many tropes and metaphors, swing in time to its various contradictions. Then on May Day, the sky filled with unlikely machines, and for the first time that anyone could remember, all of us managed to cry.

Figure 3.1   Screenshot of *Radio Salience*. Copyright Stuart Moulthrop.

is not in question, and it could in fact serve as a narrative report of events. That is, the potentially fantastical aspects of "unlikely machines" filling the sky notwithstanding, the detailed chronological progression (transpiring over a period of months) actually casts doubt upon the likelihood of its status as the recapitulation of a dream. What is missing, perhaps, is the link between the airborne spectacle of the unlikely machines and the viewers' emotional response to them (in the form of tears of joy or wonder we presume). In this scene and elsewhere throughout the text we often find that the images, carefully rendered in their realistic human detail, pull us toward a sense of human subjectivity; they humanize the text rather than dehumanizing it. By contrast, the computer-automated voice-overs tend to pull us away from it, ultimately confounding any conception of embodied perspective or point of view. We are in turn left to a hurried analysis of the kinetic text to negotiate between these poles. Above all, the entire text presents us with a system whose content is equally cryptic and whose beauty is certainly felt and appreciated more than it is understood.[13] In contrast to the "unlikely machines" in the sky, however, its content is generated by a machine that has become perhaps all *too likely* in our own homes and workplaces.

In terms of our own perspective, of course, it would be misleading to refer to an *overall* experience, as a totalizing vantage point is perpetually deferred. The movement of the interface restricts what we can see both spatially, at the level of the panels, and also temporally, by way of the transient text. In turn, we are left to consider not the big picture—that is, the way in which all the elements interrelate to form a coherent whole—but rather which elements are salient, why they resonate over and above others, and how they resolve into something recognizable and meaningful. The patterns we find might include anything from the many depictions of (often unclothed) human subjects—especially in light of the textual references to "legible flesh" that obliquely encourage our attempts to "read" them—to the scattered references to games of chance that reflexively describe the machinations of the text itself.

Nevertheless, amid the multilingual play of noise and epiphany on the airwaves, the constant ebb and flow of images, and the alignments and misalignments they deliver, the text maintains both a clear rhythm in the regularity of its transitions and a clear logic in its system of rewards and punishments. Feeding this behavior, moreover, is not some bottomless bowl of multimedial soup, but rather a predefined selection of elements called up from a delimited database. *Radio Salience* is an example of circumscribed randomness—where randomness plays out according to the rules of a system, as it must in any aesthetic object in order for it to function as such. Whether we attribute the commonality of these media elements to, for instance, the constraints of the image-editing software or the individual consciousness of the artist on the day, the orchestration of the semiotic channels in time—and more specifically what we see and how we see it—is best attributed to the process of cybernetic narration. Although these semi-otic channels never coalesce, in Chatman's sense, into a *singular* coherent narrative stream, we can nonetheless invoke the notion of cybernetic narra-tion whenever we locate meaningful connections between the technological and the literary—or what Moulthrop has called the "executable and the lyrical" (2010).

Much like the role of narrators in print, the presence of a cybernetic narrator can be more or less overt. For example, the agent of cybernetic nar-ration is perhaps most pronounced—even deviously so—during a textual segment that begins, "There is no software update from Real to handle this content". The content that follows, which includes elephants delivering tele-grams, is most certainly "unreal", but beyond the play on the name of the popular media software platform, there is an even further indication that "this content" takes on a dual meaning, referring both to the fictional scene and, reflexively, to the actual performance of the textual machine. When I experienced this scene, on multiple occasions, the delivery of the text (both its appearance on screen and its voice-over) paused, as if crashing momen-tarily, effectively enacting an allusion to the software problem mentioned in the text. Thus, the selections—and transgressions—of cybernetic narration can be at once artful and algorithmic.

Outside of the black box operations of the text, the most palpable pro-cess of selection, of course, belongs to the reader, who marks the occasion when, in the structuralist sense, the paradigmatic status of database ele-ments become syntagmatic as they are experienced sequentially. In fact, despite its clear parallels to twentieth-century poetic practice, there may be another more suitable literary precedent for *Radio Salience*, one that better accounts for the reader's dual role as participant and audience. The mono-logist Spalding Gray spoke of his obsessive habit that involved switching off his radio before leaving his home each morning only after he heard a word or phrase that was somewhat uplifting, or at least something he felt was not an explicit harbinger of doom. In perhaps his best-known monologue, *Swimming to Cambodia* (1987), he describes the origins of the routine:

> It started innocently enough. I literally could not go out of my apart-ment until I turned my little KLH radio off on a positive word. I was there all morning some days.
>
> "The stock market is rising." Click. I could go out.
>
> " . . . consider moving the Marines to safer posi . . . " Click. I could go out.
>
> "You may go to a doctor that belongs to the AMA but it doesn't necessarily mean you're going to the best." Click. I could go out. (Gray 1987)[14]

Not only does Gray intervene in the data flow in a way that is meaningful to him, he also creates a pattern via the thematic resonance of the terms "rising", "safer", and "best". In perhaps much the same way, today's media consumers struggle to select salient bytes of information and integrate them meaningfully into their lives. Selecting too much—indeed, *seeing too much*—is tantamount to selecting nothing at all, as we can become so overwhelmed by the task that we are stunned into inactivity. Ultimately, there is a need to decide when to unpack and sort the content and when to simply let the data wash over you and, like Moulthrop's dreamer, "appreciate the heft" of the system's "many tropes and metaphors" (see Figure 3.1).

CONCLUSION

Both *The Jew's Daughter* and *Radio Salience* require a theory of perspective that not only attends to the multimodal quality of digital fiction but also accommodates the phenomenological process of reader intervention in the interface. At the same time, both texts attest to the utility of concepts from extant literary and narrative theory in understanding the vantage points in and on the fictional worlds they project. The notion of cybernetic narration offers one way to explain how the kinetic and multimodal effects of digital fictions cohere with or even motivate their focalizations. More generally, an ongoing challenge for digital fiction is to establish itself beyond the fallacies that denude it of any literary potency in the classical sense (that they are never read the same way twice, or that they never end) and at the same time avoid the equally problematic fallacy that positions "hypertextual" writing or reading as always already the norm for literary texts. Navigating between foundations and innovations in careful analyses of these literary machines is an ongoing task for readers of digital fiction in turn.

NOTES

1. For a discussion of "making it new in new media" in the context of Ezra Pound's notorious credo, see Pressman (2008).
2. Ensslin (2012) proposes a literary-ludic continuum based on Hayles's notion of deep and hyper attention.
3. In 2007, Ensslin and Bell edited a special collection titled "New Perspectives on Digital Literature: Criticism and Analysis" for the online journal *Dichtung-Digital* that focuses on the close analysis of a range of creative media (see http://dichtung-digital.mewi.unibas.ch/index.htm, Number 37).
4. James introduces the idea in the Preface to *The Portrait of a Lady*, which was originally published in 1881.
5. Ciccoricco (2007: 177–86) addresses the mythological parallels of these inter-texts in detail.
6. The name itself feeds into yet another network of allusions, one that positions the homeless J as a ghost of the beheaded John the Baptist (with *J*

poignantly signaling the "decapitation" of that name) and, extra-diegetically, calls to mind the abbreviation Richard Ellmann uses for "James Joyce" in his well-known biography—not to mention the first initial of the author of the text at hand.

7. Banfield describes narratives representing the perspectives of a "collective or class consciousness" whereby a "single point of view [is] held by more than one individual" (96). Stanzel describes how a "reflectorized teller-character temporarily becomes [a] collective voice" (172). His description is closer to what occurs in *The Jew's Daughter* in that it involves the movement of vantage points across levels of narrative communication.

8. This critical gesture would apply regardless of whether the kinetic text is predetermined to be the same each time or, as in some of Morrissey's later "dynamically evolving" works, generated *variably* on the fly based on user input and algorithmically determined output (see Ciccoricco 2007: 175–176).

9. For a discussion of the problem and an alternative approach to the notion of the implied author that draws on a cognitive science framework, see Margolin (2003).

10. See Ciccoricco (2012) for an introduction of the concept of cybernetic narration and its application to Erik Loyer's "The Lair of the Marrow Monkey" and Young-Hae Chang Heavy Industries' "The Last Day of Betty Nkomo".

11. There is no obvious way to cite specific nodes in the interface; unlike much Web-based digital fiction, the nodes of the text are not titled, numbered, or individuated bibliographically.

12. The relationship of text to image as a corresponding (or anchoring) gloss compared to an image and text relation as a "mutually informing" semantic unit is analogous to Barthes's distinction of "anchorage" and "relay" respectively (1977: 38–41).

13. "Content", for Moulthrop, would be the wrong word here. In a recent reading at the 2010 University of North Dakota Writers Conference, he articulated what he sees as the difference between "data art" and "content art" and described *Radio Salience* as a possible precursor for data art: "Content is something wrapped up, something in shrink wrap. Something with a stock-keeping unit attached to it . . . a mark. Data is that which flows. . . . Data permeates. Data circulates. It's processed" (Stierman 2010).

14. The text is my own transcription of a filmed version of the monologue.

WORKS CITED

Aarseth, E. (1997) *Cybertext: Perspectives on Ergodic Literature*. Baltimore: Johns Hopkins University Press.

Bal, M. (1997) *Narratology: An Introduction to the Theory of Narrative* (2nd edition). Christine van Boheemen (trans). Toronto: Toronto University Press.

Banfield, A. (1982) *Unspeakable Sentences: Narration and Representation in the Language of Fiction*. Boston: Routledge & Kegan Paul.

Barthes, R. (1977) *Image Music Text*. Stephen Heath (trans). London: Fontana Press.

Bell, A. & Ensslin, A. (2011) " 'I know what it was. You know what it was': Second-Person Narration in Hypertext Fiction". *Narrative* 19. 3: 312–329.

Bolter, J.D. & Grusin, R. (1999) *Remediation: Understanding New Media*. Cambridge, MA: MIT Press.

Bordwell, D. (1985) *Narration in the Fiction Film*. Madison: University of Wisconsin Press.

Chatman, S. (1990) *Coming to Terms: The Rhetoric of Narrative in Fiction and Film*. Ithaca: Cornell University Press.

Ciccoricco, D. (2012) "Focalization and Digital Fiction". *Narrative* 20. 3: 255–276.

Ciccoricco, D. (2007) *Reading Network Fiction*. Tuscaloosa: University of Alabama Press.

Drucker, J. (2008) "Graphic Devices: Narration and Navigation". *Narrative* 16. 2: 121–139.

Ensslin, A. (2012) "Computer Gaming". In *The Routledge Companion to Experimental Literature*. J. Bray, A. Gibbons, and B. McHale (eds). London: Routledge, pp. 497–511.

Frank, J. (1945) "Spatial Form in Modern Literature". *Sewanee Review* 53: 221–240.

Gray, S. (1987) *Swimming to Cambodia*. Montreal: Seville Pictures.

Genette, G. (1980) *Narrative Discourse*. J. E. Lewin (trans). Oxford: Basil Blackwell.

Harpold, T. (2003) "The Contingencies of the Hypertext Link". In *The New Media Reader*, N. Wardrip-Fruin and N. Montfort (eds). Cambridge, MA: MIT Press, pp. 126–138.

Hayles, N. K. (2007) "Hyper and Deep Attention: The Generational Divide in Cognitive Modes". *Profession 2007*. The Modern Language Association of America.

Hayles, N. K. (2008) *Electronic Literature: New Horizons for the Literary*. Notre Dame, IN: University of Notre Dame Press.

Herman, D. (2009) "Beyond Voice and Vision: Cognitive Grammar and Focalization Theory". In *Point of View, Perspective, and Focalization: Modeling Mediation in Narrative*. P. Hühn, W. Schmid, and J. Schönert (eds). Berlin: Walter de Gruyter, pp. 119–142.

Hocks, M. E. & Kendrick, M. (eds). (2003) *Eloquent Images: Word and Image in the Age of New Media*. Cambridge, MA: MIT Press.

Jahn, M. (1999) "More Aspects of Focalization: Refinements and Applications". In *Recent Trends in Narratological Research: Papers from the Narratology Round Table*. J. Pier (ed). Tours: GRAAT, pp. 85–110.

Joyce, M. (2000) *Othermindedness: The Emergence of Network Culture*. Ann Arbor: University of Michigan Press.

Margolin, U. (2003) "Cognitive Science, the Thinking Mind, and Literary Narrative". In *Narrative Theory and the Cognitive Sciences*. D. Herman (ed). Stanford, CA: Publications of the Center for the Study of Language and Information, pp. 271–294.

Mitchell, W. J. T. (1986). *Iconology: Image, Text, Ideology*. Chicago: University of Chicago Press.

Mitchell, W. J. T. (2008). "Visual Literacy or Literary Visualcy". In *Visual Literacy*. J. Elkins (ed). New York: Routledge, pp. 11–30.

Morrissey, J. (2000) *The Jew's Daughter* [online]. Last accessed 13 February 2013 at URL: http://www.thejewsdaughter.com

Moulthrop, S. (2007) *Radio Salience* [online]. Last accessed 13 February 2013 at URL: http://iat.ubalt.edu/moulthrop/hypertexts/rs/

Moulthrop, S. (2010) "Mind the Gap: Print, New Media, Art". Reading: Stuart Moulthrop. 41st Annual University of North Dakota Writers Conference. March 26.

Page, R. (2008) "Work 1: *Inanimate Alice*, by Kate Pullinger and Chris Joseph". *Magazine électronique du Centre International d'Art Contemporain de Montréal* (CIAC) 30 [online]. Last accessed 13 February 2013 at URL: http://magazine.ciac.ca/archives/no_30/oeuvre1.htm

Parker, J. (2001) "A Poetics of the Link". *electronic book review* 12 [online]. Last accessed 13 February 2013 at URL: http://www.altx.com/ebr/ebr12/park/park.htm

Pressman, J. (2008) "The Strategy of Digital Modernism: Young-Hae Chang Heavy Industries' Dakota". *Modern Fiction Studies* 54. 2: 302–326.

Pullinger, K. and Joseph, C. (2005) *Inanimate Alice* (2005) [online]. Last accessed 13 February 2013 at URL: http://www.inanimatealice.com/episode1/

Rettberg, S. (2002) "The Pleasure (and Pain) of Link Poetics". *electronic book review* [online]. Last accessed 13 February 2013 at URL: http://www.electronic bookreview.com/thread/electropoetics/pragmatic

Rettberg. S. (2009) "Communitizing Electronic Literature". *Digital Humanities Quarterly* 3. 2 (Spring 2009) [online]. Last accessed 13 February 2013 at URL: http://digitalhumanities.org/dhq/vol/3/2/000046/000046.html

Ryan, M.-L. (2003) "Cognitive Maps and the Construction of Narrative Space". In *Narrative Theory and the Cognitive Sciences*. D. Herman (ed). Stanford, CA: Publications of the Center for the Study of Language and Information, pp. 214–242.

Ryan, M.-L. (2005) "Narrative". In *Routledge Encyclopedia of Narrative Theory*. D. Herman, M. Jahn, and M.-L. Ryan (eds). London: Routledge, pp. 344–347.

Schoenbeck, R. (2010) Entry for "Radio Salience". Electronic Literature Directory (ELD) [online]. Last accessed 20 August 2011 at URL: http://directory.eliterature. org/node/765

Stanzel, F. K. (1984) *A Theory of Narrative*. Charlotte Goedsche (trans). Cambridge: Cambridge University Press.

Stierman, M. (2010) (transcription) [online]. Last accessed 13 February 2013 at URL: http://www.undwritersconference.org/Moulthrop_2010.html

Walker, J. (2000) "Do You Think You're Part of This? Digital Texts and the Second Person Address". In *Cybertext Yearbook 2000*. M. Eskelinen and R. Koskimaa (eds). University of Jyväskylä, Finland: Research Centre for Contemporary Culture. [online]. Last accessed 13 February 2013 at URL: http://jilltxt.net/txt/do_ you_think.pdf

4 Seeing into the Worlds of Digital Fiction

Daniel Punday,
Purdue University Calumet, U.S.

INTRODUCTION

Although critics have long recognized that digital fiction challenges many of our assumptions about fictional worlds, usually those challenges are thought to arise from the multiplicity of the text's events. This is especially the case in what Ryan (2006) refers to as "ontological" digital texts, which include most computer games, where users can change the outcome of the story.[1] But even in exploratory hypertext fiction like Michael Joyce's *afternoon* (1987), where users are merely uncovering events that have already happened, digital fiction's primary innovation has been assumed to be the variability with which we encounter those events.[2]

Overlooked in this discussion are the unique ways in which the worlds of digital fiction are accessed by the user.[3] Programmers who create commercial software are, of course, deeply concerned with the accessibility of the program; guidebooks for the creation of computer and video games regularly extol the importance of keeping the interface simple (Pedersen 2009: 22–23; Adams 2010: 211–212) and discuss different ways of designing an onscreen "channel of information" to be intuitive and predictable (Schell 2008: 234–236). Academic critics working on new media have been slow to follow the lead of these commercial developers and attend to how we access the world of a digital fiction. The issue of accessibility is, however, central to possible world theory. As Ryan (1991) explains, drawing on Kripke, "[A] world is possible in a system of reality if it is accessible from the world at the center of the system" (31). This understanding of accessibility emphasizes the logical consistencies between one world and the next, but it also reminds us that inherent to the idea of a possible world is our ability to understand the conditions upon which we are to enter it. The disinterest among scholars working in new media about our methods of accessing digital fiction may in part be the result of early commentary that emphasized "virtual reality" and user immersion (see Murray 1997). Early celebration of such narratives assumed that the goal was to make the user's contact with the story seamless, and that technological innovations would bring us stories that we encountered without a user interface (UI).

Like so many imagined futures for digital fiction, this one did not come to pass. It is an obvious element of any electronic text that users encounter a UI in a way that readers of a traditional book or viewers of a film do not. It is true, of course, that publishers make design decisions about the layout of the book, and that DVD films occasionally introduce some interface choices for the viewer of a film. But these UI elements are generally marginal to the experience of narratives in these media.[4] In contrast, the design of the UI is a much more consistently central element of the experience of digital fiction. In this chapter, I want to place my primary emphasis on the first word in the phrase *digital fiction*. Although critics like Ryan (1991, 2001), Juul (2005), and Bell (2010) have described the nature of fictionality in digital fiction, little attention has been given to the digital interface through which we encounter those worlds. I will concentrate primarily on the computer interface, although my observations apply to video game consoles and even mobile devices. Although this interface is central to the what we think of as digital fiction—hypertext narratives like *Patchwork Girl* (Jackson 1995), video games like *Half-Life*, and mixed-media texts like *Inanimate Alice* (Pullinger and Joseph 2005)—the computer interface is also an element on texts that are not themselves clearly fiction, such as the lyric poem *House Fire* (Seay and Hefler 2009) or nonfictional CD-ROM encyclopedias. But I will argue that the design of the UI is especially important in digital *fiction* because it provides us with a way of grasping the design and principles of the textual world that the user is navigating—of understanding the *accessibility* of that invented world. Ultimately, as I will conclude in this chapter, digital fiction introduces a very different relationship between the user and the fictional world.

UI AND THE TEXTURE OF FICTIONAL WORLDS

Let us begin with the design of a UI from a popular computer game: *Medal of Honor: Allied Assault*, a first-person shooter with a UI design that is typical of the genre. Although the resolution and lighting of the image is somewhat dated by today's standards, this game contains the basic elements that go into most first-person shooters even today. We appear to be seeing into a three-dimensional landscape that game designers have worked to make as realistic as possible. We can move around in this landscape, and our perspective will shift so that we can see the other sides of the objects represented in this space. We can also pan our view up or down, looking at the ceiling or floor. Of course, the three-dimensional rendering is not perfect; much of the apparent three-dimensional detail on the objects of the room is in fact simply a texture or skin that has been applied to a simpler three-dimensional form to make it appear more geometrically complex than it is. But users understand that these textures are simply a compromise necessary for such complex spaces to be represented by the home computer or gaming console.[5]

There are several other elements onscreen that do not (fully) obey the logic of this three-dimensional space. The most obvious of these is the health bar in the lower left of the screen, a simple green column that has no three-dimensional logic at all. There is no attempt here to represent the health of the player in a realistic way; health data is simply translated into a number and a green bar whose height correlates to this abstract idea of health. Somewhat more complex is the compass that is located in the upper left of the screen. Obviously, compasses do not hang in the air in this way; and no attempt is made to explain why this item is able to disregard gravity. However, it is clear that the compass represents an attempt by the game designers to make this element of player information conform in some ways to the logic of the game world. The compass hangs in the air in order to represent what would happen if the user were to reach into a pocket, pull out the compass, and look at it. But it is clear that even in this sense the compass obeys the three-dimensional logic of the scene differently than our main perspective on the fictional landscape. Finally, at the bottom of this screen our weapon is shown; although the gun has a greater three-dimensional reality than the compass, our view of the gun does not change and we cannot fully lift it up to examine it from other angles. It is a fixed part of our view on the three-dimensional space that the player is supposed to occupy, but it is not available to exploration like the objects in the landscape.

The UI elements, then, obey very different relations to the three-dimensional logic of the main space that we appear to be navigating. For all that we feel that first-person shooters are immersive, it is clear that the player is encountering a host of textual elements that violate the logic of our view on the world. These elements of the UI essentially introduce different kinds of spaces. The nature of these UI spaces is, to various degrees, diagrammatic in nature. In their recent book, *The Culture of Diagram*, Bender and Marrinan describe the space of the diagram in this way:

> Most visual diagrams are ranged upon a flat, planar surface . . . but they multiply points of view by presenting arrays rather than legislating the single view of a replete spatial environment. Diagrams incite a correlation of sensory data within the mental schema of lived experience that emulates the way we explore objects in the world. They are closer to being things than to being representations of things. (2010: 21)

Bender and Marrinan go on to suggest that diagrams frequently mix heterogeneous spaces, including elements of realistic (but not necessarily consistent) perspective without any perspectival meaning (23). The same is clearly true of the UI design that we see in *Medal of Honor*. While the central space of the game obeys generally consistent three-dimensional logic, elements of the UI involve two-dimensional spaces and depend on various degrees of abstraction.

One thing that distinguishes the space of this game from the diagram as Bender and Marrinan describe it is that games generally make one of these spaces the center of the narrative experience. Where a diagram might include various elements with different spatial orientations, it is clear that all of the spaces of this game are subordinated to the central, three-dimensional space in which the player appears to be moving. This space constitutes what most players will think of as the "world" of the game, and the other spaces of map and health bar are of secondary importance. To be more specific, these secondary spatial elements are designed to provide information *about* the primary, three-dimensional space that takes up the center of the screen. Because first-person shooters are so deeply committed to the idea of visual realism, a game like *Medal of Honor* makes the centrality of this space particularly clear. But almost all digital fiction makes one space central. In the isometric space of the *SimCity* games the spatial logic of the game is very different from *Medal of Honor* but just as important. The majority of screen space is taken up by a three-dimensional image of the city landscape seen from a fixed perspective, with a smaller floating palette of commands on top of this view to the left. Here it is clear that the icons on the palette are secondary and merely provide information about this central city space, which constitutes the world in which we are playing. The same is true, as well, of Storyspace hypertexts, where we clearly have a central reading space surrounded by secondary textual spaces which provide information about, but do not displace, the central text (see Figure 4.1).

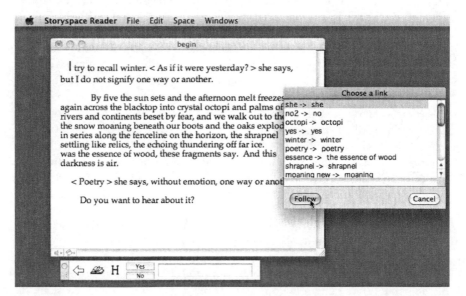

Figure 4.1   Screenshot of *afternoon, a story* by Michael Joyce. Published by Eastgate Systems, Inc. http://www.eastgate.com

In all of these cases, the UI complicates the space of the text, but also emphasizes a single, central world that we are entering.

What is the role of these secondary UI spaces, and why are they so important to digital fiction but generally absent in print-based texts? I think that Doležel's discussion (1979) of fictional worlds, and especially the role of "texture" in intentional worlds, provides us with an explanation of these secondary UI spaces. For Doležel, the fictional world is defined as the sum of the entities that exist within it: "for every narrative text, the set of its agents can be given by simple enumeration; in other words, the set is defined by extension. Moreover, we assume that in the primary world the agents exist as entities independently of any kind of designation which can be assigned to them" (197). Doležel calls this the *extensional narrative world*. Although this initial definition seems quite bland—emphasizing simply the existence of all the entities in the world—Doležel expands the concept by attributing the basic "partitioning" of the world into "the hero, his 'allies' and his 'enemies'" (197) to the extensional world as well. The extensional world in this sense is not a dumb catalog of the objects in the world but rather a structure of entities that include their properties, possible actions, and relationships: "Actions and properties are assigned to agents in the form of propositional functions. The extensional primary NW [narrative world] then appears as a set of propositional functions defined over the set of compossible [that is, logically consistent] agents" (197).

In contrast to the extensional world, the intensional world is revealed by the "texture" of the book that describes the extensional world. Doležel defines texture in this way: "[t]exture is our term for the 'wording' of the text and it comprises all lower-level units of expression as its constituents" (201). Texture becomes important in a theory of fictional worlds because it is one of the means by which we come to understand the ordering of this world, what Doležel calls "*global principles of sense organization*" (201). As an example of texture, Doležel notes the difference of naming in Defoe's *Robinson Crusoe*: "while the hero and some of his close associates are given proper names in the texture (*Robinson, Friday, Xury*), secondary agents are designated by definite descriptions (*my father, the Portugal captain, the English captain's window, Friday's father*, etc.)" (201). This difference in naming constitutes "a two-value function" that sorts the basic agents of the primary narrative world (NW): "[w]e claim that functions of this type project the extensional primary NW into its intensional correlate; therefore, they are called *intensional functions*" (202). Texture, in other words, helps us to construct an intensional world out of the many objects and agents that make up the (extensional) world. Doležel recognizes that these intensional worlds are subject to interpretive emphasis, that a single text might allow readers to project many different intensional worlds, and that these intensional worlds are ultimately the way that the extensional worlds become meaningful. Doležel summarizes this process:

> An interpreter (reader) is presented with the text in the form of its texture. On the basis of observed texture regularities, he constructs the

principles of sense organization in the form of an intensional NW. From the intensional NW he derives the extensional primary NW by following intensional functions from the intensional to the extensional world. In such a way, the intensional narrative world is the prime target of semantic interpretation, while the extensional world represents the derived "background". (204)

It seems clear here that following the basic events of the story means grasping the actions and properties of agents in the extensional world. Conversely, it is by recognizing how those agents are presented through the "texture" of the story that we are able to understand the meaning and value of this text.

The construction of such an intensional world is an especially important part of digital fiction and defines a way in which such worlds differ from their print counterparts. Doležel's example makes clear that during most of our reading, we are subtly picking up on the clues offered to us by the texture of the writing. We should intuitively grasp the extensional world, but may only gradually come to understand the contours of the intensional world, since they are signaled indirectly. Of course, there are many times when print narrative does provide explicit guidance about the use of a story. Genette (1997) notes that paratextual devices like an author's preface are designed to *"ensure that the text is read properly"* (197; emphasis in original)—by, for example, warning against interpreting a fictional story as a *roman à clef* (216–217). But in most instances print narrative can guide its readers through the more subtle clues that Doležel describes, and which the reader may not grasp until a second or third reading. Digital fiction can usually not afford to be so indirect, especially when the user must make informed and even strategic choices to move the text forward. If we concentrate for the moment on texts that function in what Ryan (2006) calls the ontological mode, in which "the decisions of the user send the history of virtual world on different forking paths", we can see that a player needs to *act* to move the story forward and influence its outcome. In a first-person shooter game like *Medal of Honor*, the player must (among other things) shoot enemies, collect objects, and navigate the landscape. It is crucial that the player grasps these rules immediately because they cannot be gradually understood over the course of the story like the emergence of texture in a printed narrative. We might recall in this sense Laurel's (1993) simple characterization of the computer desktop as having the "capacity to *represent action in which humans could participate*" (1). Because we are acting, the rules of this world need to be clear. It seems to me that these UI clues are equivalent to the texture that Doležel associates with the naming conventions in *Robinson Crusoe*. Indeed, many combat games quite literally use naming to guide character actions, printing allies' names in one color and enemies in another. The health bar and bullet count of *Medal of Honor*'s UI do the same thing: they define the contours of the world and the rules for our actions within it. These features of the UI are elements of the *intensional* rather than *extensional* narrative world because they emphasize the meaning of the basic actions and properties in these worlds. Users all understand the qualities of human beings and how they are sorted into enemies and allies (to use Doležel's example) without recourse to the UI, but as we move beyond this level of basic competency toward the *strategy* of progressing through this text (e.g. can I survive a fight in this situation?) we are dependent on the extensional narrative world's intensional qualities and implicit rules. Grasping these rules is essential to navigating the world successfully, but often they are arbitrary. In *Medal of Honor* bullets have number but not weight (we move no slower with a full clip of ammunition) just as characters are sorted by name but not by nationality in *Robinson Crusoe*. Sometimes players must intuit these rules by trial and error, but most games reveal their general rules and principles through UI design.

FICTIONAL WORLD TEXTURE SHAPED BY
THE PROGRAMMING ENVIRONMENT

So far, I have emphasized a relatively narrow range of digital fiction—primarily commercially produced video games. I would like to move back to games before the graphical era, and to consider how this model of fictional world texture applies to the textual worlds of interactive fiction (IF). Because IF can be read using one of many "interpreter" programs that process the core story code and present it to the user, IF makes the presence of the IU in the experience of the story especially obvious. Different IF interpreters will present the story in different ways, allowing users to alter the font size and color; others will even keep track of the commands that have been entered or allow the user to record notes.[6] These UI elements work like those that we see in graphical computer games, because they make evident the texture of a world where, for example, success is defined by how many things can be accomplished in as few commands as possible.

IF is particularly interesting for making clear the link between the underlying programming code and the fictional world's texture. IF is written using special coding languages that, while easy to use, limit the nature of the games that can result. IF is generally defined as a series of spaces (usually called *rooms*) that can hold objects. Objects in turn have a variety of properties that effectively make them behave as if they were different kinds of things. For example, the *Inform* programming language allows writers to create objects, supporters (such as tables), containers (such as a chest), and devices (which can be turned on or off). In IF, characters generally function like very specialized objects that can have properties, hold objects, and respond to conversational cues. IF writers have managed to use this relatively limited set of coding options to create remarkably inventive stories and fictional worlds. Nonetheless, any player who has spent much time with IF quickly realizes that there are well-defined contours to such fictional worlds.[7] When entering a room, the player might *examine* objects for more information, *talk to* characters to try to prompt a conversation, *open* containers to see inside, or *pick up* objects for use in later parts of the game.[8] The world of IF is, in general, a world defined by discrete "rooms" and by the finding and possessing of objects. Of course, individual texts can refine and sharpen these general qualities of IF fictional world texture. In *A Change in the Weather* (1995), Andrew Plotkin has used the game's ability to count moves to create a world in which timing is fundamentally important to progressing. Users must arrive at a cave and then wait for the "rainy night" to occur. Once it is night, users must be in the right location when the lightning strikes so that they can see the landscape and pick up objects. At another point in the game, the user must be at a bridge when a fox "yips" to be able to dig in a particular spot. The result is an extraordinarily difficult game in which success is tied to the smallest quirks of timing. Such timing depends on the fundamental role of discrete "moves" in IF programming.

Although the graphical UI and the nature of IF coding are very different elements of this variety of digital fiction, both show the importance of users' grasp of the digital fictional world's texture. Although readers of print texts might recognize the texture of the fictional world in which they are immersed only on the second or third reading of the story, users in most digital fiction will only be able to progress in the work if they grasp the importance, for example, of collecting objects and taking them to the right place where they can be used.[9] Once we recognize the link between our UI on the game and the coding by which that game is created, it is easy to see how we can extend this understanding of world texture to Storyspace hypertext.

Like IF, the Storyspace development environment provides a general texture for the fictional worlds created using it. Users move from lexia to lexia following different linking words, and those links may be limited according to conditions like the history of the user's movement through the text. Like all of the texts that I have discussed so far, Storyspace also uses its UI to expose this texture. Users can display a list of the available linking words within a given lexia. Some hypertexts go further and allow users access to a visual representation of the many lexias that make up the story. These design options for authors make particularly clear the degree to which UI design allows users to grasp texture. The frustration that many users have expressed with some hypertext narratives (see Douglas 2000) likewise shows that such works sometimes have a very different attitude than video games toward the importance of using UI to reveal fictional world texture. Different genres demand different levels of patience from their users.

But Storyspace also makes clear a limitation in the way that I have been talking about the texture of a fictional world. In IF, the nature of the code with which designers have to work exerts a fairly strong influence on the fictional world because the actions and story elements are determined by that code. Even though *Change in the Weather* feels very different from a simple exploration game like *Zork*, the experience of these worlds is relatively similar since their building blocks are the same. In Storyspace, however, the design environment exerts a much weaker influence on the story, since the only requirements are that discrete bits of text must be displayed on the screen, and some method of linking to the next one must be enabled. Many critics have argued that what Aarseth has called the "Storyspace school of hypertext" (1997: 85) ultimately repeats much the same reading experience,[10] but it is clear that our understanding of the texture of the world is at least as likely to depend on the language used in individual lexias than on the programming system used to organize them.

We might be tempted to say that the crucial difference between our grasp of the texture of a fictional world in Storyspace and IF is the greater potential sophistication of the language or literary aspirations of its authors, but I think that more important is the degree to which users are required to act in these texts. An exploratory hypertext, like all of the fiction of the Storyspace school, functions much like a traditional print novel, in which players may grasp the texture of the world only after many rereadings.[11] IF that is more exploratory than ontological often reveals its texture grudgingly as well. In Emily Short's dialog-based *Galatea*, for example, there are no objects to pick up, rooms to explore, or puzzles to solve; we are challenged to coax the central character into telling us the story of her background. Likewise, graphical exploratory digital fiction like *Myst* and the more recent *Syberia* may require some puzzle solving and collecting objects, but as long as players cannot die or make irreversible choices, texture can emerge gradually. *Myst* is a particularly good case in point, since the static nature of the world seems to be designed to allow users gradually to come to understand its rules and, especially, world texture. Until the very end of the game, there is no way that users can "lose", and most will go back and forth over the same ground until they gradually figure out how to progress to new spaces. Users of the game learn that one of the simplest ways to discover the puzzles that must be solved is to move the mouse around the screen and wait for the pointer icon to change into a small hand, indicating that this item can be manipulated in some way. This basic sorting of active and static elements of the fictional world is a classic example of fictional world texture, and is conveniently signaled through the tactile metaphor of the mouse-controlled hand (see Bell, this volume).

Different degrees of programming sophistication impact this texture in different ways. In IF and Storyspace, the coding system is relatively simple, and so its influence on the texture of the story is relatively direct. Current commercial games usually write their own graphics engines, and so their creators can define the nature of the fictional world in much more specific and varied ways. Digital fiction can emphasize the uncertainty about the basic rules of the fictional world by minimizing the UI design, or can make the world's texture clear by providing explicit UI information.

CONSTRUCTING TEXTURE ACROSS MULTIPLE WINDOWS

It is hardly revolutionary to claim that our experience of the worlds of digital fiction is different from those of print. But most critics have talked about these worlds in terms of their variability based on the player's ability to affect the direction of the plot and the events in the world.[12] This chapter has suggested something rather different: our experience of these digital fictional worlds is different from print because the way that we access these worlds is different.

I have argued that when we read a printed text, we generally grasp the texture of the story gradually and through the implications of the author's description of the world. Such a text essentially provides a single-window access on the story: texture is implied while the story is doing the basic work of describing objects, settings, and events. Some digital fiction works in much the same way. As I have just suggested, *Myst* generally forces players to guess at the reactive elements of the landscape presented in the story's single window.[13] But most digital fiction provides multiple streams of information. Often these are literally multiple windows—as we see in *SimCity*'s information palate or in the inventory panel of most first- or third-person action games. Other games overlay information onto the main screen of the game—like *Medal of Honor*'s compass or health bar. In all of these cases, we are experiencing a fictional world by processing multiple streams of information that reflect entirely different forms of representation.

Such multiple windows have, of course, been long associated with electronic media. Bolter and Grusin (1999) explain, "[T]he practice of hypermediacy is most evident in the heterogeneous 'windowed style' of World Wide Web pages, the desktop interface, multimedia programs, and video games" (31). But such studies almost always describe the aesthetics of such "windowed" spaces according to what they refuse to do: they depart from the immersive experience of traditional representation and force the user into self-consciousness. For Bolter and Grusin, "[t]he multiplicity of windows and the heterogeneity of their contents mean that the user is repeatedly brought back into contact with the interface, which she learns to read just as she would read any hypertext" (33). Lanham (1993) describes this as shifting from looking *through* the work to looking *at* it (15). These critics agree that such hypermediated works disengage us from any one stream of information. Landow (1997) memorably goes on to link such disengagement to deconstruction, intertextuality, and Barthes's notion of the "writerly" (32). But it is hard to reconcile these claims of disengagement and self-awareness to the utter immersion that so many players find in video games; health bars and overhead maps don't seem to disengage the *Halo* player from the fictional world in the slightest. It seems clear that in some way or another players still work to construct a space and coherent sense of the world in many works that nonetheless deploy "windowed" media. Critics working in new media have, I think, been guilty of conflating the design of the UI with the nature of the fictional world represented. While a chaotic UI in a book or game *may* indicate a chaotic or incoherent world, it is just as likely that a coherent world exists behind UI complexity. More broadly, we should not assume that differences in the nature of the UI mean that our goal isn't the same in both: to develop a coherent and complete understanding of the fictional world. Much of the pleasure of understanding a world and appreciating its rules carries over from print to digital fiction.

Although players and readers alike work to construct a coherent world, the process of that construction is often different in print and digital fiction, and these differences subtly color the pleasure that we take from experiencing fictional worlds in these two media. Users in digital media process different types of information to build up a coherent image of a single world. Players move between a three-dimensional representation of a room that the player occupies and two-dimensional orientation provided for the player through a map, abstract (and perhaps numerical) information about the player's health or perhaps even progress through the game. Processing these multiple streams mimics some of the work that we would traditionally do in puzzling out the texture of a storyworld. But books rarely depend on such secondary informational streams. It is certainly true that some print narratives require gathering together different forms of information. A first-time reader of *The Lord of the Rings* might refer to the map of Middle-Earth that Tolkien has placed at the beginning of his novel. The reader of a play might refer back to a cast of characters listed at the beginning to keep track of their relations, or the reader of a novel like *One Hundred Years of Solitude* or *Shame* might reference the family trees printed at the beginning of each text. Diligent readers might even go outside of the printed text to fill in gaps in their background, consulting an atlas when reading a novel set in an unfamiliar country or an encyclopedia to understand the historical background for an event in a story. But all of these activities—while not foreign to print—are marginal. *Most* novels don't require us to consult maps or family trees. More importantly, such information is never required as an ongoing element of the reading of the story. Readers might consult other sources of information to deepen their understanding of the story's background, or consult a map to understand what is going on the first time through the story, but these sources are ultimately *remedial* and provide information that an ideal reader would already have.

At the beginning of this chapter I argued that digital fiction makes one screen central, and usually treats it as our threshold into the "world" of the story. It is clear, however, that this centrality frequently conflicts with the importance of other streams of information, which can undermine this central space and significantly complicate our understanding of what makes the worlds of these digital fictions coherent. In a print text, everything in the fictional world is there because it is referenced in the text itself.[14] In most digital fiction, information exists in these secondary informational streams that has no role in the primary screen, even if that secondary system is as minimal as the list of available links in *afternoon* or hints about selectable objects in *Myst*. If a player kills an enemy and loots some valuable object from the body, that object may well never appear in the main, three-dimensional space at the center of the screen. In other words, the basic, extensional game world is represented completely by no one stream of information. This also creates the possibility of inconsistency between these streams. For example, many computer games make little attempt to reconcile the appearance of the onscreen avatar and the inventory that character is supposed to be carrying. In one of the recent *Monkey Island* adventure games, our svelte central character Guybrush Threepwood is carrying (among other things) a four-foot pole, a large U-shaped glass tube, and a weathervane, which are shown in a separate inventory screen. Two streams of information—one provided by the main screen showing our avatar, and the other represented in his inventory—clearly describe the fictional world in incoherent ways. Juul (2005) has noted that video games routinely create incoherent worlds—for example, when they give players three lives (123–130). This incoherence is a common part of most games that involve character inventory, since they rarely integrate those items fully into the game's main screen. But users do not experience these worlds as impossible or chaotic; they understand that certain types of inconsistency are the result of the rules of different streams of information. Critics have long since moved on from early claims in works like Sherry Turkle's *Life on the Screen* (1995) that encountering stories through an electronic medium produced simple immersion. We have come to recognize, for example, that our relationship to onscreen avatars is much more complex than a simple matter of identification.[15] Users seem to have little trouble holding these different kinds of information and ways of engaging with the text in their minds at the same time.

CONCLUSION: DESCRIBING WORLD ACCESSIBILITY IN DIGITAL FICTION

At the outset of this chapter I noted the importance of how we access fictional worlds, and over the course of this discussion I described the unique qualities of that access in digital fiction. Our access to this world depends on being able to grasp its texture, the subtle rules by which the world is organized. This chapter has offered a method for describing world accessibility in digital fiction. Most digital fictions will designate one space as the "world" of the story. We can describe the structure of accessibility by accounting for how the relevant features of that space are identified and sorted by secondary UI spaces. We can further characterize the structure of fictional world accessibility by defining the relationship between the primary and secondary UI space. Some texts create overlapping and tightly integrated informational streams, such as the consistency between the central reading space of *afternoon* and the list of available links in a secondary window.

Others, however, offer relatively independent streams with the potential for localized incoherence, such as the inconsistent space of the *Monkey Island* main and inventory screens.

I have also offered principles for understanding the tolerance for confusion and indirection in digital fictional world accessibility. I have argued that a fundamental factor in the design of digital fiction's UI and the nature of our access to the fictional world is the degree to which users act in this world. Exploratory texts can allow texture to emerge gradually in much the same way that it does in a printed text. In ontological texts, where users must act to shape the direction of the story, texture normally will be revealed more explicitly. Users can grasp texture in two interrelated ways. Some forms of digital fiction depend on well-established conventions that help users to understand the texture of these worlds. These conventions may be built right into the programming languages by which these texts are created—as is the case of IF and Storyspace authoring environments. In digital fiction that demands a higher degree of user action—especially when some actions can lead to failure in the game—UI design will normally need to provide much more detailed information about the world's texture right at the outset. This will especially be the case when the users of such texts cannot fall back on conventional limitations or programming conditions that determine the shape of the fictional world. Such digital fictions will normally do more work to reveal the fictional world texture to the user.

NOTES

1. Ryan explains: "In the *exploratory* mode, users navigate the display, but this activity does not make fictional history nor does it alter the plot: users have no impact on the destiny of the virtual world. In the *ontological* mode, by contrast, the decisions of the user send the history of virtual world on different forking paths" (2006: 108).
2. For example, in *The Possible Worlds of Hypertext Fiction*, Bell (2010) analyzes hypertext as textual "fragments that are linked in predetermined paths" (3).
3. I will use this term in place of a more medium-specific one like "reader" or "player" to describe someone who interacts with digital narratives in any form. In addition, emphasis on the *user* reinforces my interest in the design of the *user interface* for these texts.
4. Of course, many examples of such innovative "user interfaces" in print text come to mind. Part of Aarseth's (1997) goal in coining the term "ergodic" literature was to emphasize that print texts like Queneau's *Cent Mille Milliards de Poèmes* can be nonlinear and allow users to act on them. Landow has called such print texts "proto-hypertexts" (1997: 38).
5. This is, of course, true of other forms of seemingly realistic representation as well. Goodman (1976) gives the example of perspective in painting: "By the pictorial rules, railroad tracks running outward from the eye are drawn converging, but telephone poles (or the edges of a façade) running upward from the eye are drawn parallel. By the 'laws of geometry' the poles should

also be drawn converging. But so drawn, they look as wrong as railroad tracks drawn parallel" (16).

6. For a client with these features, see Zoom, whose record-keeping features are described at http://www.logicalshift.co.uk/mac/zoom/manual/progress.html. Last accessed 13 February 2013.

7. For an interesting attempt to develop IF in very different terms, see Nick Montfort's Curveship project: http://curveship.com/. Last accessed 13 February 2013.

8. Such actions are so routine and typical that a recent documentary about text adventure games is called *Get Lamp*.

9. Of course, given my broad definition of the term in this chapter, there are forms of digital fiction that do not require significant user activity in order to progress, such as the film-like design of Young-Hae Chang Heavy Industries' *Back in the ROK* (2009) or Ichikawa, Dvorak, and Croft's *Outrances* (2009). In this case, texture can emerge gradually in the manner of a print text.

10. Ryan (2006) offers a sympathetic reading of the productive ways that the design limitations of the Storyspace system can be used (136–147). See also Hayles's (2008) interpretation of the "evolution" of Joyce's writing from the Storyspace *afternoon* to the Web-based *Twelve Blue* (60–70).

11. This is the basis for J. Yellowlees Douglas's discussion of *afternoon* (2000), for which she finds closure only after reading the story four times. See also Ciccoricco (2007) on the role of rereading in "network fiction" (27–31) and Ensslin (2007) on the issue of "revis(itat)ion" in reading hypertext (41–42).

12. See for example Aarseth's discussion (1997) of how different scriptons are generated from a smaller number of textons in the cybertext (62). See also Ryan's (2006) discussion of "interactive architectures" that allow for multiple routes through a story (100–107), and Manovich's distinction (2001) between linear narrative and the database, which can be accessed and explored in many different ways (225–228).

13. In this regard, it is no surprise that the original packaging of the game (1993) adopted novel-like conventions, designating the creators Rand and Robyn Miller as its "authors" and emphasizing immersion in the game: "*Myst* is real. And like real life, you don't die every five minutes. In fact, you probably won't die at all. There are no dead-ends, you may hit a wall, but there is always a way over or around. Pay attention to detail and collect information, because those are the pieces of the puzzle that you'll use to uncover the secrets of *Myst*."

14. There is, of course, a complex debate about what it means for something to be "in" a fictional world. To what extent should we merely infer that some place or person exists in the fictional world if it is unmentioned by the narrative? Ryan (1991) has provided a widely influential solution to this problem by her "principle of minimal departure": "we reconstrue the central world of a textual universe . . . as conforming as far as possible to our representation of the AW [Actual World]" (51). In other words, unless stated otherwise, we assume that the fictional world is consistent with what we know about the actual world. But Ryan goes on to consider some complicating cases, such as the question of whether the knights of a chivalric romance should be understood to carry money. Ryan goes on to argue that an object is transferable from the actual world to the fictional world only if, among other things, "the text names as a member of [the fictional world] at least one individual or geographical location belonging to the AW" (53). In other words, money only gets into the chivalric romance if the text makes some reference to this type of object. Thus, despite the importance of inferences

based on our knowledge of the actual world, the fictional world still depends
fundamentally on what is referenced in the text itself.
15. For a good discussion of the complexity of this identification in the case of
the game *Tomb Raider*, see Flanagan 2002.

WORKS CITED

Aarseth, E. J. (1997) *Cybertext: Perspectives on Ergodic Literature.* Baltimore: Johns Hopkins University Press.
Adams, E. (2010) *Fundamentals of Game Design* (2nd edition). Berkeley: New Riders.
The Adventure Company. (2002) *Syberia.* Chicago: DreamCatcher Interactive.
Bell, A. (2010) *The Possible Worlds of Hypertext Fiction.* Basingstoke, UK: Palgrave.
Bender, J. and Marrinan, M. (2010) *The Culture of Diagram.* Stanford: Stanford University Press.
Bolter, J.D. and Grusin. R. (1999) *Remediation: Understanding New Media.* Cambridge, MA: MIT Press.
Ciccoricco, D. (2007) *Reading Network Fiction.* Tuscaloosa: University of Alabama Press.
Doležel, L. (1979) "Extensional and Intensional Narrative Worlds". *Poetics* 8: 193–211.
Electronic Arts. (2002) *Medal of Honor: Allied Assault.* Redwood City, CA: Electronic Arts.
Ensslin, A. (2007) *Canonizing Hypertext: Explorations and Constructions.* London: Continuum.
Flanagan, M. (2002) "Hyperbodies, Hyperknowledge: Women in Games, Women in Cyberpunk, and Strategies of Resistance". In *Reload: Rethinking Women + Cyberculture.* M. Flanagan and A. Booth (eds). Cambridge, MA: MIT Press, pp. 435–454.
Genette, G. (1997) *Paratexts: Thresholds of Interpretation.* Jane E. Lewin (trans). Cambridge: Cambridge University Press.
Goodman, N. (1976) *Languages of Art: An Approach to a Theory of Symbols.* Indianapolis: Hackett.
Hales, N.K. (2008) *Electronic Literature: New Horizons for the Literary.* Notre Dame, IN: University of Notre Dame.
Ichikawa, S., Crofts, T.H., III, and Dvorak. J. (2009) "Outrances". *Born Magazine.* Last accessed 13 February 2013 at URL: http://www.bornmagazine.org/projects/outrances/
Jackson, S. (1995) *Patchwork Girl* [CD-ROM]. Watertown, MA: Eastgate Systems.
Joyce, M. (1987) *Afternoon, a story* [CD-ROM]. Watertown, MA: Eastgate Systems.
Jull, J. (2005) *Half-Real: Video Games between Real Rules and Fictional Worlds.* Cambridge, MA: MIT Press.
Landow, G.P. (1997) *Hypertext 2.0: The Convergence of Contemporary Critical Theory and Technology.* Baltimore: Johns Hopkins University Press.
Lanham, R.A. (1993) *The Electronic Word: Democracy, Technology, and the Arts.* Chicago: University of Chicago Press.
Laurel, B. (1993) *Computers as Theatre.* Boston: Addison-Wesley.
Manovich, L. (2001) *The Language of New Media.* Cambridge, MA: MIT Press.
Maxis. (1993) *SimCity 2000.* Redwood City, CA: Electronic Arts.
Miller, R. and Miller, R. (1993) *Myst.* Mead, WA: Cyan.
Murray, J.H. (1998) *Hamlet on the Holodeck: The Future of Narrative in Cyberspace.* Cambridge, MA: MIT Press.

Pedersen, R. E. (2009) *Game Design Foundations* (2nd edition). Sudbury, MA: Wordware.

Plotkin, A. (1995) *A Change in the Weather*. Last accessed 13 February 2013 at URL: http://www.wurb.com/if/game/235

Pullinger, K. and Joseph, C. (2005) *Inanimate Alice*. Last accessed 13 February 2013 at URL: http://www.inanimatealice.com/index.html

Ryan, M.-L. (1991) *Possible Worlds, Artificial Intelligence, and Narrative Theory*. Bloomington: Indiana University Press.

Ryan, M.-L. (2006) *Avatars of Story*. Minneapolis: University of Minnesota Press.

Schell, J. (2008) *The Art of Game Design: A Book of Lenses*. Amsterdam: Elsevier.

Seah, A. and Hefler, F. (2009) *House Fire*. Last accessed 13 February 2013 at URL: http://www.bornmagazine.org/projects/house_fire/

Short, E. (2000). *Galatea*. Last accessed 13 February 2013 at URL: http://www.wurb.com/if/game/1326

Telltale Games. (2009) *Tales of Monkey Island: Chapter 1, Launch of the Screaming Narwhal*. San Rafael, CA: Telltale Games.

Turkle, S. (1995) *Life on the Screen: Identity in the Age of the Internet*. New York: Simon & Schuster.

Value. (1998) *Half-Life*. Bellevue, WA: Sierra Studios.

Yellowlees, D. L. (2000) *The End of Books—Or Books without End? Reading Interactive Narratives*. Ann Arbor: The University of Michigan Press.

Young-Hae Chang Heavy Industries. (2009) *Back in ROK*. Last accessed 13 February 2013 at URL: http://www.yhchang.com/BACK_IN_THE_ROK.html

Section II

Social Media and Ludological Approaches

5 Playing with Rather than by the Rules

Metaludicity, Allusive Fallacy, and Illusory Agency in *The Path*

Astrid Ensslin,
Bangor University, Wales

INTRODUCTION

Our contemporary media landscape has seen boundaries between arts and genres blur increasingly in the past decade. It is no longer possible to talk about specific digital art forms in terms of clear-cut categories—least of all digital narratives, which integrate written and spoken language, animation, still images, video, audio, games, hypertext, and hypermedia in multifarious ways, and with various aesthetic effects. Nevertheless, each artifact tends to be labeled, or referred to, by its maker by a specific genre tag, such as Flash *fiction*, multimedia *narrative*, poetic *game* or interactive *drama*. Despite this tendency, and depending on their individual expertise, political agenda, and unique experience of a digital artifact, author-programmers, readers, players, and critics don't always agree on these labels. Jason Rohrer's memento mori mini-game, *Passage* (2007), for instance, has often been likened to poetry (e.g. Thompson 2008; Magnuson 2009), although it doesn't feature a single verbal item. Kate Pullinger et al.'s *The Breathing Wall* (2004) is based on a sequentialized hypertext narrative but has at its core a breathing game, which releases—to the successful breather—essential clues for solving the murder mystery it narrates, and it communicates to a large extent through still and animated images, blended with spoken text (Ensslin 2009, 2011a). Regardless of its tendency to cause terminological ambiguity and controversy, the interface between digital writing, audiovisual art, and game programming has proven to be one of the most prolific breeding grounds for digital artists and writers in the twenty-first century thus far, and this chapter seeks to showcase the importance of this merger for contemporary narratology and other forms of text and media analysis.

Like numerous new media scholars (e.g. Gee 2007; Jenkins 2005; Tavinor 2009), I assume that video games are an art form in their own right, and that some contemporary games—especially art games—have specific literary-fictional qualities that can be close-read using a mixture of narratological, stylistic, semiotic, and ludological analytical principles. Although this doesn't make them novels or short stories, it places them on a continuum with other hybrid digital artifacts that combine ludic and literary qualities. Typical examples of such ludic-literary hybrids are digital fictions with game-like components, such as geniwate and Deena Larsen's *The Princess Murderer* (2003), Kate Pullinger and Chris Joseph's *Inanimate Alice* (2005–2008), and Steve Tomasula's *TOC: A New Media Novel* (2009). They exhibit a variety of ludic devices, such as a performance meter called "Princess Census" (*The Princess Murderer*), point-and-click mini-games (*Inanimate Alice*), and an interactive musical clock, which operates as a navigational device (*TOC*).

Digital fiction is born digital, which means it is "written for and read on a computer screen that pursues its verbal, discursive and/or conceptual complexity through the digital medium, and would lose something of its aesthetic and semiotic function if it were removed from that medium" (Bell et al. 2010: n.p.). The Digital Fiction International Network, which formulated this definition, further details in the same publication that this excludes certain digital art forms that are akin to digital fiction but can't be analyzed as such. These include nonfictional blogs and other Web 2.0 forms of "life narratives", but also paper-under-glass artifacts such as e-books, which read in the same, quasi-linear way in print and digital form and can therefore be printed. Importantly, the above definition also excludes "games we can't 'read', or rather games where there is no dynamic relationship between the gameplay (rules) and its themes (representations) that we can read into, reflect on, or interpret" (Bell et al. 2010: n.p.). Quite literally, "reading" here refers to linguistic decoding as well as any abstract or metaphorical meanings of the term, such as reading music, visual arts, or the procedural rhetoric of a video game (Bogost 2007).[1] Hence, video games aren't by definition exempt from literary, digital fictionality (see Ensslin 2014). Rather, to qualify for analytical engagement under the "digital fiction" umbrella, they need to exhibit specific elements of readability, which include the written and/or spoken word and particular aspects of textuality that facilitate or even call out for stylistic, narratological, *and* ludic analysis.

To provide an example of how literary-fictional video games might be examined systematically, this chapter will offer an analysis of the literary art game, *The Path*, by Tale of Tales (2009a). I will begin by examining the question of why a digital artifact that—in its subtitle ("a short horror game")—explicitly refers to itself as a game can or indeed should be included in a volume titled *Analyzing Digital Fiction*. To do so, I shall first explore the ludic-literary continuum (see Ensslin 2012) and provide a working definition of literariness for digital fiction. I shall then go on to explain how *The Path* meets these criteria, thus underscoring its hybrid status between art game and digital literary narrative. This will be followed by an explanation of my analytical framework, which develops Ryan's idea of functional ludo-narrativism (Ryan 2006: 203).

The final and most extensive section of this chapter offers a systematic ludo-narratological reading of *The Path*. It is informed theoretically by the Situationist concept of *détournement*, which combines processes of aesthetic appropriation and subversion "[u]sing play as a practice to transcend rigid forms and to break constraints" (Dragona 2010: 27). In particular, the analysis will take into account three etymological variants of playfulness (from the Latin "ludere"): (1) *metaludicity*, that is, the ways in which *The Path* thematizes and problematizes game mechanic features typically occurring in commercial blockbusters, such as high-speed action, navigability, achievement, and reward, and interweaves them with plot and character development; (2) *allusive fallacy* in the sense of design features that use intertextuality, pro- and analepsis as disconcerting rather than cohesive narrative and navigational devices; and (3) *illusory agency* (MacCallum-Stewart and Parsler 2007), which refers to projecting false impressions of player freedom and impact on the development of the game and its underlying fictional world.

GAMES AS LITERARY FICTION

There is no doubt that, first and foremost, games exist to be played. However, some serious game artists have shown that it is possible to experiment with other forms of cultural expression, such as visual and literary arts, and embed them in ludic structures so as to create specific aesthetic and hermeneutic effects in players. Likewise, digital writers have experimented with ludic structures and embedded them in their fictional and poetic artifacts. What results is a rich ecology of hybrid digital artifacts that defy clear categorical boundaries and challenge recipients' transmedia abilities and analysts' critical repository. To allow for systematic scholarly engagement with this hybrid ecology, I have, in my earlier work (Ensslin 2011b, 2012), suggested a textual continuum between ludic digital literature and literary video games. Ludic digital *literature* is primarily "read" and foregrounds overstructured (or deliberately understructured) oral or written language, yet it also features ludic elements in order to simultaneously subvert or exploit them. Literary computer *games*, by contrast, are primarily played (and often explicitly referred to as "games" in the title or front matter) but feature some distinctive poetic, dramatic, and/or narrative-diegetic elements, which demand from players a hermeneutic stance that facilitates the close reading of ludic and textual structures and the simultaneous reflection on subludic and subtextual layers of meaning. Prominent examples include Jason Nelson's *ArcticAcre* tetralogy (2007–2009) and Gregory Weir's *Silent Conversation* (2009).

As ludic-literary hybrids in the digital sphere exhibit a wide variety of semiotic codes, of which verbal language is a constitutive one, literariness here needs to be understood in the sense of experimental *verbal arts*. Such works include texts that employ and foreground spoken and written language in unconventional ways and embed them, kinetically and multimodally, in what are essentially digital *Gesamtkunstwerke*, rather than following a rigid paper-under-glass trajectory. The term "literary", thus, has to be dissociated from print and its implications for reception (e.g. sequentiality, closure and two-dimensionality) and production. Rather, it should be understood in the sense of "visual poetry", "interactive drama", and, of course, *literary* digital fiction; in short, artifacts that aim to "knock . . . down the verbal structures of linear [print] discourse and [to] melt . . . different poetics into a hybrid tradition" (Beiguelman 2010: 409).

Of particular importance in this quasi-iconoclastic, experimental paradigm is the degree to which computer games implement the ideas of *détournement* and (playful yet serious) deconstruction, and thematize and/or problematize—linguistically, multimodally, or otherwise—the essence of (digital) gameplay. As Dragona puts it,

> [u]sing play as a practice to transcend rigid forms and to break constraints is a distinctive feature of today's game-based art. Artists working in the field are playing with the rules, rather than playing by rules; they modify or negate instructions, structures, aesthetics and norms, seeing contemporary gameworlds as a reflection of the contemporary digital realm. (2010: 27)

In computer games/gaming as literary art, then, literary and poetic techniques are employed in order to explore the affordances of rules, feedback, challenges, performance monitoring, and other ludic mechanics.

My methodological approach differs somewhat from Marie-Laure Ryan's distinction between "*narrative game*, in which narrative meaning is subordinated to the player's actions, and the *playable story*, in which the player's actions are subordinated to narrative meaning" (2009: 45). Ryan's concept of narrative game is a much more inclusive one than that of literary video games, and covers commercial blockbusters such as *Half-Life* and *Grand Theft Auto* as well as narrative nonprofit indie games. By the same token, Ryan does not define playable stories in literary terms but rather in terms of emergent gameplay, where players create their own stories, for instance, by making characters enact a sequence of events in *The Sims*, or by deciding on a specific reading path in hypertext fiction. Ryan bases her distinction on Caillois's (1979) typology of games, which assumes a spectrum between highly structured, rule-driven games (*ludus*) and games that operate in a largely unstructured, improvised and spontaneous fashion (*paidia*). In Ryan's view,

> [w]hile ludus inspires narrative games, the spirit of paidia infuses playable stories. In a playable story there is no winning or losing: the purpose of the player is not to beat the game, but to observe the evolution of the storyworld. Playable stories induce a much more aesthetic pleasure than narrative games because the player is not narrowly focused on goals. (2009: 46–47)

This seems to make perfect sense with regard to Ryan's own theoretical framework and textual spectrum. Nevertheless, as my analysis of *The Path* will demonstrate, the situation relating to ludic-literary hybridity is significantly more complex.

THE PATH—A "LITERARY" HORROR GAME?

The Path by Tale of Tales (2009a) is an art game that transmediates the Perrauldian tale of "Little Red Riding Hood" (*"Le Petit Chaperon Rouge"* 1961 [1697]). It replaces the linear plot of the original folk narrative with a gameworld placed in a contemporary gothic setting and increases the original character repository by introducing six female protagonists at different stages of adolescence. The player can choose, for their player-character, between six sisters aged between nine and nineteen, whose names are all quasi-synonyms of the color red (Robin, Rose, Ginger, Ruby, Carmen, and Scarlet) and who are dressed in various hues of saturated red and black. They all have their own age-specific personalities and ways of expressing them. Robin, the youngest, is a lively young child dressed in the famous Grimmsian red cap, and loves playing in the woods. Wolves are "her favorite kind of animal" (Tale of Tales 2011). Rose is a precocious eleven-year-old who enjoys and enthusiastically protects the beauty and innocence of Mother Nature. She wears a black dress with a red hemline and bright red stockings. Thirteen-year-old Ginger is a tomboy full of wild ideas. Determined never to grow up, she tends to get completely absorbed in gameplay. She wears black Indian feathers in her red hair, and the two studded red belts wrapped loosely around her short black pantsuit give her the appearance of a bandit. Ruby, the "goth", is a pessimist and nihilist. Her black leg brace suggests an injury, but we do not learn why the enigmatic fifteen-year-old is really wearing it. The only color she allows in her appearance is in the black-and-red stripes of her shirt. Seventeen-year-old Carmen is aware of her beautiful body and the effect it has on the male onlooker. She enjoys flirting and dreams of a man who will hold and protect her. Her tight black-and-red shirt and leggings and swinging gait underscore her sexual appeal. Scarlet, finally, is the oldest in a family "with an invisible mother" (Tale of Tales 2011). Being responsible for her younger sisters takes its toll, and she longs for a calmer life and the company of a like-minded individual. Her outfit (long black trousers and red turtleneck top) and orderly hairstyle display a level of formality that reflects maturity and seriousness.

Each sister's version of Little Red Riding Hood represents one level of the game and starts in exactly the same way: by leaving the big city to pay a visit to their grandmother, who lives in a dark forest. The only instruction the player-character (PC) obtains at the beginning of each level is to "go to grandmother's house" and to "stay on the path". The path unfolding in front of the PC leads through the woods straight to grandmother's house, and getting there without straying into the forest is not a challenge at all. Upon entering the house without having explored the woods, however, the player is confronted with an unsatisfactory situation: she is told by the final scoreboard that she hasn't collected any items or opened any doors, but what seems most disturbing is that she hasn't encountered the wolf, for which reason she has failed. The game's feedback thus communicates to the player that it is desirable if not mandatory to confront the wolf, and quite clearly that there is no other way of succeeding than to stray from the path into the woods to collect items, experience places, and interact with objects and characters, no matter how seriously such behavior breaks the minimalistic rule set of the game.

Each character's story and destiny are thus unconditionally reliant upon encounters with the mythological wolf, which manifests itself in various physical and abstract shapes and forms. Robin is killed by a literal wolf while attempting to play with it in the graveyard; Rose drowns in the misty lake, the dangers of which she underestimates; tomboy Ginger's wolf is a female peer (the Girl in Red), who confronts her with her own femininity (Tale of Tales 2010), an internal conflict that is mirrored symbolically in the wire fencing and electric pylons strewn across the field of flowers. Ruby is tempted by a young man in the playground, who offers her cigarettes and possibly seduces and rapes her, although only the former is shown in the game.[2] Similarly, Carmen is seduced by a sturdy forester, with whom she consumes alcohol at a campsite and who later rapes and kills her. Scarlet's temptation, finally, is perhaps the most subtle and mysterious one, as she is carried away playing the piano in the ruined theater.

FROM MYTH TO GAME

The story of "Little Red Riding Hood" has seen uncountable adaptations and remediations around the world. The recent Disney and Hollywood blockbusters *Hoodwinked* (Edwards et al. 2005; Disa 2011) and *Red Riding Hood* (Hardwicke 2011), alongside TV commercials such as the serialized Sky Broadband adverts in the UK, are only some indicators of the timeless appeal of Perrault's and the Grimms' notorious tale (Zipes 2011). As documented by Zipes (1993; cf. Dundes 1989), the tale's fascination lies primarily in its thematic concern with violence and rape, which has inspired numerous popular and literary narratives, driven by its psychoanalytical and gender-theoretical implications. Especially since the latter half of the 20th century, writers such as Olga Broumas, Tanith Lee, Sally Miller Gearhart, and Anne Sharpe have offered lesbian and feminist takes on the symbolical subordination, exploitation, demonization, and victimization of the three generations of females featuring in the original story. Most of them have at their core a critique of male fantasies of sexual and domestic domination and of the concomitant moralization of female conduct.

The transmediation of "Little Red Riding Hood" offered by Auriea Harvey and Michaël Samyn, the Belgian developer team behind *The Path*, has a distinct cognitive-developmental trajectory. It exploits the educational potential of immersive gameworlds to trigger in players reflections on human cognitive, physical, and emotional development and to reflect upon the significance of trauma for human emotions and understanding. The six characters symbolize the process of adolescent maturation, which is full of temptations, failures, disappointments, and other negative experiences. By enacting a series of traumatic experiences, which no one wishes to have for themselves, the game enables players to empathize with the characters and to draw conclusions for their own lives and those of others—their children, for example.[3] Similarly, the game itself shows how the human brain deals with post-traumatic stress. After each girl's symbolic death, they find themselves lying outside grandmother's house in the rain, and having dragged themselves into the house, or rather a surrealist rendering of it, a similarly surrealist, dark and threatening cut scene is triggered, which provides further hints of what actually happened to the girl and the psychological and physical trauma to which she has been exposed before dying.

LITERARY GAMEPLAY

The gameplay of *The Path* is deliberately straightforward. It requires a minimum number of keystrokes, and most of the time the player simply uses the movement controls (e.g. mouse buttons or cursor keys) to move the character forward. According to the developers, the game "offers an atmospheric experience of exploration, discovery and introspection through a unique form of gameplay, designed to immerse you deeply into its dark themes" (Tale of Tales 2009b: n.p.). A so-called slow game (Tale of Tales 2009b; Westecott 2010), *The Path* foregrounds certain aspects of computer game aesthetics for critical purposes. It defies quick action: although players can switch between walking and running, the overall speed at which the character moves through the game world is extremely slow, and objects to interact with few and far between. The slow pace of character movement and low density of interactions enable players to reflect upon the thematic issues surrounding the narrative and thematic trajectory of the game, as well as the implications of fast-paced, unreflected gameplay.

Being a slow game, *The Path* situates itself in opposition to commercial blockbusters and the blind frenzy surrounding run-of-the-mill shooters and other popular genres. It foregrounds emotional, philosophical, and hermeneutic processes, and it does so by using a variety of techniques. Slow movement and the impossibility and undesirability of winning this game are only two albeit significant components of its metaludic if not antiludic agenda. More important for this chapter is the fact that the game exhibits a number of *literary* devices, which underscore its indebtedness to the literary canon it follows and the structural and aesthetic effects they can evoke in the player. Firstly, the game's macrostructure is labeled with fictional and dramatic terms. It consists of three "acts": Act 1, "The Red Apartment", forms the opening to each level and features the characters that the player can choose from at any stage of the game. It demonstrates how many lives, or sisters, the player has left to play as, thereby underscoring the gothic feel of the storyworld. Act 2, "The Forest", represents the main site of gameplay as the PC meanders through the woods in search for collectible items and adventures, and where she meets her instantiation of the wolf. Whenever the PC is near an interactive item, a short cut scene is triggered, which details what happens in the interaction, such as picking up a skull from the graveyard or climbing a tree. Act 3, "Grandmother's House", starts as soon as the PC has reached the front door of the building. It is a semi-interactive cut scene, in which the player can only move forward, by repeatedly pressing any key or button. This part will inevitably end in the final traumatic cut scene and be followed by the enigmatic scoreboard.

The game's three-act structure is overlaid with chapter labels for each level. Each final scoreboard says "End of chapter x", thus suggesting the player has performed a reading rather than playing activity. Clearly, chapter labels are fairly common even in commercial games. However, the player's avatar changes with each chapter, and *The Path* does not involve any "real" point scoring leading to level-ups and character development over time, as is the case, for instance, in computer role-playing games. It thus follows a horizontal, nonhierarchical rather than vertical level architecture, which brings it closer to a collection of short stories, or chapters in a novel, than a standard video game. Finally, the gameplay experience resembles the close, or deep attention paid to the details of a fictional, autobiographical narrative far more than the achievement-oriented hyper attention (Hayles 2007) afforded and demanded by most video games.

Curiously, despite its narrative trajectory, the game does not feature any spoken or written dialogue between characters or between PC and non-player characters. Likewise, the player isn't guided by any voice-over or written instructions throughout. Apart from the sparse instructions at the beginning, the name labels for characters in Act 1, and the written scoreboard at the end of each level, hardly any verbal language is used. This augments the importance of a very unusual device occurring in multiple places throughout Act 2: little snippets of interior monologue, which are worded so as to match each character's stage of cognitive and emotional development, and to act as a mimetic device for their unique personalities. Upon entering the ruined theater, for instance, Scarlet muses philosophically that "[a]rt is where the nobility of humanity is expressed. I could not live in a world without it". By contrast, Robin's interior monologues are linguistically and intellectually less sophisticated. In the graveyard, she monologizes, "People die. It's hard to imagine for a kid like me. They die and we put them in the ground. Like flowers". Hence, no matter how short and abrupt, interior monologues serve an important lyrical and characterization purpose, thus corroborating the literary feel of the game.

Finally, the peritextual environment surrounding the game reinforces its literary atmosphere. The game's official website (Tale of Tales 2011) features each sister's blog and a number of fictional entries written by them, as well as comments from various fictional and actual visitors. Again, the style of writing has been adapted to the age of each character, and the entries convey additional personal, emotional, and anecdotal information about their fictional authors. Eerily, each LiveJournal, as they are called, ends around the same date—between January and April 2009—paralleling the time leading up to the release of the game. This metaleptic device (see Bell, this volume), which bridges the ontological gap between the players' actual world and the fictional world of the game, suggests that the girls' fictional deaths are to be understood as "real" within the fictional world of the game, no matter how virtual or metaphorical they may appear in the hermeneutic process.

TOWARD FUNCTIONAL LUDO-NARRATIVISM

In *Avatars of Story*, Ryan calls for "a functional ludo-narrativism that studies how the fictional world, realm of make-believe, relates to the playfield, space of agency" (2006: 203). Such a combined approach aims to examine how elements of game design, gameplay, narrative and textuality concur to evoke distinctive receptive and interactive experiences, thus "do[ing] justice to the dual [ludic and textual] nature of videogames" (Ryan 2006: 203; cf. Juul 2005; Dovey and Kennedy 2006; Ensslin 2011b). As Ryan does not detail what exactly a functional ludo-narratological framework might entail, I shall use this section to map out its core analytical principles. The following section will then exemplify the synthetic nature of this approach by examining three structural aspects of *The Path*.

According to Ryan (personal correspondence, 10 August 2011), a full-fledged theory of functional ludo-narrativism

> should emerge bottom up from studies that ask of games: to what extent do the player's actions contribute to the progression of the plot, and to what extent is the plot imposed on the player through cinematic cut scenes and other non-interactive means. Another important question to ask for each particular game is: how dependent on a (built-in) narrative structure is the player's entertainment?

In other words, a functional ludo-narratological analysis needs to address one or more of the following questions:

- How important are the underlying storyworld and story arc for gameplay and player entertainment?

- How are the player's actions embedded in the narrative, and what actions does he or she need to perform to drive the narrative forward?
- What kind of balance (if any) does the game exhibit between gameplay, cut scenes and other noninteractive narrative devices?
- What type(s) of plot does the game feature (Ryan 2008)—epic (event and hero-oriented), tragic (conflict and relationship-oriented), and/or epistemic (problem-solution and quest-oriented) plots?
- What are the relationships and interactions between PC(s) and NPCs (nonplayer characters), if any, and how do they contribute to the development of the narrative?

At a more *literary* and textual level, however, these questions may be of lesser interest than the following:

- How are aspects of gameplay and textuality reflected upon and employed creatively and/or critically by the game designers to achieve certain aesthetic and media-critical effects?
- How are standard gameplay mechanics modified through metafictional and metaludic devices, thus impacting in various ways player entertainment and other aspects of gameplay experience? What impact do these modifications have on navigation and agency?
- How are textual (and specifically linguistic) devices typically found in literary fiction, poetry, and drama employed aesthetically?
- What kind of lusory attitude (Salen and Zimmerman 2004: 98) is required of the player for "successful" literary gameplay?

For literary (art) games, then, it is important to move onto a meta-level of interpretation, which looks at how gameness is reflected upon creatively, and what artistic means are used by the developers to achieve the intended effects in players.[4]

PLAYING WITH THE RULES: METALUDICITY, ALLUSIVE FALLACY, AND ILLUSORY AGENCY IN *THE PATH*

Having outlined, in a previous section, some of the main literary aspects of *The Path*, I shall concentrate, in my following analysis, on three ludo-narratological techniques that underline the game's subversive and self-reflexive remit more generally: metaludicity, allusive fallacy, and illusory agency. All three of them merge aspects of game mechanics and storyworld in the sense of how ludic and narrative meanings are woven into an audiovisual interactive experience. All three concepts are derived, etymologically, from the Latin verb *ludere* (to play) and denote various aspects of *ludus* (serious, rule-based, structured play) and *paidia* (improvised, unstructured, frivolous play; Caillois 1979). Metaludicity refers to aspects of a game whose purpose it is to make players reflect critically upon game mechanics and gameplay. Allusive fallacy combines the idea of "alluding" (literally, to play at, or refer to something via word play) with that of purposeful deception. Players who are subjected to allusive fallacy are deliberately misled in a game—for instance, by deceptive semiotic clues. Illusory agency, finally, contains another deceptive aspect: the idea of illusion, or playful mockery by means of false appearances. Illusory agency in a ludo-narratological context refers to "a facet of the game design which appears to allow the player free reign and personal choice, but in fact guides them along rigid lines through a relatively linear narrative" (MacCallum-Stewart and Parsler 2007: n.p.).

METALUDICITY

The Path's game manual (Tale of Tales 2009b: 3) opens with the pretext "[t]here is one rule in the game. And it needs to be broken. There is one goal. And when you attain it, you die." The game's explicit mission statement is thus dually subversive: breaking the rule is constitutive of gameplay, and successful gameplay equates to in-game suicide, which runs counter to the survival and defeat trajectory of most commercial games. The rule that has to be broken is to "[g]o to grandmothers house" and to "stay on the path" while doing so. As mentioned previously, the aim of the game is for the PC to explore the woods as extensively as he or she can, to collect as many items on the way and to encounter as many adventures, including the wolf, as possible. The game's ultimate success, however, relies solely on meeting the wolf, as any number of collected items or opened doors won't suffice to obtain "success" as feedback on the scoreboard. Thus, the subtextual message of the game, which is that symbolic death is inevitable in adolescent maturation, is manifested through the mechanics of having to interact with the wolf for success. The leveling up one would expect, however, does not take place. Rather, players move from sister to sister at free will, much as in the process of reading the chapters of a novel, or the lexias of a hypertext, and as soon as one full gameplay cycle is completed and all six sisters have died, the player is encouraged to start again.[5]

Despite being a highly narrative game, which borders generically on adventure or survival horror games, *The Path* does not feature any surprise encounters. Nor does it require players to develop any specific gameplay skills: "[t]here are no ticking clocks or monsters to defeat. No hard puzzles will ever halt your progress. Most activities in the game are entirely optional and voluntary" (Tale of Tales 2009b: 3)—except for encountering the wolf. Thus, the player can direct their attention from kinetic performance to semiotic decoding and hermeneutic understanding.

The fact that *The Path* is a slow game allows players to reflect extensively on their experience and to hypothesize about the game's inherent message. Although the PC can switch from walking to running, this will have negative effects on their overall vision, as the camera angle moves up by several in-game meters, thus obscuring many potentially useful visual clues in the forest.[6] Furthermore, the PC's meanderings through the forest are often completely uneventful for several minutes if not hours. Finding and picking the mysterious white flowers on the way will point the PC in the direction of an interactive item, but the process of picking them is slowed down through cut scenes triggered by each interaction with a flower item.

The Path is a game that can't, and doesn't want to, be won. At its core lies its subtextual and subludic message: the trials and tribulations related to adolescent maturation and the toll they take on young people's personalities and self-image. Therefore the designers suggest that players "try working **with** the game, rather than **against** it" (Tale of Tales 2009b: 13, emphasis in original) and develop a lusory attitude that will be conducive to reading gameplay in the context of its narrative and symbolical framework.

A final example of *The Path*'s metaludicity is the way it manifests the developmental process from *paidia* to *ludus* (Caillois 1979). The former concept is closely associated with the naivety and randomness of child's play, while the latter reflects the rules of adulthood a young person acquires in the course of their adolescence. The six sisters' personalities mirror this evolution, from Robin's love for playing in the woods, through Rose's affinity to nature, Ruby's nihilism, and Scarlet's mature sense of responsibility. Likewise, each character represents "the rules of play" involved in human life in a different way: Robin subscribes to the rule-less nature of child's play, Rose to the mysteriously aesthetic laws of nature, Ginger to the alleged game of life she explores through play, Ruby to the brutal laws of (human) nature and society, Carmen to the enticing rules of flirtation, and Scarlet to the social rules of etiquette.

ALLUSIVE FALLACY

The second ludo-narratological principle I would like to explore is allusive fallacy in the sense of semiotic devices deployed as misleading clues in *The Path*. Of particular importance for this undertaking is the game's interface. Once diverged from the path to grandmother's house, the PC finds herself in an impermeably dense forest. Little specks of light and dust in the air and on the ground, as well as scattered rays of sun seem to suggest navigational clues, yet the mist in the distance seems to conceal where the PC's trail (depicted as the dotted line in Figure 5.1) is leading. As the trail simply depicts the PC's past itinerary through the woods, it does not indicate where she needs to turn to discover any interactive items. Only when she is within a certain range of an interactive area or objects does it appear in the distance. By the same token, the trail only appears every one hundred in-game meters, thus impeding precise navigation.

Figure 5.1 Screenshot of Ginger's trail in *The Path* (first play-through)

Figure 5.2 shows the gaming interface during the second and any further play-throughs. It now depicts visual, iconic clues about sites to visit (indexed by the lake and field of flowers icons in the left-hand margin), and about the locations of the wolf (represented by a paw in the bottom right hand corner). Somewhat less clear-cut are such symbolic devices as the white twirls all around the margins. The steadily moving Girl in White (a dynamic navigation aid) is symbolized by the sharp white twirl immediately to the left of the paw, yet without consulting the manual, players are unlikely to fathom out immediately how to read the somewhat cryptic symbolic devices. Indeed, the larger, blurred twirls are likely to remain a mystery throughout, thus contributing to the allusive fallacy of the game.

Most strikingly, however, whenever the PC approaches an item that is allocated to another sister, a close-up of that sister is superimposed on the interface (Figure 5.3). That said, this ludic interpretation isn't obvious to players who haven't read the manual. Indeed, to the implied close reader/player, this device doesn't just operate as an intertextual hint to another chapter of the game and/or a ludic pointer toward inoperability, but indeed a proleptic or analeptic device alluding eerily to another sister's past or forthcoming suffering and death.

Figure 5.2   Screenshot of Ruby's interface in *The Path* (second play-through)

Figure 5.3   Screenshot of *The Path*: Carmen's image superimposed onto Ruby's failed interaction with the security fence

In their entirety, the allusive devices deployed in the game have a strangely disconcerting effect on the player, especially if they have embarked on the game without reading the manual. They cannot help the feeling that they are somewhat aimlessly meandering through the woods, and that their trajectory increasingly directs them to the frightful yet inevitable encounter with the wolf.

ILLUSORY AGENCY

Generally speaking, rules are there to structure gameplay and to provide a sense of direction as well as the winning and termination conditions of a game (Adams 2010). The fewer rules there are, the simpler a game usually is, and this simplicity tends to be emphasized by the design of the interface and gameworld. Going by the straightforward rules of *The Path*, one might assume that they structure the gameplay experience by limiting it to the game's explicit rule and goal. This, however, is not the case. As noted above, following the straightforward path to grandmother's house results in failure, and the aim of the game is for players to explore and reflect on the game world as they wonder through the woods.

The seemingly endless *mise-en-scène* unfolding before the PC in Act 2 requires a large degree of agency, of strategic thinking, exploring, and trial and error. There isn't a prefabricated narrative path to follow, except for the suggestive age sequence of the six sisters. They can, however, be played in any order.

Upon closer inspection, however, the sense of agency evoked by the sandbox-like, endless woodlands diminishes. Once the player realizes that his or her main objective isn't to complete a repository, to collect all white flowers, or to seek to unlock the doors in grandmother's house, but rather to reflect upon the significance of the symbolic wolf and the player's interaction with it, the infinity of the woods begins to appear insignificant, and so does the agency it seems to engender. After all, the path to the wolf is signposted throughout from the second play-through onward, and there is only one way of interacting with him (as with any other units in the game): through letting go of all controls once near him and letting the ensuing cut scene tell the rest of the story. Thus, the sense of illusory agency conveyed by the game is caused by the loss of ludic and narrative meaning inherent in player agency, and a much stronger sense of nonagency takes over, which is underscored by the feeling of inevitability relating to trauma and death.

CONCLUSION

As this chapter has sought to demonstrate, a systematic ludo-narrativist analysis of a literary-fictional game like *The Path* can uncover its metaludic agenda and the ways in which game designers play with, rather than by, rules and other ludic devices to achieve specific aesthetic effects and a genre-critical stance in the player. I have shown that *The Path* deserves a place in a volume dedicated to digital fiction because it situates itself firmly in the creative and critical canon surrounding its urtext ("Little Red Riding Hood"), and offers a new take on its much debated sexual connotations, psychoanalytical interpretations, and feminist concerns. *The Path* offers a postmodern pluralistic and procedural approach to victimized female identity and enacts different versions of the underlying fairy tale theme to expose the temptations and dangers facing young people—especially females—at different stages of adolescence. I have further demonstrated how the game employs a range of distinctly literary elements by employing the written word in particular as mimetic devices—to paint character portraits of the six sisters—and as paratextual tools framing the game in terms of a three-act (closet) drama and a six-chapter novel. The LiveJournals further serve as a metaleptic tool to diminish the ontological gap between the actual world of the player and the fictional world of the game.

My eclectic ludo-narratological analysis has explored the metaludic mechanics and narrative structures, as well as aspects of allusive fallacy and illusory agency in the game. As a whole, the techniques used by Tale of Tales to evoke a reflective stance in their players operate at various levels of ludicity and textuality. The feeling of confusion and trepidation conveyed by the game's gloomy atmosphere is augmented specifically by misleading interface items, pro- and analepsis, and the vexing fallacy of pervading a seemingly infinite gameworld without being able to evade one's own fatal destiny.

On a final note, more bottom-up analyses are needed of narrative and specifically *literary* video games to further refine and systematize the methodology of functional ludo-narrativism. Furthermore, the analytical repository will need to be able to include games that are poetic and/or dramatic rather than primarily fictional-narrative in style and structure. What remains crucial, however, is the close relationships between ludic and textual devices and how they are co-deployed to allow an integrated approach to close reading and close play.

NOTES

1. For a somewhat broader definition of games as digital fiction, see Punday (this volume).
2. An alternative or even complementary interpretation would be that, after taking the drugs, Ruby is involved in a car accident, as suggested by imagery used in the ensuing Act 3.
3. The game is "unsuitable for children", according to the game manual. Although it only alludes to violence and sexuality, "the overall melancholy mood of the game and the potentially unsettling course of events" may upset preadolescent players (Tale of Tales 2009b: 3).
4. For a collection of essays discussing how this may be achieved in games as art and art games more generally, see Catlow et al. (2010).

5. Strictly speaking, each game cycle ends with an Epilogue, in which the PC is the mysterious Girl in White that each sister meets on several occasions on her journey through the forest. Whilst in the sisters' chapters, the Girl in White acts as a navigational device to take the pausing player back on the path, the same character becomes playable in the Epilogue. This part of the game, which takes place in pouring rain, summarizes all previous chapters by allowing the PC to revisit all interactive sites in the woods, yet interaction with them is no longer possible. Act 3, which uses the same semi-interactive principles, is distinctly less noir, yet again revisits all six sisters' traumas.

6. The running experience differs depending on the type of controls that are used. The moving camera angle occurs when using the mouse to run. When using the cursor keys, the interface becomes blurred, and the system is likely to crash after a few seconds.

WORKS CITED

Adams, E. (2010) *Fundamentals of Game Design*, 2nd ed. Berkeley, CA: New Riders.

Beiguelman, G. (2010) "The Reader, the Player and the Executable Poetics: Towards a Literature beyond the Book". In *Beyond the Screen: Transformations of Literary Structures, Interfaces and Genres*. J. Schäfer and P. Gendolla (eds). Bielefeld: Transcript, pp. 403–425.

Bell, A., Ensslin, A. Ciccoricco, D. Laccetti, J., Pressman, J., and Rustad, H. (2010) "A Screed for Digital Fiction". *electronic book review* [online], 07 March. Last accessed 7 August 2011 at URL: http://www.electronicbookreview.com/thread/electropoetics/DFINative

Bogost, I. (2007) *Persuasive Games: The Expressive Power of Videogames*. Cambridge, MA: MIT Press.

Caillois, R. (1979 [1958]) *Man, Play, Games*. M. Barash (trans). New York: Schocken Books.

Catlow, R., Garrett, M., and Morgana, C. (eds). (2010) *Artists Re:Thinking Games*. Liverpool: Liverpool University Press.

Disa, M. (2011) *Hoodwinked Too! Hood vs. Evil*. Los Angeles, CA: Blue Yonder Films.

Dovey, J. and Kennedy, H. (2006) *Game Cultures: Computer Games as New Media*. Maidenhead: Open University Press.

Dragona, D. (2010) "From Parasitism to Institutionalism: Risks and Tactics for Game-Based Art". In *Artists Re:thinking Games*. R. Catlow et al. (eds). Liverpool: Liverpool University Press, pp. 26–32.

Dundes, A. (ed.) (1989) *Little Red Riding Hood: A Casebook*. Madison: University of Wisconsin Press.

Edwards, C., Edwards, T., and Leech, T. (2005) *Hoodwinked*. Los Angeles, CA: Blue Yonder Films.

Ensslin, A. (2009) "Respiratory Narrative: Multimodality and Cybernetic Corporeality in 'Physio-cybertext' ". In *New Perspectives on Narrative and Multimodality*. R. Page (ed). London: Routledge, pp. 155–165.

Ensslin, A. (2011a) "From (W)reader to Breather: Cybertextual Retro-intentionalisation in Kate Pullinger et al.'s *Breathing Wall*". In *New Narratives: Stories and Storytelling in the Digital Age*. R. Page & B. Thomas (eds). Lincoln, NE: University of Nebraska Press, pp. 138–152.

Ensslin, A. (2011b) *The Language of Gaming*. Basingstoke: Palgrave Macmillan.

Ensslin, A. (2012) "Computer Gaming". In *The Routledge Companion to Experimental Literature*. J. Bray, A. Gibbons, and B. McHale (eds). London: Routledge.

Ensslin, A. (2014, forthcoming) *Literary Gaming*. Cambridge, MA: MIT Press.

Gee, J. P. (2007) *Good Video Games + Good Learning: Collected Essays on Video-games, Learning and Literacy*. New York: Peter Lang.

geniwate and Larsen, D. (2003) *The Princess Murderer*. Last accessed 30 April 2010 at URL: http://www.uiowa.edu/~iareview/tirweb/feature/june03/larsen_geni/prin.html

Hardwicke, C. (2011) *Red Riding Hood*. Hollywood, CA: Appian Way Productions.

Hayles, N. K. (2007) "Hyper and Deep Attention: The Generational Divide in Cognitive Modes". *Profession* [online] 13: 187–199. Last accessed 27 April 2010 at URL: http://www.mlajournals.org/doi/pdf/10.1632/prof.2007.2007.1.187

Jenkins, H. (2005) "Games, the New Lively Art". In *Handbook of Computer Game Studies*. J. Goldstein and J. Raessens (eds). Cambridge, MA: MIT Press, pp. 175–189.

Juul, J. (2005) *Half-Real: Video Games between Real Rules and Fictional Worlds*. Cambridge, MA: MIT Press.

MacCallum-Stewart, E. and Parsler, J. (2007) "Illusory Agency in *Vampire: The Masquerade—Bloodlines*". *dichtung-digital* [online] 37. Last accessed 6 January 2011 at URL: http://www.brown.edu/Research/dichtung-digital/2007/Stewart%26Parsler/maccallumstewart_parsler.htm

Magnuson, J. (2009) "Life in a Bottle". *Necessary Games: Games Considered for Meaning and Significance* [online], 16 August. Last accessed 10 August 2011 at URL: http://www.necessarygames.com/reviews/passage-game-free-download-independent-linux-mac-os-x-windows-art-game-abstract-singleplayer

Nelson, J. (2007) *ArcticAcre* [online]. Last accessed 30 August 2011 at URL: www.arcticacre.com

Perrault, C. (1961 [1697]) *Perrault's Complete Fairy Tales*. A. E. Johnson & Others (trans). London: Penguin.

Pullinger, K. & Joseph, C. (2005–2009) *Inanimate Alice*. Last accessed 7 May 2009 at URL: http://www.inanimatealice.com

Pullinger, K., Schemat, S. and babel. (2004) *The Breathing Wall* [CD-ROM]. London: The Sayle Literary Agency.

Rohrer, J. (2007) *Passage*. Last accessed 10 August 2011 at URL: http://hcsoftware.sourceforge.net/passage/

Ryan, M.-L. (2006) *Avatars of Story*. Minneapolis: University of Minnesota Press.

Ryan, M.-L. (2008) "Interactive Narrative, Plot Types, and Interpersonal Relations". In *Interactive Storytelling: Proceedings of 1st ICIDS 2008*. N. Szilas and U. Spierling (eds). Berlin: Springer, pp. 6–13.

Ryan, M.-L. (2009) "From Narrative Games to Playable Stories: Towards a Poetics of Interactive Narrative". *Storyworlds: A Journal of Narrative Studies* 1: 56–75.

Salen, K. and Zimmerman, E. (2004) *Rules of Play: Game Design Fundamentals*. Cambridge, MA: MIT Press.

Tale of Tales. (2009a) *The Path*. Last accessed 25 July 2010 at URL: http://tale-of-tales.com/ThePath/downloads.html

Tale of Tales. (2009b) *The Path* manual. Last accessed 11 August 2011 at URL: http://cdn.steampowered.com/Manuals/27000/ThePATH-UserManual.pdf?t=1308077606

Tale of Tales. (2010) "The Path Post Mortem". Last accessed 2 April 2012 at URL: http://tale-of-tales.com/blog/the-path-post-mortem/

Tale of Tales. (2011) *The Path* website. Last accessed 12 August 2011 at URL: http://tale-of-tales.com/ThePath/

Tavinor, G. (2009) *The Art of Videogames*. Malden: Wiley-Blackwell.

Thompson, C. (2008) "Poetic *Passage* Provokes Heavy Thoughts on Life, Death". *Wired* [online], 21 April 2008. Last accessed 10 August 2011 at URL:

http://www.wired.com/gaming/gamingreviews/commentary/games/2008/04/gamesfrontiers_421?currentPage=all

Tomasula, S. (2009) *TOC: A New Media Novel*. Tuscaloosa, AL: University of Alabama Press.

Weir, G. (2009) *Silent Conversation*. Last accessed 30 August 2011 at URL: http://armorgames.com/play/4287/silent-conversation

Westecott, E. (2010) "Playing with the Gothic: If you go down to the woods tonight . . . " In *Artists Re:thinking Games*. R. Catlow et al. (eds). Liverpool: Liverpool University Press, pp. 78–81.

Zipes, J. (1993) (ed.) *The Trials & Tribulations of Little Red Riding Hood* (2nd edition). New York: Routledge.

Zipes, J. (2011) "They'll Huff and They'll Puff", *Times Higher Education Supplement*, 16 June 2011, 45–46.

6   140 Characters in Search of a Story
Twitterfiction as an Emerging Narrative Form

Bronwen Thomas,
Bournemouth University, UK

INTRODUCTION AND BACKGROUND

Twitter is a social networking and microblogging service set up in 2006 that restricts users to messages or "tweets" consisting of no more than 140 characters. Despite this seeming limitation, Twitter has become a highly influential means of disseminating news and providing updates on "trending" or hot topics. The Twitter website promises users "instant updates" and "real-time information" but customized to their individual interests ("what's new in your world") and with the added bonus of helping create a "positive global impact" (www.twitter.com 15/7/2011). Twitter has been credited with kick starting and organizing various social and political campaigns and uprisings (particularly the so-called Arab Spring), while its other main use to date has been to provide users with updates and stories about their favorite celebrities (Page 2012). Users can choose to access their Twitter accounts via a range of devices including smartphones. They can also select from a wide range of Twitter clients or applications, and each user chooses who it is he or she wishes to "follow". Once a user has elected to follow another user, every tweet he or she posts appears in his or her timeline. Users can choose to "retweet" their posts to others in their network, adding links or content to the original tweet as necessary.

From the outset, the creative potential of Twitter has been evident, particularly in the design of user profiles and the practice of devising witty and satirical hashtags to generate trending topics: #wheresthegovernment, widely used in the summer of 2011, mocked both the British Prime Minister and his deputy for being away on holiday during various national and international crises. In addition, a whole host of spoof or fake celebrity accounts have emerged, offering entertainment (@MrsStephenFry, the "poor downtrodden wife" of gay author and actor, Stephen Fry) and, occasionally, searing commentary on current affairs (@DrSamuelJohnson, purporting to recount the insights of the eighteenth-century English author and essayist). The storytelling potential of Twitter has also been recognized, both in the sense of stories emerging from individual tweets, but also as a process of co-construction (Page 2012) as users retweet stories to their network of contacts. Page's study of celebrity tweets draws on models of oral narration (especially Labov 1972 and Ochs and Capps 2001) to try to establish whether there is anything new or unique about the way in which stories emerge on Twitter. She focuses on the way in which Twitter grounds the stories told in the here and now but also encourages users to see tweeting as a kind of performance, allowing for all kinds of creative interplay between their offline and online selves.

My analysis will focus on examples of "Twitterfiction" where an authorial figure of some kind creates stories specifically tailored to the format for his or her followers. This use of Twitter may be traced back almost to its origins, and can be contextualized with reference to other short narrative forms such as the Japanese *keitai shosetsu* (cell-phone fiction), or the drabble from the world of fanfiction, where users are restricted to writing a story of no more than 100 words. One of the earliest examples of the form was Matt Richtel's 2008 "Twiller" (http://twitter.com/mrichtel), which harnessed the "real-time" claims of the form to heighten the suspense of his crime thriller. Richtel used the basic scenario of having his central character narrate his story via tweets, providing followers with short bursts of information and the tension that arises from knowing that the protagonist has no more clue as to how events will turn out than they do. However, this strategy meant that there was very little explicit continuity between or across tweets, resulting in a reading experience that offered little possibility of immersion or absorption in the narrative.

METHOD

This chapter will provide a close analysis of two distinct forms of Twitterfiction. The first section will focus on what is known as the "shorty" or "Twister" where each tweet provides a self-contained narrative. The second section will take the serialized form as its focus, where the narrative unfolds across tweets, and so requires different skills and activities from its users, especially powers of recall and an intense attachment and commitment to the characters and fictional worlds on offer. As discussed in the introduction to this volume, this kind of "bottom-up" approach ensures that claims about the form are grounded in practice, and are verifiable.

Digital fiction often poses a challenge to the models and concepts of classical narratology, particularly those that are prefigured on notions of wholeness, coherence, or the unity of the narrative text. Although digital fiction also implicitly challenges the idea that these kinds of models can truly be universal, they can provide a useful starting point for analysis. We can trace back to Aristotle's *Poetics* the notion that narrative plots are based on some kind of complication that disrupts an initially orderly situation, resulting in a crisis, and usually ending with some kind of resolution.

Numerous theories have provided variations on this basic trajectory—for example, Todorov (1971) who claimed that narratives take us from a state of equilibrium through to a period of disequilibrium, before returning us once more at the end of the narrative to a reinstatement of the initial equilibrium.

In the case of Twitterfiction, as we will see, the narrative structure of the stories taken out of context may appear rather conventional, but I will argue that they may nevertheless challenge basic concepts of order, chronology, and causality in a number of ways. In particular, the idea that readers are motivated by a desire for an end to the narrative (Brooks 1992) becomes questionable when that end is uncertain and subject to constant revision and deferral. Similarly, the very notion of reading as a structured, focused, linear activity is challenged by the fact that each reader of a Twitterfiction has a unique experience shaped by his or her own choices about who or what to follow, making it impossible to predict how this surrounding content influences the interpretation of individual tweets.

It could also be argued that Twitterfiction destabilizes the relationship between author and reader. One of my main interests is in the kind of reading experience the form facilitates, so I will be drawing on reception theory, specifically the work of Iser (1974, 1979), which is concerned with how readers process narratives and display active engagement with fictional texts. Iser's notion of gap filling allows for the possibility that narratives are made to have meaning by individual readers, as they journey through a text and bring their own interpretations to bear, while his concept of the "implied reader" is useful for understanding what kind of role is expected of the reader in terms of genre, background knowledge, and so on. Iser's theories have been especially influential in the analysis of serialized forms, but they have also become increasingly relevant to the study of new media, where the idea that readers or audiences actively participate in the negotiation of meaning has become so central. Iser's work has also provided an important starting point for studies (e.g. Rustad 2009) interested more broadly in the competencies and interpretive communities associated with specific forms of digital fiction.

My approach in the analysis that follows is multifocal in the sense set out in the introduction, paying close attention to the specific affordances and context of Twitterfiction, especially aspects of the interface and the use of multimodal devices. To this end, I draw on theories and concepts from media and cultural studies, particularly work which engages with the narrative structures of new media forms and their audiences. This facilitates an approach that is not narrowly confined to print-based models, and that focuses on the situatedness of texts as part of a wider, ongoing experience for participants. My analysis will therefore engage with studies of both new and "old" media, particularly television, which offers many interesting comparisons with Twitter with its emphasis on "real time", its segmentation of content, and its creation of a sense of an ongoing narrative "flow" (Williams 1974), providing a metanarrative comprised of seemingly unconnected discrete parts. Twitterfiction may also be understood with reference to the increasing prominence of what media theorists call micronarratives (Jenkins 2004), evident as structuring mechanisms across a range of broadcast media forms, but also video games and other narratives based on new media technologies. In terms of its mode of narration, Twitterfiction continues the trend in the media noted by Margolin (1999) whereby there is a near overlap of action and narration, representing a shift toward an aspiration to "Tell as you live" rather than "live now, tell later". With this form of what Margolin terms "concurrent narration", the reader is provided with a sequence of "NOW moments", a key aspect, I shall argue, of the medium-specific experience that Twitterfiction offers.

THE TWISTER

Arjun Basu (@arjunbasu) has acquired a large number of followers (163,562 as of February 20, 2013) and won the "Shorty" award in 2010 for his "Twisters", which he has published daily since October 2008. These narratives mainly focus on the day-to-day lives and relationships of an unnamed man and woman, with a high proportion of stories about sex, kids, food, and bodily functions of various kinds. The stories are entirely self-contained, making them perfect for users to browse and to retweet to others. As well as posting his Twisters, Basu occasionally comments on news events and provides links to other sites featuring his own work and that of others. Basu seems to choose to present himself as a self-deprecating individual both in the information he gives out about himself in his profile ("Shorty Award winner [though I'm not that short]"), and in his choice of profile picture, which sees him clutching his forehead and looking somewhat perplexed.

Basu's stories offer his followers a predictable pattern, adopting a fairly conventional plot structure but with the emphasis usually on the complication or crisis. Most Twisters feature a change of state for at least one of the central characters, and while they often provide some sense of resolution, this tends to be quite far removed from the traditional happy ending, providing instead a sense of resignation or disillusionment:

> They entered the car a family. [Initial Situation.] They drove many miles and ate lots of bad food. [Complication/Crisis.] They were no longer a family. [Resolution.] (July 16, 2011)

Another common strategy employed by Basu is the twist in the tale or "reveal", facilitated by the fact that the characters in his stories often seem to barely know one another, and so tend to get themselves tied up in various kinds of misunderstanding:

> She shook with a kind of religious fervour, at least he had thought so, but in truth she just needed to pee really really badly. Like really. (January 18, 2011)

The tone is conversational, and the effect created is often one of overhearing an intimate exchange or the private thoughts of one of the characters, placing the reader in a privileged position in relation to the two characters.

Basu's Twisters offer his followers a steady stream of easily digestible stories, making no great demands of the "implied reader" in terms of background knowledge, and requiring no great commitment, as the user does not need to keep up with all of the tweets. The fact that the Twisters are frequently retweeted suggests that followers not only enjoy the stories but want to share them with their network of acquaintances, and Basu has emerged as a prominent spokesperson for Twitterfiction, with numerous interviews appearing online (e.g Sniderman 2010). However, the repetitive nature of the Twisters is not to everyone's taste, as is evident from some of the tweets posted in response:

> I'm a huge fan of your posts. I wonder, though, if you aren't stuck in a bit of a male vs female dichotomous rut. #punintended. (@Kylealanhale, July 7, 2011)

Basu is by no means alone in offering standalone stories on Twitter,[1] and though he defends the craft involved in adhering to the constraints of Twitter ("Practice makes perfect", cited by Sniderman 2010), he is much more circumspect when it comes to questions about whether what he does can be counted as "art". Certainly, the fact that the Twisters are self-contained and so short means that the writing is more exposed and open to scrutiny, were they to be examined in isolation. However, as was suggested earlier, this would be completely contrary to the aims and objectives of a medium-specific approach to new media narratives, or one that is multifocal in its outlook. In the case of Basu's Twisters, we need to understand the affordances of Twitter and the kind of relationship that exists between users. Twitter is all about updating and responding instantaneously to what is happening, and so it may be understood as part of a broader impulse to collect and seek out new content noted by new media theorists such as Walker Rettberg (2008) or Jenkins (1992), or as yet another example of the contemporary phenomenon of frenzied archiving (Currie 2007). However, in practice it can be quite tricky to trace tweets back across timelines, or to fully capture the activities of commenting and retweeting. It is also vital to remember that individual tweets appear in a timeline alongside tweets from all sorts of different sources, requiring constant adjustments from users in terms of the kind of response appropriate to the content.

Basu's Twisters fit comfortably within the paradigms familiar to users of Twitter, and offers the same sense of sharing an ongoing experience that is provided by following other contributors and threads. Basu works within and against the seeming restrictions of Twitter but also partakes of that sense of constant updating that helps create for users a sense of anticipation and excitement whenever they access their accounts. In terms of their structure, Twisters may be compared to jokes or to advertisements (Rubin cited in Sniderman 2010), short narrative bursts providing instantaneous entertainment, where repetition and predictability are virtues rather than vices, and where the relationship between addresser and addressee is more often than not informal and conversational. It would be easy to dismiss such storytelling as the kind of "*Triviallitteratur*" (Petrucci 2003) that poses a threat to the established notion of reading as a serious and demanding activity. However, as Cavallo and Chartier (2003) argue, to understand the kinds of shared competencies emerging around new forms of telling and reading stories, we must consider the historicity of ways of using, comprehending, and appropriating texts, allowing us, for example, to recognize that the idea of reading while engaged in other activities such as traveling, can be traced back as far as ancient Greece. Readers of electronic text are much more accustomed to reading messages in movement and in disjointed fragments (Petrucci 2003), and it is possible to see the rise of this "anarchical reader" as a liberating rather than a negative development in the history of reading. Of course, there will always be those who question the value of such narratives, or who contest the myth of a shared reality that some of the hype about social media has generated (Couldry 2004), but as with the evolution of any new medium, adapting it for the purpose of storytelling seems to be a primary impulse for users.

Although Basu has chosen to work within the restrictions of only having 140 characters to play with, some of his Twisters make use of the facility Twitter gives its users to create links to content elsewhere. For example, the following tweet was linked to Instagram where a photograph of the landscape being described has been inserted:

> This was the grey city, a place he could not run from if he tried. What are you thinking? she asked him. I'm thin. (April 26, 2011)

Tagging and embedding links provide users of Twitter with the ability to offer their followers the possibility of more content without detracting from the sense of immediacy and epigrammatic directness that has become a virtue of the restrictions of the form. From the point of view of the storyteller, it provides an opportunity to extend the narrative outward, and to offer readers the experience of seemingly discovering new content for themselves, exploring and roaming beyond the hub of the tweeted narrative, to replicate the kind of accretive, boundary-challenging activity (Alexander and Levine 2008) that has become such a feature of online behavior since the advent of Web 2.0.

SERIAL FORMS

Alongside the freeform variety of storytelling of the Twister, serial forms of narrative have emerged on Twitter, arguably providing a greater sense of participation for followers, allowing them to engage in a kind of "episode foraging" (Rosenberg 1996) where it appears as though they are able to seize control of the direction of the narrative, and carve out their own reading pathways. Most commonly, serial forms are used on Twitter to retell classic tales and epics of various kinds, providing readers with an ongoing, unfolding narrative in an experience that can extend into weeks, months, and even years. Attempts have been made to retell stories from the Bible in the form of tweets (@TweetTheExodus), while @MiddleEarth-Days offers its followers updates on what is happening "Today in Middle Earth", matching its timeline to that of Tolkien's *Lord of the Rings* trilogy. This kind of storytelling seems more designed to reward the loyalty of followers and to offer them the reassurance that this is an experience that potentially can fill their lives for some time. Fanfiction has provided ample testament to the staying power of fans of epic narratives such as Tolkien's, as well as the desire of fans to have "more from" as well as "more of" (Pugh 2005) the fictional worlds to which they are so attached, through subversion and rewriting. With Twitter, loyalty is rewarded with frequent tidbits, the potential to connect with other followers, to comment on what is being offered, and to partake of the story as of some kind of journey or shared experience where much of the thrill derives from the uncertainty about exactly what is to come next. Of course, in the case of the Bible and the *Lord of the Rings*, the trajectory of events has already been mapped out, and the characters who reappear are (in theory at least) already familiar to followers. Nevertheless, followers of these tweets seem to relish the opportunity to relive these stories via Twitter, with the language and form of the tweets helping to (re)create those "NOW moments" that are so intrinsic to the medium.

Epicretold

Epicretold (@epicretold) is the brainchild of a colleague of mine at Bournemouth University, Chindu Sreedharan. It came about after we had a conversation in the summer of 2009 about *keitai shosetsu*, after which Chindu decided to attempt to retell the Indian epic, the Mahabarata, via Twitter. He continues to refer to his narrative as a "twiction", though I have opted here for the more widely used Twitterfiction. *Epicretold* attracted considerable attention as soon as it appeared, with articles appearing in *Time* magazine, as well as in a number of Indian newspapers. However, it was from the outset a very ambitious project, making great demands not just of the author, but also of his readers. Unlike Basu's followers, the readers of *Epicretold* have to retain information between tweets, and the author has to do enough to sustain their interest across gaps of weeks and even months. Nevertheless, the experience provided is arguably even closer to that of "following" an individual or a Twitter thread across a stretch of time. Moreover, for users familiar with blogs and other kinds of "distributed narrative" (Walker 2004), tracking a narrative dispersed across time, space, and different media is nothing new, nor is the notion of reading or viewing a given narrative as part of a network of possibilities, as is the norm with services such as YouTube.

The specific context of narration for *Epicretold* could also be said to offer users something close to the experience of audiences of the epic in its oral form, and indeed, *Epicretold* retains many of the techniques and stylistic features of oral tellings, in particular its digressions, the focus on the "tellable" (Labov 1972) and on the actions of the protagonists, and the possibility of near "real-time" interactions between the storyteller and his or her audience. But *Epicretold* might better be understood as displaying the kind of "secondary orality" described by Ong (1982), where the affordances of media technologies are harnessed to recreate the effect of the oral storytelling situation, and to mitigate for the fact that users are actually distanced from each other and are unable to rely on the aural and visual signals available when participants are in close physical proximity with one another. For example, television has been argued to perform a "bardic function" (Fiske 1987), offering viewers a unique kind of "nowness" that comes from being part of an audience living through events and situations alongside the performers on our screens.

The Twitter profile for *Epicretold* acknowledges that this version of the epic is indebted to Prem Panicker's (2009) retelling of the narrative from the point of view of Bhima, itself "adapted from" M. T. Vasudevan Nair's *Randamoozham* (1984). Therefore, while the narrative is based on events and characters familiar to millions, the author is constantly reiterating that this is a retelling rather than a faithful recapitulation of the epic, and that "[t]he fun lies in reimagining incidents, recasting characters" (@aboutepicretold, September 19, 2010). Panicker's retelling of Bhima's story was published as a blog initially, and hence it took the form of a distributed narrative told in installments. Written as a series of "episodes" with short paragraphs and a great deal of dialogue, Panicker's narrative focuses on offering the reader a glimpse into the daily lives of the characters from the epic, and so employs a realist mode rather than the fantasy or melodrama more common in traditional versions.

Epicretold shares this desire to involve the reader in the daily lives of the main characters and is also episodic in structure. The narrative begins, conventionally, with the childhood of the hero, and offers a child's perspective on events, suited both to creating suspense for the reader, as Bhima is not always aware of the significance of what he is witnessing, and to the format of the narrative, as the narrative is made up of short bursts of information. Like Panicker's novel, *Epicretold* relies quite heavily on the speech of characters, which, along with the use of the first person narration, contributes to the effect of orality.

Epicretold also draws on some of the tried and tested devices of the serialized narrative, in particular the use of the cliffhanger:

> That day Father had wandered off with Aunt Madri, laughing. Mother sat by the window, still, silent. Then I heard the wailing. (@epicretold, July 29, 2009)

As in the above example, the narrative also makes extensive use of flashbacks and flashforwards. Thus whereas Basu's narratives incorporate within a single tweet plot twists and changes of state, from the outset *Epicretold* has to provide its readers with a strong narrative hook that will bring them back for more. Information and elaboration are deliberately withheld, with the gaps between tweets providing ample opportunity for readers to reflect on what they have already been told (in Iser's [1979] terms, "retention"), and to anticipate what is to come (Iser's "protension"). As Kafelnos (1999) demonstrates, the idea of succession is key to understanding narrative and its representation of sequential events. *Epicretold* relies on readers holding on to this notion that the narrative is progressing, and that the events narrated are linked according to some kind of cumulative design. However, as I shall argue, this is problematized by the specific context of reception of Twitter, which places the emphasis on the moment rather than on structuring events according to some sense of before or after.

The continued appeal of serial forms has been well documented, particularly in relation to television narratives (Fiske 1987) and, more recently, long-form multistrand narratives (Mittell 2007), where the teasing and testing of the viewer becomes almost a game in its own right, and an important source of pleasure (Warhol 1999). Morson (1999) bases his concept of the "processual narrative" largely on the serial form, arguing that it facilitates contingency and the possibility that a narrative may be influenced by real events taking place over the course of its narration. In the case of *Epicretold*, the author has made some concessions to his readers in terms of offering a sense of an overall design—for example, organizing the tweets into chapters, providing links to a website providing "Field Notes",[2] and also rearranging the tweets in chronological order for "The End of Childhood".[3] He has also set up a separate Twitter account (@aboutepicretold) in which he offers a running commentary on his progress and responds to queries raised by his followers. These often concern matters of style or voice—for example, where he consults followers as to whether he should switch to narrating in the past tense (@aboutepicretold, August 9, 2009). However, he also adopts a playful attitude, relating his experience of writing *Epicretold* to his offline activities, and telling his "gang" that the narrative will be "As long as it takes to tell the story" (@aboutepicretold, July 29, 2009).

Bhima is a warrior character from the Indian epic, and so it is important to acknowledge that the genre here is also quite different from Basu's Twisters. Coupled with this, the author's background as a journalist interested in the reporting of war helps provide a context for understanding why it is that his narrative has an urgency and immediacy about it that is so in keeping with the stated aims of Twitter. Most tweets in *Epicretold* use the present tense, immersing the reader in the action and creating the impression that we are being updated on events as they happen. As was said earlier, because it is focalized through Bhima's perspective, there are many gaps in knowledge and a very strong sense that the future is unpredictable and uncertain. This is established from the very first tweet:

> I can't help staring at the lady with the black cloth over her eyes. I feel disturbed, scared–but I can't look away. (@epicretold, July 27, 2009)

In many ways, the style is reminiscent of the diary or journal, where entries provide an account of the day's events close to when they took place. Moreover, the very idea of the "presentification" of the past (Ricoeur 1985) may be said to be intrinsic to storytelling, even where the outcome of events may be known, both for the purposes of suspense, but also so that the reader can share in the experiences of the characters and the decisions and dilemmas they face. However, as was said earlier, in order to understand how this works on Twitter, we have to look at how the tweets are received as well as how they are produced.

Twitter presents users with a good deal of information both about when tweets have been composed but also how they are composed, that is, in terms of the particular device used. In the case of *Epicretold* we can see that the tweets have been sent from a laptop and from a smartphone, and each tweet carries a precise time stamp, dating it and allowing the user to track back to earlier tweets if necessary. As was said earlier, these tweets will appear in a timeline alongside content from many other, diverse sources, and while it is possible to predict with someone like Arjun Basu that we will get at least one tweet a day, with *Epicretold*, tweeting has been much more sporadic and unpredictable. Twitter relies on a logic of "not first things first but the newest things first" (Song 2010) and, unlike perhaps most narratives, focuses on what has just happened rather than what happened in the beginning.

In terms of trying to understand what kind of reading experience we have here, it is helpful, as Rustad (2009) has demonstrated, to draw on more recent work by Iser (1993: 276), which offers the possibility not just of reading as a "game that ends when the meaning has been found", but of reading as exploration, driven and played by chance, not by confirmation or predictability. As has already been acknowledged, *Epicretold* retells a story already familiar to millions, but the mode of its retelling helps to recreate this sense of exploration and unpredictability. In a much earlier work, Iser (1972) argued that modern texts are often so fragmentary that the reader's attention is almost exclusively occupied with the search for connections. In turn, this impacts on the status of the text, which becomes a dynamic rather than a static object, unfolding, Iser suggests, as a kind of living event, so that the expectations of the reader must be continually modified. Once again, this conceptualization of reading seems particularly apt for understanding the specific experience Twitter offers its users, and the ways in which this has been adapted for the purpose of telling stories.

Despite the impact that *Epicretold* initially created, things slowed down considerably in 2010–2011, with barely an increase in the number of followers during this time (1,635 as of July 20, 2011) or the number of tweets published (595 as of the same date). This slowing down has prompted the self-confessed "lazy author" (epicretold Facebook 2013), to appeal to his followers via Facebook to help him keep up the momentum. Chindu has maintained a dialogue with his readers from the outset—for example, exhorting them to "read ER as a story, fiction" (@epicretold, September 19, 2010). Many of his followers come from the Indian subcontinent, and so it is not uncommon for them to take issue with some matter of interpretation, or factual accuracy. It might be expected, therefore, that the "implied reader" here is one who is already familiar with the epic and with its main plotlines, though as no knowledge of other characters or events from the Mahabarata is assumed, it is by no means the case that those without any familiarity with its tales are excluded. Nevertheless, readers of *Epicretold* could have been under no illusion from the outset that this would be a protracted affair but also an experiment in adapting a traditional tale to a form whose features and uses are still evolving to meet the needs of its users. In a sense there are no shortcuts here. Reading the author's digests of the tweets, or accessing them as an individual timeline or stream, creates a rather artificial experience, which removes the narrative from the hustle and bustle of Twitter, and its distinctive sense of happenchance and being in the moment with multitudes of users across the globe.

In an age of transmedia storytelling, it is perhaps no surprise that Twitterfiction both draws on but also feeds back into narratives in other media. As was suggested earlier, retellings and spoofs constitute a major part of the activity on Twitter, outweighing attempts such as Basu's to create "original" stories designed for the medium. Instead, it seems that for many tweeters, it is the challenge of adapting material, and particularly preexisting stories, to this form of communication that represents much of its appeal. In this respect, the creative response to Twitter shares some similarities with the activities of fans online, as they take familiar and beloved fictional worlds and stretch and subvert them as part of a playful attempt to see how far they can go. Nevertheless, as I have argued elsewhere (Thomas 2010), we should not assume that the movement is unidirectional from "old" to "new" media. In the case of *Epicretold*, the author is under contract to produce a book based on his tweets, but is finding that it is no simple task to try to capture or remediate the experience of Twitter in print form. Attempts have been made to publish books based on tweets—for example, the highly successful *Twitterature* (Aciman and Rensin 2009)—but only by making the tweets fit the demands of the printed page, removing any sense of a distinctive interface, and presenting the tweets as a linear, chronological stream, making them appear more like short, epigrammatic paragraphs, and taking away any sense of "liveness" or dynamism.

CONCLUSION

The questions posed by this kind of narrative are much the same as those facing any kind of digital fiction: is there anything really new here, and will people still want to read and reread the stories once the novelty has died down? New media theorists often stand accused of avoiding confronting issues of quality and value for fear of seeming élitist and of importing standards and criteria from "old" to "new" forms (see, for example, Thomas 2011). However, Lunenfeld (2000) has suggested that we are moving toward what he calls an "aesthetic of unfinish", away from static conceptions of the work of art as a finished artifact toward a dynamic engagement with the work in progress where it is precisely the process of creativity as much as the end result that is the focus of attention. The notion of processurality (Ensslin 2007: 37) also allows for the recasting of the reader/viewer/user not as passive consumer of already-formed objects but as a participant in an ongoing experience in which his or her contribution is key. We can see this at work with Twitterfiction, both in the interactions that take place between author and readers and also in the activities of retweeting, sharing, and linking. Twitter, like many other forms of social media, becomes a part of the daily ritual of users, where it is not so much the quality or even the quantity of output that matters most, so much as the reassurance that there will be constant updates, and that followers will be kept "in the loop" about any new developments.

As with many variants of digital fiction, particularly interactive narratives, a key question raised by Twitterfiction is that of control or agency. To some extent, authors can control both the content of their tweets and their distribution, and yet they cannot control when a tweet will be picked up or read by follower, nor can they predict how a tweet will be accessed (i.e. by which device) or what other content (textual and visual) may surround a tweet as it appears in the individual timelines of each and every follower. Similarly, though followers elect to receive updates from these authors, they cannot predict when these tweets will appear in their timelines, and they are completely powerless to affect the pace at which the narrative proceeds, other than by contacting and prompting the author. However, once the content is posted, they can retweet, add links, and communicate with other followers to provide a running commentary on the narratives and to create some sense of participation.

At the time of writing, Twitter is gaining more and more influence both in terms of the sheer number of people who are signed up for the service, but also in the impact it is having not just on reporting but on helping to shape world events. Given the restrictions that the form imposes on its users, and the complexities of the interface, this is perhaps surprising. Yet as with many kinds of new media, its success is largely due to the creativity of its users, and the ways in which they help shape and manage its evolution and its functions. Storytelling drives much of this activity, whether that is stories about world affairs, celebrity gossip, or the personal lives of users, shared, discussed, and disseminated with anyone who is a part of their network. Alongside this, there is an appetite, it seems, to step into fictionalized worlds existing in parallel with the stories taking place in "real time", both as a diversion perhaps from those realities, but also as an opportunity for absorption in a narrative NOW that offers users both familiar tales presented in new formats, and the possibility of participating in an emerging form in which the relationships between teller, tale, and audience are there to be discovered and shaped, rather than being fixed and immutable. As more and more of us search for stories on Twitter, it is likely that we will discover new genres and modes of storytelling, but also new modes of participation and customization, as the boundaries between authors, characters, and readers continue to blur and merge.

NOTES

1. See for example www.very-short-story.com.
2. See http://www.chindu.net/reports-on-research/field-notes-on-epicretold/.
3. See http://www.chindu.net/reports-on-research/the-end-of-childhood/#story.

WORKS CITED

Aciman, A. and Rensin, E. (2009) *Twitterature: The World's Greatest Books Retold through Twitter*. London: Penguin.

Alexander, B. and Levine, A. (2008) "Web 2.0 Storytelling: Emergence of a New Genre". *EDUCAUSE Review* 43. 6. Last accessed 20 February 2013 at URL: http://www.educause.edu/EDUCAUSE+Review/EDUCAUSEReviewMagazineVolume43/Web20StorytellingEmergenceofaN/163262

Brooks, P. (1992) *Reading for the Plot: Design and Intention in Narrative*. Cambridge, MA: Harvard University Press.

Cavallo, G. and Chartier, R. (2003) "Introduction". In *A History of Reading in the West*. G. Cavallo and R. Chartier (eds). Cambridge: Polity Press, pp. 1–36.

Couldry, N. (2004) "Liveness, 'Reality', and the Mediated Habitus from Television to the Mobile Phone". *The Communication Review* 7. 4: 353–361.

Currie, M. (2007) *About Time: Narrative, Fiction and the Philosophy of Time*. Edinburgh: Edinburgh University Press.

Ensslin, A. (2007) *Canonizing Hypertext: Explorations and Constructions*. London: Continuum.

epicretold Facebook (2013). Last accessed 20 February 2013 at URL: http://www. facebook.com/pages/epicretold/116105872179

Fiske, J. (1987) *Television Culture*. London: Methuen.

Iser, W. (1972) "The Reading Process: A Phenomenological Approach". *New Literary History* 3. 2: 279–299.

Iser, W. (1974) *The Implied Reader*. Baltimore, MD: Johns Hopkins University Press.

Iser, W. (1979) *The Act of Reading*. Baltimore, MD: Johns Hopkins University Press.

Iser, W. (1993) *The Fictive and the Imaginary: Charting Literary Anthropology*. Baltimore, MD: Johns Hopkins University Press.

Jenkins, H. (1992) *Textual Poachers: Television Fans and Participatory Culture*. London: Routledge.

Jenkins, H. (2004) "Game Design as Narrative Architecture". Last accessed 20 February 2013 at URL: http://web.mit.edu/cms/People/henry3/games&narrative.html

Kafelnos, E. (1999) "Not (Yet) Knowing: Epistemological Effects of Deferred and Suppressed Information in Narrative". In *Narratologies: New Perspectives on Narrative Analysis* D. Herman (ed). Columbus, OH: Ohio State University Press, pp. 33–65.

Labov, W. (1972) *Language in the Inner City*. Philadelphia, PA: University of Pennsylvania Press.

Lunenfeld, P. (2000) "Unfinished Business". In *The Digital Dialectic*. P. Lunenfeld (ed). Cambridge, MA: MIT Press, pp. 6–23.

Margolin, U. (1999) "Of What Is Past, Is Passing, or to Come: Temporality, Aspectuality, Modality and the Nature of Literary Narrative". In *Narratologies: New Perspectives on Narrative Analysis*. D. Herman (ed). Columbus, OH: Ohio State University Press, pp. 142–166.

Mittell, J. (2007) "Film and Television Narrative." In *The Cambridge Companion to Narrative*. D. Herman (ed). Cambridge: Cambridge University Press, pp. 156–171.

Morson, G. S. (1999) "Essential Narrative: Tempics and the Return of Process". In *Narratologies: New Perspectives on Narrative Analysis*. D. Herman (ed). Columbus, OH: Ohio State University Press, pp. 277–314.

Nair, M. T. V. (1984) *Randamoozham*. Kerala, India: Current Books.

Ochs, E. and Capps, L. (2001) *Living Narrative*. Cambridge, MA: Harvard University Press.

Ong, W. (1982) *Orality and Literacy: The Technologizing of the Word*. London: Methuen.

Page, R. (2012) *Stories and Social Media: Identities and Interaction*. London: Routledge.

Panicker, P. (2009) *Bhimsen*. Last accessed 20 February 2013 at URL: http://prem panicker.wordpress.com/2009/10/05/bhim-complete-and-unabridged/

Rettberg, J. W. (2008) *Blogging*. Cambridge: Polity Press.

Ricoeur, P. (1985) *Time and Narrative* (Vol. 2). K. Blamey and D. Pellauer (trans). Chicago, IL: Chicago University Press.

Petrucci, A. (2003) "Reading to Read: A Future for Reading". In *A History of Reading in the West*. G. Cavallo and R. Chartier (eds). Cambridge: Polity Press, pp. 345–367.

Pugh, S. (2005) *The Democratic Genre: Fanfiction in a Literary Context*. Bridgend: Seren Books.

Rosenberg, J. (1996) "The Structure of Hypertext Activity". *Proceedings of the Seventh ACM Conference on Hypertext*. New York: ACM, pp. 22–30.

Rustad, H. K. (2009) "A Four-Sided Model for Reading Hypertext Fiction." *Hyperrhiz: New Media Cultures* 6. 1: 1–17.

Sniderman, Z. (2010) "Arjun Basu's Twister". *The Garret*. Last accessed 28 July 2011 at URL: http://www.thegarret.org/?p=186

Song, C. (2010) "The Reverse Chronology of a Blog and Its Implications". *Ellephanta*. Last accessed 20 February 2013 at URL: http://ellephanta.wordpress.com/2010/01/10/the-reverse-chronology-of-a-blog-and-its-implications/

Thomas, B. (2010) "Gains and Losses? Writing it All Down: Fanfiction and Multimodality". In *New Perspectives on Narrative and Multimodality*. R. Page (ed). London: Routledge, pp. 142–154.

Thomas, B. (2011) "What Is Fanfiction and Why Are People Saying Such Nice Things about It?" *Storyworlds* 3: 1–24.

Todorov, T. (1971) "The Two Principles of Narrative". *Diacritics* 1. 1: 37–44.

Walker, J. (2004) "Distributed Narrative: Telling Stories across Networks". Paper presented at AOIR 5.0, Brighton, UK. Last accessed 20 February 2013 at URL: http://jilltxt.net/txt/distributednarratives.html

Warhol, R. (1999) "Guilty Cravings: What Feminist Narratology Can Do for Cultural Studies". In *Narratologies: New Perspectives on Narrative Analysis*. D. Herman (ed). Columbus, OH: Ohio State University Press, pp. 340–355.

Williams, R. (1974) *Television: Technology and Cultural Form*. London: Fontana.

7 Amnesia: The Dark Descent
The Player's Very Own Purgatory

Susana Tosca,
IT University of Copenhagen, Denmark

INTRODUCTION

This chapter analyzes *Amnesia: The Dark Descent*, "a game about immersion, discovery and living through a nightmare"[1] by applying a methodology based on relevance theory (Tosca 2000). In *Amnesia*, the player controls Daniel, a character who has no memories and is given to understand that his amnesia is self-inflicted. In real time, he has to save himself from terrible dangers by exploring a castle linked to his own dark memories. The game has won multiple awards, even though it deviates from the genre's usual components such as cut scenes, staged fights, and static puzzles, thus suggesting that gamers are ready for works where suspense, understood as a "cognitive state of uncertainty" (Carroll 1996: 71), is the driving force for action. The search for meaning—who Daniel is, why he inflicted amnesia upon himself, what happened in the castle, and how can we escape—is literally the goal of the game. Plot intrigue and basic questions about identity and morality blend into each other and are eventually solved at the same time. Immersion is not only audiovisual but also largely semantic, as the player has to ponder the meaning of clues, text fragments, and events (such as the resolution of dynamic puzzles and attacks of monsters) at every step.

There is already quite a body of work concerned with the analysis of narrative in computer games and hypertextual narratives. However, the two camps have run parallel to each other, rarely meeting, even though many of the topics, such as the importance of choices, are of common interest.[2] In "A Pragmatics of Links" (Tosca 2000), I proposed an analytical framework based on relevance theory in order to explain the movements of meaning inherent to the hypertextual reading praxis. My aim was to describe reading as a process, and to illustrate the kind of "work" done by readers who, even though they cannot be said to be co-creators of the text, do make active decisions in piecing their stories together. Players of story-based computer games also search for meaning, and implicatures[3] form the background for all decisions about movement and action.

In this chapter I intend to expand the relevance theory framework to the medium of computer games because it has the potential to successfully address the different levels of a hybrid product such as *Amnesia*. By hybrid narratives, I mean fictions where the game element and the story element are equally important, and couldn't be analyzed comprehensively by exclusively focusing on either interaction rules or narrative alone. It is also an aim of this chapter to address the nature of hybrid digital narratives, to show how hypertexts and narrative games can share analysis models and to propose a methodology that can tackle the latter successfully.

A Pragmatics of Links

My previous work on reading hypertext (Tosca 1999, 2000) is based on the idea that traversing links is not an empty spring in the void, but that the act of choosing a link and getting to the other side prompts readers to actively search for meaning. This can be exploited by authors, who can create expectations that are then met or twisted in surprising ways. Burbules (2001), for example, looks at links as classical tropes or figures of speech such as metaphor, metonymy, or synecdoche. For him, links are "rhetorical moves that can be evaluated and questioned for their relevance. They imply choices; they reveal assumptions; they have effects—whether intentionally or inadvertently" (Burbules 2001: 117). It is only natural therefore that readers ponder over the meaning of links, facilitating enriching creative processes.

My notion of a pragmatics of links (Tosca 2000), based on the linguistic theory of relevance (Sperber and Wilson 1986), tries to explain how this pondering occurs. Relevance theory is based on implicatures (Grice 1961: 3), or the information that lies behind linguistic utterances and can be inferred by the audience according to the context of communication. For example: two people are in a room, and the one sitting further away from the open window says: "It is cold in here". It can be interpreted literally, but if we ask ourselves what the speaker is trying to achieve in that context, a very likely implicature is that she is asking the other person to close the window. All linguistic utterances can be interpreted in this way, by searching for their relevance in the specific context, not only in the context of everyday communication but also in the interpretation of poetry, which I have earlier compared with the interpretation of links in hypertextual navigation (Tosca 1999).

To illustrate this we can pick the beginning of a famous poem, *The Waste Land*, by T. S. Eliot, and its "April is the cruelest month, breeding". Here the reader is surprised and shocked. April is a spring month, and it usually has positive associations, as it does in other great works of literature (for example, the informed reader might relate it to Chaucer's *Canterbury Tales*). But cruel? The reader will work hard trying to make sense of that line, in what I have called elsewhere (Tosca 2000) a centrifugal expansion of meaning

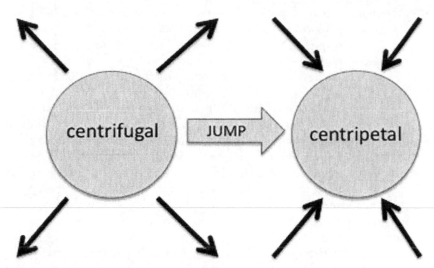

Figure 7.1   Movements of meaning in poetry and hyperlinks

or search for contexts in which that sentence makes sense. By centrifugal, I mean moving away from the center so that from one clue, an array of meanings is produced (see Figure 7.1). The second verse "Lilacs out of the dead land, mixing" will provide a temporary anchor for those meanings. This is what I call a centripetal movement (Tosca 2000), as in moving toward a center. That is, from one clue, the multiple meanings are reduced to a "correct" one given the context (see Figure 7.1). Here our interpretations are guided in the direction of death, which is the theme of the first part of the poem. An anchor in this sense is an utterance that helps the reader choose the appropriate relevant context, thus effectively reducing the amount of possible interpretations. Still, the violent contrast between "breeding" and "dead" will keep readers on their toes, as they will not yet be entirely sure of what the author wants it to mean, that is, what is the intention behind the utterance. Admittedly, *The Waste Land* is an almost too-perfect example, since the poem is all but unequivocal, and the reader has to keep readjusting her expectations and following the expansions and contractions of meanings. But the process will be the same in less polysemic works, if less intense, and *The Waste Land* thus serves well as a means of illustrating more clearly how reading a poem is an actively interpretive process.

If we had links instead of verses, we would speculate before choosing a particular one, in a centrifugal expansion of meanings, and then experience the centripetal anchoring at having some of those meanings (or new ones) confirmed. For example, *My Body, a Wunderkammer* by Shelley Jackson (Jackson 1997) is a fictional biography of a girl, told by anchoring memories to different parts of the body. There is a text node about the girl's arms, where we read that her unfeminine muscular arms usually impress people, who ask what she does to look so sporty: "Nothing, I say, I was born this way. I get a worried look in response. They think I'm lying. Well, I'm pretty active, I say, to help them out. *I roller skate*, I play tennis."[4] The reader might wonder where the link ("I roller skate") will go, what implicatures it suggests. It could be a description of that particular sport, maybe an accident, or, even a joke, since roller skating does not give muscular arms (centrifugal expansion of meanings). When the link is activated, it takes the reader to a page where the author describes a phantom limb she claims to have.[5] The connection with roller skating is thin, as it is one of the things the phantom limb helps her with (maintaining balance), but the text is mostly about a surreal perception of being different, which is reinforced by other nodes in the text and the narrator's view of her own body. The meanings have been anchored and now reinterpreted according to the context. The author has carefully laid out those links for the reader, but she is active when traversing them. She is making meaning.

The degree to which texts encourage the productive reading activity varies with different hypertext formats, genres, and even design choices. For example, a hypertext with no visible links (like Michael Joyce's *afternoon*) would fare differently than the one I just briefly looked at. If the links cannot be found, navigation is more a matter of chance, although we might argue that in *afternoon* we try to click on the words that *could be* links, so that we also speculate in the same centrifugal way. As Simanowski so precisely puts it in his semantic approach to analyzing links: "The link is not just a means of navigation, it adds meaning to the text, it becomes text itself" (Simanowski 2004). The meaning of links is also cumulative, resulting in complex overall linking strategies such as the ones studied by Bernstein (1998) and Ryan (2001).

MEANING AND COMPUTER GAMES

How can the meaning making activity of players be accounted for? In order for relevance theory to be applicable to hypertext, I have above treated links as utterances. I will now propose that we do the same with the semantic units in computer games, be they story fragments or procedural affordances. Stories we understand, but what are procedures?

Inspired by Janet Murray's first essential property of the computer, *procedurality*, a number of authors (Bogost 2007, 2008; Wardrip-Fruin 2009; Flanagan 2009) have developed specific theories about how computer games generate meanings. The *procedural* property refers to the computer's ability to execute rules in succession and thus generate behaviors (Murray 1997). Ian Bogost proposes the term *procedural rhetoric*, defined as "the art of persuasion through rule-based representations and interactions rather than the spoken word, writing, images, or moving pictures" (Bogost 2007: ix.). So we should be able to find meaning also in computational processes, not only in the representation level of video games. To illustrate this, some[6] have used the example of the "serious" game *12th September*, created by Gonzalo Frasca.[7] In this game, the player acts as a sort of "God from above" looking at a cartoonish Middle East city with people going about their business. She has to drop bombs to kill terrorists, which is impossible without also hitting some innocent bystanders, something that will in turn spawn new terrorists, as the families of those murdered take up the fight. The player soon realizes that it is impossible to win this game. The mechanics of the game illustrate that it is useless and harmful to try to stop terrorism through war on civil population, a harsh commentary against the Bush Administration's war on terror tactics. The player of *September 12th* has only one choice (i.e. to drop bombs), but there is a delay between the act of clicking and the explosion, which means that in reality the player cannot control where the bombs drop. The repeated exercising of this captive choice causes the kind of centrifugal expansion of meanings necessary to understand the point of the game. The reader will speculate over why this is happening, the hidden implicatures behind it, and eventually find a meaningful explanation for the tragic game mechanics of the delay: we cannot control the dropping of the bombs in the same way that we cannot fight terrorism in a war from above. Consequently, behaviors, rules, and mechanics can also be interpreted as if they were utterances or poems. The strength of this process is a powerful resource for video games as a form of expression. In relation to this, theorist Miguel Sicart has remarked that the rules of video games create "the values we have to play by" (Sicart 2009: 22). Being able to grasp the game as system is a necessary premise for ethical understanding. An ethically relevant game will provide the player with moral decision power, so that she is not only free to interpret but also to discern the consequences of her actions (understand the procedurality of the system) and ultimately make a moral choice of some kind.

Amnesia: The Dark Descent: A Hybrid Product?

I have called *Amnesia: The Dark Descent* (from now on *Amnesia*) a hybrid product in the introduction to this chapter. This means that it is a "narrative game" (Egenfelt-Nielsen et al. 2008), or a game where narrative plays an important part (not all games are like this at all). The hybridity comes from it having two active levels at the same time: "the plot level and the action level. . . . The first one, that we experience on the fly, can be narrated afterwards (it is *tellable*) and makes sense as a story (complete with character motivation and feelings); the second is about solving action problems, and if it was to be narrated it would correspond to what we know as walkthroughs" (Tosca 2003: 6).

This is not the same as hypertext, or other kinds of literature, where, even though there are choices and movements of meanings as the reader searches for implicatures (as we saw above with the Eliot poem), we are lacking the action part, the procedural, or even cybertextual aspect, as Aarseth would say (1997). So we have a game *and* a story, and they are bound together and perceived in the same act of playing/understanding. Thus procedurality is inextricably linked to interpretation. *Amnesia*'s developers insist on the importance of story from the beginning; the first time we load the game, we see a few information screens, one of which has the message: "*Amnesia* should not be played to win. Instead, focus on immersing yourself in the game's world and story".

The basic premise of the lost memory has been used many times in the world of computer games:[8] Daniel, the protagonist and player-character, wakes up in a creepy Prussian castle, and the player doesn't know where he is or what has happened to him before. Soon enough he finds the first of his "notes to self" (that he has written before deliberately erasing his own memory). The player learns from it that something, a shadow, is pursuing Daniel, and that he feels guilty. It reads: "You are my final effort to put things right. . . . Redeem us both Daniel. Descend into the darkness where Alexander waits and murder him". The player needs to grudgingly embark on an exploration of the castle.

One could also say that *Amnesia* is a hybrid for reasons of genre. It is a survival horror game that doesn't quite follow the established conventions. It has adopted the "pick up objects/solve puzzles" mechanism typical of adventure games, which works so well in the survival horror genre, but its protagonist is unarmed. Usually, survival horror games are mainly about shooting all the monsters on our way and getting out of some closed location. In *Amnesia*, we have no weapons at all; Daniel is not a superhero. In fact, he is even more vulnerable than other humans would be because his sanity drops every time he is in the darkness for too long or looks at a monster, which can be felt by the avatar starting to shake and his vision becoming blurry.[9] We have to take care of him, bring him close to the light so he can regain his sanity once in a while, and make him hide when the monsters come.

The other deviation from genre conventions is that the game contains close to no cut scenes, so that the story is told through the objects we find, our spatial movements, and a few voice-overs from Daniel (and a few other characters), which usually allow us to move at the same time. The very few cut scenes are Daniel's auditory flashbacks where some location triggers a memory of what he did there in the past, and the end of the game, which works in the same "light-handed" way: we hear the voices and the information but can simultaneously move around and activate objects. Thus the player does not lose complete control at any time. Krzywinska has pointed to the loss of control in horror video games (Krzywinska 2002: 217) as mechanisms that force players to watch dangerous and horrible events that we might otherwise want to avoid. But *Amnesia* doesn't take advantage of this resource. Instead, it enforces voyeurism spatially: we need to traverse all the scenarios of horror slowly, lingering in unpleasant and disgusting places in order to find clues. We are trapped by the necessity of the mechanics of the game, in a more subtle way than cut scenes would allow for because it is the player herself who has to linger and explore against her will.

Yet another way for the developers to emphasize that the story is all-important is the absence of "save-places". The player doesn't need to worry about where these save-places are, as her progress is automatically recorded and saved by the game, so that if the character dies, the player doesn't have to begin again too far back in the story. The result is that because the fiction is not broken and the player is not reminded of the incoherence[10] of game fictions, she has the opportunity to become more immersed in the illusion and the story.

The game's atmospheric design is aesthetically flawless. It is not that the castle where the story develops is particularly beautiful or presents an exceptionally complex maze, but the combination of realistic graphics, brilliant sound design, the clever situation of puzzles, and the AI-animated monsters that prowl the rooms randomly cause an impression of vividness that facilitates immersion.

MOVEMENTS OF MEANING AT PLAY

The world of *Amnesia* is a spatial narrative of the enacted sort, in terms of Henry Jenkins, where "the story itself may be structured around the character's movement through space and the features of the environment may retard or accelerate that plot trajectory" (Jenkins 2003). In this case, the main motivation for the character's movement is the search for the answer to the question: who am I, and why am I here? This will provide the context for the movements of meaning (both centrifugal and centripetal) and shape the player's piecing together of the plot. The revelations about Daniel's past are well spaced, and it will take the player a significant degree of speculation and interpretation to put the story together, as she finds the different notes and journal entries scattered around in the rooms of the big castle. Slowly the story will emerge, and the player will continue her hunt for meanings (expanding centrifugally from the clues) as she gets in and out of many tense situations in which Daniel is about to get caught[11] by unspeakably uncanny monsters that leave him whimpering aloud, gasping for breath. The lived experience of these horrors is so intense that even though it is insinuated from the beginning that Daniel is guilty of something horrible, it is difficult to be against him because the player *is* him. When the game starts, Daniel is helpless and frail; his sanity declines rapidly when he is far from a light source, and his rapid, stressed breathing makes obvious his fear and his discomfort.

The experience of this hesitant, frightened man doesn't fit too well with the first note in which he writes of having to put things right. So the player can wonder in a centrifugal search for meanings what he has done in the past that justifies his present state. Has someone suffered because of his inaction? Has he murdered someone? Is the castle home to some dangerous secret of which he is a part? The only clues that the player has to find the appropriate implicatures are the ominous setting, the stressed breathing of the character, and the mysterious nature of that first note. The sole evidence to go by is that Daniel believes himself to be guilty of something. A bit later, the player finds the first of Daniel's diary entries, which sets the story in a new light:

> The unflinching African sun has continued to plague our expedition, making it impossible to dig until dusk. . . . Later that evening, we uncovered a passage beneath the dunes leading to a sand-covered stone structure. . . . Tomorrow, I shall lead the men into the ancient structure, hoping to reach the burial chamber. No matter what the professor is keeping from me, the dig should yield something interesting to take back to London and the British Museum.[12]

This entry anchors the speculations of the player and causes a centripetal landing of meanings: the familiar plot of the Western archeologist disturbing some ancient artifact/secret and having to pay for it dearly. The entries about Daniel and his team exploring the tomb, retrieving a strange object, and the accidents and suspicious events that befall them continue, fully meeting the player's expectations and not really interfering with her progress in any way. But later in the game, the diary entries begin to change in nature, becoming less specific, as if Daniel wants to avoid writing all the truth, opening up again for a centrifugal search for implicatures: what is he trying to hide? As the evil shadow that he awoke in Africa was about to catch up with him, Daniel travelled to Prussia and accepted the help of Alexander, the baron who owns the castle. Alexander claimed that he could restrain the shadow through a combination of rituals that involved human torture and sacrifice, and it seems that Daniel slowly turned into a disciple of that demonic figure. The diary entries are now dark and disturbing:

> I cannot believe what I have become. One of the girls escaped and I chased after her all the way upstairs. I hunted her down and. . . .
>
> What is a life worth? How many lives can I take before I surrender my own? Sure, I would kill a murderer to save an innocent. But to kill an innocent to save myself—a cold blooded murderer!

The player must make sense of these developments putting them in context with the rest of what has been experienced in the game so far. Daniel has suffered several hallucination scenes where past and present are blended in strange ways, so there could still be a doubt about the reality of what the player has just read. He also seems to write with a shred of conscience even though the acts he has committed are morally wrong. The player might thus still wonder about it all being a dream or a hallucination as the all-explaining implicature. However, the next entry anchors meanings again centripetally in an unequivocal way:

> It's not fair! I'm not to blame. I've been manipulated by that demon. He played my guilty conscience and duped me into facing the shadow alone. That vile, conspiring man. He expects me to meet my death as he steals power beyond imagining?

The old Daniel, before he drank Amnesia (which is the name of the drug that made him forget), evades his responsibilities, and the player knows now for sure that he is egotistic and morally weak. This opinion is supported by the latest discoveries in this area of the game, where the player has visited the torture chambers and seen torture instruments such as the Iron Maiden, the Brazen Bull, and many innocent dead bodies scattered about. She has also seen some flashbacks of what Daniel has done and read his notes about how to become a more effective torturer.

We might then think that moral repugnance is a sort of centripetal conclusion: the only possible emotional affordance induced by the game at this point. However, there is more, as the player doesn't only see Daniel from the outside, but inhabits him, and together they have taken some action throughout the game.

GAMEPLAY: HIDE AND SEEK

The analysis above has only dealt with the story level of *Amnesia* and how the main plot is unraveled through spatial exploration and the finding of clues. But I have not yet discussed the gameplay, the procedural part of this game, not because story and gameplay are unrelated, but for the sake of clarity in developing the argument. So what do the rules of this game allow its player to do? And does it cohere with the conclusions the player came to in her search for meaning?

At the beginning of this section, I noted that there seemed to be no choice in this game. There is only one way: into the castle, (no way out before the quest is fulfilled), and even though some rooms can be visited in different orders, there is a "level" division that prevents the player from getting into new zones before her purpose in the old zone is completed. Puzzles can only be solved in one way, and the player cannot even decide not to pick up objects because she will need every single one of them to complete her mission. When the monsters appear, the only choice is whether to run or to hide to avoid certain death. Perhaps we could look at the micro-level of the monster encounters, which are in truth the only situations that allow for a bit of strategic planning: will the player hide in a cupboard? Will she try to run past the monster? Will she just crouch in the shadows and not look? Eventually, she will learn some survival techniques by trial and error, like closing all doors behind her, looking for places to hide as the first thing when entering a room, or using the light as little as possible to avoid attracting monsters.

But this is a very small degree of freedom, and certainly not one that inspires creative searches for meanings and implicatures. The only way through the game is to revisit the very places Daniel sought to forget by drinking Amnesia. There is only the player, and the monsters, or the player/character as the monster, as it turns out. She roams across eerily empty rooms, full of discarded furniture, picking up jars of oil and tinderboxes, always making sure to have fuel for lights, as light is needed to keep sane. The flashbacks and even some of the puzzles are repulsive (like one where the player has to "vaccinate" Daniel by injecting blood from a corpse).

This lack of freedom is disturbing for the player, who not only has no option in the exploration of the scary castle; her avatar is weak and reduced to hiding and "remembering" through flashbacks and the finding of diary entries. Superficially, *Amnesia* is about surviving, about becoming good at avoiding the monsters, finding the solution to the puzzles, destroying Alexander, and finally being liberated from the shadow. But really, if we interrogate the implicatures of this kind of gameplay, it is about being trapped in a nightmare. The mechanics of this game force players into impotence and vulnerability. The many game design awards, the unanimous praise of the specialized press, and the close to 400,000 downloads of the game[13] are a testimony that the experience of claustrophobia is the procedural success of *Amnesia*, but to appreciate it, the player has to set the procedures/actions against the meandering amorality of the story as discussed above. The problematic combination of what we experience (action) and what we interpret (story) is what prompts us to ponder over the hidden meaning/implicature of the game's mode of play, such as it also happens in *The Path*.[14] This tension launches the centrifugal search for meanings that is eventually resolved in the final scene of the game, where the player manages to kill Alexander and thwart the shadow at the same time. Daniel leaves the castle saying: "It was my greatest triumph . . . and I never looked back. You think I was afraid fleeing Brennenburg? Quite the contrary. I knew it was my purgatory—hellfire made to wash my sins. There's no denying the things I've done. But I have paid my tribute. I gave them that awful man. . . . I did the right thing."

How to interpret this and find the right implicature? In the Catholic tradition, purgatory is punishment that cleanses the subject of his sins, suffering with a purpose. This is what Daniel has been through: revisiting his past evils has been torture, and killing the man who lured him to evil the necessary avenging act. The game has three possible endings, and the purgatory idea is in all of them (even if only explicitly in the "good" ending quoted above). There is a less desirable ending, where Alexander succeeds in his change of dimension and Daniel dies ("Thank you my friend. Your sacrifice won't be forgotten. You'll be celebrated . . . forever".), and a "special" ending where they both die but, at the end, Daniel is rewarded by another character, a magician ("There he is. Do you see him Weyer?[15] He deserves so much more. Please help him, I know you can. Don't worry Daniel. It will be alright".) The three endings assume that Daniel has been through much trouble and pain, *sacrifice*, and he deserves gratitude or even to live again. But will players agree? They have also been through the *Amnesia* ordeal with Daniel, and experienced his fear, his suffering, and the haunting memory of his past evils first hand. Can he be forgiven as the three redeeming endings suggest? Regardless of what each player will answer to this question, the truth is that they have been dragged through the amorality and terror of Daniel's life, and forced to act *from within* him.

Cleverly, the game has, through the gameplay and the movements of meaning created by the player, turned Daniel's purgatory into the player's purgatory. The three endings are in reality open because they give players the moral power in the very end, not in a way that changes the gameworld or the plot, but in a way that lives in them. Players have been inside a torturer and murderer, and at the same time they have been tortured (and murdered a few times), experiencing fear and distress. When does one weigh more than the other? Have players condoned Daniel's behavior at some point, and if so, how can they reconcile this as ethical beings? The questions are open; the expansion of meanings continues and is fuelled by the impeccable fusion of story and procedures.

AN ANALYSIS METHOD FOR HYBRID NARRATIVES

This chapter has proposed a close reading of a narrative computer game, explicitly framing it around a search for meanings and contexts similar to that experienced when reading hypertexts. The difference between a static hypertext and a computer game is that in the latter, we also have to take the procedural level into account: they are story *and* game, and their combination is more than a sum of the two. Some theorists have taken this double nature of narrative games into account before (e.g. Aarseth 1997; Tosca 2003, 2005; Juul 2005; Calleja 2011), and others, as noted above, have described the procedural nature of computer games as the essence of their expressive power (Bogost 2007, 2008; Wardrip-Fruin 2009; Flanagan 2009). However, these theorists have not provided a practical method to investigate how the procedural/interpretive activities could operate together in the praxis of interpreting/playing hybrid products such as narrative games. This is my contribution in this chapter.

The most novel aspect of this approach is that both texts and rules can be treated as utterances, and their meaning expanded and contracted in an adaptive process of play. Inspired by the concept of yin and yang, which illustrates the interconnectness of different things (although they are not opposites here), I suggest reforming the illustration shown in Figure 7.1 above so as to adapt it for narrative video games (see Figure 7.2).

Figure 7.2 illustrates that both story and action initiate the search for implicatures, and that they are so imbricated that interpretation is always double-sided. Key to this approach is to keep asking the question: "what does this mean/suggest"? at every step. The right implicature when interrogating story or procedures will always be partly determined by the other side. I hope to have demonstrated that this mode of inquiry leads to insights about the narrative, cultural, and ethical nature of the works that wouldn't be possible otherwise.

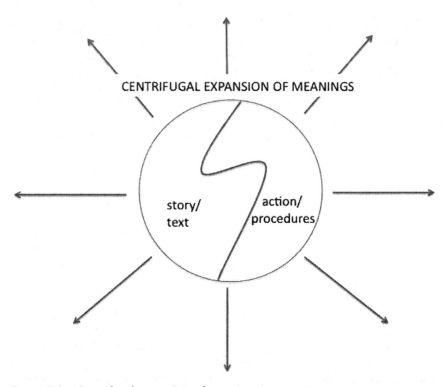

CENTRIFUGAL EXPANSION OF MEANINGS

story/
text

action/
procedures

Figure 7.2   Centrifugal expansion of meanings in narrative games

Based on my work with *Amnesia*, I can propose a method for the pragmatic analysis of a narrative computer game. It requires the following steps:

1) A systematic recording of the movements of meaning/creation of implicatures (both at the story level and the rules/procedural level) through the writing/videotaping of a player diary.
2) An analysis of player choices both at the level of story and gameplay, as well as an evaluation of the consequences of those choices.
3) A joint evaluation of the materials produced at steps 1 and 2, paying special attention to the hybrid meanings that emerge, paradoxes, and reinforcements.
4) An interrogation of the joined narrative force of the product: what is the game telling us (through representation and procedurality)?
5) An assessment of the game as a producer of cultural and ethical meanings, positioning it against a wider perspective.

As a development of my earlier take on the question of video game narratives, I would say that combining a pragmatic approach with the close reading of story/procedures gives us a much more holistic tool with which to approach hybrid narratives. *Amnesia: The Dark Descent* has been a very productive example, both aesthetically and as an object from which to develop theory and methodology, and I am confident that this method can be applied fruitfully to digital fictions with similar characteristics.

NOTES

1. From the developers' website: http://www.amnesiagame.com/#game (accessed 21 February 2013).
2. For an account of the not always peaceful reunion of literary theory and computer games research, see chapter 8: "Narrative" of Egenfelt-Nielsen et al. (2008).
3. An implicature is a technical term to distinguish between a literal interpretation of an utterance and what is really meant. It was introduced by Grice (1961: 3) and is widely used in pragmatics.
4. In the link called "arms" (Jackson 1997).
5. In the link called "phantom_limb" (Jackson 1997).
6. For example Bogost (2007, 2008), Sicart (2009).
7. Available at http://www.newsgaming.com/games/index12.htm (accessed 20 February 2013).
8. It is certainly not exclusively of this medium. For example, the film *Memento* (2000) builds up suspense in a very similar way.
9. In this respect, Ensslin, who also writes about a horror game (*The Path*) in this same volume, has aptly called *Amnesia* "an anti-survival" horror game.
10. This is Juul's term, as developed in *Half-Real: Video Games between Real Rules and Fictional Worlds* (Juul 2005: 146).
11. When he does get caught by one of the terrible monsters, the player can see how he is murdered horribly onscreen in rather unpleasant scenes. After that she has to start again a bit further back in the game.

12. Literal quote from the game, respecting syntax and punctuation.
13. Figure taken from the developers' website, http://www.amnesiagame.com/, on January 5, 2012.
14. See Ensslin in this volume.
15. A secondary character in the story.

WORKS CITED

Aarseth, E. (1997) *Cybertext: Perspectives on Ergodic Literature*. London: John Hopkins University Press.
Bernstein, M. (1998) "Patterns of Hypertext". *Proceedings Hypertext '98*. New York: ACM.
Bogost, I. (2007) *Persuasive Games: The Expressive Power of Videogames*. Boston, MA: MIT Press.
Bogost, I. (2008) *Unit Operations: An Approach to Videogame Criticism*. Boston, MA: MIT Press.
Burbules, N. (2001) "Rhetorics of the Web: Hyperreading and Critical Literacy". In *Page to Screen—Taking Literacy into the Electronic Era*. Snyder, I. (ed). New York/London: Routledge.
Calleja, G. (2011) *In-Game: From Immersion to Incorporation*. Boston, MA: MIT Press.
Carroll, N. (1996) "The Paradox of Suspense". In *Suspense: Conceptualizations, Theoretical Analyses, and Empirical Explorations*. P. Worderer, H.J. Wulff, and M. Friedrichsen (eds). Mahwah, NJ: Lawrence Erlbaum Associates.
Egenfelt-Nielsen, S., Smith, J.H., and Tosca, S.P. (2008) *Understanding Videogames*. New York: Routledge.
Flanagan, M. (2009) *Critical Play: Radical Game Design*. Boston, MA: MIT Press.
Frictional Games. (2010) *Amnesia, the Dark Descent*. Helsingborg, Sweden: Frictional Games.
Grice, P. (1961) "The Causal Theory of Perception". *Proceedings of the Aristotelian Society, Supplementary Volume* 35: 121–152.
Jackson, S. (1997) "My Body: A Wunderkammer". Last accessed 20 February 2013 at URL: http://www.altx.com/thebody/
Jenkins, H. (2003) "Game Design as Narrative Architecture". In *First Person*. N. Wardrip-Fruin and P. Harrigan (eds). Cambridge, MA: The MIT Press.
Joyce, M. (1999) *afternoon: a story* [CD-ROM]. Watertown, MA: Eastgate Systems.
Juul, J. (2005) *Half-Real: Video Games between Real Rules and Fictional Worlds*. Cambridge, MA: MIT Press.
Krzywinska, T. (2002) "Hands-on-Horror". In *ScreenPlay*. G. King and T. Krzywinska (eds). London: Wallflower Press.
Murray, J. (1997) *Hamlet on the Holodeck*. Boston: The MIT Press.
Ryan, M.-L. (2001) "Can Coherence Be Saved—Selective Interactivity and Narrativity". In *Narrative as Virtual Reality—Immersion and Interactivity in Literature and Electronic Media*. Baltimore: John Hopkins University Press.
Sicart, M. (2009) *The Ethics of Computer Games*. Boston, MA: MIT Press.
Simanowski, R. (2004) "Concrete Poetry in Digital Media: Its Predecessors, Its Presence and Its Future". *Dichtung Digital* 3. Last accessed 20 February 2013 at URL: http://www.dichtung-digital.org/2004/3-Simanowski.htm
Sperber, D. and Wilson, D. (1986) *Relevance: Communication and Cognition*. Oxford: Blackwell.
Tosca, S. (1999) "The Lyrical Quality of Links". *Hypertext '99 Proceedings*. New York: ACM.

Tosca, S.P. (2000) "A Pragmatics of Links". *Journal of Digital Information* 1. 6. Last accessed 20 February 2013 at URL: http://journals.tdl.org/jodi/article/viewArticle/23/24

Tosca, S. (2003) "Reading Resident Evil: Code Veronica X". *Proceedings of DAC03*. Melbourne: RMIT Press.

Tosca, S. (2005) "Implanted Memories or the Illusion of Free Action". In W. Brooker (ed). *The Blade Runner Experience*. London: Wallflower Press.

Wardrip-Fruin, N. (2009) *Expressive Processing: Digital Fictions, Computer Games and Spoftware Studies*. Boston, MA: The MIT Press.

8 Wreading Together
The Double Plot of Collaborative Digital Fiction

Isabell Klaiber,
University of Tübingen, Germany

INTRODUCTION

Which reader doesn't at one point or another dream of being an author? Online writing platforms for collaborative narrative fiction such as *One Million Monkeys* (henceforth *OMM*), *Protagonize, StoryPassers, Ficly,* or *WEBook* seem to offer the perfect opportunity for nonprofessionals to write literary texts and gain recognition.[1] These platforms are conceived as "creative writing communit[ies] dedicated to writing various forms of collaborative, interactive fiction. One author writes a story, poem, or other work, and others post branches or chapters to it" (*Protagonize*). Anybody may sign up under a user name to contribute text segments of usually no more than a few hundred words. Thus, literary digital fiction may be considered collaborative if a literary project is actively contributed to by several users in form of textual additions and/or alterations; commonly, it is nurtured through commentary and/or evaluation by different users. As any other form of digital fiction, it is "written for and read on a computer screen . . . [it] pursues its verbal, discursive and/or conceptual complexity through the digital medium, and would lose something of its aesthetic and semiotic function if it were removed from that medium" (Bell et al. 2010, n.p.). For the collaboratively written text itself, this is particularly true if the individual platform allows for a hypertextual structure that branches the story out into multiple versions. Furthermore, the interaction between users is based in the medium, as it takes place in blog-like sections of the respective platform as well as personalized user-profile pages, which could not be reproduced on paper.

In the following, the focus will be on interactive, all-text writing platforms whose projects are unlimited in time and where narratives are written consecutively so that the co-authors take turns. There is a variety of formats, of which the most restricted one is *fabulate*, where users together write one narrative at a time; the community rates and thus selects a chapter from several submitted versions to then move on to the next chapter. While *WEBook* adheres to linear narratives, stories on *Protagonize, OMM,* and *Ficly* may branch out into multilinear versions at the end of any contribution; thus alternative versions of a story may be introduced to any instance of the narrative, and there are multiple versions of a narrative simultaneously present. As in any multilinear story, the narrative may thus "play with the reader's notions of cause and effect, making the words and actions of the characters radically ambiguous" (Bolter 2001: 128). Furthermore, text segments may be ranked by users and commented upon. While only a few platforms allow editing, the most extended editing options are offered on *WikiStory*, where stories may be continuously revised by different users; on *Protagonize* only self-editing is possible. Thus, depending on the platform, users may read, comment on, actively contribute or add branches to, and sometimes edit ongoing narrative collaborations.

APPROACHES TO ANALYZING COLLABORATIVE DIGITAL FICTION

How are we to analyze this collaborative form of digital fiction? Simanowski's approach juxtaposes the social and the textual levels in collaborative online writing as oppositional and even mutually exclusive, so that the literary aesthetics is replaced by the social dynamics, which he calls "(un) social" (2000)[2] or "cooperative aesthetics" (2002: 61). In declaring collaborative stories to be failures if they turn out to be incoherent and/or remain unfinished, he implicitly evaluates them in relation to the unitary aesthetics of the single-handed genius author (Stillinger 1991). In spite of their amateurish quality and the fact that most stories are sooner or later abandoned, however, these participatory writing platforms are rather popular. This is because multiauthored digital fiction is rather process-oriented than result-oriented (Simanowski 2002: 42), as its main purpose seems to be not so much the final literary product but rather the act of participation itself, that is, to watch and contribute to the emerging narrative in real time.[3] The social dynamics of the collaborative process may be traced in the commentary of registered users, which accompanies the textual contributions, as well as in their evaluative ratings. Thus collaborative writing platforms seem to function primarily as social networks. Indeed, online writing platforms may be considered "communities of practice" (cf. Wenger 1998: 7), which "are groups of people who share a concern or a passion for something they do and learn how to do it better as they interact regularly" (Wenger 2006); online writing communities share a passion for collectively writing a literary text and advance in their project as they interact on the platform through rating, commenting upon, and contributing to the communal narrative.

In the following, however, it will become evident that an aesthetics that looks at the literary and social realms separately is not fully fit to account for the inherent dynamics and complexity of collaborative digital writing. Therefore, an approach to collaborative digital fiction is suggested here that correlates the analysis of the social dynamics with that of the textual dynamics. Instead of privileging one aesthetic at the expense of the other and speaking of their mutual "replacement", they may be analyzed in terms of a "double plot", which allows for a focus on their interdependencies and takes both social *and* textual dynamics for integral components of collaborative writing. Using this kind of dual approach permits us to better understand how the fundamental dilemma of collaboration is tackled: absolute liberty typically results in unreadable texts, while regulations contradict the principle of equal creativity for all participants (Heibach 2003: 174). The double-plot analysis allows us to trace how users try to balance out these oppositional interests on the level of the text and that of interaction.

THE "DOUBLE PLOT" OF COLLABORATIVE DIGITAL FICTION

In a dynamic "double plot", the interaction between the users may be considered the "story behind the story", which runs parallel and is immediately connected to the literary narrative; thus the story of the collaboration forms a secondary or meta-plot that is closely related and complementary to the primary literary narrative.[4] This "double plot" is displayed on screen in form of the literary text and the paratextual blog-like commentary, where users comment on the narrative and their own or others' ways of contributing to it; in fact, hardly any contribution remains uncommented. This double-plot structure of collaborative narratives may be represented in a revised communication model derived from Chatman (1978: 151) as shown in Figure 8.1.[5]

In collaborative fiction, the far "sender" end is not occupied by the authors but rather by the administrator or provider of the collaborative platform, who does not only control the facilities and functions of the platform but also employs the multiple-author format as an incentive for the users to read and participate. Presumably, the strategic highlighting of the participatory format as well as the space provided on such platforms for elaborate comments, profile pages, etc. feed the users' interest in the

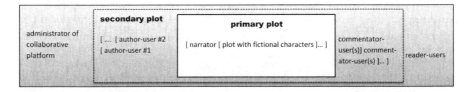

Figure 8.1 Communication model of the double plot in collaborative narratives

social dynamics as much as the stories themselves. Furthermore, while Chatman locates author and reader as fixed entities on the far ends of the extra-textual realm of communication, in collaborative digital fiction the extra-textual realm is occupied by the users in their flexible roles (cf. Page 2012: 125) of "author", "commentator", and "reader", between which a single user may switch back and forth. Thus, in contrast to Chatman's fixed positions of author and reader being connected in a mono-directional way, the connection between the collaborating digital users is multidirectional and dynamic (cf. Ben-Arie 2009: 153). In Figure 8.1, this flexibility of roles and the permeability between the level of the secondary plot and the level of the sender/recipient are indicated by a dotted line between the various active and passive roles available, where author-user and commentator-user are actively engaged in the writing process, while the reader-user is not.[6] In as far as users flexibly adopt and drop different roles, they function as actants or "characters" in "the story behind the story". According to Page (2012), participants in collaborative online projects adopt different roles such as the "reviewer" providing retrospective (usually positive) evaluation, the "editor" critically checking the quality of the text, the "collaborator" being concerned about the interaction, the "creator" as the most prolific contributor, and the "convenor" initiating the project and maintaining its collaborative nature (130–134). Page's typology thus provides a set of "stock characters" for the secondary plot of a collaborative project.

Regardless of their interdependency, the two plot levels are fundamentally different from each other in quality and ontological status: the fictional plot is narrativized while the second-degree plot of the interaction between the users belongs to virtual life and is not diegetically represented but exclusively "shown" (cf. Prince 2003: 89) in the meta-fictional commentary accompanying the primary narrative. Furthermore, as Page (2012) asserts, in digital collaborative fiction, "comments will not necessarily influence the text of the narrative, and the stories can be read without reference to the comments that accompany them. But while the completed story can be read as a detached artifact without reference to the commentary, the story could not have been produced without the commentary. Narrative production is inextricably linked to the surrounding talk that evolved episodically along with the story content" (122). Therefore, rather than considering the interaction between the users merely supplementary in the hierarchy of textual production, commentary should, due to this interrelatedness, be read as an integral and highly significant part and thus a second plot level of the emerging narrative at large. The user, it seems, reads collaborative fiction for the double experience of immersing herself in the "primary plot" and her being aware of its constructedness by taking in the "secondary plot". A similar double focus has been well established since the beginnings of digital fiction (cf. Lanham 1993, 47ff.): "[i]n exploring a hypertext the reader oscillates between looking through the prose of each episode and looking at the junctures or links between episodes" (Bolter 2001: 137f.). In online writing projects on *OMM* or *Protagonize*, however, drawing the readers' attention to the junctures between the textual segments is much more than a customary strategy of digital narrative, as here the junctures are elaborated and spelled out as the plot of the interaction between the users of the collaborative project in their changing roles. Furthermore, the double focus on the narrative itself and its genesis seems indeed to be a core interest users take in collaborative digital fiction.

In the double-plot structure, narrative coherence on both plot levels needs to be taken into consideration. In the Aristotelian tradition, a well-made plot represents a harmonious whole in which everything has a purpose: "As readers, we are all prophets. When we are engaged in a well-made novel, we know in advance many things we could not know in life. Should the story be nearing its end, we rule out certain events as impossible because they would make the narrative incoherent. Incidents that would make no sense thematically will not occur. We look for loose ends to be tied up and outstanding mysteries to be resolved. The fact that the work has been designed provides something close to a guarantee that an overall pattern is traced. [. . .] In life we lack such guarantees" (Morson 1999: 283). The fact that the secondary plot of social interaction belongs to (virtual) life and not fiction does not only make participation in online writing projects particularly attractive; it also makes them a shifting terrain. Real- and virtual-life events do not necessarily form a unitary whole; instead, life is contingent and open-ended. It is characteristic of collaborative writing that different authors may have different agendas for the same story, which leads to a more or less confrontational struggle over its narrative trajectory. Although multilinear pathways help to ease some of the confrontation,[7] often co-authors try to shift the focus, tone, or narrative trajectory as they write, which in turn is then subject to commentary. Therefore, while in spite of these challenges the primary plot still tends to aim at the emulation of a well-made story,[8] the secondary plot does not: the interaction of the authors (as quasi-characters of the secondary plot) represents a truly open-ended process in which it might never be settled which author's ideas for a story eventually persist. For Morson (1999), "[G]enuine process allows for more than one alternative at some or all moments [. . .] for the moment possesses what Bakhtin calls *eventness*. [. . .] When time is open in this way, each moment contains a *field of possibilities*. Some possibilities are more likely to be actualized than others, but none is inevitable" (279; original emphases). Therefore, the "story behind the story" may be radically contingent, incoherent, and open-ended. When the contingency of the secondary plot of the authors' interaction with each other "spills over" into the primary narrative and is reflected by its inconsistencies and contingencies, the literary collaboration is less likely to fulfill the established aesthetic standards of a well-made narrative.

In the collaborative writing process, decisions about characters and their constellation, the plot trajectory, the tone of narration, etc., are continuously made; what has not yet been occupied for the narrative by earlier authors is available to later ones. However, it is important to note that already established aspects of the narrative may be and are also changed. Indeed, in collaborative fiction writing, authors often usurp already occupied meaning and appropriate it for their own version of the story, thus jeopardizing the narrative unity of the emerging primary plot (cf. Simanowski 2002: 33). Therefore, the narrative coherence of the primary plot in collaborative fiction heavily depends on the successive authors' faithfulness to the already existing parts of the story. Although coherence is, of course, a fuzzy concept (cf. Toolan 2013), if we "consider . . . narratives as developing wholes" (Phelan 2002: 211), then Phelan's conceptualization of "narrative progression" is particularly useful.[9] This means "the synthesis of both the textual dynamics that govern the movement of narrative from beginning through middle to end and the readerly dynamics that both follow from and influence those textual dynamics" (Phelan 2007: 3).[10] The correlation and eventual resolution of the instabilities occurring within the story and tensions created by the discourse of a text are determining factors for its coherence, or for what Booth (1983) calls the "implied promise" of what will come later in a narrative (128). In collaborative fiction, it is often exactly this implied promise that is at stake at the transition from one author's contribution to the next, and mostly with regard to plot as the emerging stories tend to be heavily plot-driven rather than concerned with developing character, exploring language, etc.

Narrative coherence is particularly precarious in collaborative online projects. For projects with a hypertextual structure that allows for multiple versions of a story, this is partly due to their digital properties: as Tyrkkö (2009) notes, "[H]ypertexts [in general] challenge coherence not only by being . . . open-ended, but also by actually transforming themselves in the course of—and because of—each reading" (3). In collaborations, authors quickly lose control over their own version of the text and expose it to the creative appropriations not only by their subsequent co-authors but by the readers' individual hypertextual reading processes as well. Even if a collaborative digital story follows a linear structure, all participants in a writing project in their respective roles—authors, readers, commentators, and rating members—are immediately involved in the formation of the coherence of the primary plot as they continue the story in their own way, confirm or question certain "implied promises" of a text segment, etc. A user may not only flexibly take on all of these roles; she is also always a reader first before she becomes a co-author who creatively appropriates the already existing text for her own ideas of the story; in turn she will expose her own work to the subsequent appropriation of other co-authors and commentators. Due to these variable forms and degrees of writerly/readerly participation, the participant of a collaborative online writing project may truly be considered a "reader-author" or a "wreader".[11] It is, on the one hand, the interplay between multiple wreaders and emerging narrative, and on the other hand, the interaction of multiple wreaders that evoke the double plot in collaborative fiction.

Due to the collaborative format as well as the editing function and the often multilinear narrative structure, narrative coherence on the primary plot level of collaborative digital fiction proves to be unstable, progressive, reversible, and collective—in short, highly precarious. Rettberg (2005) summarizes the "principle limitation" of a collaborative narrative as follows: "Putting voice and style aside, the success of the story depends on continuity and causality, and on implicit contracts between the various contributing writers to respect the ontology presented in the early chapters in producing the later chapters" (101). Indeed, the precarious coherence of collaborative online writing is often disrupted by various factors, ranging from the individual authors' vanities to under- or overreading. Readers, willy-nilly, underread and overread narratives by "invariably . . . overlook[ing] things that are there and put[ting] in things that are not there" (Abbot 2008: 86). The unfinished text casts the resolution of instabilities and tensions as always potentially in reach, often without ever fully realizing it, so that narrative coherence is ever emerging.

Since the secondary plot of the collaborative process is closely interrelated with the narrativization of the primary plot, collaborations on *OMM* with their alternative branches allow us to trace the authorial interaction on both plot levels. The secondary plot of the interaction among the users branches out along the multilinear primary plot and evolves in respective subplots. This interrelatedness of the two plot levels becomes particularly evident when narrative coherence on the primary plot level is disrupted: where narrative branches are abandoned, the secondary plot breaks off too.

THE DOUBLE PLOT IN MULTILINEAR COLLABORATIVE DIGITAL FICTION

This interrelatedness of the two levels of the double plot may be illustrated with "Hejira", a story on *OMM*. The platform *OMM* expired over the summer of 2011—as most material on the Web it is of a transitional nature. Yet it is still of interest as the multilinear stories on this platform in general and "Hejira" in particular lend themselves to the double-plot analysis in a way that collaborative multilinear stories on most other platforms do not. The occasional multilinear story on other platforms typically either breaks off after just a few segments (e.g. on *Ficly*) or is not as narrativized (e.g on *Protagonize*) as the usually more "literary" narratives on *OMM*.

"Hejira" was launched on March 25, 2008 by Bill Wagner,[12] one of the platform's most prolific members. It was frequently commented upon and contributed to from its first day until December 2008. Altogether there are thirty-nine text segments in eleven story lines. The story starts with the protagonist Nyssa returning to her childhood home, which she left in her teens under conflicted, yet unspecified circumstances. What users make of this beginning ranges from a sentimental journey into a rose-tinged childhood, to the story about a prodigal daughter seeking peace with her family, to her return to an empty house haunted by ghosts of the past, some of which are psychologically explained and some not. Thus its genre is romance, horror, or mystery novel. None of the narrative branches of "Hejira" has ever been concluded. Before users choose narrative paths, they explicitly enjoy the openness of the story's beginning (cf. Marla McMain, March 25, 2008; cf. little lemon, March 26, 2008); Jack Bellhouse, for instance, "like[s] it because it is open, and it doesn't have a clear genre yet" (March 27, 2008). And indeed, the range of "directions [the primary plot] could go" (March 27, 2008) proves to be almost unlimited, just as it is the case for the secondary plot, where the users will soon take on the social roles within their communal project as it evolves.

Much of the commentary on "Hejira" helps to integrate the rather heterogeneous continuations of the story after Nyssa's return to her childhood home into a common enterprise. Bill Wagner, the initiator of the story, gives this type of support several times—for example, when at a rather early stage he praises the "snippet [of another author for] really captur[ing] Nyssa's trepidation [Wagner] was trying to set with the opening snippet": "Totally different direction than I was heading, but I like it" (March 25, 2008). Wagner in the role of the convenor thus not only enforces a sense of community among the co-authors, but he also stresses the connection between different narrative segments. Other comments both express respect for the work of previous authors and praise how they tie in with what has been written before—for example, when Tina Todd asks Penny J. about her segment: "In paragraph three, second sentence, funerals is plural. Intentional or typo? I'd love to add a snippet, but that one little "s" makes a big difference. Really like how mom pulls Nyssa on the carpet [. . .] . Pulls up the theme from prior snippet, and creates some continuity" (April 10, 2008). Such respectful interaction among the co-authors strengthens the communal quality of the project without impairing the authority of the individual authors over their own part(s) of the narrative. Accordingly, when Penny J. answers that "[t]he 's' was intentional" (May 18, 2008), she implicitly confirms her authority over the meaning of her own textual contribution.[13]

The communal quality of collaborative fiction is further sustained by the fact that very little commentary on *OMM* is critical, and if so, it is uttered with caution and many disclaimers such as "[m]aybe [i]t's just in my head" (May 16, 2008), as to not affront any of the co-authors.[14]

Typically, individual users play different roles and may also flexibly switch between them. The role of the editor is in "Hejira" filled primarily by Jack Bellhouse, but also by Rachel Wintner. To attenuate his criticism he often offers it as questions—for example, when he mildly complains about a plot cliché by asking: "Why is their [sic] always a mysterious funeral? Is death the only reason people come home?" (May 27, 2008; cf. Rachel Wintner, April 12, 2008). At other times Jack Bellhouse downplays his critique by embedding it in praise, such as when after an enthusiastic comment he adds that the "only negative [he] see[s] is some verbal cliches [sic]" (March 27, 2008).[15] Even in the case of outright inconsistency, users put their criticism very politely: "I have a question—if the mother died 'nearly three years ago', then why is the funeral now?" (Katherine Dexley, March 29, 2008), and others still offer encouragement in the face of such obvious blunders by claiming they still "think it's a good start. :)" (Ariana Amdulah, April 19, 2008). Thus, much of the commentary accompanying the collaborative process has a clearly community-sustaining function. A perhaps more honest expression of the users' opinion may be found in their rating activity, which for this particular segment, with 2.20 bananas out of 5.00 and an average rating in "Hejira" of 4.01, is extremely low.

Due to this user-determined netiquette on *OMM*, the secondary plot usually does not include much conflict unless some direct mismatch, incoherence, or deviation from the users' literary expectations occurs in the primary plot. The typical reaction on the secondary plot level is the abandonment of the respective story line. In a branch called "Forever and Always", for instance, Nyssa is dissolved in tears over the sentimental memory of how as innocent children she and a neighborhood boy promised lifelong friendship to each other. Although two users praise the depiction of the children (May 10, 2008), the sentimental plot and mawkish tone seem to be too cliché-laden for any of the co-authors to continue from here. In "Flood of memories" (March 26, 2008), another branch succeeding the segment of the prodigal daughter, Nyssa is returning home ruefully; instead of providing some information on the past events and Nyssa's apparent guilt, however, the following segment "Forgiveness" (March 30, 2008) continues with her mother suddenly forgiving her without any further explanation of what for or why. With the unexpected erasure of all of Nyssa's previously elaborated concerns and guilt, the central plot instability of her role as prodigal daughter up to here is prematurely resolved so that the suspense deflates and the narrative focus is unexpectedly shifted from the past to the future of the story. There are not only no comments on this snippet, but the branch was also abandoned—apparently no other user felt encouraged to build up new narrative tension from here.[16] As open criticism seems to be against *OMM* netiquette, complete silence among the users upon a contribution may in cases such as these indeed be a form of implicit disdain. The same telling silence may be found on the dead-end snippet "Hallucinations and

Dreams" (December 9, 2008), where the narrative, after having followed the conventions of a mystery novel for nine sections, suddenly turns out to be a hospital novel about a schizophrenic woman.

In contrast to such telling silence, supportive comments put users into a communal relation with other users, e.g. when they are "officially hooked on this story now" (March 29, 2008), and others agree, "Hooked too—nice work so far" (May 16, 2008), or when in turn users thank others for their praise: "Thank you, Bill! I'm so excited you liked it" (March 30, 2008). Dialogic commentary in retrospect may establish different kinds of relationships between the users: in the last example, Jenny Rock's gratefulness answers to Wagner's praise, who as the initiator of the story and one of the most active "monkeys" on the platform has a celebrity status; her gratefulness thus establishes a hierarchical mentor-student relationship between Wagner and herself. Jacko duo, on the contrary, does not express gratefulness or awe that establishes a hierarchical relationship, but rather answers as on par with Wagner: after his comment: "Nice snippet! The girl is creepy . . ." (June 2, 2008), jacko duo simply responds: "isn't she"? (June 3, 2008). When Halfmoonorange joins this brief conversation with: "Yeah . . . the whispered bit is absolutely my favorite part", jacko duo feels fully understood by Halfmoonorange (ibid.). They also negotiate whose turn it is, e.g. when Katherine Dexley connects primary with secondary plot by announcing her next contribution: "WOW. awesome snippet, very hard to add to. But, I'm sure I will [. . .]!" (April 9, 2008). Thus through commentary regarding the primary plot level Jenny Rock, Bill Wagner, Halfmoonorange, jacko duo, and Katherine Dexley form a virtual community of practice, i.e. of co-authors on the secondary plot level, where they claim their turn or acknowledge, support, encourage, and criticize each other all in support of their common project "Hejira".

THE DOUBLE PLOT IN LINEAR COLLABORATIVE DIGITAL FICTION

As multilinearity apparently reduces confrontation among the collaborators and disperses the secondary plot into as many branches as there are on the primary plot level, it seems likely that the secondary plot is more tightly knit in linear collaborations. The linear *Protagonize* story "The Smart Ones" (TSO), which was actively contributed to between January and May 2009, is a case in point: it consists of forty-two linear narrative segments by five co-authors, where each segment has at least one, often two, alternative, yet unrealized, branches. This rather coherent science fiction time-travel story revolves around the super-intelligent Elizabeth Quinn who encounters her two older selves of 2019 and 2029; together they try to prevent the also super-intelligent Jason Petrovsky from achieving global dominance in the future. In the end the three Elizabeths realize they cannot change history (or the future) but only open up alternative "branches" of multilinear reality. While not all users feel that this is a proper ending (QQube, October 1, 2011), the story has never been continued after this point.

The 172 direct comments on the evolving story as well as the conversations on the co-authors' profile pages bear witness to the complex and dynamic relations among them. The "characters" of the secondary plot are the initiator of the story m3LaVirtuosaScotlandesa (m3), who contributed fifteen segments to the narrative, danda with ten story entries, Eric Rountree (aka Faltarego)[17] with nine segments, Sharon Flood (aka moonwalker)[18] with six, and farrago with one contribution. Their roles may be categorized along Page's typology (2012: 130–134) so that m3 functions not only as the "convenor", but also together with danda as the "creator" of the story, Faltarego as an "editor" and moonwalker as a "collaborator". However, their functions in the collaboration clearly exceed these stock-character roles, which becomes evident in the secondary plot.

Their commentary immediately reflects their interaction as collaborating co-authors, most of whom knew each other before they joined the project: from mutual commentary on their *Protagonize*-profile pages it is evident that m3 knew Faltarego as well as moonwalker, and danda knew Faltarego too. This means that most of the actants of the secondary plot are on friendly terms from the very start while others are mere "peripheral participants" of this particular community of practice (Wenger 1998: 167), such as Cookies Cream (January 29, 2009), ElizaFalk (ibid.), or Tranzient, who occasionally or briefly commented on a segment, but neither do they get actively involved in extended discussions, nor do they ever contribute a text segment of their own. Thus Tranzient, for instance, praises m3 and danda: "This is great stuff you two—you keep posting and I'll keep reading :)" (February 3, 2009). After m3's beginning, she and danda alternate for twelve chapters and grow more and more familiar with each other; this becomes evident when danda after the ninth narrative segment calls m3 "Gwen" (February 2, 2009)—a gesture with which danda tries to relate to the "real" person behind the *Protagonize* pseudonym; similarly, he welcomes Faltarego to the team of co-authors calling him by his "real" first name "Eric" (February 12, 2009). The ping pong–like exchanges of narrative segments as well as the participating authors' comments make it obvious that "it's [. . .] a pleasure [for them] adding to this story" (danda February 1, 2009) and that they enjoy the challenge as well as their own curiosity about any next segment: "how is [Elizabeth] gonna get out of *this* mess?!" (February 9, 2009). By the time m3 admits that she is "stuck on" how to continue, she clearly considers "The Smart Ones" the common project of danda and herself: she explicitly asks him whether he "would [. . .] be too terribly put off if [she] stepped back on this one [i.e. the next segment] and see if someone else would be interested in sequeling" (February 15, 2009); she then invites Faltarego to "add[] onto [sic] any branches" of TSO, which he does (February 18, 2009). The three work in concert for the following thirteen chapters, where they frequently cheer or "poke" each other into continuation. In addition Faltarego takes on the role of the supportive editor and mentor, telling danda to use more contractions in dialogue to make it sound less formal (February 20, 2009) and offering m3 stylistic advice on the usage of active and passive voice, word choice, etc. (February 24, 2009). In his constructive criticism, Faltarego offers his particular skills to this community of practice—"I'm big on dialogue" (February 20, 2009)—to ensure a consistent narrative tone and style as well as a realistic depiction of characters (e.g. in their speech). In response to his criticism, his co-authors report back to the "editor" promising to "fix it" (April 17, 2009) and readily revise their own text segments to improve the project at large.

Furthermore, their exchanging personal information indicates their increasing familiarity, e.g. when danda discloses his being an Indian immigrant to the US (March 17, 2009), or when m3 announces that she is currently taking the SAT for college admission (May 3, 2009).[19] After a short period as a peripheral participant, moonwalker cautiously asks m3 for permission to join the "closed circle" of co-authors (March 21, 2009). M3, as the creator and convenor of the story, heartily welcomes her: "go right ahead!" (March 21, 2009). Moonwalker proves a particularly sensitive collaborator, always connecting to and seeking explicit consent from the others: "Hellooo? Is anybody there? Please tell me I haven't gone and killed this fabulous story just by adding to it. M3? Faltarego? Danda?" (March 31, 2009). From the way all three co-authors immediately report back to moonwalker (ibid.), it becomes evident how very important their lively interaction is for each one of them as well as the project at large.

This significance of the secondary plot is exactly what farrago, the last author to join, ignores: he fails to connect to the already established authors of TSO before throwing in his chapter unsolicited; he does not realize his mistake until after he has added to the narrative (May 20, 2009). Although farrago's contribution annihilates Faltarego's cue at the end of the preceding segment (May 12, 2009), he does not so much interrupt the primary plot. Indeed, it took the other co-authors an entire week to brood over Faltarego's particularly challenging segment without any results (May 14, 2009). It is rather that farrago apparently missed the discussion between Faltarego and m3 on their profile pages during that week about how to proceed from there (May 17, 2009). Upon farrago's failure to connect to the established co-authors before joining them, Faltarego admits that he "get[s] a little '*Gulp*— Uh-oh' reaction when [he] see[s] a new name crop up on something that's been around as long as this story has" (May 21, 2009). Although he placably adds that the newcomer delivered a worthy continuation (ibid.), farrago seems to feel alienated enough to not return. Finally, moonwalker (May 23, 2009) and Faltarego (May 25, 2009) write the last two segments of the story. While m3 welcomes Faltarego's final contribution as "precisely what [she] was thinking" (May 25, 2009), she never writes a follow-up; nor does anybody else, although m3 and moonwalker remain active for another two months encouraging danda, Faltarego, and each other to continue the story (July 31, 2009). Interestingly, they do not encourage farrago to return and thus, via secondary plot, practically exclude him from the entire project. All four established co-authors individually continue to collaborate on other projects and thus continue the secondary plot in their own "branches" of the larger *Protagonize* community.

CONCLUSION

In "Hejira" and "The Smart Ones" it has become evident that through analyzing collaborative digital fiction in terms of a double plot, the double role of the participants as "wreaders" may be accounted for: in contributing to, reading, commenting, and rating the primary text, they are truly "wreaders", whose interaction with each other constitutes a secondary plot. In collaborative writing projects, both plot levels are equally important: instead of the social aesthetics replacing the literary aesthetics, they immediately influence each other, as has become evident in the various dead-end branches in "Hejira" and farrago's unsolicited contribution to "The Smart Ones". In multilinear projects, the tolerance among co-authors for deviations and inconsistencies is greater than in linear narratives where a single incoherency may ruin the entire primary plot and bring the secondary one to a halt. However, alternative story lines as in "Hejira" also result in the co-authors' reduced commitment to the entire project beyond "their own" branch. In linear projects such as "The Smart Ones", once the co-authors have formed a team, it seems they may be joined by others only after previous Web-based social interaction with the already established co-authors and/or upon their permission. In conclusion, a double-plot analysis offers a perspective on collaborative digital writing projects that neither reduces them to "pure literature" nor to "pure social networking", since they are really the dynamic combination of both.

To a certain extent the double-plot analysis may also be applied to offline literary collaborations in the round-robin format and with clearly identifiable text contributions. However, in offline projects there is usually very little evidence of the secondary plot beyond the literary text itself. Yet, readers may still reconstruct the secondary plot from its traces in the literary text, especially where the transitions between authors do not run entirely smoothly. A famous case in point is *The Whole Family* (1908) initiated by William Dean Howells and continued by eleven other writers, where the power struggles between the authors are immediately reflected in revisionary characterizations, the complete invalidation of an entire chapter via a character's "misunderstanding", and metafictional complaints on the "misbehavior" of individual co-authors. There are, however, fundamental differences in the parameters for the secondary plot in offline collaborations:

usually there is a limited number of professional writers involved, who typically complete the project as they are under contract for it. Furthermore, the participants in offline collaborations have multiple roles too, as the co-authors are always also readers of the chapters preceding their own. However, usually there is no established format for rating and commenting on individual contributions, nor is there usually evidence of their negotiations, which renders the secondary plot almost intangible beyond the literary text itself. Therefore, while the double-plot analysis surely highlights a typical aspect of collaborative fiction writing in general, it seems to particularly capture a characteristic of collaborative digital writing: here the secondary plot features prominently in the commentary realm of the platforms, and the double focus of the projects on both plots seems to be an incentive for users to read and participate.

NOTES

1. For different definitions of collaborative offline writing, see Ede and Lunsford (2001) and the essay collection edited by Leonard et al. (1994).
2. Simanowski comes to the conclusion that the interaction between collaborating authors is often "unsocial" rather than mutually supportive because it is heavily shaped by their power struggles for dominance over the text (ibid.).
3. Hence these texts lose attractiveness once they are abandoned or (very rarely) finished.
4. The double-plot analysis may also be applied to collaborations in the wiki format, such as the wiki novel *A Million Penguins* (*AMP*) by Penguin Books and De Montfort University, which was active for five weeks in 2007 and where the secondary plot of the users' editing and inserting links was visible in the "history function". Mason and Thomas (2008) describe the social aesthetics of this wiki novel with the Bakhtinian concept of the carnival, which within a strictly limited period of time "subverts and reverses the established order because all who [partake are] equal and all [are] members of a collective" (Mason and Thomas 2008: "Research", 17). While this concept proves useful for *AMP*, it is not so for collaborative online formats that are unlimited in time, like *WikiStory*, which does not reach the carnivalesque complexity, speed, uncontrollability, and inscrutability of *AMP*. "Ray-Ban Man" on *WikiStory*, for instance, develops very slowly and is less of a mass phenomenon: while it has been viewed over 2,500 times, it was from May 2008 through October 2009 revised only five times by only three users; commentary rarely exceeded monosyllabic and technical descriptions.
5. For how the primary plot may evoke multiple implied authors, see Klaiber (2011). For how the paratextual cues on the authors' identities are discursively constructed, see Page (2012: 125–127).
6. For hypertextual projects with multiple versions, however, it may be argued that the reader-user contributes to the final version of the text after all by choosing her individual path through the links.
7. Simanowski describes collaborative writing as confrontation between egotists (2002: 32). However, whether or not online writing projects are

confrontational very much depends on the collaborative format and also the netiquette of the individual platform. In fact, multilinearity rather *discourages* confrontation. While in offline collaborations usually only one final version of the narrative may be realized and the narrative text is therefore more contested among the authors, in multilinear online formats, several versions of the same story may exist side by side; this openness takes the confrontational edge off the collaborative enterprise.

8. While "early hypertext fictions by Joyce and others have worked to subvert the ideals of clarity and propriety in narrative[, . . . and t]heir rhetoric [. . .] relied heavily on the violation of the expected and conventional order" (Bolter 2001: 129), collaborative online projects usually do not aim at reader disorientation or the violation of clarity and causality, but tend to emulate traditional literary conventions.

9. Coherence is here understood as mostly the effect of the complex narrative dynamics that in the course of narrative progression interrelate textual features with implied values. These do not become fully manifest unless they are progressively being realized by the reader while reading.

10. "Closure [. . .] refers to the way in which a narrative signals its end, whereas completeness refers to the degree of resolution accompanying the closure. Closure need not be tied to the resolution of instabilities and tensions but completeness always" (Phelan 2002: 214). Furthermore, "all parts of a narrative may have consequences for the progression, even if those consequences lie solely in their effect on the *reader's understanding* of the instabilities, tensions, and resolution" (212).

11. What Landow says about the user in "networked textuality" is particularly true for online writing projects on platforms such as *OMM* and *Protagonize*, where the "technology [of the platforms] transforms reader-authors or 'wreaders', because any contribution, any change in the web created by one reader, quickly becomes available to the other readers", who in turn may comment or contribute themselves (Landow 1994: 14, cf. 2006: 234; Simanowski 2001).

12. All original user names are replaced by pseudonyms to protect the users' identity, except for those authors who explicitly gave their permission to mention their real names or real usernames; this is accordingly indicated.

13. In spite of this authorial "permission" for Tina Todd, this section is not continued by her, probably because more than five weeks elapsed before Penny J. answered.

14. Netiquette styles vary considerably from platform to platform: while the social aesthetics of *OMM* prove astonishingly harmonious, *Protagonize*, for instance, seems to allow for more direct critique of creative work.

15. Similarly, Ben Darey first praises a phrase to then place his critique: "that was AWESOME. no doubt.. loved the snippet, except for a few million dollar words.. the [sic] sound nice if you know how to pronounce them, but they are tedious and even offensive if you have to pick up the Webster's to figure them out" (April 8, 2008).

16. Similarly, the inconsistent depiction of Nyssa's character may be held responsible for the abandonment of a snippet where she all of a sudden turns out to be a victim of her family although previously she has been presented as being full of guilt and regret (April 10, 2008)—again there are not comments and no follow-up segments.

17. Eric Rountree (aka Faltarego) explicitly gave his permission to mention his real name and real username.

18. Sharon Flood (aka moonwalker) explicitly gave her permission to mention her real name and real username.

19. Rather than being verifiable facts about the "real" offline identity of a user, personal and private information here primarily serves the discursive constitution and authentication (Williams and Copes 2005: 85) of the respective user's "cyberself" (Waskul 2003) as a member of the larger platform community in general and the particular project-specific community in particular, here as collaborator on TSO.

WORKS CITED

Abbott, H.P. (2008) *The Cambridge Introduction to Narrative* (2nd edition). Cambridge: CUP.

Bell, A., Ensslin, A., Ciccoricco, D., Rustad, H., Laccetti, J., and Pressman, J. (2010) "A [S]creed for Digital Fiction". *electronic book review*, 7 March. Last accessed 20 February 2013 at URL: http://www.electronicbookreview.com/thread/electropoetics/DFINative

Ben-Arie, U. (2009) "The Narrative Communication Structure in Interactive Narrative Works". In *ICIDS 2009*. I.A. Iurgel, E. Zagalo, and P. Petta (eds). Berlin/Heidelberg: Springer, pp. 152–162.

Bolter, J.D. (2001) *Writing Space: Computers, Hypertext, and the Redemption of Print* (2nd edition). Mahwah, NJ: Lawrence Erlbaum.

Booth, W.C. (1983 [1961]) *The Rhetoric of Fiction* (2nd edition). Chicago, IL: University of Chicago Press.

Chatman, S. (1978) *Story and Discourse: Narrative Structure in Fiction and Film*. Ithaca, NY: Cornell UP.

Ede, L., and Lunsford, A.A. (2001) "Collaboration and Concepts of Authorship". *PMLA* 116. 2: 354–369.

Ensslin, A. (2007) *Canonizing Hypertext: Explorations and Constructions*. London: Continuum.

Fabulate.com [online]. Last accessed 31 March 2011 at URL: http://www.fabulate.co.uk/ (terminated project; site expired)

Ficly.com [online]. Last accessed 30 September 2011 at URL: http://ficly.com/

Heibach, C. (2003) *Literatur im elektronischen Raum*. Frankfurt a.M.: Suhrkamp.

Klaiber, I. (2011) "Multiple Implied Authors: How Many Can a Single Text Have?" *Style* 45. 1: 138–152.

Landow, G.P. (1994) "What Is a Critic to Do? Critical Theory in the Age of Hypertext". In *Hyper/Text/Theory*. G.P. Landow (ed). Baltimore: Johns Hopkins UP, pp. 1–47.

———. (2006) *Hypertext 3.0: Critical Theory and New Media in an Era of Globalization*. Baltimore, MD: Johns Hopkins UP.

Lanham, R. (1993) *The Electronic Word: Democracy, Technology and the Arts*. Chicago: Chicago UP.

Leonard, J.S., Wharton, C.E., Davis, R.M., and Harris, J. (1994) (eds). *Authority and Textuality: Current Views of Collaborative Writing*. West Cornwall, CT: Locust Hill.

Mason, B. and Thomas, S. (2008) *A Million Penguins Research Report*. Institute of Creative Technology [online]. Last accessed 31 December 2010 at URL: http://www.ioct.dmu.ac.uk/projects/millionpenguinsanalysis.html (site expired)

Morson, G.S. (1999) "Essential Narrative: Tempics and the Return of Process". In *Narratologies: New Perspectives on Narrative Analysis*. D. Herman (ed). Columbus: Ohio UP, pp. 277–314.

One Million Monkeys [online]. Last accessed 7 July 2011 at URL: http://www.1000000monkeys.com/ (terminated project; site expired)

Page, R. E. (2012) *Stories and Social Media: Identities and Interaction.* New York: Routledge.

Phelan, J. (2002) "Narrative Progression". In *Narrative Dynamics: Essays on Time, Plot, Closure, and Frames.* B. Richardson (ed.). Columbus, OH: Ohio State UP, pp. 211–216.

———. (2007) *Experiencing Fiction: Judgments, Progressions, and the Rhetorical Theory of Narrative.* Columbus, OH: Ohio State UP.

Prince, G. (2003) *Dictionary of Narratology.* Lincoln, NB: University of Nebraska Press.

Protagonize.com [online]. Last accessed 15 October 2011 at URL: http://www.protagonize.com/

Rettberg, S. (2005) "All Together Now: Collective Knowledge, Collective Narratives, and Architectures of Participation". In *Digital Experience: Design, Aesthetics, Practice: Proceedings of the 2005 DAC Conference.* IT University of Copenhagen, pp. 99–109 [online]. Last accessed 20 February 2013 at URL: http://retts.net/documents/cnarrativeDAC.pdf

Simanowski, R. (2000) "'Beim Bäcker': Collaborative Sex und soziale Ästhetik". *Dichtung-Digital* [online] 9. Last accessed 20 February 2013 at URL: www.dichtung-digital.de/2000/Simanowski/15-Feb

———. (2001) "Autorschaften in Digitalen Medien". *Text + Kritik* 152: *Digitale Literatur*: 3–12.

———. (2002) *Interfiction: Vom Schreiben im Netz.* Frankfurt a.M.: Suhrkamp.

Stillinger, J. (1991) *Multiple Authorship and the Myth of Solitary Genius.* New York: OUP.

StoryPassers.com [online]. Last accessed 2 October 2011 at URL: http://www.storypassers.com/

Toolan, M. (2013) "Coherence". In *The Living Handbook of Narratology.* P. Hühn et al. (eds). Hamburg: Hamburg UP [online]. Last accessed 24 June 2010 at URL http://hup.sub.uni-hamburg.de/lhn/index.php/Coherence

Tyrkkö, J. (2009) "Hypertext and Streams of Consciousness: Coherence Redefined". In *Internet Fictions.* I. Hotz-Davies, A. Kirchhofer, and S. Leppänen (eds). Newcastle: Cambridge Scholars, pp. 2–22.

Waskul, D. D. (2003) *Self-Games and Body-Play: Personhood in Online Chat and Cybersex.* New York: Lang.

WeBook.com [online]. Last accessed 15 October 2011 at URL: http://www.webook.com/

Wenger, E. (1998) *Communities of Practice: Learning, Meaning, and Identity.* Cambridge: CUP.

———. (2006) "Communities of Practice: A Brief Introduction". Last accessed 20 February 2013 at URL: http://www.ewenger.com/theory/

Williams, P. and Copes, H. (2005) "'How Edge Are You?' Constructing Authentic Identities and Subcultural Boundaries in a Straightedge Internet Forum". *Symbolic Interaction* 28.1: 67–89.

WikiStory.com [online]. Last accessed 15 October 2011 at URL: http://www.wikistory.com/wiki/WikiStory_Home

Section III

Semiotic-Rhetorical Approaches

9 (In-)between Word, Image, and Sound

Cultural Encounter in Pullinger and Joseph's *Flight Paths*

Hans Kristian Rustad,
Hedmark University College, Norway

The Middle East protests that started in December 2010 in Tunisia—known as the Arab Spring—demonstrated the destabilizing power of the World Wide Web. Following the tragic incident of the man who burned himself to death in protest at his treatment by police, a revolutionary wave of mass demonstrations emerged in the Arab world. The protests were not only in the streets however; social media such as blogs and Twitter played a significant part in disseminating information and voices to the Arab people and to the rest of the world. The power of these digital forms of communication within the Arab Spring represent some of the most obvious examples of how the World Wide Web enables ordinary people to make their views known, and for the subaltern to write back. Networked and digital media offer new solutions for postcolonial theory, whether by—as the use of social media during the Arab Spring shows—permitting individual voices to be heard, or—as this article will demonstrate—by dismantling simplified binary oppositions such as "we" and "the other", "first" and "third world". Such opportunities are not as easily offered by print. Landow (2006) writes, for instance, that during a research stay in Zimbabwe, he learned that the intellectuals there produced a lot of criticism that "remained unknown to European and American postcolonialists because it never entered the distribution channels for printed books and periodicals outside Africa" (345).

The modern novel, argues Landow, is a literary genre that derives from print culture, which makes it a major colonial imposition on the "the other" (350). Fiction that needs to be read in networked and programmable media represents a movement from print to digital. It represents a movement that brings radical changes in conceptions of the immigrant and the colonialized. This is not to say that digital fiction provides authenticity on behalf of the colonialized. Rather I would claim that digital fiction represents new possibilities for telling stories about migration and presenting cultural encounters. Its multimodal dimension represents a movement away from print novel as the dominant Western genre for literature about migration, and hence an equalization of different modes of representation. Similarly, the network media and the multilinear structure represent a potential dissolving and dissemination of the authorial voice because it can offer a place for different voices to emerge and thus resist simple and unitary models of subjectivity.

This chapter presents an analysis of Kate Pullinger and Chris Joseph's *Flight Paths* (2007).[1] It focuses on how the interaction between different semiotic modes contributes to exploration of issues surrounding immigration and cultural encounter. "Cultural encounter" is here understood as encounters between characters from different cultures as a result of migration.[2] More precisely I will explore how immigration and the cultural encounter in *Flight Paths* are represented via the multimodal interplay of text, video, photography, music, and sound, and I will therefore approach *Flight Paths* from a semiotic point of view. Semiotic theory is concerned with the properties of signs and their functions—in other words why and how (some) things signify. A semiotic resource, or "representamen", as Peirce (1956) calls it, "is something which stands to somebody for something in some respect or capacity" (99). Since *Flight Paths* is a multimodal work, I will look not only at what and how a semiotic resource in the work represents something else but also how the different modes work together. On the one hand, this calls for theory that explores the relation between different modes, such as the theory of word and image provided by Mitchell (1996), and semiotic theory, such as that of Barthes (1977) and van Leeuwen (2005). On the other hand, when approaching the multimodal dimension of *Flight Paths*, the analysis requires an awareness of the historical context of the relation, or *encounter*, between modes and between art forms.

FLIGHT PATHS

Flight Paths is a hybrid literary work about immigration, written by Pullinger and Joseph with contributions from readers. It is a story about Yacub and Harriet and their encounter, represented through written text, video, photography, graphics, music, and sound effects. Yacub is a stowaway on an airplane from Pakistan, on his way to the 'promised land' and Harriet is a London housewife. They meet at the parking lot outside a supermarket just as Yacub falls off the landing gear of the airplane and lands on Harriet's car. The fall totally destroys the car, but bizarrely Yacub survives the fall without injury. The incident is presented through a mixture of pictures and sounds, which, along with a short and surprising dialog between Harriet and Yacub, creates a surreal atmosphere.

The narrative is comprised of five parts entitled: "Yacub in Dubai", "Yacub at the airport", "Harriet driving", "Dark mass", and "Paths crossing". The five episodes could be read in any order, but are numbered from one to five and organized on the front page in a manner that implies an intended sequence for readers. Each episode contains a linear sequence of events, and the reader proceeds through these events by clicking on the Urdu symbol for "go" or "forward".

In short, the narrative develops from a clichéd binary opposition of the poor black man and the rich white woman, and ends in a complex mix of structures that exceed binary models and presents the encounter between the two as what we might call the borderline of the present. Here *Flight Paths* evokes Bhabha's notion of migration in our globalized contemporary culture: "in the *fin de siècle*, we find ourselves in the moment of transit where space and time cross to produce complex figures of difference and identity, past and present, inside and outside, inclusion and exclusion" (1994: 2). According to Bhabha, the knowledge of "the other" is not to be discovered through established concepts and conventional (binary) models. Knowledge of "the other" appears when one moves beyond these models, that is, away from the center and toward the margin. According to Bhabha, one has to enter the Third Space to be able to negotiate identity, subjectivity, agency, nationness, cultural value, and binary opposition such as black and white, first and third, host and immigrant.

> It is that Third Space, tough unrepresentable in itself, which constitutes the discursive conditions of enunciation that ensure that the meaning and symbols of culture have no primordial unity or fixity; that even the same signs can be appropriated, translated, rehistoricized and read anew. (1994: 55)

The Third Space is obviously not a concrete space, but an in-between space that belongs neither to the one nor the other.

In addition to the narrative about Yacub and Harriet, *Flight Paths* uses Web 2.0 technologies to tell its immigration story. This makes it possible for readers to participate in the work by submitting their contributions, and thus to offer some solutions to the postcolonial dilemma concerning how to write fiction about immigrants. More specifically, the five fiction episodes of *Flight Paths* are linked to a website created in *Netvibes*, a Web-based page aggregator application that brings together content like photos, videos, social networks, etc., from online sources in a single page. The website also allows readers to give feedback or contribute to *Flight Paths* by adding photos, sounds, or videos, or by telling their own story about immigration. It also serves as an exhibition site where submitted works can be explored, and provides information about *Flight Paths*'s authors, other contributors, and additional information about airplane stowaways.

WORD, IMAGE, AND SOUND: A SHORT
HISTORICAL APPROACH

Contemporary digital fiction is to a great extent hybrid and multimodal, combining art forms and semiotic systems. It also draws on conventions, traditions, and strategies that can be identified as belonging to traditionally separated art forms and media, such as film, graphics, music, and literature.

As a result, it inscribes itself in the history of the different art forms (and media) and in the historical discussion of the relation between art forms.

Hayles (2002) describes contemporary digital fiction, or what she also refers to as "the second generation" of electronic literature, as multimodal, containing more visual and auditory attributes than "the first generation", that is, the early work of hypertext fiction and poetry that were primarily text-based. According to Hayles the shift from first to second generation took place around 1995, with Shelley Jackson's *Patchwork Girl* (1995) as an "appropriate culminating work" (Hayles 2008: 7) of the first generation. The shift from first to second generation should not be seen as a break (see e.g. Ciccoricco 2007). Rather, multimodal digital fiction has increased extensively over the last decade as a consequence of both the development of hypermedia software and more general tendencies in contemporary art and literature. Indeed, works like *Victory Garden* (Moulthrop 1991), *Iaktagarens förmåga att ingripa* (*The watcher's ability to interfere*, Tallmo 1992), and *Patchwork Girl* have a literary form that is to a great extent determined by print literature, but they also contain visual and sound material that makes them early examples of *multimodal* digital fiction.

In her discussion of the second generation, Hayles emphasizes the capabilities of the Web. "With the movement to the Web," she argues, "the nature of electronic literature changed as well" (Hayles 2008: 6). Of course, to some extent the development of literature is influenced by technological advancements (c.f. Kittler 1986). But we might also see the development in literature and other art forms as a driving force for generating new technology. It seems reasonable to say that digital fiction is both dependent on a technological development and is an answer to an aesthetic development and perhaps an aesthetic need. Consequently, as a literary form where different art forms combine, digital fiction not only inscribes itself in a technological context, but it must also be seen in relation to historical tendencies in art and literature.

Digital fiction is thus an aesthetic practice that advocates the relation and combination of different art forms. In that sense it corresponds with the tradition of "*Ut pictura poesis*", a tradition based on the Roman poet Horace's work *Ars poetica* (published c. 18 BC; here from Horace and Brink: 1971), which emphasizes the similarities between art forms. In *Ars poetica* Horace compares painting and literature and points out that when it comes to content and function, the two have much in common. In an Aristotelian mimesis perspective, they both, according to Horace, strive for an imitation of human action. He therefore sees the value of making art forms collaborate in their representation of something else.

Throughout the history of the relationship between art forms there has also been a tendency toward a more normative approach concerning the art forms' hierarchical value as art. This is for instance the case in Lessing's *Laokoon: Oder über die Grenzen der Malerei und Poesie* (1766). Lessing here argues for a clear distinction between art forms, and claims that art forms such as painting and literature should not be mixed. The reason for keeping the two separate, according to Lessing, is that they are based on two different organization principles. Paintings are spatial and thus best suited to represent the world spatially, while literature (most often) is temporal and should then represent events that unfold in time. Lessing advocates keeping the two art forms distinct because he believes that they are each based on different semiotic systems. As a result he perceives a fundamental relation between, for instance, literature and music because both unfold in time. While literature and music are based on different semiotic systems, they are both temporal art forms. Thus, both, according to Lessing at least, are suitable for representing sequences of events.

WORD, IMAGE, AND SOUND: AN ANALYTICAL APPROACH

The Laokoonian approach to the separation of art forms has been both maintained and challenged by contemporary theorists (e.g. Greenberg 2001 [1940]; Barthes 1977; Mitchell 1996; van Leeuwen 2005; Hayles 2008). In his analyses of art practice, art critic Greenberg (2001 [1940]) uses Lessing as a starting point for arguing for purity in arts. He claims that purity "in art consists in the acceptance, willing acceptance, of the limitations of the medium of the specific art" (566). Greenberg's point is that each art form defines itself in relation to its medium, and artists should therefore accept and be true to the limits of that medium. Painting, which is the art form that Greenberg is most concerned with (his main purpose is to advocate purity in the early twentieth-century avant-garde and abstract paintings) should accept the flatness of the canvas and not make use of techniques to create illusions of depth.

A similar argument for the separation of photography and literature is made by Valéry in his essay "The Centenary of Photography" (1980 [1936]). On the one hand Valéry's contribution needs to be seen in light of the high modernists' call for purity in art, but at the same time Valéry argues that written language must be used for what it does best:

> If photography, which is now capable of conveying colour and movement, not to mention depth, discourages us from describing, it is because we are thus reminded of the limits of articulate language and are advised, as writers, to put our tools to a use more befitting their true nature. (193)

In other words, since photography is the best medium for capturing the detail of an object, the function of literature should, according to Valéry, be abstraction.

Less normative and more descriptive approaches are found in contemporary visual theory (e.g. Barthes 1977; Mitchell 1996; van Leeuwen 2005).

Mitchell (1996), for example, identifies the relation between word and image as either "word as image" or "word vs. image" (54). The former denotes a congruent and unified interaction between the two, which Mitchell describes as "their tendency to unite, dissolve, or change places" (54). The latter, on the other hand, signifies a tension and divergence between word and image: "word vs. image denotes the tension, difference, and opposition between these terms" (54). A text that follows this logic would then guide the reader's attention toward the differences between the modes. A relation described as "word vs. image" can then open up for a *liminal* space, or what I earlier referred to as the Third Space. When the tension highlights the differences between the modes of representation, this could be qualified as a liminal space because the aesthetic and interpretative outcome of this tension is something that does not belong to either.

No matter how the relation between modes is defined, we need to remember that these relations do not all sit in fixed categories. Mitchell (1996), for example, explains that the relation between modes should be seen as a dialectic trope where the identified relations always resist constancy. In that sense, there is always a tension between congruency and divergence: "[b]oth of these relations, difference and likeness, must be thought of simultaneously as a vs/as in order to grasp the peculiar character of this relationship" (54). "Vs/as" here denotes that the one relation between words and images always appears simultaneously. A systematic approach to the multimodal dimension of digital fiction must thus consider a whole set of relations and distinctions that are at play in the work. Moreover it is the dynamic play between these relations that enables us to call attention to why and how these make a difference. In the following analysis, I am going to apply the theoretical concepts outlined above to *Flight Paths* in order to show how the multimodal dimension of digital fiction can be examined systematically.

READING THE MULTIMODAL INTERPLAY: A CULTURAL AND GEOGRAPHICAL LEITMOTIF

In *Flight Paths*, videos, photographs, graphics, music, sound, and written texts are to a great extent collaborating, particularly in the two first episodes. In episodes one and two, we read about Yacub going to Dubai to find employment, so that he can support his family, and also about Yacub climbing into an airplane's landing gear to go to the UK to get a job. In episode one, Yacub narrates in the first lexia: "I went to Dubai from my home because I heard I could earn good money". The music which could be identified as or gives association to Arabian music, places Yacub culturally and geographically, and thus confirms the information given to us from the written language and the visuals. The episode contains pictures of workers and skyscrapers in Dubai. Further, when, for example, Yacub refers to a

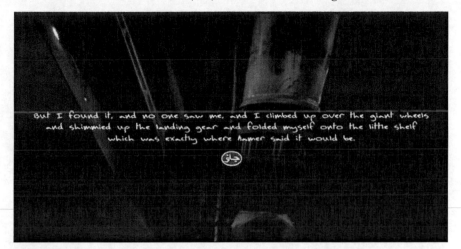

But I found it, and no one saw me, and I climbed up over the giant wheels and shimmied up the landing gear and folded myself onto the little shelf which was exactly where Ammer said it would be.

Figure 9.1 Screenshot from *Flight Paths'* episode three, where Yacub is about to enter the airplane's landing gear. Original image by Paul Hart, http://www.flicker.com/people/atomicjeep

man who has told him about the workers' camps in Dubai, a picture of a man appears concurrently.

In the first two episodes, the different modes of representation support each other in a congruent relationship. We might say that they are used for what they can do best, based on their "functional specialization" or what social semiotic theory often refers to as "affordances" (Van Leeuwen 2005).[3]

One of the pictures in the "Yacub at the airport" lexia shows a detailed and close-up view of the airplane's wheels and landing gear where Yacub finds a small place to hide. Here the picture represents the location where Yacub will stay, as well as depicting an authentic view of the landing gear and putting us in an immediate relation to the object. As a homodiegetic narrator, Yacub provides us with a first-person account of the scene. His narrative is then combined with photographical images in a manner that evokes Valéry's notion of the relation between photography and language, as described above.

Indeed the photography provides a kind of window to reality. Bolter (2006) argues that "most digital artists today reject the aesthetic of transparent representation" (110). At the same time, however, he also puts forward the notion that "our popular culture wants transparency in the texts" (110). Transparency then stages a single and homogeneous "realistic" world that gives the reader the impression of seeing through the complex representation. According to Bolter and Grusin (1999), transparency is a strategy that permits the reader to forget the media in question and the semiotic resources as representations for something else. It gives the reader the impression of being in an "immediate relationship to the contents of that medium" (23–24). The semiotic resources appear not as manipulated but as natural. This is the case when Yacub climbs into the plane's landing gear. In the screenshot above (see Figure 9.1), we are positioned in an immediate relation to the landing gear. Through the first-person point of view, the photography creates an illusion, as if we are facing the landing gear in real life, and not through a computer screen.

In episode three, "Harriet driving", the dominant relation between modes is still congruent; however, congruency here follows a different strategy to those enacted in episodes one and two. The narrative shifts from the point of view of Yacub to the point of view of the London housewife Harriet, a move that is also geographical and cultural (from East to West). Here different video clips represent Harriet's view of Richmond, London, as she drives to the supermarket. We are, in other words immediately, through the work's multimodal dimension, placed in a different cultural milieu to the one presented by Yacub. The videos and the photographs loop and are presented in multiple windows. The music is also more typically Western compared to the music in episode one. It marks the geographical and cultural shift, as well as the shift in point of view, and situates both the reader and the event in a Western context. The written narrative is focalized through Harriet and presents her thoughts and reflections on the Western society that she is part of, and we learn that she and her family live affluently.

Since the different modes of representation appear in distinct frames and windows in episode three, the fragmented arrangement acts reflexively. Instead of providing a "window out to the world" (c.f. Bolter and Grusin 1999: 31), the modes compete for our attention, and, instead of being a text that offers a place (or a screen) where we can immerse in the content, we notice the modes at play, as well as how they are combined. This makes it explicit that what appears on the screen is a representation and appears as a consequence of a play between media and between sign systems. In the combination of media and modes, we are asked to enjoy and take pleasure in the media and the mediation process.

The change of narrator and point of view, as well as the visual and aural differences between episode one and two, on the one hand, and episode three, on the other, emphasize the contrast between the poor and the rich world. This contrast is even more accentuated with Harriet's ironic opening remark concerning the wealth in the Western world; she needs to go to the supermarket, "otherwise my family will starve". Harriet here establishes herself as a counter voice: "While there are plenty of wars and cataclysms happening elsewhere, as far as I can see, stuck as I am in the one-way system, Richmond is its usual placid, well-fed self this week". This cultural and geographical contrast, which appears in the analysis of the multimodal interplay, is as we shall see also highlighted by the composition of the screen in episode four.

READING THE COMPOSITION

In episode four, "Dark mass", the relationship between the modes is different from the first three episodes. Here the world of Yacub and the world of Harriet are represented on the same screen, which is divided into two segments, with Yacub lying in the dark room in the airplane's landing gear, represented on the left side, while Harriet, who is shopping at a supermarket, is represented on the right. Yacub's side of the screen is black, as an iconic representation of the dark room that Yacub is stuck in on his flight. The black screen also implies that Yacub's destiny is not very hopeful (statistically airplane stowaways seldom make it to the intended destination). The written text underscores the fact that Yacub's chances are small: "I am crushed into this too small space; I have been here for an eternity. . . . Freezing hot, then burning cold". In contrast, the right-hand side of the screen shows a picture from inside a supermarket, as if representing the view of Harriet as she shops.

One of the most common or conventionalized interpretations of the relation between information on the left and on the right in a Western society is described by van Leeuwen (2005) as the relation between given and new information. In relation to horizontal organization, van Leeuwen writes that "the distinction between left and right has been an important source of meaning and often also of morality" (201). He points out that "the element placed on the left will be presented as though it is given, that is, although it is something already known to the receiver. . . . The element on the right will be presented as new, that is, as something not yet known to the receiver" (204).

Reading the composition in episode four in a Western context would imply reading the information on the left-hand side as familiar and the information on the right-hand side as new and unknown. In that sense, Yacub and his cultural context should appear as known, while Harriet and her Western context should be the unknown culture. This makes sense because we have already been introduced to Yacub and his situation. In other words, as Western readers we are asked to identify with Yacub. But representing an immigration story in a multimodal digital work makes the idea of known-unknown more complex. Seeing and reading from Yacub's point of view would mean following the Arabian convention and reading the composition from right to left. The Western idea of known-unknown is thus turned upside down. It is not likely that a western reader would read the composition following the Arabian convention because the conventional reading direction of left-right is simply too strong. Still, *Flight Paths* presents a bi-directional idea of given and new in which the subject positions are not fixed, but float between known and unknown, between given and new, and between "I" and "the other".

Even if Yacub is being identified with the familiar perspective, it should be underlined here that *Flight Paths* is written and edited by Western authors. The work's utilization of technological affordances like Web 2.0, as mentioned in the introduction, underscores that *Flight Paths* is a narrative whose ambition is to present an immigration story that provides an alternative view on immigration to what Said (1978) calls "Orientalism", that is, the West's construction of the colonized. By creating a work and a platform where people can contribute by adding movies, photographs, audio, etc., *Flight Paths* aspires to be less a story about immigration presented solely from the point of view of the Western author and more a work with a potential of bringing in different voices and giving pluralistic perspectives on immigration.

IN-BETWEEN SIGNS, IN-BETWEEN CULTURES

Flight Paths is, as pointed out, an immigration story, not about settlement in a new country, but about the journey to a new country. A central motif in *Flight Paths* is therefore the transition. After traveling from Pakistan to Dubai, and then returning to his home, Yacub starts on his journey from Pakistan to the UK. The screen composition in the first part of episode four emphasizes that *Flight Paths* is, predominantly, a story about an immigrant, focusing on Yacub as he travels from one country to another. In this sense, the left-right organization puts weight on the transfer, that is, that Yacub is traveling from the East to the West, represented onscreen as the left and the right.

The journey motif is fairly common in literature, with Homer's *Odyssey* being the archetype of a literary journey: the protagonist goes on a journey, faces trials and tribulations, survives the problems, and gets rewarded. The reward could be something physical, but the main reward—the real reason for the journey—is the gaining of new experiences and confirmation of strength. In other words, it is not the reward itself that is the goal for the journey; rather, it is traveling and meeting new people and new situations. In *Flight Paths*, the transition is imperative for opening up the Third Space and the cultural encounter that takes place.

Yacub's main goal is to arrive in the UK, just like it was Odysseus's goal to return home to Penelope. And there is nothing in the story about his journey that tells us that he has gained new experiences (except learning that the room with the landing gear is too small and too cold) or learned new things about himself. Hence Yacub could be classified as a flat character with hardly any development. Still, the places where the different events take place connote change, transaction, and interaction, and involve vehicles which transport the protagonists from one place to another. Yacub is on an airplane, Harriet is driving her car, and she is in a supermarket and later on a parking lot. These are places where changes, new experiences, and negotiations of identity take place. Rather than being a means for psychological growth, the journey and the places of the events give hope and indicate that a cultural transition will happen.

The climax of the journey is Yacub's fall from the airplane in the last part of episode four. As the aircraft puts the gear down to prepare for landing, Yacub loses his grip and starts falling. Harriet, who is moving toward her car with her loaded trolley, simultaneously stops and looks up into the sky: "and then for some reason, I have no idea why, I look up, into the clear blue autumnal sky". She sees Yacub falling. This is a climax because he literally falls toward the ground and certain death, but also because the fall is the entrance, the threshold, to the cultural encounter. The climax and dramatic turn of the narrative is anchored by the multimodal interplay. The music and sound effects are cut short and interrupted by a sharp, piercing noise that lasts for a couple of seconds before stopping to leave silence. With the appearance of the sharp sound, the border that until this point has divided the screen in two, disappears and is replaced with a video of a blue sky. The audiovisual changes thus represent the dramatic change in Yacub's circumstances. With the silence and the video of the blue sky, Yacub's and Harriet's thoughts appear as written text on the screen. There is no panic reaction. Harriet, who has discovered a black dot falling from the sky, freezes. Yacub shows no sign of fear, but stays calm and self-controlled as if this is what he has wished for: "Suddenly, I am released. . . . I am set free".

The event takes place neither in the airplane, nor in the supermarket, nor on the parking lot, but in-between these two locations. This in-between space is a threshold that opens up for the cultural encounter that is soon to happen. According to Skaret (2011: 46), literature about cultural encounters often contains thresholds, which she reads as liminal spaces, that is, as in-between spaces where cultural change and encounters take place. In this space, Skaret points out, there are movements between different cultures, identities, values, categories, etc. Bhabha defines liminality as the place where differences cease to exist:

> The stairwell as liminal space, in-between the designations of identity, becomes the process of symbolic interaction, the connective tissue that constructs the difference between upper and lower, black and white. The hither and thither of the stairwell, the temporal movement and passage that it allows, prevents identities at either end of it from settling into primordial polarities. (Bhabha 1994: 5 cited in Skaret 2011: 47)

As mentioned earlier, Third Space can be understood as the presence of an in-between space that does not belong to either of the two cultures. It is in this in-between space that the negotiation of culture and cultural identity takes place because borders between cultures are blurred or no longer exist.

For Yacub, the sky, the open space between him and the Earth, is a way— if not the only way—down. But the sky is also something more than just a passage. It is neither heaven nor Earth, but something in-between the two. It is a space where culturally constructed and inherited dichotomies cease to exist. In that sense, Yacub's fall represents a threshold leading to the impending cultural encounter.

Yacub's destination is the parking lot. "I'm here, at last", are his last words at the end of episode four. He crashes into Harriet's car, and the screen goes black, accompanied by a crashing sound. Despite the fact that Yacub falls from an airplane and lands on Harriet's car, he survives the fall and suffers no injuries. Harriet describes this as follows: "He looked perfect, lying there, the roof of my car like a crumpled velvet blanket. Not dead at all". The parking lot is significant for understanding what happens in this encounter. Just as the sky can be seen as a threshold or in-between space, the parking lot is a space that is in-between because it is neither the supermarket nor home. It is hardly a destination in itself, but rather a space in-between, a transitional place that people pass through to get somewhere else.

The way the modes are combined in episode five indicates that the parking lot represents such an in-between space. The music and the visuals are no longer leitmotifs that help us to situate the events in a defined place. While in the first three episodes, places are represented through music, video, and photography, in episode five the semiotic resources as cultural and geographical indicators are blurred. They do not represent cultural differences, but rather the merging of what until now have been represented as divergent cultures. The car wreck appears on the screen in a blurring combination of graphics and photographs so that the realistic and unrealistic appear inseparable on the screen, both representing and not representing the object. Likewise the music in the episode blends with the sound of an aircraft as well as noises from a supermarket and a parking lot. Simultaneously past and present appear as one: the airplane represents the past (i.e. the sound that Yacub hears while stuck in the airplane's landing gear), and the sound of supermarket trolleys being pushed over a parking lot represents the present. The mixture of sounds from different events, places, and times thus emphasizes that the world of Yacub and the world of Harriet have collided and opened up for an in-between space where differences such as time, place, culture, East-West, native-immigrant, and host-guest, have merged.

HEGEMONIC INDETERMINACY

Flight paths can be seen as presenting a rather naïve and harmonic view on immigration, where differences concerning language and cultural baggage are presented as uncomplicated. In the cultural encounter at the parking lot, the language is no longer a barrier for communication. The same goes, it seems, for Yacub's cultural background. One could of course argue that an immigrant's cultural background is something that prevents smooth immigration, but in the encounter between Harriet and Yacub, this is not an issue.

The use of English as the dominant language for communication opens up for a criticism of the work for being too Anglocentric. Ashcroft et al.

(2004) for instance remind us of the power of the English language "with its signification of authority" (7). Still, the communication situation emphasizes the Third Space in the sense that it embodies changed conceptions of language, space, and time. As this analysis has shown, in *Flight Paths* it is predominantly videos, photographs, music, and other sound elements rather than written language that represent and highlight different cultures and their merging. That Yacub speaks in fluent English following his crash to the ground ("And then he sat up and said, in perfect English [in that tiny moment I remember being surprised by this], 'Am I dead?' ".) implies that the differences between Yacub and Harriet are predominantly nonverbal. The fact that they communicate in perfect English not only highlight the work's view on English as the global language, but it also suggests that Yacub has left his position as an immigrant and fully become an English citizen. This is critical for the understanding of the cultural encounter in *Flight Paths*, and the divergence between the work's use of language and the work's audiovisual dimension. While pictures and sound elements merge and give room for the appearance of a Third Space, the language is in opposition to this appearance. *Flight Paths* then establishes Yacub as an immigrant, but simultaneously conceals this position in his dialogue with Harriet by giving him a hegemonic position.

The only indication of differences in the language situation is emphasized in the use of different typography. Yacub's and Harriet's voices are given in written language, but they are represented in different fonts. Yacub's voice is presented on the screen in italics, while Harriet's voice is in regular font. The italics, in other words, are a semiotic resource that serves to mark that Yacub and Harriet speak different languages. When they meet in episode five, both voices are represented in regular font, which signifies not only that they speak the same language (which is English according to Harriet), but that the differences between them no longer exist. The lack of italics as a signifier of different languages here underscores the floating of subject positions. Yacub is no more an immigrant than Harriet is, and Harriet is no more a host than Yacub.

The narrative ends with a cultural encounter that deconstructs what Bhabha calls primordial polarities. The somewhat surrealistic dialogue between Harriet and Yacub in the end underlines a hegemonic indeterminacy. The boundary between host and guest is blurred when Yacub suggests that they should go to Harriet's place and eat. Harriet does not respond to Yacub's suggestion with hostility. Rather she behaves as a welcoming host and takes Yacub home for a meal. According to Skaret (2011: 125), in postcolonial theory, hospitality is recognized as a form of gift that can be given to others.[4] Harriet is the Western citizen and the one that in normal circumstances has the opportunity to invite Yacub home. After the crash, Harriet is for obvious reasons in some sort of shock and not able to think clearly and react. She relates: "But there was only silence. The sound of my breathing. The sound of me staring. The sound of me not knowing what to do". But when Yacub invites himself home to her place, Harriet immediately, and with no sign of intolerance or prejudice, replies: "'okay' . . . 'we'll get a taxi'".

In the scene, both Yacub and Harriet have some agency. The power is in other words not something that belongs to Harriet, as a Western citizen, but something that must be seen as a dynamic feature that continually alters between Harriet and Yacub. By letting Yacub invite himself home to Harriet, *Flight Paths* offers a view on immigration and cultural encounter that makes the border between host and guest, native and immigrant, blurry. Food is here a semiotic code that indicates subjectivity and cultural capital, and it is a means to transform nature (raw meat) into culture (prepared meat) (see e.g. Lèvi-Strauss 1986; Chandler 2002). In this scene, it serves as a manifestation of a social interaction. By letting Yacub in a relatively polite way invite himself home to Harriet's house for a meal, *Flight Paths* shows that food is a means for social and cultural encounter and a shared cultural code—something that they have in common.

AN ENCOUNTER IN-BETWEEN

Two questions have been explored in this chapter: 1) To what extent does *Flight Paths* utilize the potential of networked and programmable media to overcome some of the postcolonial challenges in its story about immigration and cultural encounter? and 2) What kind of immigrant story is *Flight Paths*?

To understand the postcolonial situation, Landow (2006) argues for a new aesthetics, one that represents a change from the linear, univocal, closed, authoritative narrative that involves passive encounters to a nonlinear, multivocal, open, and nonhierarchical narrative. He argues that the value of social and networked media is its multivocality and its invitation to decentering and redefinition of identities and cultures. Landow writes that new media "provides a paradigm, a way of thinking about postcolonial issues that continually serves to remind us of the complex factors at issue" (356). By opening up for different voices, combined in a hypertextual network structure, and presented through verbal, visual, and aural modes of representation, digital fiction offers a place for negotiation of (cultural) differences. *Flight Paths* is organized in a linear sequence. In that sense, it does not exploit the potential offered by the media to combine different languages, cultures, histories, and experiences in complex hypertextual structures that might change our conceptions of these. Still, as I have argued, *Flight Paths*'s multimodal dimension creates a narrative composed of semiotic in-between spaces where homogeneity is rejected in favor of multivocality and heterogeneity. In these semiotic in-between spaces, meaning, personal identity, and history are mixed. In that sense, our notion of these might be negotiated. The tension between the verbal language's and the other modes' representation of the cultural encounter therefore reminds us of the complexity and challenge involved in presenting a story about immigration.

To understand what kind of immigrant story *Flight Paths* is, and how the cultural encounter appears in the work, it is necessary to read and interpret the multimodal interplay and the arrangement of the semiotic resources on the screen. This, as I have argued, is where the cultural encounter is represented. The different journeys that take place in the work allow us to read *Flight Paths* as an immigration narrative about cultural encounter. Yacub travels first to Dubai and then to the UK, and the different modes in the work as well as the interactions between them contribute to this postcolonial reading. The visuals represent the different places in Dubai, at the airport, in the streets of Richmond, or at the supermarket. Similarly, the music and different sounds anchor the events to different places and cultures. In other words, the modes draw attention to cultural differences. At the end of the work, these differences cease, and the two characters' situation and experiences are equalized in the cultural encounter that appears as an in-between space. Again the multimodal interplay here highlights the encounter as taking place in such an in-between space. Sounds and visuals merge, so that the border between the different cultures blurs, again allowing Yacub's world and Harriet's world to integrate. Instead of making the difference between the cultures the main focus, *Flight Paths* ends with a focus on the new elements that arise in the encounter. Here, the audiovisual modes force us to pay less attention to one of the two worlds, and instead immerse ourselves in the combination of the two and in-between the two. A third culture appears that is neither of the two. Hence it is fair to say that multimodality has provided digital fiction with new affordances for representation including, as this analysis of *Flight Paths* has shown, immigration and cultural encounters. The incident and the encounter at the parking lot in episode five function as an interlinking network where the generic feature cannot be equated with any of the predefined cultures.

NOTES

1. Since this chapter was written, Pullinger and Joseph have added a new episode to *Flight Paths*. This sixth episode called "Jack meets Yacub" has not been taken into consideration in the present analysis.
2. In her doctoral dissertation about cultural encounter in picture books, Skaret (2011) defines cultural encounter in a similar way.
3. "Affordances" is defined by van Leeuwen (2005) as "the potential uses of a given object, stemming from the perceivable properties of the object" (273).
4. Skaret here refers to Rosello's book, *Postcolonial Hospitality* (2001) as a crucial work for the development of knowledge about hospitality.

WORKS CITED

Barthes, R. (1977). "The Rhetoric of the Image". In *Image, Music, Text*. London: Fontana Press.
Bhabha, H. (1994). *The Location of Culture*. London/New York: Routledge.
Bolter, J.D. (2006). "The Desire for Transparency in an Era of Hybridity". *Leonardo* 39. 2: 109–111.
Bolter, J.D. and Grusin, R. (1999). *Remediation*. Cambridge: MIT.
Chandler, D. (2002). *Semiotics: The Basics*. London/New York: Routledge.
Ciccoricco, D. (2007). *Reading Network Fiction*. Tuscaloosa: University of Alabama Press.
Greenberg, C. (2001 [1940]). "Towards a Newer Laokoon". In *Clement Greenberg: A Critic's Collection*. K. Wilkin et al. (ed). Princeton: Porland Art Museum.
Hayles, K. (2002). *Writing Machines*. Cambridge: MIT.
Hayles, K. (2008). *Electronic Literature: New Horizons for the Literary*. Notre Dame, IN: University of Notre Dame.
Horace, Q. and Brink, C.O. (1971). *The "Arc Poetica"*. Cambridge: Cambridge University Press.
Jackson, S. (1995). *Patchwork Girl*. Watertown, MA: Eastgate Systems.
Landow, G. (2006). *Hypertext 3.0*. Baltimore: Johns Hopkins University Press.
Levi-Strauss, C. (1986). *Introduction to Science of Mythology*. London: Penguin books.
Kittler, F.A. (1986). *Grammophon, Film, Typewriter*. Berlin: Brinkmann & Bose.
Mitchell, W.J.C. (1996). "Word and Image". In *Critical Terms for Art History*. R. Nelson and R. Shiff (eds). Chicago: University of Chicago Press.
Moulthrop, S. (1991). *Victory Garden*. Watertown, MA: Eastgate Systems.
Peirce, C.S. (1956). *The Philosophy of Peirce: Selected Writings*. J. Buchler (ed). London: Routledge and Kegan Paul.
Pullinger, K. and Joseph, C. (2007). *Flight Paths*. Last accessed 20 February 2013 at URL: http://www.flightpaths.net/
Rosello, M. (2001). *Postcolonial Hospitality: The Immigrant as Guest*. Stanford: Stanford University Press.
Said, E. (1995 [1978]). *Orientalism: Western Conceptions of the Orient*. London: Penguin Books.
Skaret, A. (2011). *Litterære kulturmøter. En studie av bildebøker og barns -resepsjon*. Ph.D. dissertation. Oslo: University of Oslo.
Tallmo, K. E. (1992). *Iakttagarens förmåga att ingripa*. Stockholm: Nisus Publishing.
Valéry, P. (1980 [1936]). "The Centenary of Photography". In *Classic Essays on Photography*. A. Trachtenberg (ed). New Haven: Leete's Island Books.
Van Leeuwen, T. (2005). *Introducing Social Semiotics*. London/New York: Routledge.

10 Figures of Gestural Manipulation in Digital Fictions

Serge Bouchardon,
University of Technology of Compiègne,
France

INTRODUCTION: THE MANIPULABLE DIMENSION IN DIGITAL CREATION

At the end of the 1990s, online advertising banners depended essentially on animation. However, in recent years, there have been an increasing number of online advertisements that also call on an active manipulation on the part of the user. It may be a question of moving an element on the screen (e.g. bannerblog 2009a), of activating a link (e.g. bannerblog 2009b), or even entering text via the keyboard (e.g. tippexperience 2010). In all these cases, we can describe the advertising banners in question as *interactive*, whether it is a question of apprehending existing content, of activating other content, or of creating new content by introducing new data (Bouchardon 2009).

In the domain of literary and artistic digital creation, interactive works have already existed for several decades. In an *interactive* creation, manipulations by the reader are often required so that they can move through the work. Such manipulations, in these interactive digital creations, are not radically new, and there are many examples of literary works that require physical interventions on the part of the reader; for example, in Raymond Queneau's *Cent mille milliards de poems* the reader must construct sonnets from a number of individually printed lines of poetry. Aarseth (1997) proposes the term "ergodic literature" to describe this kind of work, arguing that "in ergodic literature, *nontrivial effort* is required to allow the reader to traverse the text" (1). Yet while some print fictions do require that the reader provide some physical input, what is somewhat new in interactive digital works is the fact that it is the text itself, and not only the physical medium, which acquires a dimension of manipulation. Thus a digital text, as well as being a text provided for reading, can also provide an opportunity for manipulation (Ghitalla et al. 2004). It is this particular dimension—the manipulation of the text as well as other semiotic forms—that opens a large field of possibilities in interactive digital creations.

Currently, theorists lack the tools, and in particular the semiotic tools, to analyze this sort of creative work. The aim of this chapter is thus to propose a method for semiotic—and in particular semio-rhetorical—analysis of manipulations in digital creations, notably digital fictions. I will limit the field of study to online creations, in the twin domains of creative advertising and literary and artistic creation. To this end, I will first of all address the gesture of manipulation in digital creations. I will then propose a model—based on a bottom-up approach—for the analysis of gestural manipulations.[1] Utilizing this approach, I will end with the study of *figures of manipulation* in digital creations.

THE GESTURE OF MANIPULATION
IN DIGITAL CREATIONS

Gesture and Meaning

Jeanneret (2000) claims that the simple act of turning the page of a book "does not suppose *a priori* any particular interpretation of the text. . . . [B]y contrast however, in an interactive work the fact of clicking on a hyperword or on an icon is, in itself, an act of interpretation" (113). Jeanneret further suggests that the interactive gesture consists above all in "an interpretation realized through a gesture" (121). However, the distinction that Jeanneret proposes between turning a page and clicking on a hyperlink is not necessarily obvious and could be criticized. Moreover, we are stretching the limits of *interpretation* quite dramatically if we really accept that all clicking is interpretative (see e.g. Tosca this volume, Rustad 2009). Despite these caveats, we can nevertheless point out that, in an interactive work, the gesture acquires a particular role, which fully contributes to the construction of meaning.

Let us illustrate this point with the short digital fiction *Don't touch me*. This work displays a photograph of a woman lying on a bed (see Figure 10.1), as a voice—that of Annie Abrahams, the author—starts telling a story. The narrative is about a dream that Annie Abrahams had when she was a teenager. This dream can be interpreted as the sometimes painful transition from teenage to adulthood about a young woman exposed to the gaze and the desire of men. Being passive, looking and listening without using the mouse is not always easy for the interactor, who is often prompted to click compulsively. If the interactor rolls the cursor over the image, the image seems to resist the reader. Text immediately appears on the screen expressing the woman's refusal ("don't touch me"), the woman changes her physical position, and the vocal tale immediately stops and restarts from the beginning. On the fourth attempt of a *caress* with the mouse, the window closes.

Figure 10.1 Screenshot of *Don't touch me*. LAL Annie Abrahams

The story *Don't touch me* has a vocal, visual (the young woman displayed), and *written-textual* dimension (the three messages of refusal). It also has a gestural dimension: it is through the action of the user that the vocal narrative makes sense. This is an interactive story that is based on a play between interactivity and narrativity (cf. Ensslin 2012). Interactivity prevents narrativity insofar as the gesture of the user stops the narrative. The author also plays on the apparent incompatibility between narrativity and interactivity to teach the user to resist his desire to click, but also to apprehend differently the representations—especially online—of the female body. The vocal narrative can only be interpreted through the gesture of the user: it makes sense because it is interactive. But how can we analyze the functioning of this gesture of manipulation in a more systematic way?

A Repertoire of Gestures

In the manipulation of interactive online creations, we are dealing with a range of different gestures: clicking, double-clicking, right-clicking, moving the mouse (or moving the finger on the track-pad), maintaining the pressure of the finger, lifting the finger, tapping a key on the keyboard, but also sometimes breathing or speaking into a microphone, moving the head in front of a webcam, etc. Given this diverse range, we need a repertoire of gestures that acknowledge that these acts appear as distinct units. We are nevertheless faced with a difficulty: the gestures involved in digital manipulation are constantly evolving and depend on the available devices. In this respect the *wiimote* (the controller for *Nintendo*'s *Wii* console) has led to a considerable evolution in the repertoire of gestures that are available to a player. But even without considering video game consoles or the virtual reality devices available on digital installations, the simple fact of being able to use two fingers for zooming/dezooming with the track-pad of the latest Macintosh computers offers unprecedented possibilities for manipulation in online creations.

With other devices, the repertoire of gestures will clearly be even wider than with just the mouse-keyboard input. This is the case for the manipulation gestures available with interactive tables (cf. Wobbrock et al. 2009), or yet again when interacting with a 3D tactile desktop.[2] But to the extent that we limit our study to the analysis of online creations, we will be above all concerned with the standard input interfaces of mouse and keyboard, while recognizing that certain websites already propose the possibility for navigating with other input interfaces such as the webcam, the microphone, or indeed any sort of everyday object in experiments with augmented reality (e.g. a box of breakfast cereal[3]).

If we wish to abstract ourselves from the contextual dimension of technological innovations, we can pose the following question: can a gesture, considered as a distinct unit, also be considered as a meaningful unit, independently of the context in which it is inscribed and/or the media resource to which it is applied? I wish to put forward here the idea that there may be expectations linked to a certain gesture performed in a certain context. The context recreates a situation that has already been encountered and in which a certain gesture has given rise to a relevant result. It is thus the gesture in a given context that is linked to an expectation, and not the gesture in itself: for example, the expectation is different when one clicks to validate a choice or when one clicks on a hyperlink. These expectations are in part the fruit of the construction of conventions. Thus, the *roll over/roll out*, by which a media resource can be made to appear/disappear, can trigger the expectation of an unveiling (Bouchardon 2008). Just as there may be significant features linked to movements in an animated sequence (Saemmer 2009), we can speak of the *possible significant features* linked to the gesture of manipulation in context.

THE ANALYSIS OF THE GESTURE OF MANIPULATION

Gesture and Action

The *gesture* is considered here as a single unit (pressing a key on the keyboard or the mouse button, elementary movement of the mouse, etc.), and the single unit is linked to a material interface. The *action* is considered as a sequence of gestures (for example, *drag and drop*) and has a more global meaning linked to a double coupling with a context and a process. Often, the relevant medium (with which the gesture interacts) is indeed a process and not the final result. Even more than in the case of animation, manipulation brings into play what Bootz (2004) calls the "depth of the device": in the case of manipulation, the signs are fundamentally "dual" signs, which bring into play elements that are situated both on the side of the program and on the side of the screen.

With the aid of this approach to gestures, I will now propose a model for the analysis of gestures of manipulation in online digital creations. This model is the result of a bottom-up approach. Alexandra Saemmer, Philippe Bootz, and myself have analyzed a corpus of one hundred advertising banners and twenty literary digital creations to build this model.

The Five Levels of Analysis of Manipulation

I will now propose terminology that makes it possible to distinguish five levels in the articulation of signs, which correspond to five levels of analysis. I will illustrate this five-level model by analyzing an advertising banner, considered here as a short interactive narrative. The advertising banner for the Amanco company (bannerblog.com 2009c) contains an image of a toilet cubicle. Within the cubicle viewers see a cistern and a chain with a handle, which dangles from the ceiling, inscribed with the word "pull". The image and text encourage the interactor to pull the chain and consequently flush the toilet by pulling the mouse toward him- or herself while keeping the button pressed, hence mimicking the action of pulling the chain of the cistern downward. Once the chain is pulled, a violin and hands appear from the bottom of the toilet bowl and music is played on the violin. The slogan, "Not every sound deserves to be heard", and the name of the product, "silentium PVC soundproof pipes", both appear. If the interactor pulls on the chain again, another instrument appears from the bottom of the toilet bowl. Overall, three instruments (a violin, a saxophone, an accordion) follow one another.

THE GESTEME

The gesteme is the first and lowest level of articulation and corresponds to a distinct semiotic unit. It results from the coupling of a physical act and an input interface (for example, the act of moving the mouse or pressing a key[4]). In the Amanco advertisement, the interactor presses the button of the mouse (after having positioned the cursor on the word "pull"), keeps it pressed while moving the mouse, and then releases the button. We have here several gestemes that intervene in this manipulation: pressing the button, moving the mouse, releasing (the reverse of pressing).

THE ACTEME

The acteme is constructed on the basis of the gestemes. It corresponds to a sequence of gestemes and results from the coupling between the gesteme and the process on which the manipulation bears. There are three types of actemes (which are distinguished by the coupling of the sequence of gestures and the process which is *manipulated*):

- Actuator (change of state).
- Parametor (setting a parametric process); for example, the use of a scrollbar makes it possible to move horizontally or vertically through an interface.
- Perturbator (a co-managed process) in which, for example, a program can take control and/or perform an act that seems incompatible with the user's instructions.[5]

In the Amanco example above, there are two actemes: a parametor (I pull) and an actuator (I release), which simultaneously trigger the appearance of a musical instrument and the associated sound.

THE SEMIOTIC UNIT OF MANIPULATION (SUM)

The actemes are combined to form semiotic units of manipulation (SUMs). In the Amanco example, the two second-level actemes together constitute a single SUM: *pull-release*. Following Peirce (1987), Klinkenberg (2000) recalls that icons are signs that are "motivated by resemblance" (193) so that in the icon, something from the physical world is recognized as such. In the same way, the SUMs bring to mind actions in the physical world. For example, the SUM "scratch" could recall the action of scraping a surface. The SUM is thus *iconic* with respect to situations of manipulation in everyday life; it carries *features of iconicity*. In the Amanco advertisement, it is indeed interesting to note the *iconic* dimension of the SUM. The interactor is encouraged to make a gesture with the mouse that *resembles* the gesture in real everyday life when he/she pulls a toilet chain.

MEDIA COUPLING

Media coupling results from the coupling of the SUM with the media context. The SUM, as we have seen, exhibits an iconic dimension. However, it is only through its coupling with actual media that the significant features are realized (see Figure 10.2). The realization of these features depends on the text, the image, or the sound to which the gesture is applied, as well as the multimedia context and the cultural environment of the reader. The wider the domain of intersection between the significant features of the gesture and

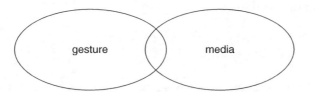
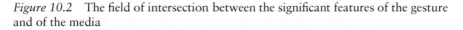

Figure 10.2   The field of intersection between the significant features of the gesture and of the media

the media to which it is applied (and the more the combination of features that are mobilized corresponds to the expectations of the reader related to the immediate context and his reading habits), the more the construction of meaning derives from what we may call *conventional coupling*.[6] When the field of intersection between the significant features of the gesture and of the media is diminished, there arises a differential between the expectations of the reader and the state actually accomplished by the manipulation: in this case we speak of *nonconventional coupling* (for example, the gesture of clicking on a link does not result in any activation, or a delayed activation, or yet again the activation of a multiplicity of elements).

Every coupling between a SUM and the media is by nature "pluri-codal", in the sense that it brings into play a number of "sub-statements each of which refers to a different code" (Klinkenberg 2000: 232).

There are three sorts of coupling:

- Simultaneous (simultaneous coupling between a gesture and the media)
- Consecutive (coupling between a gesture and the media which closely precede and/or follow it)
- Deferred (coupling between a gesture and a media result which is very distant in time)[7]

In the Amanco advertisement, we can identify two media couplings (one is simultaneous, the other is consecutive):

- The coupling of the SUM *pull-release* with "pull" and with the image of a toilet-flush (a conventional coupling)
- The coupling of the SUM *pull-release* with the incongruous appearance of the violin considering the media context, here the toilet bowl (nonconventional coupling)

This second coupling takes into account the initial state, the manipulation gesture, and the final state. In the final state, a violin appears instead of water after having pulled the toilet chain. The appearance of the violin in the toilet bowl is incongruous considering the media context, but also perhaps with respect to the interactive gesture: I pull downward and something arises upward (in this case, a violin). The general isotopy (toilet bowl, confined space) reinforces the media couplings.

INTERACTIVE DISCOURSE

This is the level of a complete interactive sequence of media couplings. We are here at the level of "discourse" (Klinkenberg 2000). Indeed it is often by taking into account the whole interactive discourse that the gesture of manipulation becomes fully meaningful. In the Amanco example, after the interactor has pulled the chain a first time, an expectation is created: pulling the chain causes a violin to appear. One can speak of a perturbation of the expectation when it is another instrument that appears the second time (a saxophone), then the third time (an accordion). The *actuator* of level two is then reinterpreted as a *perturbator*. The user may think that there is a random choice between the various instruments. However, if he or she continues to actuate the flush handle, he or she realizes that the sequence, violin–saxophone–accordion, is always the same. He or she can finally reinterpret the *perturbator* as a *parameter*. The strength of this advertisement lies in its capacity to encourage the user to play and to replay the sequence so as to discover whether or not his or her expectations will be fulfilled.

FIGURES OF MANIPULATION IN DIGITAL CREATION

We have seen that the *semiotic units of manipulation*, in context, constitute *media couplings* (a media coupling results from the coupling of the semiotic unit of manipulation with the media context). Nonconventional media couplings give rise to figures. According to Genette (1966), a figure can be considered as "a gap between sign and meaning" (209). Klinkenberg (2000) defines a rhetorical figure more precisely as "a *dispositif* producing implicit meanings, which result in polyphonic utterances" (343). In interactive and multimedia writing, the polyphonic dimension of the figure also relies on the pluri-codal nature of the content.

Digital literary and artistic works, notably digital fictions, do indeed largely call upon what we may call *figures of manipulation*. If we come back to our first example, the digital fiction *Don't touch me* by Annie Abrahams, we can identify a nonconventional coupling between a SUM (*Move*) and the media context insofar as there is a gap between the expectations of the interactor when he or she moves the mouse cursor and the result obtained with this manipulation (until the final white screen). The *caress* on the picture of the woman with the mouse cursor only interrupts and then brutally stops the course of the piece, giving rise to what could be called a *figure of interruption*.

Anonymes: A Figure of Lability

I shall now analyze in detail first a figure of manipulation from another short piece and then a whole interactive narrative based on figures of manipulation. I will take as an example the French creation entitled *Anonymes version 1.0* (anonymes.net). *Anonymes version 1.0* is an online fiction made of twenty-four scenes that can be accessed sequentially or nonsequentially. Each scene deals with the theme of anonymity and the building of identity, and each scene is interactive: it is through the gesture of the reader/interactor that the scene can unfold. I shall focus in particular on the first scene, entitled "*Nom-dit*".[8] On the homepage, a reactive zone constituted by the text "Anonymes" (anonymous) allows the user to access this first scene. A video turns in a loop, representing a man who gets up from an armchair, apparently so as to avoid being filmed. An accompanying soundtrack (maybe footsteps, or simply the *noise* of the video) also plays in a loop. A window is presented to the interactor accompanied by a text: "Type your name". The scene is thus waiting for an action by the interactor.

The interactor types a letter; but this letter, instead of remaining in the window, "flies off" and disappears from the window. The interactor is tempted to type in another letter, in particular to test whether the functioning will be the same. The second letter flies off too. The interactor can then rapidly type in several letters—a complete word—to see the letters dispersed over the space of the scene (see Figure 10.3). We arrive at a result similar

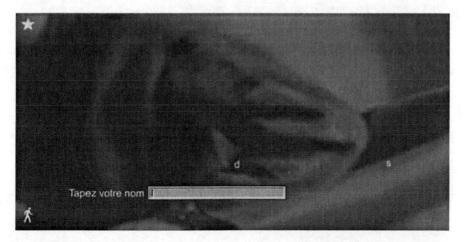

Figure 10.3   Screenshot of *Anonymes* version 1.0, scene "Nom-dit". anonymes.net

to that of certain kinetic poems (letters spread over the space and in movement), but here the letters result from an action by the user (introducing
data via the keyboard).

The meaning of this scene (the letters of a name that fly off and disappear, unavoidably) can be seen in relation to the title of the whole creation,
Anonymes. The figure that results from the gesture (the impossibility of
inscribing one's name) is an echo of the video (a man who tries to avoid the
field of the camera) and maybe also the soundtrack (sound of footsteps that
move away). This scene does not have an end: we will remain anonymous
indefinitely. The interactor does nevertheless have the possibility of returning to the homepage (via an icon in the top left corner of the screen), or to
pass on to the next scene (via an icon on the bottom left).

To employ our terminology, the *SUM* mobilized here consists in "activating" (in punctual fashion, by pressing the keys of the keyboard). But this
manipulation only takes on its full meaning when situated in the context
of the *media coupling*, or even in the whole of the *interactive discourse*.
We also witness a nonconventional coupling with the process of inscribing
letters on the screen (here, the letters that fly off), to the extent that the
functioning of the typing window is diverted from its usual function. The
functioning of the typing window is part of the "encyclopaedia" (Klinkenberg 2000) of the user of a digital interface. In Klinkenberg's terminology,
"encyclopaedia" refers to the knowledge mobilized by the reader; the encyclopaedia mobilized here depends on the ergonomics of man-machine
interfaces and not on a linguistic semiology. A typing window conventionally makes it possible to type in a sequence of alphanumerical characters
via the keyboard, without having the letters disappear in the course of the
capture. Here, however, the window does make it possible to capture the
letters of a text, but not to conserve them. The expectation of the user is
thus disturbed.

Let us now analyze the process of construction. The typing window,
associated with the text "Type your name", suggests that the program is
waiting for the gesture of typing a character on the keyboard. Now when
one types a letter via the keyboard, one "inscribes" something that, at least
in one's expectation, will be conserved. In online administrative and business forms, the typing windows in which one is asked to give one's identity
are indeed often entitled "inscription" or "register". The possible significant features linked to the action (typing a character on the keyboard) and
the media context (the typing window associated with the text "Type your
name") are: *inscription, save*. Here, however, the letters that have been
typed in fly away and disappear. We have here then the suppression of one
possible significant feature—(lasting) *inscription*—because of the flight and
disappearance of the letter. It is possible to type in characters, but not to
inscribe them.

I form the hypothesis here that the construction of an interpretation occurs in particular with the repetition of a gesture. The functioning of this

nonconventional coupling does indeed depend on the repetition. It is by repeating the gesture (here, typing letters on the keyboard) that the user progressively constructs the meaning of the scene (and understands that it is not simply a bug). In order to come to this conclusion, he or she will take into account the whole context of the media and the interface. The media video (+ sound) then makes it possible to give a meaning to the scene. The content of the video (a man going away) takes on a meaning, as does its form (an indefinite loop). Indeed, possible significant features of a video loop are: *circularity, constantly repeating itself*. The significant feature of the video loop ("circularity") is superposed with the significant feature "inscription" (adjunction and then suppression). The form of the loop is associated here with the letters that unavoidably disappear from the typing window: caught up in this circularity, any seizure and any lasting inscription are impossible (we could also consider that the inscription on the screen is multiplied, but that it has no permanence). We have here a pluri-codal construction between the significant feature "circularity" (the video loop) and the feature "inscription" (gesture coupled to the data capture window). The reader can draw the conclusion: "I will remain anonymous".

Other interpretations are also possible. For example, at the level of the creation, we may consider that what is shattered here is the illusion of participating in the work. The reader cannot participate (although he or she does participate in the visual rendering, but only for him- or herself). What is portrayed here is a reflection on the interactivity and the contribution of the reader in so-called participatory works.

At a second level, it is necessary to resituate this scene in the totality of a discourse, by taking into account this preliminary interface, but also the whole set of the other scenes in this "version 1.0". On the homepage, one can see bees turning endlessly on the background of their hive. They too seem anonymous in the hive, but they also have an identity linked to what they are doing (queen, workers, drones), and consequently to their position in the hive. One can access the first scene by clicking on the corresponding cell of the honeycomb, or else by clicking on the title of the piece ("Anonymes"), which also constitutes a reactive zone (passing over it triggers the text "Enter"). It is this media context of interaction that must also be taken into account in the analysis of this figure, which could be called a *figure of disappearance*.

Loss of Grasp: An Interactive Narrative Based on Figures of Manipulation

Numerous interactive digital fictions play on the expectations of the reader by resorting to nonconventional media couplings, which can be analyzed in terms of figures. I shall now focus on the figures of manipulation to be found in an entire digital fiction called *Loss of Grasp*[9] (Bouchardon and Volckaert 2012). *Loss of Grasp* is an online interactive narrative in English, French, and Italian. In this creation, six scenes tell the story of a character who is losing grasp on his life. In the first scene, the reader/interactor unfolds most of the narrative by rolling over the sentences that appear on the screen; each time a sentence is rolled over, a new sentence is displayed. However, during the first scene, when the sentence "Everything escapes me" appears, the mouse cursor disappears. The reader can keep rolling over each sentence, but without the reference point of the mouse cursor. Through this nonconventional media coupling, the reader experiences loss of grasp with his or her gestures.

The second scene stages the meeting of the character with his future wife, twenty years earlier. While the character "ask[s] questions to reveal her", the reader can discover the face of the woman by repeatedly moving the mouse cursor over the screen. These movements leave trails of questions which progressively unveil her face. The questions themselves constitute the portrait of the woman (see Figure 10.4).

In the third scene, twenty years later, the character can't seem to understand a note left by his wife; he asks: "love poem or break up note"? The reader can experience this double meaning with gestures. If he or she moves

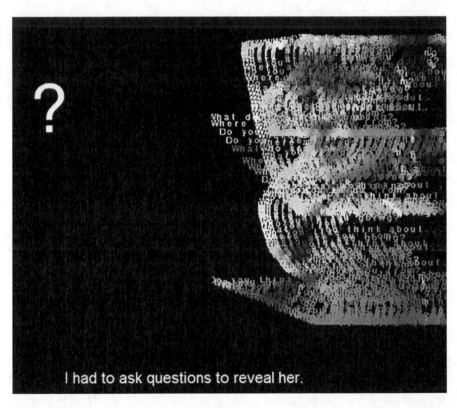

Figure 10.4   Screenshot of Loss of Grasp, second scene

the mouse cursor to the right, the text will unfold as a love poem; if he or she moves the cursor to the left, the order of the lines is reversed, and the text turns into a break up note (see Figure 10.5).

In the fourth scene, the protagonist's teenage son asks his father to read an essay he has written on the notion of "hero". But the protagonist is unable to focus on the words and "can only read between the lines". If the reader clicks on the words of the essay, sentences appear—made up of letters from the text itself—such as:

I don't love you.
You don't know me.
We have nothing in common.
I don't want anything from you.
You're not a model for me.
I want to make my own way.
Soon I will leave.

Paradoxically, the gesture of focusing on the text makes it fall apart and lets an implicit meaning appear (see Figure 10.6).

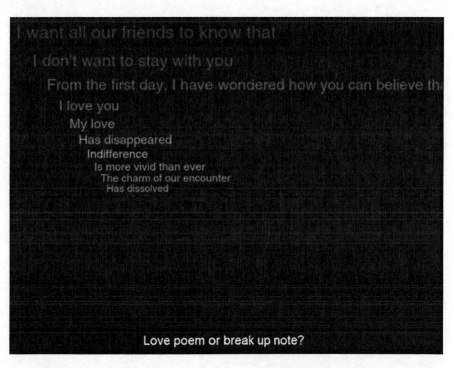

Figure 10.5   Screenshot of Loss of Grasp, third scene

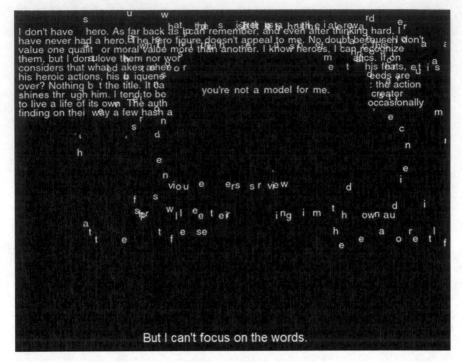

Figure 10.6   Screenshot of Loss of Grasp, fourth scene

In the fifth scene, even the character's own image seems to escape him. Via the webcam, the image of the reader appears on the screen. He or she can distort and manipulate it. The character/reader thus "feel[s] manipulated", as written on the screen.

In the last scene, the protagonist decides to take control again. A typing window is offered to the reader, in which he or she can write. However, whatever keys he or she types, the following text appears progressively:

I'm doing all I can to get a grip on my life again.
I make choices.
I control my emotions.
The meaning of things.
At last, I have a grasp . . .

Here again, the reader is confronted with a figure that relies on a gap between his or her expectations while manipulating and the result on screen. Thus through his or her gestures and through various figures of manipulation—which could as a matter of fact appear as variations on a *figure of loss of grasp*—the reader experiences the character's *loss of grasp* in an interactive way.

CONCLUSION

In order to analyze interactive and multimedia digital creations, notably digital fictions, we need specific tools of semiotic analysis. The five-level analysis model presented in this essay has above all the heuristic aim of displaying the specificities of gestural manipulation in a digital creation and the role these manipulations play in the construction of meaning.

The gesture of manipulation allows for conventional and nonconventional couplings with a range of media. Nonconventional couplings give rise to figures. This essay is thus set in the context of an approach aiming at the formalization of a rhetoric of interactive writing.[10] We can put forward the hypothesis that there are indeed figures of rhetoric that are specific to interactive writing (Bouchardon 2011). We are dealing here with a category of figures in its own right—in addition to the classical figures of diction, of construction, of meaning, and of thought—that we can call "figures of manipulation". Two points are to be emphasized here. On one hand, the notion of "figure" can—and this is what is new—take into account the gestures of the reader. On the other hand, interactive writing relies on figures of manipulation to a greater extent than other figures of meaning such as tropes. In a more general way, then, this chapter aims at making a contribution to the unveiling of the specificities of interactive writing.

NOTES

1. This model is directly inspired by a proposition by Philippe Bootz. This essay owes much to a collective reflection in the framework of a research group—composed of Alexandra Saemmer, Philippe Bootz, Jean Clément, and myself—on the semiotics and the rhetoric of digital creations.
2. See, for example, gizmodo.com (2009).
3. Dassault Systèmes and Nestle are collaborating on an augmented reality project in which they aim to "transform . . . [a] cereal box into an interactive 3D augmented reality game that mixes real and virtual worlds" (Dassault Systèmes 2009).
4. One can decompose a continuous movement (such as moving the mouse) into different gestemes. Thus, a *mickey* is a unit of measurement for the movement of a mouse cursor, equivalent to 1/200 inch, or eight pixels. This unit makes it possible to distinguish between different gestemes in the physical manipulation of the mouse.
5. The concept of a perturbator also invokes Ensslin's (2007) notion of the "third generation cybertext", which emphasizes the role that machine code can play in taking control over the user. See, for example, Rozendaal (2012), in which certain works play on the discrepancy between the manipulation of the mouse and the displacement of the arrow on the screen (visibility, appearance, speed, meaning, direction, etc.). (See also Bootz 2005.)
6. See Saemmer in this volume for more details concerning conventional or nonconventional couplings.

7. This last sort of coupling facilities what Bootz (2004) calls "double reading".
8. *"Nom-dit"*, literally "name-said", but there is a play on words here with the phonetically close expression *"non-dit"* (i.e. "unspoken").
9. This digital fiction won the New Media Writing Prize 2011.
10. Classical rhetoric comprises five main parts: invention, disposition, elocution, action, and memory. Elocution is particularly attached to the literary and aesthetic aspect of the discourse. This is the aspect that is retained by "restricted rhetoric". This expression comes from Michel Pougeoise: "Amongst the advocates of this rhetoric that can be described as 'literary' because it is interested essentially in the study of figures and style, we must mention J. Cohen, G. Genette, H. Morier as well as the μ group" (Pougeoise 2001). We are interested here in this restricted rhetoric: posing the question of a rhetoric of interactive writing amounts to posing the question of a specificity of this writing in terms of style and in particular of figures.

WORKS CITED

Aarseth, E. (1997). *Cybertext, Perspective on Ergodic Literature*. Baltimore: John Hopkins University Press.
Abrahams, A. (2003) *Ne me touchez pas/Don't touch me*. Last accessed 7 February 2012 at URL: http://www.bram.org/toucher/index.htm
anonymes.net (n.d.) *Anonymes version 1.0*. Last accessed 20 February 2013 at URL: *http://www.anonymes.net/anonymes.html*
bannerblog.com (2009a) Last accessed 20 February 2013 at URL: http://www.bannerblog.com.au/2009/09/commbank_finances.php
bannerblog.com (2009b) Last accessed 20 February 2013 at URL: http://www.bannerblog.com.au/2009/09/fas_twitter.php
bannerblog.com (2009c) Last accessed 20 February 2013 at URL: http://www.bannerblog.com.au/2009/09/toilet.php
Bootz, P. (2004). "der/die Leser/Reader/Readers". In *p0es1s. Ästhetik digitaler Poesie/The Aesthetics of Digital Poetry*. F.W. Block, C. Heibach, and K. Wenz (eds). Ostfildern-Ruit: Hatje Cantz Verlag, pp. 93–121.
Bootz, P. (2005) *rabot-poète*. Last accessed 20 February 2013 at URL: http://epoetry.paragraphe.info/artists/oeuvres/bootz/rabot.htm
Bouchardon, S. (2008) "The Rhetoric of Interactive Art Works". *DIMEA 2008* Conference, 10th-12th September, Athens, Greece, ACM Proceeding Series vol. 349, 312–318.
Bouchardon, S. (2009). *Littérature numérique: le récit interactif*. Paris: Hermès-Lavoisier.
Bouchardon, S. (2011). "Des Figures de Manipulation dans la Création Numérique". *Protée* 39. 1: 37–46.
Bouchardon, S. and Volckaert V. (2010) *Loss of Grasp*. Last accessed 20 February 2013 at URL: http://lossofgrasp.com
Dassault Systèmes (2009) "From Cinema Screen to Cereal Box with 3DVIA". Last accessed 20 February 2013 at URL: http://www.3ds.com/company/experiential-marketing/augmented-reality-kungfupanda2/?xtmc=cereal&xtcr=1
Ensslin, A. (2007) *Canonizing Hypertext: Explorations and Constructions*. London: Continuum.
Ensslin, A. (2012) "Computer Gaming". In *The Routledge Companion to Experimental Literature*. J. Bray, A. Gibbons, and B. McHale (eds). London: Routledge, pp. 497–511.

Genette, G. (1966) *Figures 1*. Paris: Seuil.
Ghitalla, F., Boullier, D., Gkouskou-Giannakou, P., Le Douarin, L., and Neau, A. (2004) *L'Outre-Lecture: Manipuler, (s')Approprier, Interpéter le Web*. Paris: Editions du Centre Georges Pompidou.
gizmodo.com (2009) "BumpTop 3D Desktop Gets Unique Multi-Touch Gestures". Last accessed 20 February 2013 at URL: http://gizmodo.com/5371913/bumptop-3d-desktop-gets-unique-multi+touch-gestures?autoplay=true
Jeanneret, Y. (2000) *Y a-t-il Vraiment des Technologies de l'Information?* Paris: Editions Universitaires du Septentrion.
Klinkenberg, J.-M. (2000 [1996]) *Précis de Sémiotique Générale*. Brussels: De Boeck.
Peirce, C. S. (1978) *Ecrits sur le signe,* collected, translated and commented by Deledalle G. Paris: Seuil.
Pougeoise M. (2001) *Dictionnaire de Rhétorique*. Paris: Armand Colin.
Queneau, R. (1961) *Cent Mille Milliards de Poèmes*. Paris: Gallimard.
Rozendaal, R. (2012) *RR*. Last accessed 20 February 2013 at URL: http://www.newrafael.com/websites/
Rustad, H. (2009) "A Four-Sided Model for Reading Hypertext Fiction". *Hyperrhiz 06*. Last accessed 20 February 2013 at URL: http://www.hyperrhiz.net/hyperrhiz06/19-essays/80-a-four-sided-model
Saemmer, A. (2009) "Aesthetics of Surface, Ephemeral and Re-Enchantment in Digital Literature: How Authors and Readers Deal with the Lability of the Electronic Device". Cyberliteratures of the World, *Neohelicon* 36: 477–488).
tippexperience (2010) *YouTube*. Last accessed on 20 February 2013 at URL: http://www.youtube.com/watch?v=4ba1BqJ4S2M
Wobbrock, J. O., Morris, M. R., and Wilson, A. D. (2009) "User-Defined Gestures for Surface Computing". *Proceedings of the 27th International Conference on Human Factors in Computing Systems*. Boston, MA: ACM, pp. 1083–1092.

11 Hyperfiction as a Medium for Drifting Times
A Close Reading of the German Hyperfiction *Zeit für die Bombe*

Alexandra Saemmer,
University of Paris 8, France

INTRODUCTION

Zeit für die Bombe ("Time for the bomb") is an award-winning hyperfiction written and programmed by the German author Susanne Berkenheger.[1] Since its publication in 1997, it has fueled many debates and comments but few "exhaustive" readings. If we consider the extent to which the critical discourse on hyperfiction has resorted to the paradigms of deconstruction, fragmentation and de-coherence, we realize that we cannot avoid questioning the feasibility of such an exhaustive analysis, which requires a thorough reading of the texts and full activation of the links contained in a work. In this chapter, I will demonstrate the possibility, interest, and limits of an exhaustive analysis, by relying on a digital reading methodology I have developed over the last few years.

The methodology used in this essay draws on the phenomenological tradition and borrows some of its key concepts from Reader Response Theory. The main objective of this theory, as articulated by Iser in his book *L'Acte de lecture* (1995 [1976]), is to study the practice of reading as an individual and social co-construction of meaning. Although one of the fundamental issues of his methodology is to take into account the role of the reader in the analysis of a literary work, Iser pays little attention to the role of the reading device (i.e. the book, pamphlet, screen, etc., that displays the text). Jeanneret (2008), however, usefully complements Reception Theory, particularly in the field of digital textuality. While emphasizing the dynamic aspects of the reading process, Jeanneret shows how the "editorial utterance", i.e. the regulatory frameworks provided by digital writing and reading tools, literally "border" the digital text.

I begin with the premise that the process of reading is influenced by a set of individual and socially shared elements, taken form the reader's "horizon of expectations" (Jauss 1990). I also argue that is guided by the "repertories" (Iser 1995 [1976]: 127) and the rhetorical strategies of the text and the device that already anticipates a mode of reception. In order to circumscribe the potential act of reading in hypertext, I will first retrace the horizon of expectations in relation to the digital device and text, potentially shared in a society at a given moment, by examining the elements of the repertory and the rhetorical strategies of a hyperlinked text (called "parent text"). I will then consider the potential expectations raised by this text in relation to the "related text". A comparison between the repertory and strategies of the parent text and the related text, with regards to the reader's horizon of expectations, will finally allow me to evaluate the potential (de-)coherences between these elements.

Through the analysis of *Zeit für die Bombe*, I will show that these potential (de-)coherences, and other potentially emerging "places of indeterminacy" (Iser 1995 [1976]: 299) between handling ("manipulation") gestures, animations, and the characteristics of the reading device, may be an important part of the aesthetics of the digital text. Manipulation gestures and textual animations may also provide the digital text with immersive effects. The oscillations and tensions between (de-)coherence, the fulfillment of the reader's expectations, and immersion in digital literature will be discussed in my conclusion.

THE REPERTORY AND STRATEGIES OF A DIGITAL TEXT

Like Iser and Jauss, I consider the act of reading as an encounter between the horizon of the text and the reader's horizon of expectations. The "repertory" of the text contains all the necessary elements to trigger this encounter, such as allusions to historical events, social conventions, models of reference, and commonly shared representations. The strategies of the text link these elements together, and delineate the conditions of perception: for example, the order in which events are narrated, the number of details, the narrative perspective, etc. In the case of hypertext, the repertory and strategies of the "parent text" especially foreshadow a place for readers and guide their comprehension of the related text. In this sense, the potential (de-)coherence of hyperlinked texts is based on the identification of the temporal or logical elements that are common to the parent text and the related text. As pointed out by Jeanneret and Davallon (2004), a hypertext conveys traces and anticipations of readings: the encounter between the parent text and the related text results from an interpretative act, performed by the author, which fully, partially, or hardly meets to the reader's expectations.

ICONIC IRRADIATIONS

Hypertext does not only establish a relation between a parent and a related text, but it is also an interactive, "manipulable" element that combines at least two different semiotic systems through the same active support: a text and a "manipulation gesture". This is also true for the animated text, which combines a text and a movement. In a research project launched several years ago at the University Paris 8, Philippe Bootz, Serge Bouchardon, and myself have been considering certain sequences of gestures as "iconic signs", more accurately called "semiotic units of manipulation". Unlike the linguistic signs, which are (in principle) characterized by an arbitrary relationship between the signifier and the signified, iconic signs, thanks to their visually perceptible or physically manipulable structure, come closer to the representation of their experienced referent. The semiotic unit "activate" (Bouchardon 2011), mobilized by the handling of a hypertext, combines, for example, a consecutive, brief, and nonrepetitive press/release gesture within an interactive zone. We believe that readers recognize this unit because they have already experienced it elsewhere—for example, by pressing the button or switch of a radio, a lamp, etc. (see Bouchardon in this volume). The signified of the unit "activate" may be circumscribed by ideas of brevity and immediate reactivity, without being subject to conscious thought: the iconic signified is rather a form with which the perceiving body enters a "mimetic resonance" (Meunier 2006: 137). I propose to call "iconic irradiation" the interaction of an iconic sign with a linguistic sign. Iconic irradiation is activated by any manipulable hypertext and reinforces the expectations of instant "revelation" (Gervais 2006): as if he or she were indeed pressing on a switch, the reader expects an immediate reaction on the interface. In some cases, iconic irradiation seems to be able to turn the text into a "pretense" of its referent: for example, the reader is encouraged to press the hyperlinked "switch" of a bomb in *Zeit für die Bombe*. With reference to paper calligram, I call such an "imitative" coupling between text and gesture "kine-gram" (*kine* from *kinetik*).

In animated text, the linguistic sign is coupled with movement. Some movements constitute the signifier of an iconic sign that we call "temporal semiotic unit" (TSU), referring to TSUs in music. As part of a research project on musical semiotics, researchers at the French laboratory MIM have identified a number of "temporal semiotic units", such as the one called "obsessional", characterized by a fast, reiterated, insisting sound (i.e. a rapidly repeated piano note) (MIM 2012). The comparison of certain visual animations (i.e. flashing animations) and certain sound units (i.e. the "obsessional" one) provides indeed a strong impression of synesthesia. The signified does not differ from this experienced referent (recalling, for example, ideas such as urgency or danger for a flashing "obsessional"). According to the reader's expectations and the actual coupling of a text with one of these movements, the (de-)coherence between the iconic and linguistic signs may then be perceived as more or less strong. In some cases (i.e. the word "heart" flashing in a love story), the word seems to be turned into the "pretense" of its referent. I propose to call this coupling a "cine-gram" (*cine* from *cinetic*) (Saemmer 2011a). Nevertheless, whenever a linguistic sign and a movement are combined within the same stimulus in an animated text, two signs of a very different nature intermingle: such a coupling shall never be considered as completely redundant.

THE REPERTORY OF THE DEVICE

The digital text is part of a reading device (e.g. a tablet, a computer) and characterized by socio-symbolic and socio-technical repertories. For example, the frequent use of *content management systems* (that is, editing systems such as blogs, which offer very constrained writing and reading frameworks), has contributed to the generalization of the "menu" at the top or in the margin of websites. Readers have thus become accustomed to this kind of structuring format, and may feel disturbed if such a menu is missing in a digital work. Another facet of the device is the program. If we take a look at the code of a "classic" (nondynamic) hypertext, we note that it invariably links a parent text to a related text. This characteristic trait of the device can enter a (de-)coherent relationship with a quite frequent representation of the hypertext advocating more freedom for the reader. Although the digital device itself has frequently been ascribed with stability and sustainability, it is also characterized by its "lability" (Bootz 2002). The computational speed significantly influences the actualization of text animations, for example. This variability can potentially result in other forms of (de-)coherence between text and movement.

POTENTIAL (DE-)COHERENCES

I have used the term "(de-)coherence" several times to describe the potentially surprising, or even contradictory relation between the repertory and strategies of a digital text, as well as the relation between the iconic and linguistic signs and the device, on the one hand, and the reader's "horizon of expectations" on the other hand. The term refers to the "places of indeterminacy", which, according to Iser (1995 [1976]), designate, for example, the temporal or logical gaps in a text. As some places of indeterminacy may be resolved during the act of reading, however, I prefer to use the term (de-)coherence, which I consider a more dynamic one. I have already mentioned the potential (de-)coherences between the parent text and related text in a hypertext. The coupling of text and movement, or text and manipulation gesture, can also be characterized by a certain degree of (de-)coherence. Finally, (de-)coherence can also arise through the social representations of a device such as the Internet and the imaginary dimensions mobilized by the textual genre (narrative text, for example), or through the technical purposes of the tool and the commonly shared ideas about the digital text. Defying the reader's expectations, the potential (de-)coherences of the digital text can acquire a critical, and even political, dimension. The readers' reaction when faced with (de-)coherence, and the mediation process eventually undertaken in order to make at least some sense from this (de-)coherence, depend on their horizon of expectations.

ELEMENTS FOR THE READER'S HORIZON OF EXPECTATIONS

The potential of a digital text unfolds through the encounter with the reader's horizon of expectations, which is both individual and social. Even if it is obviously impossible to circumscribe it exhaustively, it seems important to point out some of its elements.

THE IMAGINATIVE WORLDS OF THE INTERNET

In his book *L'Imaginaire d'Internet* (2001), Flichy underlines the influence of the Californian counter?culture of the 1980s and 1990s on the first social representations of the Web. As Cardon (2009) also points out, the Internet was considered as an alternative, open, and democratic "public space" throughout the 1980s. The idea of building online communities, without hierarchy and prejudice, became one of the most commonly shared models of reference in the 1990s: for example, a 1993 cover of *Time* magazine was entitled "Cyberpunk" (*Time* 1993). However, a paradigm shift took place around 2000. Considered as the flagship tool of the "information society" (Labelle 2001), the Internet has been more and more regarded as a "stabilizer" of information and knowledge. In a survey conducted in 2011 by the French CSA among 1,005 adults, 76 percent of the participants said they use the Internet primarily to "access information" (*Observatoire Orange Terrafemina* 2011). The idea of a free and dialogic juxtaposition of ideas on the Web has gradually been replaced by the imaginative dimension of a network where the user "checks" factual information (Wolton 2009: 55).

IMAGINATIVE DIMENSIONS OF THE DIGITAL TEXT AND HYPERTEXT

This paradigm shift can also be observed in the imaginative dimensions associated with the digital text and hypertext. Throughout the 1980s and 1990s, the critical discourse surrounding hypertext in particular often highlighted the idea of a "dialogic" hypertext, linking divergent points of view to one another, able to instrumentalize complexity (Clément 2000) and even to reflect "rhizomatic" brain activities (Bolter 1990). Hypertext was presented as a tool for positive contradiction and beneficial fragmentation. Its reading was considered an act of writing (e.g. Landow 1997). At the end of the 1990s, however, the model of reference of an "informational" hypertext, able to reduce uncertainties, gradually prevailed in the media sphere (Laborde 2010).

The representation of hypertext as an "effective" (Tosca 2000) and "predictable" (Ensslin 2007) link between "factual" pieces of information is presented as a touchstone ready to meet the reader's expectations (Charney

1994). Dialogic hypertext, however, is considered as a "gap", a "romantic" (Charney 1994) or "literary" diversion, which deliberately subverts the "transparency of interconnectedness" (Ensslin 2007: 127). A survey conducted in 2006 among 600 students at the Université Lyon 2, has confirmed this strong association of hypertext with informational expectations[2] and raises the issue of the willingness of readers to read a fictional text on a digital device.

In the same survey, 40.5 percent of students said that they only "skimmed through" digital texts. While such a rapid browsing activity seems well suited to the informational imaginative dimension, it seems less adapted to the textual strategies of narrative texts. Indeed Ryan (2006), for example, wonders how to reconcile narrativity and interactivity considering that narration presupposes the linearity of time, logic, and causality (99). The acceptance of hyperfiction also depends on the reader's models of reference. The paradigm of the "deconstructive", "anti-Aristotelian" hypertext so prevailed in the 1990s (Landow 1997: 181; Jennings 1996: 349) that Ryan considers whether hyperfiction does not act *against* the medium whenever it presents a certain degree of consistency (Ryan 2004: 330). Studying the exact role of hypertext in narration, she, however, states that the relationship between the parent text and the related text can be "temporal", making the reader travel forward or backward on the time axis of the story without endangering the temporal and logical coherence of the story (Ryan 2006: 109). Researchers such as Bourassa (2010) therefore argue for a reconsideration of the systematic association of hypertext with disorientation.

IMAGINATIVE DIMENSIONS OF TEXTUAL ICONICITY

The iconic aspects of digital texts have also been rediscussed in recent critical discourse. In the 1990s, Bolter and Grusin (1999) put forward a strong contrast between "immediacy" (associated with immersion) and "hypermediality" (associated with critical distance). Based on the "postmodern" paradigms, Bolter (1990) considers immersion as dubious because it cancels critical distance (155). According to him, hypertext is able to create a distance. Ryan (2006) also considers the position of the reader in a hyperfiction as necessarily "external" and "exploratory" (107). However, the iconic character of the manipulation gesture has been commonly neglected so that while hyperfictions such as *Zeit für die Bombe* experiment with it, (academic) readers are often torn between fascination and reluctance.

ZEIT FÜR DIE BOMBE AND ITS RECEPTION

Susanne Berkenheger's *Zeit für die Bombe* is one of the best-known textual hyperfictions in German. The pages, connected by seventy-six hypertexts, sometimes contain animated text elements. The story skillfully combines sex and crime by playing on the stereotypes of the genre. Many readers of *Zeit für die Bombe* have analyzed this hyperfiction's animated texts as "effects of presentification" (Hautzinger 1999). Despite the fact that he considers some of them as "redundant", Simanowski (2007) also analyzes the possible meaning of these animated texts. The involvement of the reader through textual "manipulation" has also been highlighted by many readers. Simanowski, for example, stresses the immersive aspect of this kind of interactivity, which sometimes even gives the reader the role of a "criminal" (1999).

Some early readers seem heavily influenced by the representation of hyperfiction as a counter-model opposed to the "classic" narration. In particular, disorientation and meandering are often highlighted. Simanowski (1999) argues, for example, that the reader does not know how the elements of *Zeit für die Bombe* are connected, what the relationships between the characters are, and what "all this may mean". Similarly, Franke (n.d.) notes that the reader can certainly select "variants" of the story, but that the narration does not help him or her to make carefully thought-out decisions: eventually, it is a "chaotic" work, he states. By contrast, Suter's (2005) reading stresses the possible coherences existing throughout the pages of this hyperfiction. According to Suter, the repeated "peregrinations" toward the hypertextual network eventually allow the reader to reconstruct the temporal and logical progression of the story. Given the differences of interpretation in these cases, what are these traces and anticipations of reading that potentially give the reader an impression of coherence or de-coherence in *Zeit für die Bombe*?

THE ACTION POTENTIAL OF THE TEXT AND DEVICE IN *ZEIT FÜR DIE BOMBE*

Digital texts seem to resist a long and meticulous reading for several reasons. The students interviewed in 2006 evoked, among other things, the discomfort caused by the reading device and the ambiguous role of hypertext, which sometimes "helps" and sometimes "disturbs" the reading. The habits related to the collecting of information, the social representations of the Internet as a stable agent of knowledge, and the imaginative dimension of the "factual" hypertext certainly play an important role in shaping the horizon of expectations as regards online hyperfictions, such as *Zeit für die Bombe*. As highlighted above, many readers also stress the fact that they only skim through digital texts. The heirs of Deconstruction have legitimized this partial reading even in the case of narrative hypertexts (e.g. Joyce 1993). A reader who only "skims through" the texts in *Zeit für die Bombe* may yet miss the fact that the parent texts often hint at the repertories of the related texts, at least partially. These hints create expectations that are often met in this hyperfiction.

A reading of the forty-seven "fixed" and forty-six "transitional" pages, connected by seventy-six hypertexts, takes about four hours. Following my reading, I summarize *Zeit für die Bombe* as follows, in order to show that such a detailed summary, based on the reconstruction of temporal and logical reconstruction, is actually possible, despite the various hyperlinks inside each of the text pages:[3] the reader just has to read and explore them all.

After the explosion of a bomb in a train station in Moscow, the young Veronika falls into a coma. On the "last" page of the website, the reader becomes aware that the interconnected storylines in *Zeit für die Bombe* reflect the conscience of the young woman, revolving around the de-coherences of her memory. *Zeit für die Bombe* is thus the story of a crazy winter day in Moscow, during which several characters meet and get lost in the streets and railway stations, a psychiatric hospital, an apartment, and a pub.

The previous summer, Veronika had an affair with Vladimir, who asked her to carry a bomb in her bag on her next visit. As she arrives at the station, she expects to be welcomed by Vladimir. However, it is Iwan, her ex-boyfriend, a student in psychiatry, who is waiting for her. He takes the suitcase. Still shocked by the unexpected meeting, Veronika runs to a taxi and forgets the bag in her haste.

Iwan stays alone on the platform. By activating hyperlinks readers have one of two options: they follow either Veronika or Iwan; if they regret their choice, they still have the opportunity to go back and explore a different storyline. The hyperlinked pages are interspersed with "transitional"[4] pages, appearing on and disappearing from the screen without the reader having any opportunity to intervene. They are often characterized by text animations and sometimes facilitate the transitions between parent texts and related texts, but they also provide a frenzied reading pace.

If readers decide to explore first the hyperlinks located on the description of Veronika's journey, they learn that she rushes to Vladimir's place. In front of the building, she runs into a blond woman (Blondie) who is just leaving Vladimir's apartment after they have made love. Blondie has left a contact lens in Vladimir's apartment.

Veronika joins Vladimir. Their passionate reunion causes Vladimir's telephone to overturn, so that the line will be engaged for a long time. Vladimir finally inquires about the bomb. Veronika remembers the suitcase. She instantly leaves Vladimir's apartment. However, just before she does, she notices the contact lens. She arrives at the station. At this moment, Veronika overhears a conversation between Blondie and her brother in a phone booth. The girl talks about her contact lens, while her brother alludes to a bomb. Veronika deduces that the two people are talking to Vladimir. Furious, she goes back to Vladimir's apartment. After a violent argument, the couple "make up in bed". Veronika leaves again to find the bomb. However, she takes the "wrong door". Activating the hyperlink on *"wrong door"*, readers find themselves on an error page. By scanning the page with the cursor, they can locate a hidden hyperlink that, once activated, is designated as a "hole through space and time". On the page to which the hyperlink leads, Veronika asks Vladimir to show her the *"right door"*. As readers activate the link, they discover Vladimir making love with Blondie. How did Blondie manage to arrive so quickly in the apartment? This temporal incoherence may strike the reader.

Profoundly disappointed, Veronika runs away again and decides to leave Moscow. All this time, Iwan had been in possession of the suitcase. Alone on the platform, he loses his mind. He is taken to a mental hospital. While his tutor considers ways to get him out, Iwan opens the suitcase and discovers the bomb. Should he press the little switch? If the reader activates the hyperlink on *"press the little switch"*, the countdown starts.

With the help of his tutor, Ivan leaves the hospital. Still groggy because of the drugs he has been given at the hospital, he enters a pub—the same pub where Blondie's brother tries to join Vladimir. Depending on the storylines they have already explored, readers know why Vladimir's line is engaged. Someone is crying *"hallooohooo"* in the pub. By activating the hyperlink placed on the cry, the reader learns that Blondie, kissing her brother effusively, has damaged the phone. The couple runs away and searches for a telephone booth. This is where Veronika will overhear their conversation. If readers followed Iwan's wandering to the same pub, they are apparently confronted with the same page containing the hyperlinked cry *"Hallooohooo"*. However, this hyperlink no longer leads to the escape of the brother and sister, but instead to Iwan leaving the pub on Blondie's orders. Depending on the path followed before by the reader, the *"Hallooohooo"* is thus addressed either to Blondie's brother or else to Iwan: thus another potential de-coherence emerges here.

While Ivan goes to the station with the suitcase in his hands, Blondie and her brother finally join Vladimir, who invites Blondie to pick up her contact lens. They make love. Veronika walks in on them and then leaves in a taxi. Veronika and Iwan arrive at the station at the same time. As Veronika pops her head out of the train window, she recognizes Iwan. For a brief moment, a reconciliation seems possible, but at this very moment, the bomb explodes, killing Iwan and thirty-two other people. Veronika falls into a coma. On the last page of the story, readers are given the opportunity to restart their exploration.

As this summary shows, rather than causing invariable disorientation, many relations of the parent text with the related text in *Zeit für die Bombe* are potentially characterized by a high degree of logical and temporal coherence, which potentially meet the reader's expectations.

POTENTIAL COHERENCES

The action potential of a first category of hyperlinks between the parent text and the related text in *Zeit für die Bombe* can be called "chronological".

The repertories of the parent text allude to an event; the activation of the related text allows the reader to discover the following episode and this straightforward temporal relation is likely to meet the reader's expectations. For example, Veronika goes past the phone booth. When she finally understands the relationship between Vladimir and Blondie, she exclaims, "*Pah*"! Activating the hyperlinked "Pah", the reader discovers Veronika's immediate reaction, i.e. she takes a cab to quickly run away from her unfaithful lover.

Besides such chronological sequences, any reader of narrative texts is used to being confronted with time warps in the story. An "analeptic hyperlink", which allows readers to learn what happened before the events told in the parent text, certainly meets their expectations if the parent text already announces such a time warp. For instance, one passage describes the reunion of Vladimir and Veronika: "Veronika is *back*". The word "back" suggests that Veronika has already been in Vladimir's apartment. After they activate the hyperlink on this word, readers discover the previous episodes of their love story.

While an "analeptic relation" allows the readers to learn what happened before, a "proleptic hyperlink" signifies a leap into the future. Further, a "synchronic hyperlink" between the parent and the related text tells the reader what happens during the events described in the parent text, at another place and/or involving another character. This relation is often combined with a delocalization and/or a change of perspective, which can meet the reader's expectations depending on the allusions already made in the parent text. For example, after their reunion, Veronika and Vladimir make love and knock the *telephone* over. The text related to the word "telephone" tells the reader what is going on at the same time at the other end of the line, in the pub where a man tries to join Vladimir.

A "delocalizing hyperlink" between the parent text and the related text is established whenever the narrated events take place in two or more different places. If the announcement of this delocalization in the parent text is explicit enough, the change of location in the related text certainly meets the reader's expectations. Delocalization is often coupled with an analeptic, proleptic, chronological, or synchronous relation. In one section of *Zeit für die Bombe*, for example, the parent text focuses on Veronika, who looks at Moscow passing by through a taxi window. Veronika suddenly wonders if "she had not just passed by *Vladimir's room*". The related text tells the reader what happens during these moments, inside the room.

Just as is the case for many "paper" stories, the narrative focus on the characters can change between the parent text and the related text, without necessarily disturbing the reader's expectations. This hyperlink resulting in a change of focus operates, for example, a change of the narrative perspective from the outside to the inside: in this case, the parent text describes a character through his or her actions, while the related text reflects his or her inner thoughts. After she made love with Vladimir, for example, Blondie decides to go *elsewhere*. The text related to the word "elsewhere" offers a chronological continuation to Blondie's move, but also an entry into her thoughts. The focus can also be shifted from one character to another.

An action potential based on the "causal hyperlink" between the parent text and the related text is often coupled with already listed relations: it explains why a character acts like this, why events unfold that way. Providing answers to questions readers potentially ask themselves during the act of reading, this action potential tends to meet their expectations. On one of the first pages, Veronika leaves the platform, and before Iwan really could understand what had happened, "she was already *gone*". In the related text, the reader discovers the following sequence and also gets some explanations for Veronika's behavior: she was expecting another man.

POTENTIAL (DE-)COHERENCES

The reading of *Zeit für die Bombe* is an autopoietic process during which the reader's repertory progressively grows. Many (de-)coherences potentially emerge between the parent texts and the related texts if the reader has not yet explored all of the hypertext, but this can be progressively solved by the activation of alternate hypertexts and a reading of the related pages. However, some (de-)coherences resist any exhaustive reading.

BETWEEN PARENT TEXT AND RELATED TEXT

One of these de-coherences is highlighted by the text itself as a "hole through space and time" (see summary above). After returning to Vladimir's apartment for the second time, Veronika finally decides to leave again in order to find the bomb. However, she takes the *"wrong door"*. After the activation of this hyperlink, an "error page" is displayed, containing the firstly hidden, but hyperlinked words *"the hole through space and time"*. A click on this hyperlink displays a related text, in which Veronika asks Vladimir how to get out of the apartment. But a shameful discovery awaits Veronika behind the *"next door"*. When the reader activates the link "next door", he or she discovers a love scene between Vladimir and Blondie. How did Blondie manage to arrive so quickly in the apartment? Even if all the pages have been read, the mystery remains.

There is another de-coherence that does not arise as we read the text for the first time but that widens during an exhaustive reading. As shown in the summary above, several narrative paths lead to a scene in the pub in which someone is crying *"Hallooohooo"* (see Figure 11.1). The *"Hallooohooo"* represents direct speech (signified by speech marks) and is also a hyperlink that can be activated by the reader. Depending on the narrative path already followed by the reader, this interpellation addresses one of two characters.

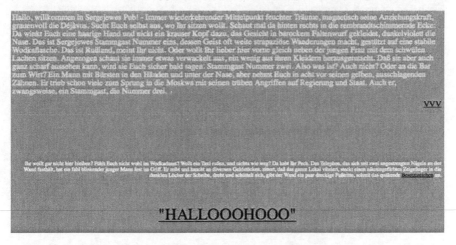

Figure 11.1   Screenshot of pub scene in *Zeit für die Bombe*

In the first case, the related text tells the reader that Blondie calls out to her brother; the breaking of the telephone and the flight of the couple ensue. In the second case, while the parent text seems to be exactly the same, the reader discovers in the related text that Blondie was calling out to Iwan. In a fiction where most events follow a logical/temporal order if all the pages and hypertexts have been explored, such a de-coherence strikes the reader in the most unexpected way.

BETWEEN TEXT AND "MANIPULATION" GESTURE

Metalepsis, transgressions between generally separate levels of fiction, is one of the most characteristic traits of *Zeit für die Bombe* (see Bell's chapter in this volume). Borges (1957) summarizes readers' confusion when confronted with metalepsis: "such inventions suggest that, if fictional characters may become readers or spectators, there is no reason why we, their readers or spectators, could not become fictional characters" (85).[5] In *Zeit für die Bombe*, the narrator addresses the characters and comments on their actions. He sometimes appears to be omniscient, sometimes hesitant. Repeatedly, the narrator addresses readers too, anticipating their reactions, urging or even directly involving them in the story.

In a hyperfiction, the metaleptic effect can be reinforced by the reader's physical involvement. The more the gesture carried out by the reader resembles the gesture made by a fictional character, the more the mimetic illusion is strengthened. For example, in an episode in *Zeit für die Bombe*, Iwan is facing the open suitcase and cannot decide whether to trigger the bomb or not (see Figure 11.2). The narrator comments: "Well,

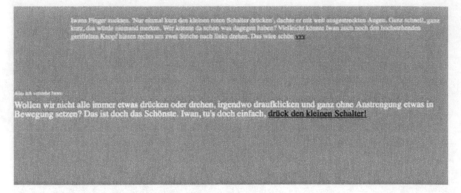

Figure 11.2   Screenshot of metalepsis in *Zeit für die Bombe*

I understand Iwan: Don't we all want to push, turn or click something to make something happen without any effort? It is the most beautiful thing in the world. Iwan, come on, do it, *press that little switch*"! This passage is characterized by both a textual metalepsis (the narrator addresses his character) and a coupling of the linguistic signs "*press that little switch*" with the semiotic unit "activate" induced by the manipulation of the hyperlink. The narrator's invitation is addressed to Iwan, but the physical activation of the hyperlinked "switch" is carried out by the reader. At the narrative level, Iwan is expected to make a pressing gesture. The reader performs the same gesture on the word. The iconic sign irradiates the word "switch" and seems to turn it, at least partially, in the pretense of its referent: the reader literally *feels* the touch of the "object" switch. It is a kind of "kine-gram": an imitative coupling between text and gesture (see categories above).

However, the potential of this coupling of text with gesture is also characterized by some (de-)coherences. First, the invitation in the parent text is addressed to Iwan, not the reader. Moreover, readers do not only press the word "*switch*", but also the word "*press*", which textualized their gesture. Finally, the transitional page appearing after the activation results in the display of the sentence "Iwan pressed", which attributes the activation gesture to Iwan and situates the event in the past tense of this story. These (de-)coherences are very characteristic of this kind of narration, which often plays with mimetic illusion by revealing its impossibility.

BETWEEN TEXT AND MOVEMENT

The fluctuation between mimetic illusion and its actual impossibility can also be observed in some couplings of text with movement. *Zeit für die Bombe* mostly experiments with fast flashing, resorting to the temporal

Figure 11.3 Screenshot of flashing text in *Zeit für die Bombe*

semiotic unit called "obsessional", a movement characterized by its fast, reiterated, and insisting nature (see categories above). After the bomb is activated, the sentence "And the bomb was ticking" appears (see Figure 11.3). The word "bomb" is flashing, and this movement seems to imitate the characteristics of a bomb. Simanowski (2007) considers this movement as redundant and suggests that we remove the verb "was ticking" ("*tickte*"). However, he does not consider the difference between *auditive* ticking and *visual* flashing.

Indeed there is a strong synesthesia between an "obsessional" sound and an "obsessional" movement (see the convergence of the "temporal semiotic units" in sound and visual creations, as explained above). However, synesthesia is not equivalent to a recovery: a removal of the words "was ticking" would make this bomb silent. In addition, the sentence describes the sound of the bomb in the past, while the bomb is presently flashing. Thus, despite perhaps initial appearances, this animation cannot really be defined as a "cine-gram", a relation based on redundancy between the action potential of the text and the movement.

In other textual animations, the potential (de-)coherence between text and movement widens. On one of the last pages of the story, the sentence "Time bursts into a thousand pieces" is again combined with a flashing movement. But this flashing barely imitates the explosion of a bomb.

BETWEEN THE TEXT AND THE DEVICE

(De-)coherences also emerge between the headers of the webpages and the texts within these pages. On the one hand, the reader is not always able to understand the allusions, injunctions, and other comments contained in the title bar, at first reading. On the other hand, the very use of the title bar for narrative purposes certainly challenges the reader's expectations: on most webpages, the title bar just briefly summarizes the content of the page.

Several passages in *Zeit für die Bombe* contain more or less explicit allusions to the reading device. Whereas the imaginative dimension of "immersive" reading seems to be linked to a necessary forgetting of the device, the device in *Zeit für die Bombe* often recalls its characteristics. For example, when the reader activates the link on "*wrong door*", the related page contains the expression "404 error", an explicit reference to the digital device. Similarly, on the first page, the reader is advised to use the "Netscape 3.XX" browser. However, the development of this browser—very popular in the 1990s—was put an end to in 2008. The unavailability of the advised device has already caused some (de-)coherences between the surface events planned by the author and the current status of the work. The remarks made by readers allow us to locate some of them. For example, on one of the last screens the hyperlinked phrase "*departure hall*" appears. In her analysis, Hautzinger (1999) discusses a pop-up window entitled "Error— Internet Explorer-Skript" which reads, "Forget it. The bomb will explode on OK"; a hyperlink is located on the word "OK". However, this pop-up is not displayed in more recent browsers. These observations on the increasing (de-)coherence between the actualizations of a digital work on different devices lead some authors to reflect on the "aesthetics of a digital ephemeral" (Saemmer 2011b) inextricably linked to the unstable characteristics of electronic reading devices.

CONCLUSION: AESTHETICS OF HYPERFICTION, BETWEEN DE-COHERENCE, FULFILLMENT OF THE READER'S EXPECTATIONS, AND IMMERSION

Jauss (1990) suggests that a work lives on, not because it raises timeless questions or because it provides permanent answers, but because of a more or less open tension between questions and answers, which reinitiates the dialogue between the horizon of the work and the reader's horizon of expectations (125). This analysis of *Zeit für die Bombe*, including the analysis of its reception, shows that the (de-)coherences between digital texts in hypertext, between linguistic and iconic signs, and between text and device have shifted according to the readers' horizon of expectations. They will keep on shifting because of the ever-changing reading habits, devices, and works themselves. If certain (de-)coherences tend to be solved through an exhaustive reading, which is perhaps facilitated by the convenience of the current reading devices, others will resist any attempt at mediation. It is perhaps precisely because the potential of *Zeit für die Bombe* does not immediately resort to the paradigms of deconstruction and fragmentation, but because the logic and temporal coherence between many episodes of this story can be rebuilt, that the still-unanswered questions really disturb the reader's expectations.

Zeit für die Bombe is characterized by a constant fluctuation between the fulfillment of the reader's expectations, an invitation to "immersive" reading, and the aesthetics of de-coherence, which defies these expectations, challenges the automatisms of perception, and creates distance. Whenever readers identify with the characters to the point where they get the impression that they are making choices on their behalf, subtle (de-)coherences infiltrate the aesthetic pleasure and disturb it, without calling it into question completely. Whenever their experience of the work finally seems to be stabilized, the logico-temporal "seams" of the story start to give way again. Just as in Jean Echenoz's and Alain Fleischer's novels, whose seemingly "classic" architecture is built on quicksand, *Zeit für die Bombe* can thus be considered as a "mediator for drifting times" (Blanckeman 2000).

NOTES

1. Pegasus award, IBM/*Die Zeit*.
2. Questionnaire-based project, led by Claire Bélisle at the Université Lyon 2-ISH. The results were collected and analyzed by Claire Bélisle, Eliana Rosado, and myself (project report ELLEN available at http://lire.ish-lyon. cnrs.fr/spip.php?rubrique88).
3. All of the quotations taken from *Zeit für die Bombe* have been translated from German to English by the author of this chapter.
4. The "transitional" pages are one of the formal innovations of this hyperfiction. Sometimes their action potential revives the reader's interest. On the last page, which describes how Veronika repeatedly plunges back into her fragmented memory, a hyperlink allows the reader to start exploring the story "from the beginning". The transitional page anticipates one of the potential issues leading to a new exploration: "What did Iwan do after Veronika's departure"?
5. Translation by the author of this chapter.

WORKS CITED

Berkenheger, S. (1997) *Zeit für die Bombe*. Last accessed 7 November 2012 at URL: http://berkenheger.netzliteratur.net/ouargla/wargla/zeit.htm

Blanckeman, B. (2000) *Les Récits Indécidables: Jean Echenoz, Hervé Guibert, Pascal Quignard*. Paris, Villeneuve d'Ascq: Presses Universitaires du Septentrion.

Bolter, J.D. (1990) *Writing Space: The Computer in the History of Literacy*. Hillsdale: Lawrence Erlbaum.

Bolter, J.D. & Grusin, R. (1999) *Remediation: Understanding New Media*. Cambridge: MIT Press.

Bootz, P. (2002) "Alire: Un Questionnement Irréductible de la Littérature". *Revista Digital d'Humanitats* [online]. Last accessed 20 February 2013 at URL: http://www.uoc.edu/humfil/articles/fr/bootz0302/bootz0302.html

Borges, J.L. (1957) *Enquêtes*. Paris: Gallimard.

Bouchardon, S. (2011) "Des Figures de Manipulation dans la Création Numérique". *Protée* 39. 1: 37–46.

Bourassa, R. (2010) *Les Fictions Hypermédiatiques: Mondes Fictionnels et Espaces Ludiques*. Montréal: Le Quartanier.

Cardon, D. (2009) "Vertus Démocratiques de l'Internet". Round table presentation "Internet et Renouveau Démocratique" (with D. Bougnoux and P. Flichy). Grenoble, 9 May.

Charney, D. (1994) "The Effect of Hypertext on Processes of Reading and Writing". In *Literacy and Computers: The Complications of Reading and Learning with Technology*. S. Hilligoss and C. L. Selfe (eds). New York: Modern Language Association, pp. 238–263.

Clément, J. (2000) "Hypertexte et Complexité". *Etudes Françaises* 36. 2: 39–57.

Ensslin, A. (2007) *Canonising Hypertext: Explorations and Constructions*. London: Continuum.

Flichy, P. (2001) *L'Imaginaire d'Internet*. Paris: La Découverte.

Franke, M. (n.d.) "Ästhetik und Technik. Literaturprojekte der Semiosphäre" [online]. Last accessed 20 February 2013 at URL: http://www.franke-matthias.de/wlbfctxt.htm

Gervais, B. (2006) "*Richard Powers et les Technologies de la Représentation: Des Vices Littéraires et de Quelques Frontiers*". *Alliage* 57–58: 226–237.

Hautzinger, N. (1999) *Vom Buch zum Internet? Eine Analyse der Auswirkungen-hypertextueller Strukturen auf Text und Literatur*. Mannheim: Mannheimer Studien zur Literatur- und Kulturwissenschaft.

Iser, W. (1995 [1976]) *L'Acte de Lecture—Théorie de l'Effet Esthétique*. E. Sznycer (trans). Paris: Mardaga.

Jauss, H. R. (1990) *Pour une Esthétique de la Réception* J. Starobinski (trans). Paris: Gallimard.

Jeanneret, Y. (2008) *Penser la Trivialité: Volume 1, La Vie Triviale des Êtres Culturels*. Paris: Hermès.

Jeanneret, Y. and Davallon, J. (2004) "La Fausse Évidence de l'Hypertexte". *Communication et Langages* 140: 43–54.

Jennings, P. (1996) "Narrative Structures for New Media: Towards a New Definition". *Leonardo* 29. 5: 345–350.

Joyce, M. (1993) *afternoon a story* [CD-ROM]. Watertown, MA: Eastgate Systems.

Labelle, S. (2001) " 'La Société de l'Information', à Décrypter!" *Communication et Langages* 128: 65–79.

Laborde, A. (2010) "Quel Imaginaire d'Internet dans la Société Française? Représentations d'Internet dans la Presse Généraliste depuis 2000". *Rapport de Recherche* [online]. Last accessed 15 January 2012 at URL: http://raudin.u-bordeaux3.fr/oat/wp-content/uploads/SYNTHESE%20IMAGINAIRE%20D\x27INTERNET.pdf

Landow, G. P. (1997) *Hypertext 2.0: The Convergence of Contemporary Critical Theory and Technology*. Baltimore: The Johns Hopkins University Press.

Meunier, J.P. (2006) "Pour une Approche Cognitive de la Signification Iconique". In *Images et Sémiotique: Sémiotique Pragmatique et Cognitive*. B. Darras (ed). Paris: Publications de la Sorbonne, pp. 133–145.

MIM. (2012) Last accessed 20 February 2013 at URL: http://www.labo-mim.org/site/index.php?2008/08/11/24-les-ust

Observatoire Orange Terrafemina. (2011) "Du 20 Heures à Twitter: Les Réseaux Sociaux Bousculent l'Info". *Observatoire Orange Terrafemina*.

Ryan, M.-L. (2004) *Narrative across Media: The Languages of Storytelling*. Lincoln/London: University of Nebraska Press.

Ryan, M.-L. (2006) *Avatars of Story*. Minneapolis: University of Minnesota Press.

Saemmer, A. (2011a) "*De la Confirmation à la Subversion: Les Figures d'Animation Face aux Conventions du Discours Numérique*". *Protée* 39. 1: 23–36.

Saemmer, A. (2011b) "Writing the Ephemeral [. . .] and Re-Enchanting the Remnants: The Lability of the Digital Device in Literary Practice". *Journal of Writing in Creative Practice* 4. 1: 79–92.

Simanowski, R. (1999) "*Susanne Berkenhegers 'Zeit für die Bombe': Die Tat des Lesers, die simulierte Zerstörung und die Redundanz der Animation*". *Dichtung digital* [online]. Last accessed 20 February 2013 at URL: http://dichtung-digital.mewi.unibas.ch/Simanowski/2-Juli-99/brief1_0_x.htm

Simanowski, R. (2007) "What Is and to What End Do We Read Digital Literature?" *Dichtung digital* [online]. Last accessed 20 February 2013 at URL: http://dichtung-digital.mewi.unibas.ch/readingdigitalliterature/proceedings-Simanowski.htm

Suter, B. (2005) *"Narrationspfade in Hyperfictions, Erzählung als Weg durch den fiktiven Raum"*. *Netzliteratur.net* [online]. Last accessed 15 January 2012 at URL: http://www.netzliteratur.net/suter/narrationspfade.htm

Time (1993) Last accessed 20 February 2013 at URL: http://www.time.com/time/covers/0,16641,19930208,00.html

Tosca, P. S. (2000) "A Pragmatic of Links". *JoDI (Journal of Digital Information)* 1. 6. Last accessed 20 February 2013 at URL: http://journals.tdl.org/jodi/article/view/23

Wolton, D. (2009) *Informer n'est pas Communiquer*. Paris: CNRS Editions.

Afterword

12 Reading Digital Fiction
From Hypertext to Timeline

Roberto Simanowski,
University of Basel, Switzerland

It has been ten years now since I published a monograph whose agenda was to give an overview of different genres of digital literature and to offer of a number of close readings of specific works (Simanowski 2002). Close readings were rare in the first wave of digital literature studies, during which general issues of the new writing space and tools, as well as taxonomic questions of the new genres of text, were discussed. In order to foster close readings I founded the online journal *dichtung-digital* in May 1999 and published my monograph *Interfictions* (Simanowski 2002) about writing on the Net, offering not only a theoretical approach to and a terminological discussion of the new forms of literature in digital media but also various case studies in the field of hyperfiction, collaborative writing projects, and kinetic concrete poetry. In the same year Hayles published her book *Writing Machines* with an extensive case study of Talan Memmott's *Lexia to Perplexia*, looking in particular at how the code supplements and comments the text; in 2003, the collection *Close Reading New Media: Analyzing Electronic Literature* by van Looy and Baetens appeared, an anthology that aimed to provide a set of case studies to illustrate and test theories developed in years of terminological and theoretical debates. These titles seemed to start a second wave of digital literature study moving from highly generalized perspectives on new media art and literature into detailed readings paying attention to the specificities of a particular work.

Despite these attempts to move scholarship toward media specific analysis, only a few books dedicated to the analysis of specific examples of digital fiction and poetry have been published since then. As the editors of this volume note in their introduction, important second-wave projects include *New Narratives: Stories and Storytelling in the Digital Age* (2011) edited by Page and Thomas, which contains some close readings of digital fictions and games, and *Reading Moving Letters: Digital Literature in Research and Teaching* (Simanowski et al. 2010), in which scholars and teachers from different countries and academic environments articulate their approaches to the study and teaching of specific examples of digital literature. To this we may add Ricardo's 2009 anthology *Literary Art in Digital Performance: Case Studies and Critical Positions*, which is based on the conference

Reading Digital Literature that I organized at Brown University in 2007, and explores specific examples of digital literature through the lens of contemporary criticism. Three books in ten years is not an abundant harvest. Why are hermeneutic endeavors into concrete examples of digital literature still so rare compared with terminological or theoretical works?

Van Looy and Baetens offer three reasons that also reappear in this volume's introductory chapter. "First of all", they argue, "there is the basic conviction that critical attention does not matter, or even that it is not appropriate to works belonging to a medium which has as one of its primary principles the absence of—literally—fixed shapes and—literally—fixed meanings" (2003: 7). The potentially fractured narrative structure of digital literature, the issue of narrative closure in multilinear narrative, and low level of reader absorption—the "unreliable narration", as Ensslin (2012a) aptly calls it—seems challenging for many practitioners of literary studies, whose main orientation is determining signs. While new hermeneutic approaches start from the assumption that such determination can never end or always has to be deconstructed respectively, the literally unfixed sign in digital literature causes an additional theoretical and methodological challenge.

"Second", van Looy and Baetens continue, "there is the idea, which is not entirely false, that hyperfiction is born on the margins of a medium, the computer, which is still considered a number cruncher rather than a literary device" (2003: 8). In their response to this idea, van Looy and Baetens refer to Aarseth's conviction that "the emerging new media technologies . . . should be studied for what they can tell us about the principles and evolution of human communication" (Aarseth 1997 quoted in van Looy and Baetens 2003: 8). Of course, these technologies should also be looked at with regard to the principles of the aesthetic communication involved. However, it is equally important to focus on the interface rather than the code. Code is without doubt an indispensable element in every discussion of digital literature because everything happening on the screen is first and foremost subject to the grammar and politics of code. In many cases and in many different ways, it is important to understand what has been done and what can be done on the level of code to understand and assess the semantics of a digital artifact. However, a preoccupation with code threatens to divert our attention from the actual meaning of an artifact. It encourages claims such as the notion that everything in digital media is actually literature because everything is represented as alphanumeric code or, on the contrary, that the computer can't be a literary device, for it will always be a number cruncher.

If we focus on the interface instead of the code, then a number of salient issues emerge that need to be taken into account in a semiotic-rhetorical approach to digital literature. This book's introduction lists some of them: "salience (tone, color, foregrounding, etc.), compositional principle (left-right, top-bottom, center-margin, etc.), positioning of the reader-viewer, modality, transitivity, and framing (that is, the sense of connection-disconnection through the use of frame lines, empty spaces, etc.)". Other important issues stem from classical rhetoric and conventional taxonomy that can and should—appropriately modified—be applied to describe the stylistic devices of digital literature. What do, if we may ask with Saemmer (2010), "kinaesthetic rhymes" and "kinetic allegory" look like, and how do we treat "transfiguration" (morphing one word into another), "interfacial antagonism" (where the media content provoked by the interactive gesture is contrary to the announced and expected content), or "interfacial pleonasm" (where the interactive gesture does not provoke the emergence of additional information)?

Additional questions arise in relation to the literary function(s) and the ethics of a link. If the undermining of established grammatical rules constitutes poeticity or the "literary", as Saemmer argues, is literariness of linkage established by incongruous, seemingly "irrelevant" links? To what extent does such deviance from common use run the risk of being perceived as a malfunction? To what extent does the *literary* collide with media *literacy*? Saemmer concludes that only consistency between a detected incongruity and the context helps decide whether one is confronted with a bug or rather with an intentionally created figure, and demands a stabilization of the destabilization. It will, and this is the (practical) consequence of such a theoretical perspective, be important to understand that certain grammatical rules of digital language, i.e. the relevance of links, are creatively dismissed on the behalf of the poetic function of the digital text.

In this context it should be stressed once again that the term *digital* in digital literature relates to the medium of its production and not to the semiotics of its material. Because language consists of discrete signs, one could say that literature is always the result of digital encoding, contrary to images or sound that are based on nondiscrete signs. This is the basis for some linguists' objections to the prevailing expansion of the term language to nonlinguistic signs such as images. They are not based on "a combinatory system of digital units, as phonemes are", as Barthes holds in his essay "Rhetoric of the Image" (1991: 21). However, in the case at hand, both concepts of language, the linguistic as well as the nonlinguistic, apply. Because digital literature by definition is different from traditional print literature—if the only difference is the form and place of presentation, one may rather speak of digit*ized* literature—it also has to surpass semiotic digitality characteristic of traditional literature and text in general. This takes place by connecting discrete linguistic signs to nondiscrete signs such as visual, sonic, and performative elements. The characterization of the term *digital literature*, therefore, points to the technological and not the semiotic notion of the medium: digital literature is *not* digital with respect to the aspect of expression but with respect to its way of presentation, the former being described as *primary digitality* (discrete-distinctive signs), the latter as *secondary digitality* (digitalization of signs as consequence of the computer)

(Hiebel 1997: 8). However, in contrast to digitized literature, digital literature does not simply use digital technology for reason of distribution but rather makes aesthetic use of the features of this technology. To put it this way: digital literature is technologically digital because it stops being print in a semiotic way. The result of this characterization is a shift from linguistic hermeneutics to a hermeneutics of intermedial, interactive, and performative signs. It is not just the meaning of a word that is at stake but also the word's interaction with tactile, visual, and sonic signs, as well as the meaning of the performance of the word on the monitor that may be triggered by the reader's action.

To be sure, looking at the interface rather than focusing on the code does not mean ignoring the politics of coding. As I have argued elsewhere (Simanowski 2010: 8), "In digital art, the demands or constraints of technology may give rise to unintended situations and signals with no connection to the work's significance. A specific feature may actually be a bug the artist was not able to fix, or it may be there for other nonaesthetic reasons". An example I explore in the same publication is the interactive drama *Façade* (2005) by Michael Mateas and Andrew Stern. The authors describe the personalities of Grace and Trip, the characters the player interacts with, as self-absorbed and giving the gist of their statements during the first seconds, in which the player can't interrupt, instead of working toward it. This, Mateas and Stern state, allows Grace and Trip to believably ignore player inputs that are unrecognized or unhandleable and requires the player to react to the characters' utterances rather than the other way around. Hence, the personalities of the characters are designed according to technological constraints. What in a traditional text would reveal something about the characters in the story in this context instead points to certain characteristics of the underlying technology.

I also argued that, in a dialogue generated by the computer as in the case of *Façade*, the text presented needs to be as conventional as possible. Although the actual artwork in computer-generated work such as *Façade* is not the text but the text machine, the virtuosity of the programmer can only be proven by making us forget the programming. It is a paradoxical relationship of immediacy and hypermediacy (Bolter and Grusin 1999): while looking *through* the medium, we are actually looking *at* the medium. Any alienation—if, for example, Trip offers a martini, the player says, "Martini works for me", and Grace comments, "Don't let's talk about work!"—makes us aware of the machine behind the dialogue. Since absurdity is still the default nature of text generators, we will inevitably perceive any alienation not as reference to Beckett or Dada but as a flaw, which needs to be fixed unless one welcomes such unintended absurdity as genuine part of a computer-generated text. However, the authors or programmers can prove their craftsmanship only by making the generator produce text as conventional as possible. The message of text machines, to allude to McLuhan's famous phrase, is mainstream literature. A digital hermeneutics has to take into account the possibility of such technological determinism. Needless to say, we therefore must not forget in analyzing the aesthetic of digital fiction the technology used to produce it.

As a third reason that there are so few close readings of digital literature, van Looy and Baetens note, "[W]e often hear the argument that hyperfiction has not yet produced enough interesting works to justify a turn towards a more literal and literary tackling of the material" (2003: 8). The editors correctly object to this argument, engaging with Ryan's claim that even in the case of lack of quality, close analysis is worthwhile because, "for the literary scholar, the importance of the electronic movement is twofold: it problematizes familiar notions, and it challenges the limits of language" (Ryan 1999 quoted in van Looy and Baetens 2003: 8). Even works of so called mediocre quality—and perhaps precisely these—can shed light on the extent to which digital literature can handle its material in a meaningful and convincing way and help us understand where potential traps and pitfalls may lie.

This of course requires developing analytical tools for approaching hyperfiction and the other genres of digital literature. The volume at hand has to be credited for taking up this challenge not only on a theoretical level but also for exercising the analysis of digital fiction with respect to specific examples. It will be interesting to see how the tools offered are adopted by other scholars and how the close readings presented are answered by other close readings of the same works or inspire close readings of other works. Rather than reviewing the outcome of this undertaking myself, I want to suggest future areas of research for the field. I do so by picking up two remarks from the introduction that seem crucial to me for the future not only of digital fiction but also of fiction in digital media.

The editors state, "[T]o comprehend and critically reflect on the aesthetic interplay between hyper and deep attention, we need methods that can capture the way the text invites those kinds of attention. We need to look at the text, but we will also need to consider media-specific attributes such as interface design, software versus hardware mechanics, links, images, sound, and so on". The issue of digital media and hyper attention has been discussed in recent years, especially in cognitive science. Thus, in *Proust and the Squid: The Story and Science of the Reading Brain*, Maryane Wolf, professor of child development at Tufts University, announces the loss of deep reading and with it the loss of deep thinking (2007). Based on Wolf and other studies in neuroscience, American journalist and cultural critic Nicholas Carr, in *The Shallows: How the Internet Is Changing the Way We Think, Read and Remember* (2010), wonders about a world where the mind no longer immerses itself in the universe of a book but only looks for key phrases before leaving for the next sensation. In the same spirit French Philosopher Bernard Stiegler claims in *Taking Care of Youth and the Generations* that the shift from "deep attention" to "hyper attention" by modern psychotechnologies such as video games, MP3 files, and Facebook leads to watchfulness without reflection. The "psychotechnologies by the programming industries", he argues, "destroy attention and consciousness", which is a crucial threat to social and cultural development (2010: 179). More recently, the German neurobiologist Martin Spitzer has been bringing the problem to the attention of a broader audience. He has been using talk shows and interviews to accuse, with bold and populist statements, digital media of causing "digital dementia", which is also the title of his latest book (2012).

The issue of hyper attention and the loss of deep reading has been discussed mostly with respect to its psychological, social, and political ramifications, rather than by writers and scholars of literature, with the exception of recent articles, for example, those by Hayles (2012) and Ensslin (2012b). The inevitable questions for the scholar of literature are: what are the consequences of such social and cultural development for reading and writing? How do literature and art react to this process? Do they approve of it by adjusting their poetics to our current fast-paced culture, which is intensified by digital media? Do they invite a critical perspective on the status quo as the purpose and mission of art and literature have often been defined? What role is the cultural technique of reading going to play at all if power browsing, multitasking, and permanent online connectivity make the long-established contemplative reading session increasingly obsolete?

I have discussed the issue of hyper attention with respect to the replacement of text by other media or turning the text itself, by stripping it of its linguistic value, into another medium at several occasions using the term "transmedial cannibalism" (2010, 2011: 42–53). In a close reading of *Still Standing* (2005) by Bruno Nadeau and Jason Lewis, I argue that this work—which requires the audience to stand still in front of a screen in order to read a text forming across the screen—unconsciously surrenders to the same fast-paced culture it intends to challenge. The work treats the moment of standing still itself as an event by keeping it as short as possible, although eye tracking would allow refreshing the text once it has been read again and again, thus extending the time the audience is required to stand still and truly testing their patience (2011: 49ff.). Can similar contradictions be detected in other works? What are the aesthetic strategies implemented in other artifacts to defend and exercise the vanishing culture of deep reading?

In this context, one also has to explore the potential consequences of reading applications such as *readmill* that make the new environment of text, the e-book, go social. This app by Henrik Berggren, launched in 2011, takes advantage of the e-book's connectedness to the Internet by allowing users to share their "reading data": their favorite books and their favorite sections of a book. Users can browse other users' highlights from the same book they are reading and engage in a discussion with them (of course, their profile will be available and may reveal more about their reading habits). What Berggren, who himself is not a literary scholar but a programmer, considers an enhancement of the reading experience, others, among them certainly Carr and Stiegler, may see as its end because it contradicts the mode of immersive reading in favor of immediate sensation. Nevertheless, one can easily imagine how readmill.com could be bought out by larger players in the digital marketplace, such as Amazon, Google, Apple, or Facebook, and how this so-called "social reading" would widely and deeply change the way we read. We can also easily imagine that statistical data about what readers like most and least, where they slowed down their reading, where they left the text for browsing the Internet (and what sites they went to) may determine the production and trading of (electronic) books and (digital) literature. How do fiction writers react to such a fundamental reconstruction of the reading environment? How do scholars include the data available about the digital reading experience into their analyses of a text's structure and meaning? How will writers allow their writing to be determined by those data?

The second part of this volume's introduction that I want to underline is the claim that "creative new media are increasingly blurring conventional generic boundaries, thus becoming hybrid forms of experimental literary and media art". I certainly agree with the editors' notion that, while the first generation of digital literature focused on hypertextuality, the second focused on visual and auditory attributes. This should not come as a surprise, since the medium's increasing power of "crunching numbers" offered more and more new features, and since this has been the tendency in the contemporary art and literature more in general. On the other hand, the internal narrational aporia of hyperfiction—the lack of a well-designed, authoritative mono-linear text structure supporting immersion and suspense—soon made scholars suggest taming the hypertextual. Thus, as early as in 2000, Marie-Laure Ryan saw the future of hyperfiction in more "instant satisfaction" through "relatively self-contained lexias such as poems, aphorisms, anecdotes, short narrative episodes" and in shifting focus from alternative navigation toward other aesthetic features: "Give up on the idea of an autonomous 'literary' genre, and take greater advantage of the multi-media capability of the electronic environment", including the "hybridization with computer games" (2000).

However, the central feature of the next generation of digital literature may be "to blur the lines between fiction and faction", as Mark Amerika proposed under the term of *(h)activity* over a decade ago (2000). A famous example is the fiction *Ally Farson* (ShadowMan Films 1999–2000), an allegedly true story of a female serial killer operating in 1999, that uses alleged documentary video footage and supposedly official websites of the police department as well as newsgroups on which "police officers" answer the questions of skeptical readers. A most recent, quite different example is *Common Tongues* by John Cayley and Daniel Howe (2009–), a work that assembles Beckett's *How It Is* by searching online for three- or four-words phrases from the Beckett text in contexts that are *not* associated with Beckett. *Common Tongues* uses the mechanisms of search engines in order to find the words of an authorized text where they are still, if only momentarily, associating freely. Hence, the work addresses questions of ownership and copyright by exploring the mutual determination of algorithmic and statistical models of reading on one hand, and human reading on the other.

While *Common Tongues* is a conceptual work, Facebook's Timeline is a "narrative" environment dealing with similar issues without addressing them. The Timeline has been introduced by Facebook with the slogan: "Timeline. The story of your life. All your stories. All your apps. Express who you are", and it has been considered the diary of the twenty-first century (Fricke 2011). The Timeline is not a diary in that that it doesn't present the personal description—or expression—of personal experiences. Rather, experience inscribes itself in real time into the Timeline. If you share a YouTube video with a Facebook friend, the link is sent to your friend and the sharing is reported in your Timeline if you allow the system to do so. In this automated autobiography you don't report the action explaining its reason and aim, but the action reports itself. Although the status line and the *life event* section allow for personal comments and narrative composition, this option seems to be rarely used. The Timeline has narratological consequences in three ways. First, the "writing" of the autobiographical story is outsourced to the computer by the algorithm used by Facebook and its partners in order to store the data on the Timeline. Second, accounting returns to its etymological origin when it still meant counting, i.e. each event counts regardless of its importance to a specific way of perceiving events and giving meaning to them. The fact that datasets are not meaningful with respect to a narrative guarantees their completeness, since they can't contradict or disturb any narrative. Third, the meaningful reading of the data is outsourced to the reader. The Timeline seems to make popular what Nicholas Felton, who documents his life statistically as *Annual Reports*, calls "numerical narrative" (2011). The Timeline also seems to approve Lev Manovich's assumption, expressed more than ten years ago, that database and narrative as two different modes of making sense of the world are increasingly competing for the same territory of human culture (2001: 225). This development opens new areas of future research for the field of digital fiction and narration and raises some interesting issues such as: what are the consequences for writing after blurring the lines between fiction and faction if the database becomes the symbolic form of our age and if the task of narration is outsourced to the reader?

There are other aspects to be considered in the scholarship of digital writing. Even without *readmill*, writing online is writing the network. The author meets her readers; she can't escape their comments, their critique, their two cents; she can't help learning how and to what extent her audience understands the text and to what extent she failed to get her message across. Another facet of digital technology is the undermining of copyright. The author, we hear, has to become her own manager. It will be interesting to investigate how this new demand changes the business of writing. But writing within digital networks starts before the feedback of the network. It starts with the computer and with technologies such as Google determining the way we use language. Digital technologies are not only machines we use to "do" language—they determine how we do it. They represent and undertake an evolution of writing and literacy. If scholarship in the field of digital literature looks for new analytical tools for approaching multimodal compositions as self-referential aesthetic objects by way of computer aided close readings searching, collating, and indexing its object, this may be considered a new New Criticism based on a computational or quantitative turn. However, more than ever before, we have to take into account that text is not autonomous but has to be understood in its historical and medial context. This is true even more so when writing occurs within social networks and is based on digital technologies provided and controlled by private companies. Hence, we may also say we need a new New Historicism. The challenge to the task of analyzing digital literature will be to reconcile both schools on behalf of the new subject.

WORKS CITED

Amerika, M. (2000) "Network (H)activity. Interview with Mark Amerika". *dichtung-digital* 14. Last accessed 20 February 2013 at URL: www.dichtung-digital. de/Interviews/Amerika-3-Nov-00

Barthes, R. (1991) *The Responsibility of Forms: Critical Essays on Music, Art, and Representation*. Berkeley: University of California Press.

Bolter, J.D. and Grusin, R. (1999) *Remediation: Understanding New Media*. Cambridge, MA: MIT Press.

Carr, N. (2010) *The Shallows: How the Internet Is Changing the Way We Think, Read and Remember*. London: Atlantic Books.

Cayley, J. & Howe, D. (2009–) *Common Tongues*. Project website last accessed 21 May 2013 at URL: http://thereadersproject.org/index.php?p=installation/ rts2012/commontongues.html

Ensslin, A. (2012a) ' "I Want to Say I May Have Seen My Son Die This Morning': Unintentional Unreliable Narration in Digital Fiction". *Language and Literature* 21. 2: 136–149.

Ensslin, A. (2012b) "Computer Gaming". In *The Routledge Companion to Experimental Literature*. J. Bray, A. Gibbons, and B. McHale (eds). London/New York: Routledge, pp. 497–511.

Felton, N. (2011) Lecture: *Numerical Narratives*. At UCLA Department Design, Media, Arts. 15 November. Last accessed 21 May 2013 at URL: http://video. dma.ucla.edu/video/nicholas-felton-numerical-narratives/387

Fricke, C. (2011) "Schön-schreckliches Tagebuch des Lebens". *Focus.Online*, September 26. Last accessed 20 February 2013 at URL: www.focus.de/digital/ internet/facebook/tid-23736/facebooks-neue-timeline-im-ersten-test-schoen-schreckliches-tagebuch-des-lebens_aid_669090.htm

Hayles, N.K. (2012) "How We Read: Close, Hyper. Machine". In *How We Think. Digital Media and Contemporary Technologies*. Chicago/London: University of Chicago Press, pp. 55–83.

Hiebel, H. (1997) *Kleine Medienchronik: Von den ersten Schriftzeichen zum Mikrochip*. Munich: Beck.

Manovich, L. (2001) *The Language of New Media*. Cambridge, MA: MIT Press.

Mateas, M. and Stern, A. (2005) *Façade* [online] Last accessed 21 May 2013 at URL: http://www.interactivestory.net/

Nadeau, B. and Lewis, J. (2005) *Still Standing* [online]. Last accessed 21 May 2013 at URL: http://collection.eliterature.org/2/works/nadeau_stillstanding.html

Page, R. and Thomas, B. (eds). (2011) *New Narratives: Stories and Storytelling in the Digital Age*. Lincoln, NE: University of Nebraska Press.

Ricardo, F. (ed.) (2009). *Literary Art in Digital Performance: Case Studies in New Media Art and Criticism*. New York: Continuum.

Ryan, M. L. (2000) "Immersion and Interactivity in Hypertext". *dichtung-digital 10*. Last accessed 20 February 2013 at URL: www.dichtung-digital.de/2000/Ryan/29-Maerz

Saemmer, A. (2010) "Digital Literature—A Question of Style". In *Reading Moving Letters: Digital Literature in Research and Teaching. A Handbook*. R. Simanowski, P. Gendolla, and J Schäfer (eds). Bielefeld: Transcript, pp. 163–182.

ShadowMan Films (1999–2000) *Ally Farson* Last accessed 21 May 2013 at URL: http://www.allyfarson.com/

Simanowski, R. (2002) *Interfictions: Vom Schreiben im Netz*. Frankfurt am Main: Suhrkamp.

Simanowski, R. (2010) "Digital Anthropophagy: Refashioning Words as Image, Sound and Action". *Leonardo, Journal of the International Society for the Arts, Sciences and Technology* 43. 2: 159–163.

Simanowski, R. (2011) *Digital Art and Meaning: Reading Kinetic Poetry, Text Machines, Mapping Art, and Interactive Installations*. Minneapolis/London: University of Minnesota Press.

Simanowski, R., Gendolla, P., and Schaefer, J. (eds). (2010) *Reading Moving Letters: Digital Literature in Research and Teaching*. Bielefeld: Transcript.

Spitzer, M. (2012) *Digitale Demenz: Wie wir uns und unsere Kinder um den Verstand bringen*. Munich: Droemer Knaur.

Stiegler, B. (2010) *Taking Care of Youth and the Generations*. Stanford: Stanford University Press.

Van Looy, J. and Baetens, J. (eds). (2003) *Close Reading New Media: Analyzing Electronic Literature*. Leuven: Leuven University Press.

Wolf, M. (2007) *Proust and the Squid: The Story and Science of the Reading Brain*. New York: Harper.

Contributors

Dr. Alice Bell is Senior Lecturer in English Language and Literature at Sheffield Hallam University (UK). She is Principal Investigator of the Digital Fiction International Network (founded with funding from The Leverhulme Trust) and of Ontological Metalepsis and Unnatural Narratology, a collaborative research project undertaken with Jan Alber and funded by the British Academy. She is the author of *The Possible Worlds of Hypertext Fiction* (Palgrave-Macmillan, 2010) and has had articles published on digital fiction, narratology, and stylistics in *Storyworlds*, *Narrative*, *Style*, *Journal of Narrative Theory*, *Contemporary Stylistics* (Continuum, 2007), *New Narratives* (Nebraska, 2012), and *A Poetics of Unnatural Narrative* (Ohio State, 2013).

Dr. Serge Bouchardon graduated with a degree in literature from La Sorbonne University (Paris, France). After working as a project manager in the educational software industry for six years, he wrote his dissertation on interactive literary narrative and is currently Associate Professor in Communication Sciences at the University of Technology of Compiègne (France). His research focuses on digital creations and in particular digital literature. His publications include *Un Laboratoire de Littératures— Littérature Numérique et Internet* (Editions du Centre Pompidou, 2007) and *Littérature Numérique: Le Récit Interactif* (Hermes Science Publishing, 2009).

Dr. David Ciccoricco is a lecturer in the English Department at the University of Otago in Dunedin, New Zealand. His research is focused on contemporary narrative fiction, with a particular emphasis on emergent forms of digital literature and network culture in general. He is the author of *Reading Network Fiction* (University of Alabama Press, 2007), a book on the first and second waves of digital fiction, and has articles published in *Electronic Book Review*, *The Routledge Companion to Experimental Literature* (Routledge, 2012), and *Intermediality & Storytelling* (Walter de Gruyter, 2010).

Professor Astrid Ensslin teaches at Bangor University's School of Creative Studies and Media. Her main publications include *Canonizing Hypertext: Explorations and Constructions* (Continuum, 2007); *Language in the Media: Representations, Identities, Ideologies* (Continuum, 2007); *Creating Second Lives: Identity, Community and Spatiality as Constructions of the Virtual* (Routledge, 2011); *The Language of Gaming* (Palgrave, 2012); and articles in *Narrative, Storyworlds, dichtung digital, Electronic Book Review, Language and Literature, Journal of Gender Studies, Language and Data Processing, Language Learning Journal* and *Corpora*. She is Principal Editor of the *Journal of Gaming and Virtual Worlds* (Intellect) and Investigator of various funded projects on digital fiction and computer gaming.

Dr. Isabell Klaiber is Associate Professor in American Literary and Cultural Studies at the University of Tübingen, Germany. Her fields of research are nineteenth- to twenty-first–century American culture and literature with a focus on gender studies, African American studies, cultural iconicity, drama, and narratology. Her current research project is on literary collaboration from the nineteenth century to online-writing projects. Her publications include *Kulturelle Leitfiguren: Figurationen und Refigurationen* (co-editor, Duncker & Humblot, 2007) and *Gender und Genie: Künstlerkonzeptionen in der amerikanischen Erzählliteratur des 19. Jahrhunderts* (Wissenschaftlicher Verlag, 2004).

Dr. Daniel Punday is Professor of English at Purdue University Calumet. He is the author of *Narrative after Deconstruction* (State University of New York Press, 2002); *Narrative Bodies: Towards a Corporeal Narratology* (Palgrave, 2003); and *Five Strands of Fictionality: The Institutional Construction of Contemporary American Writing* (Ohio State University Press, 2010); and *Writing at the Media Limit: Searching for the Vocation of the Novel in the Contemporary Media Ecology* (University of Nebraska Press, 2012). He has had articles published in journals including *Electronic Book Review, Poetics Today,* and *Style.*

Dr. Hans Kristian Rustad is Associate Professor in Literature and New Media Communication at Hedmark University College, Norway. His research interests are digital literature, contemporary poetry in Scandinavia, intermediality, and literary techno-critique. He is a member of Electronic Literature Organization and a founding member of the *Digital Fiction International Network*. His publications include *Tekstspill i hypertekst* (Agder University College, Kristiansand, 2008); "A Four-Sided Model for Reading Hypertext Fiction" (*Hyperrhiz*, 2009); "*der vårgras brydder*": *Nye lesninger av Åsmund Sveens dikt* (Oplandske bogforlag, Valset, 2010); "Nordic Electronic Literature: Tradition, Archiving, and

Cultural Valuation", in *Spiel* 29 (2010) "A [S]creed for Digital Fiction" (*electronic book review*, 2010), and *Digital Litteratur* (Cappelen Damm Akademiske, Oslo, 2012).

Dr. Alexandra Saemmer is Associate Professor of Information and Communication Sciences at University of Paris 8. Her current research projects focus on semiotics and aesthetics of digital media, reading, and writing on digital supports. She is the author and editor of several books and articles on digital literature and arts, including *Matières Textuelles sur Support Numérique* (Publications de l'Université de Saint-Etienne, 2007); *E-Formes 2: Les Littératures et Arts Numériquesau Risque du Jeu* (co-editor, forthcoming, Publications de l'Université de Saint-Etienne); and *E-Formes 1: Ecritures Visuelles sur Support Numérique* (co-editor, Publications de l'Université de Saint-Etienne, 2008). She has articles published in *Reading Moving Letters: Digital Literature in Research and Teaching* (Transcript Verlag, 2009) and *Perspectives on Digital Literature* (West Virginia University Press, 2010).

Dr. Roberto Simanowski is Professor for Media Studies at the University of Basel, Switzerland, before which he was a Research Fellow at Harvard University and the University of Washington, and Professor for German Studies at Brown University. He is the founder and editor of dichtung-digital.org, editor of three books on digital literature, and author of four books on digital culture. His publications include *Reading Moving Letters: Digital Literature in Research and Teaching: a Handbook* (co-edited, Transcript, 2010) and *Digital Art and Meaning: Reading Kinetic Poetry, Text Machines, Mapping Art, and Interactive Installations* (University of Minnesota Press, 2011).

Dr. Bronwen Thomas is Senior Lecturer in Linguistics and Literature in the Media School at Bournemouth University, where she teaches New Media Narrative and leads a Narrative Research Group. She is co-editor with Ruth Page of *New Narratives: Stories and Storytelling in a Digital Age* (University of Nebraska Press, 2012) and has published a number of articles on hypertext fiction and Internet fanfiction in journals including *Narrative*, *Storyworlds*, and *dichtung-digital*.

Dr. Susana Tosca is Associate Professor at the IT University of Copenhagen. Her current research focus is on digital reading across platforms and genres, transmedial storytelling, and digital reception processes. She has published widely on hypertext, digital literature, and computer games. Her last book, the second edition of the successful *Understanding Video Games*, has just been published by Routledge.

Index